Sisterhood
Situation

Sisterhood Situation

Janette McCarthy Louard

sepia

BET Publications, LLC
http://www.bet.com

SEPIA BOOKS are published by

BET Publications, LLC
c/o BET BOOKS
One BET Plaza
1900 W Place NE
Washington, DC 20018-1211

All Kensington Titles, Imprints, and Distributed Lines are available at special quantity discounts for bulk purchases for sales promotions, premiums, fund-raising, and educational or institutional use. Special book excerpts or customized printings can also be created to fit specific needs. For details, write or phone the office of the Kensington special sales manager: Kensington Publishing Corp., 850 Third Avenue, New York, NY 10022, attn: Special Sales Department, Phone: 1-800-221-2647.

ISBN: 1-58314-259-2

First Printing: October 2003
10   9   8   7   6   5   4   3   2   1

Printed in the United States of America

OCT - - 2003

With God, all things are possible.

This novel is dedicated in loving and enduring memory of my father,

Dr. Voldie Osmond McCarthy

ACKNOWLEDGMENTS

I began writing this book after my beloved father passed away, and I can say without equivocation or exaggeration that this book would not have been completed had it not been for the love, support, guidance and encouragement of my family and my friends. I would like to thank the following angels in my life: my husband, Ken, for loving me even when it wasn't easy and for not letting me give up on my dreams; my darling son, Jamaal, for teaching me the lesson of love over and over again; Michael, for the joy he has brought into my life; my mother, Brenda, for her example of grace under pressure, strength in hard times, and above all, her example of fierce love for her family; Paul, Barbara, Mark, Naimah, Khadijah, Michelle, Micah, the wonderful McCarthy and extended family; the fabulous Louard and Louard-Michel women—Agnes, Rita, Diane and Olivia Grace—for setting a shining example; the Michel family for their kindness to me; my sistergirls—Kathi, Molly, Lessie, Robyn, Latisha, Joyce, Stephanie, Diane, Guilene, Charmaine, Sarah, Vonda, Angie, Charleen—all of whom elevate the concept of friendship daily; Frank and Marla, who crossed over from friends to family a long time ago; the Primes family for sustaining me with good food and good love; my church, for keeping me in their prayers during this time; my agent, Denise Stinson, for her great work; my incredible editor, Glenda Howard King; author Margaret Johnson Hodges for her advice and kind words; all those who took the time to read *Mama's Girls,* thank you for your support. And as always, I would like to thank my father, Dr. Voldie Osmond McCarthy, for more than this page or this book could possibly contain. I thank you, Daddy, for showing me what unconditional love is, for being a living example of a strong and loving man, for teaching me what honor means, for passing on your stories and your many sayings to me, for waiting at the Port Authority until my bus pulled off for school, for lifting me up all those many years whenever I fell down. I will love and honor you forever, Daddy. Sweet dreams!

Fall Semester

Chapter 1

Reva

Reva Nettingham knew that the impeccably manicured lawn, green foliage, the surrounding hills and the sparkling blue water of the lake that split the Middlehurst College campus into two distinct halves were impressive to most people. Folks tended to appreciate colleges that could pass for exclusive country clubs. For Reva, however, Middlehurst was a little too perfect. Everything was in its proper place, or if not, would soon be. The buses that transported the students around the five hundred acre campus always came on time. Stray soda cans or other offending debris that might occasionally litter the campus grounds were picked up promptly. As she did often during the past three years at Middlehurst, Reva longed for the confusion of New York. She longed for litter, quirky people, even bus drivers that pulled away from the curb as you were running towards the bus. She longed for imperfection.

The majority of students at Middlehurst fell into three categories—middle class, upper middle class or too rich to care. The scholarship students who needed that weekly stipend that came from campus jobs, students like Reva, who could not depend on a telephone call home to solve financial problems, were few and far between. Reva had never seen so many folks with money. She had certainly never seen so many affluent African Americans. She had grown up under the misapprehension that just about all African Americans were like herself—struggling and trying to make it. Meeting people that looked like her but who had summer homes, or who came from generations of money, was an eye opening experience. It was one thing to feel out of place with the majority student body, but it was quite another to feel out of place with her own people. Thank God for Precious. She and Precious represented a decidedly underrepresented group at Middlehurst—the poor and the black.

There were many times that Reva thought about transferring to another college, a college in a more urban environment, an environment in which she would just blend in with the rest of the student body. Although this particular idea was seductive, there was no other place that she had encountered that afforded her a full academic scholarship. Her mother could not afford to send her to college. Middlehurst had opened its doors to her without question. She remembered how during her on campus interview, her mother Sugar, who never met a thought she didn't care to share with the rest of the world, had told the academic dean "this place is nice and all, but we can't afford it—so it's seems like a big waste of time to drag us up here." Reva had been thinking the same thing, but the tact gene that prevented Reva from voicing her opinion, had skipped Sugar's generation. A full scholarship, book stipend and guaranteed on-campus job had sealed the deal. She was stuck here at Middlehurst—in her gold prison, as Reva often referred to the college.

Still, when the longing to be in a place where she was more comfortable got to be too much, she would cling to the one thing that made Middlehurst bearable—her girls. She'd met her best friends here at Middlehurst. Most people had one best friend. She had three—Precious, Opal and Faith. Before coming to Middlehurst, Reva had never cultivated close female friendships. Her mother, Sugar, a beautiful, complicated and competitive woman had raised her to view other girls with mistrust. It was not until her freshman year at Middlehurst that Reva realized just how wrong her mother was. Meeting Precious, Opal and Faith had been like a drowning man finding a sturdy life boat. They had laughed together, cried together, faced good, bad and crazy times together. They knew each others' dreams and kept each others' secrets. Without her girls, as Reva referred to them, she would be lost, and that, if nothing else, would keep Reva grateful to Middlehurst College. Still, she didn't have to like the place.

Precious

The journey from Lenox Avenue, Harlem to Middlehurst College lasted approximately four hours and thirteen minutes, but Precious Averyheart would tell anyone who asked that this particular journey had taken a lot longer than that. During the last three years, Precious had looked around at the impeccably landscaped grounds, the campus with its newer, more modern buildings and the traditional Tudor style dormitories and school buildings; she had looked at the faces of young women whose lives were as different from her own, as night is from day, and whose traditions she did not share or, at times, understand; and at the expansive green lawn that sloped down from her third floor dormitory room—and she had wondered how the hell she got here. She was a long way from 125th Street and Lenox.

She had never intended to go to a single sex college. At the beginning of her freshman year she had called Middlehurst a "girls' school," but she had been quickly reprimanded by her English Literature teacher, Miss Corrigan, who had snapped at her in front of the entire class, "there are no girls here at Middlehurst, Miss Averyheart. We are all women. You'll be best served if you remember that." It was not the last time Miss Corrigan had corrected her. Each year Precious would take a Corrigan class, determined to show Cutthroat Corrigan, as she was widely known at Middlehurst, that a girl—no, woman— from Harlem could excel at English Literature. Each year, Miss Corrigan would hand her a B, not a B+ or B-, but a B, always with a sarcastic comment written on Precious' exam papers. This semester, Precious had registered for another Corrigan class, and she was determined to get the A that she knew she deserved. She just hoped that Corrigan finally saw things her way.

Precious had intended to go to City College in New York, a fine institution that was just a few blocks north from where she grew up, but her father had different intentions. From the moment Roosevelt Averyheart lay fresh eyes on Middlehurst College, all thoughts of City College were summarily dismissed. "This is why I cleaned other folks' bathrooms," he had declared, "so I could send you someplace like this."

Roosevelt Averyheart had been a janitor since before his only child was conceived. He had worked in a clothes factory in the Bronx, and he was not ashamed to say that while he had done all right for himself, after all he had raised his daughter alone since her mother walked out fifteen years ago, he wanted better for his daughter. He wanted better for his Precious.

Roosevelt turned deaf ears to Precious' misgivings. First, Middlehurst was far from diverse. There weren't many black folks here, and the few black students that crossed Middlehurst's threshold did not grow up in single parent households in Harlem. They did not have janitors for fathers or crackheads for mothers. These folk were strictly middle class or otherwise upwardly mobile, the kind of black folks that vacationed in Martha's Vineyard, the kind of folks to whom the word achievement came naturally.

"I won't fit in here," Precious had wailed.

"I didn't raise you to fit in," Roosevelt had responded. *"I raised you to set standards, baby girl."*

New York City was home. She was born and bred there, and Precious intended to die there. Middlehurst, Massachusetts was a small New England town with not much else going for it except Middlehurst College. There was one movie theatre, a couple of stores, three churches, a bank and a post office. Everything else re-volved around the college. She was used to the hustle of Harlem. This sleepy town was not going to do it for her.

"It's too far from New York."

"And that's supposed to be a problem?"

The prevailing uniform of pastel shirts and khaki pants was un-nerving. Izod shirts, LL Bean shoes, plaid skirts, and the ubiquitous combination of pink and green were a far cry from her typical uni-form of blue jeans, T-shirt, and black boots.

"I hate khaki pants."

"You can wear a dashiki every day for all I care—but you'll be wearing it at Middlehurst."

Precious could have rebelled. She could have chosen to go to City College or another college. Her father would not have stopped her, but Precious knew that he would have been disappointed. In the end, she had given in. No matter what, she did not want to be another in a long line of disappointments for her father. The disappointment had started with her mother, and had gone on from there. She knew how much hurt her father lived with on a daily basis and she wasn't going to add to that hurt. She chose Middlehurst for the same reason she chose everything else in her life, to make Roosevelt Averyheart proud.

In the end she had grown to love this place. Everything that she had worried about now seemed inconsequential to her. She felt safe here. Middlehurst was a place where other people didn't mock her dreams. If she told folks that she wanted to be an astronaut who built houses on Mars, she wouldn't be surprised if some well meaning pro-fessor would smile and say "good for you." Outside, the bells from Mayhew Chapel were ringing. Every day at four o'clock the chapel bells rang. Tradition was big at Middlehurst, and for someone who did not grow up with any particular family traditions, there was some-thing reassuring in knowing that no matter what, the bells of Middlehurst rang at four—even if the world were coming to an end.

Opal

Opal Breezewood stared at the diamond ring on the fourth finger of her left hand. It looked strange there as if some foreign object had

descended on her slim, brown fingers. Beside her, her boyfriend—
no, fiancé, she was going to have to get used to that word—was smiling. Jordan Garvey had a lot to smile about. Smart, good-looking,
wealthy and with a good disposition, Jordan was her parents' dream
son-in-law. Her family had all breathed a collective sigh of relief when
she left her last boyfriend, Adrian. *"Inappropriate,"* was the word her
mother had used to describe Adrian, and Opal was inclined to agree,
but not for the same reasons as her mother. Her mother viewed
Adrian's aversion to school work, and his habits of disappearing for
weeks on end with suspicious eyes. Adrian was a high school dropout
who never quite had any logical or plausible explanations for all the
money that he so freely spent. For Opal, Adrian's inability to be faithful was the most serious of his flaws. Fidelity was not a concept that he
cared to understand, and if during their two year relationship there
was one day Adrian hadn't gotten high, it was news to her. After finding him last year with yet another woman whom he claimed didn't
mean anything to him, Opal had said good-bye.

She had been surprised when Jordan immediately expressed an interest in becoming more than the friends they had been since childhood. Their families had known each other for years, ever since
Jordan's family had bought the house next door to their summer
house in Martha's Vineyard. Jordan was a few years older than Opal
and he was a contemporary of her brothers. But looking back, he had
always seemed to be around, hanging out in the periphery of her life.
He had always been polite and sometimes overly solicitous, but Opal
hadn't given him a second thought until, influenced by her parents,
she'd accepted Jordan's invitation to accompany him to a friend's
wedding.

She'd fallen easily into a relationship with Jordan. He was everything that Adrian wasn't: dependable, faithful, smart and genuinely
interested in her opinions. He was the perfect boyfriend. Roses and
other sweet smelling flowers were delivered to her regularly . He got
along with her parents, and her girlfriends. He listened to her problems without checking his watch or keeping one eye on the television.
He made her laugh when she was down. He went to church regularly,
without anyone forcing him to do so. He was in his second year at
Harvard Business School, and he was gorgeous. He was, as everyone
agreed, a great catch. Still, there was something missing. She didn't
want Adrian back, but there were times when a very small voice
buried someplace deep inside would wonder whether she was with
Jordan simply because she was afraid of being alone.

She'd always had a boyfriend. Opal knew that she was considered
to be good-looking. She wasn't vain about it. She looked like her
mother and her mother was a beautiful woman. Beautiful women

usually had men in their lives, or men clamoring to be in their lives. Opal was no exception. But she'd never intended to be engaged in her senior year of college. She had plans, dreams. Dreams of seeing the world. Dreams of studying art history at the Sorbonne. Dreams of traveling through Africa. Dreams of living abroad, being apart from a family that spent most of their spare time together. Sometimes that togetherness got to be too much.

Opal had surprised herself by accepting Jordan's proposal. She knew it was coming. Jordan had told her from the start of their relationship that he was serious about her. This was not a casual relationship for him. He told her that he'd loved her since she was eight years old and he was twelve and he'd seen her with her Michael Jackson afro, chasing seagulls at the Inkwell, their favorite beach in Martha's Vineyard. A month before his actual proposal, Jordan had informed her that he was going to propose. She'd been silent then, her mind racing as she tried to figure out how to best let him down. She still wanted Jordan in her life, she just didn't want a husband, especially a husband that she was not sure she was in love with.

The proposal had come when they were sitting on the same beach where Jordan had fallen in love with her. The sun had set and the popular Inkwell beach had been deserted except for a few people. Jordan had held her hand and as they sat snuggled in a blanket, staring at the fading sun rays dancing on the Atlantic Ocean, Jordan had asked her to marry him. The feeling of his warm, strong hands in hers, the sight of the Atlantic, the laughter of children playing nearby and the undiluted love she saw in Jordan's eyes had been her undoing. *"Yes,"* she'd surprised herself, even as she knew that she should say no. *"Yes, Jordan Garvey. I'll be your wife."*

"What are you thinking about?" Jordan's voice interrupted disturbing thoughts.

"Nothing," Opal lied with a smile.

"Hmm . . ." said Jordan, reaching over with his free hand and holding hers. With the other hand he maneuvered his dark blue Porsche through traffic. They were heading back to Middlehurst after spending Labor Day weekend with their families in Martha's Vineyard. "I just don't like to see a frown on my future wife's pretty face."

Future wife. The words felt like a noose around her neck.

"Don't worry," said Jordan, as if he read her thoughts. "I know it's a lot to get used to. I've known that I was going to marry you since I was twelve years old. You just need a little time to catch up."

Opal smiled at him. It was almost impossible to feel bad when she was in Jordan's company.

"I've just been a little tired," Opal said. This was partially the truth. She had been feeling tired and out of sorts lately. She hadn't told anyone about the lump she had found underneath her breast last month. It was small and hard—the size of a small pebble. Immediately, she'd known that she was in trouble. Her grandmother had died of breast cancer—she knew what the symptoms were, but she'd put off going to the doctor. She knew she was being foolish, but she was afraid. She wasn't familiar with the taste of fear and she wasn't sure how to deal with it. She had always attacked life and its problems head on, she didn't know any other way, but now she was afraid—too afraid to go to the doctor.

"You need to go to the doctor," Jordan said, as if reading her thoughts. "You've been feeling out of sorts for a while now."

"You sound like my mother," Opal replied.

"Good, there's two of us who have sense, so maybe it's time to join the party."

In the distance Opal could see the gray towers of the Middlehurst campus. She felt a familiar drop in the pit of her stomach. Opal had never quite made peace with Middlehurst. She'd only gone there because her mother was an alumna—family pressure would be the only reason that she would go to an all women's college. True, if she hadn't gone to Middlehurst, she wouldn't have met Precious, Reva and Faith—but the previous three years had not been easy for her. The Art History Department did not have many African Americans there and although the professors and other students went out of their way to make her feel welcome and comfortable, Opal still felt alienated.

"I'm hungry," Opal lied. "Let's stop somewhere and eat," she said, in an effort to delay the inevitable reentry back to college life.

"Trying to spend some extra time with me?" asked Jordan with a chuckle.

Opal smiled back at him. "Absolutely."

Jordan slowed his car down. "There's a seafood place near here that makes great lobster rolls. You game?"

"Always," said Opal, looking over at her fiancé. She wondered when the feelings she knew that she should have towards Jordan would finally materialize.

Faith

Faith Maberley stared at Hope and Charity. For a fleeting moment she wondered what it would be like to be an only child. There was only one year between herself and the twins, but most folks thought that they were triplets. They looked alike, spoke with the same hoarse voice, had the same nervous laugh and they had only just recently stopped dressing alike—in a fit of rebellion against their West Indian mother, who had yet to forgive them. Hope and Charity had grown up following her everywhere, and college was no exception. Faith had chosen to go to Middlehurst because it was several hundred miles away from Shaker Heights—the upscale Cleveland suburb where she had grown up. Hope and Charity had followed her there the very next year. Faith had finally drawn the line when Hope and Charity tried to follow her to her dormitory. Still, Hope and Charity found their way entirely too often to her dorm room.

Faith watched as Charity rifled through her closet in an attempt to find something she could wear on yet another hot date. When does the child have time to study, she wondered. Hope was lying on Faith's twin bed, talking about something that made no sense to Faith, except that the conversation dealt with Bob Marley, Malcolm X and rap music. Hope's conversations usually had no defined beginnings or endings. They simply meandered until Hope, or the listener, eventually gave up showing any interest in the topic at hand. Who would think that a five hundred acre campus would not be large enough to get away from her sisters?

Faith's mother had urged her children to love each other. From birth, the importance of family was practiced and preached in the Maberley clan. But there were times when the appeal of being the solitary child proved almost irresistible.

"What's this?" Charity held up an almost empty bottle of Riesling wine. "And what's it doing in your closet?"

Damn. Charity was as good as a bloodhound. If you wanted something to stay hidden, don't have Charity Maberley around. Her family were Baptists, and Baptists, according to her mother, did not drink alcohol. There were times when Faith saw the logic in this, usually the day after she'd had a close encounter with a few too many glasses of her favorite Riesling wine. Faith knew that her family was worried, but they were just overprotective, opinionated Baptist folks. A drink or two was her way of unwinding.

"It's a wine bottle, Charity," said Faith. "You don't need to wave it in front of my face like a flag."

"I know what it is," said Charity, doing an accurate imitation of their mother, with one hand on her hip and her head cocked to the side. "It's an almost empty bottle."

"Did you drink the whole thing by yourself?" asked Hope, sitting up in the bed.

"Not that it's any of your business," Faith replied, "but no, I didn't drink it alone. I shared it with Reva and Precious.

That was a lie. Reva and Precious were just as worried about Faith's drinking as her sisters were. The last thing they would share with her was a bottle of wine.

"Faith, you drink too much," said Charity, her voice quiet.

"No sermons this afternoon, please," said Faith.

"She's right," said Hope. "You do drink too much. Mama says . . ."

"Look, I don't want to hear what Mama says about anything right now . . . I have three chapters of biology to read before the first class tomorrow—so I'd appreciate it if you two would leave now so I can study . . ."

"Are you kicking us out?" asked Charity, indignant, and momentarily forgetting the bottle she was holding.

"I wouldn't put it that way," said Faith, taking the opportunity to take the bottle from Charity's hand. "I'm just trying not to flunk out of college my senior year."

Hope snorted. "Drinking is not the way to elevate your grade point average . . ."

Faith put the almost empty Riesling bottle in the trash can, then she opened her door to emphasize that it was time for her annoying little sisters to go.

Hope shook her head. "You're lucky we love you, girlfriend."

Charity wasn't so kind. "I don't see you kicking your friends out of your room—you're just mad because we found that bottle, and Faith, you know you drink too much, girl . . ."

"Out." Faith had had enough. She knew where this particular road would lead them. If she listened to her family, she'd be in Alcoholics Anonymous already. Yes, she liked to drink, and there were times she drank to excess but she could stop at any time. She was anything but an alcoholic. Folks, starting with her family, needed to keep their minds on their own business.

Hope left without saying a thing, but Charity had to get in a parting shot.

"Chicken merry, the hawk is near," said Charity, before she slammed the door. It was one of their mother's favorite sayings, and it signified that no matter how merry things might be, there was trouble coming around the corner. Faith shook her head. She loved her sisters. She loved her mother. She loved her father. She loved her friends, but everyone needed to stay out of her business.

Opal

Opal sat on the windowsill in her dormitory room and waved her left hand in the air. It still felt odd seeing the diamond on her fourth finger. After Jordan had gone back to Cambridge, she'd called her girlfriends to come to her dorm room. She hadn't seen them since summer break began and she was anxious to break her news to them.

Jordan had wanted to remain with her while she told her girlfriends of her engagement, but Opal had been firm in sending him back to his apartment. There were some things she wanted to do alone and this was one of them. Sometimes Jordan's unrelenting focus on her was oppressive. He hovered around her like a mother hen who was afraid that her chick would flee the nest. She had been relieved to see him go. After spending the last three days with him at his family's place in Martha's Vineyard, she wanted some time away. She knew that it was not a good sign to be relieved when your fiancé left your presence, but she was certain that most brides-to-be had some doubts. Didn't they?

Her friends lounged around her small dormitory room. Faith was lying on the floor, with Reva sitting next to her. Precious sat on the bed. Opal waved her left hand at them again.

"Oh, my God," Faith shrieked, "you're engaged!"

Opal was quickly surrounded by her three friends. Her ring was examined and the appropriate exclamations were made.

"How big is your rock?" asked Faith.

"Four carats," Opal replied calmly. "It's too big."

"When did this happen and why didn't you call us?" asked Precious.

"He asked me three weeks ago at the Vineyard."

"Three weeks ago!" Faith cried. "You kept this from us for *three weeks!*"

"I wanted to tell you in person."

Reva walked over to Opal's narrow twin bed and sat down. "Opal, the last time we talked, you told me that you weren't sure about Jordan."

"Oh, for heaven's sake, Reva, don't rain on her parade!" said Faith.

Reva ignored her. "Opal, are you sure about this?"

Trust Reva to get right to the point. Opal was not sure about Jordan. She was not sure about anything. She had a perfect man— handsome, smart, funny, kind, passionate where it counted. Still, the love she knew she should feel for Jordan hadn't come yet, but she was still waiting. Three weeks ago, she'd said yes to Jordan's proposal. What did it take to make her happy, she wondered. She was a favored child, her parents' long awaited daughter. Like Jordan she was rich, good-looking and smart. People looked at her with envy as if her pedigree was an automatic ticket to the good life. If they only knew that she couldn't remember the last time she'd truly known happiness, joy. Thank God for her girlfriends, at least with them she had moments of happiness, although these moments were always chased by a nagging feeling that something wasn't quite right with her world. She just didn't know the source of her disquiet.

Opal turned on her brightest smile. "I'm sure about my decision," she said. "Jordan is a good man."

Faith and Precious sat down beside Reva on the bed. Opal remained sitting on her windowsill. The leaded glass windows were open, and she could hear pieces of conversation coming from the courtyard below. There was a warm September breeze that she knew was only temporary. In a few weeks, the breezes would get decidedly cooler, as summer gave way to fall.

"I know he's a good man," said Reva, "but do you love him?"

"Reva, let it go," said Faith. "Just be happy for Opal."

"I do love him," said Opal. *I just don't know if I'm in love with him.*

"We're happy for you," said Precious.

"Let's have a drink to celebrate," Faith laughed.

Everyone in the room stared at Faith, but it was Reva who spoke the words that were on everyone's mind. "Faith, have you lost your mind?"

Faith raised both hands in mock protest. "Hey, I was just kidding."

"Your drinking is nothing to joke about," Precious said quietly. Opal knew that Precious was thinking of her own mother's addiction to crack.

"Bad joke," said Faith, whose smile disappeared as she noticed that no one was joining in on the joke.

Opal had first noticed Faith's drinking their freshman year, but it wasn't until junior year, after Faith's two episodes of blacking out, that Opal realized that Faith had a drinking problem. Her assessment of Faith's drinking problems were confirmed by a call from a Boston jail last spring, after Faith had gotten arrested for driving while intoxicated. Opal's father, a Boston lawyer and politician, had convinced the judge to drop the charges in exchange for mandatory alcohol abuse counseling sessions. Opal, Reva and Precious had all taken turns going to the counseling sessions with Faith. After she'd completed the program, Faith promised she'd never have another drink. Opal hoped that she'd keep that promise.

"I tell you what," Opal said, in an attempt to diffuse the tense air in the room. "I've got some heavenly hash ice cream in the refrigerator downstairs . . . that could definitely constitute a celebratory meal."

"I'm on a diet," said Precious.

"Girl, no one wants a bone but a dog," said Opal. Opal was tall and thin. She ate whatever she felt like and never gained an ounce. A good metabolism and a high strung personality probably attributed to Opal's slender shape. Despite this, Opal was Precious' biggest defender. She refused to let anyone talk about Precious' weight, including Precious herself.

"That's right," Faith chimed in. "Thick is in!"

"Big women unite!" said Reva, joining her friends. She knew how down Precious was about her weight.

Precious started laughing. "All right, we can have the damn ice cream. Enough, already!"

"You all are going to be my bridesmaids," said Opal, as if they had no say in the decision.

The room got quiet, and Opal could swear that even Reva looked misty eyed, although later, she thought that it was just a trick of the lighting.

Finally, Faith spoke. "I look good in pastels."

"I've got to lose some weight," Precious said.

Reva stood up and walked over to Opal. She looked as if she wanted to say something, but wasn't quite certain how to begin. Then, Reva hugged Opal. Opal felt strong arms hold her. Tight. Just as quickly, Reva pulled away, then she said, "Just don't put me in any of those ugly bridesmaid dresses."

Chapter 2

Precious

Middlehurst College was founded in 1832 by the Middlehurst family, a prominent Boston family of abolitionists. The Middlehurst family, who made their considerable fortune in the shipping industry, were committed to the idea of social justice and as a result, Negroes, as black people were then called, were accepted to Middlehurst College from its inception. In 1832, there were two young women of African descent at the College, which was almost unheard of. Despite the best intentions of Middlehurst College, the number of black women who attended the college did not greatly increase until the 1970s, when the doors seem to swing open a little wider, and the normal one percent of students of African heritage swelled to almost ten percent, where it now stood, give or take few percentage points.

Precious was well acquainted with the history of Middlehurst College, as well as the history of the Middlehurst family, whose fates were often intertwined. Every freshman was expected to take a course on the history of the college. She had even gone to a tea where a few select students were invited to meet some of the Middlehurst descendents. *"How nice it is to see you people are doing so well here at Middlehurst,"* the septugenarian Middlehurst had beamed at her. Precious had bristled at the "you people" reference and had kept her placid smile in place without responding. The truth was, that while Precious did well at Middlehurst, as she had done well at every other school she'd attended, many other African American students did not fare as well as she did. There were few African American students that shared her

high grade point average, and even fewer shared her love and connection to the college. Most felt in some way that they did not fit in.

Precious remembered that that had been her fear also, but the college had come to be a part of her. She loved the bells that rang at four
o'clock every day; she loved the Wednesday afternoon teas with the
alumnae; she loved the traditions of the college; she loved sitting in
her favorite chair in Wadsworth Library, right by the window that
looked over the lake; she loved the process of learning; and most of
all, she loved being in a place where she was not ridiculed for her love
of learning. She had grown up in a neighborhood where people who
liked going to school were viewed with suspicion, or worse, derision.
Looking back, she realized that most of the people in her old neighborhood were so defeated that they could not see a way out. Education
and all that it offered was a dream that most considered out of their
reach. Precious knew that if she did not have her father in her corner,
she, like the rest of the children in her neighborhood, would have
given in to the inevitability of failure.

Roosevelt Averyheart refused to let his daughter fail. He cleaned
toilets, worked two jobs, and took jobs that other people would have
walked away from, because he did not want his daughter to fail. Even
after her mother left them to pay homage to the siren call of the crack
pipe, Roosevelt refused to be defeated. He taught his daughter to
read when she was three years old. He taught her to love jazz, playing
his vintage Sarah Vaughan and Billie Holliday records. He told her
stories about black people—W.E.B. DuBois, Zora Neale Hurston,
Malcolm X, Martin Luther King, Jr., Muhammad Ali—who had
achieved success in education, sports, theatre, science, and the arts.
"If they could do it," was his constant message, *"then there's no reason why
you can't either."*

By the time she was seven, he made Precious read to him from the
New York Times and the Bible, King James Version, thank you very
much, every day. He also insisted that she learn a Bible verse every
day. Often, he would come home from his job, dirty and tired, but he
would always ask *"what'cha learn today, Precious Pie?"* Once, in exasperation, she'd replied *"nothing, Daddy, I didn't learn anything today."* She
was tired of studying every day. The other kids around the block got
to play, but she had to always study. Even with her good grades, her father insisted that she make it her business to learn something new
every day. She remembered that it had been a hot summer day, and
she had leaned out of her fourth floor apartment window looking at
the kids on the block run screaming, laughing, hurling themselves
through the water of an open fire sprinkler. *"Come on down, Precious!"*
They had called. *"Your Daddy ain't here. Come on down."* But Precious
shook her head no. The last time she disobeyed her father, her back-

side paid for it, and she didn't want a repeat performance. But by the time her father got home, the old familiar resentment that her father seemed to always expect more from her than other parents did from their own children, had surfaced. The other kids at school could bring home C's and D's. When Precious brought home a B, her daddy was disappointed.

"What'cha mean you didn't learn anything today?" Her father's tone had been mild, but his dark eyes were hot. Her daddy was in general an even tempered man, but you didn't want to cross him. He had a bad temper. He'd gotten in trouble over his temper, but that, he would say with a rueful smile, was another life.

Throwing caution far away, Precious had stuck her chin out, striking a defiant pose, right hand on right hip. *"I just didn't feel like learning anything today, Daddy. It was hot and I was tired."*

"It was hot and you were tired?" her father asked her, still keeping his tone mild.

Precious nodded her head, but something in the way her father looked at her made her pose a little less defiant.

"I'll tell you what hot and tired is, Precious," her father had said, moving closer to her. *"Hot and tired is cleaning thirty-five bathrooms, with no kind of ventilation. It's hauling other people's garbage when it's ninety-five degrees outside and a whole lot hotter inside. It's mopping more floors than you can count. It's . . ."*

"I get the picture, Daddy," she'd said quietly.

"Do you now, Miss Lady?" He asked. Daddy only said "Miss Lady" when he was annoyed.

"Yes, Daddy, I do."

"There's nothing wrong with working, even if it's cleaning up other people's mess," said Roosevelt Averyheart. *"An honest job is just that—and what I do takes care of you and takes care of me. But I want more for you, Precious. I want so much more—don't you want more for yourself?"*

She was ashamed. She knew how hard her father worked for her, and here she was acting plain old ungrateful—acting like her mother.

"I'm sorry, Daddy."

"Yes, you are," replied Roosevelt Averyheart. *"Now go on in your room and open that big old encyclopedia that I got you last Christmas and find out something new about this world that you live in—and once you've found it out, come on back and we'll talk about it."*

"O.K., Daddy."

Roosevelt had been right about Middlehurst just as he had been right about insisting that she learn something new every day. By the time she got to Middlehurst, one of the most elite schools, a member of the so-called Seven Sisters, Precious Averyheart, a girl from Harlem who went to public schools all her life, could keep up with, if not surpass, a lot of students who went to better schools. Roosevelt had been proud, but he'd been even prouder when he saw that his Precious took Middlehurst for all it gave.

Precious wished that Reva, Faith and Opal shared her love for Middlehurst. Reva hated the place, Faith tolerated Middlehurst, and Opal was just plain old indifferent—but then again, it seemed to Precious that Opal was indifferent to most of the blessings that came her way. She loved Opal like a sister, but she was spoiled. Her family had done a good job in spoiling the much beloved and only daughter. Most people assumed that when Precious disapproved of things Opal said or did, she was jealous. It was easy to see why folks thought that jealousy entered the picture. Opal had a lot of attributes that Precious would have been jealous about if she were that kind of person. First, Opal was beautiful—knockout, model, ought-to-be-in-movies beautiful. With beautiful skin, the color of burnished copper, and dark red hair, courtesy of some long forgotten Scotch-Irish ancestor, Opal was a striking figure. She had large piercing dark brown eyes, which seemed to look right through you, as if she could see something you were trying to hide. Her prominent, jutting cheekbones evoked her Indian ancestry and her full, wide lips, the color of crushed berries, came straight from the Motherland. If this were not enough, Opal had two dimples that magically appeared any time she smiled. Precious had seen those dimples get Opal out of a world of trouble.

Years of playing tennis (she had been offered tennis scholarships to no less than five schools), had kept her frame long and lean. Everyone else had put on pounds since freshman year, but Opal remained slender, to the envy of most people around her. Opal was tall—almost six feet in her stocking feet. She became a veritable giant when she wore her usual four-inch black patent leather pumps. With her tall stature, her wild, curly red hair, which she refused to tame or to perm, and her flair for wearing her favorite color, black, Opal made a dramatic figure around campus. She was smart, rich and had a wicked sense of humor, and despite her aversion to makeup, her natural beauty was difficult to ignore. But Precious, whose admittedly pleasant good looks could never compare to Opal, was not jealous of her. Precious had learned a long time ago from her mother's experience the futility of wanting what someone else had.

Still, Opal annoyed her at times. It didn't seem right that a person who had as much going for her as Opal did was so nonchalant about her many blessings. Opal had two parents who worshipped her. She was the youngest and the only daughter in a family of five. Her brothers, who all went to various Ivy League schools, were protective and adored their baby sister. She had a fiancé who was fine, rich and decent. Everyone loved Jordan, except, it seemed, Opal. It seemed to Precious that Opal was only making time with Jordan—eventually, Precious was sure, he would go the way of other discarded men who lived on only in memories and old photo albums. Opal just didn't know a good thing even if it bit her on the hand.

Precious turned her attention back to present matters. It was almost time for the four o'clock tea. There were few people who looked like Precious that showed up for the weekly teas. Precious knew that her friends were amused by her devotion to these teas. Precious herself wondered why something that started out by accident, for she had only gone to the first tea to keep an appointment with a professor who wanted to talk to her about a case study, evolved into something regular and something to which she looked forward. The weekly teas were held in the very grand Faculty House, located at the edge of the lake. The Faculty House reminded Precious of the house in *Gone With The Wind*—stark white with four imposing pillars in front. In warmer months, the teas were held on the lawn under a billowing white tent, in case the capricious New England weather turned nasty. In colder months, the teas were held in the House's front parlor or in the adjoining wood-paneled library.

As it was an unusually warm late September day, the tea was going to be held on the lawn. Precious hurried down the path behind her dorm—a shortcut. It was quarter to four and she hated being late. One of the many lessons Roosevelt Averyheart had taught his daughter was the value of time, other people's time as well as her own. Precious walked down the steep hill that led to a path that cut through the campus, eventually reaching the Faculty House, which was located on the north side of campus. She could have taken one of the campus buses but it was a beautiful afternoon and the sun felt good on her face. If she hurried she'd make it just in time for Reverend Ward's blessing of the tea.

Opal

"What do you mean you have a lump underneath your breast?" Reva's voice was sharp. "And more to the point, why haven't you gone to see the doctor?"

"Would you please keep your voice down," Opal sighed. Trust Reva to make everything sound so dramatic. They were sitting at a table at the Student Center—the place where everyone eventually gravitated to—as Opal would often joke, the epicenter of the campus. The Student Center was a good place for resting before or after classes, gossiping, and drinking some pretty good coffee.

"You're worried about the level of my voice?" Reva asked, one eyebrow arched, clearly signifying annoyance.

Opal took a sip of her coffee, which was now significantly cooler, and bordering on cold. It tasted bitter to her, but she had greater things to worry about besides her cold coffee. "I shouldn't have told you anything. You're making a big deal out of this."

Even as the words left her lips, Opal tasted the bitter taste of fear. She could feel her heart start to quicken. *Stop it,* she commanded herself. *Stop thinking the worst.*

"What does Jordan say about all this?" Reva asked.

"I haven't told him. You're the only person I've talked to about this . . ."

"You haven't told Jordan!" Reva did not let Opal finish her sentence. "Opal, you are engaged to the man. You're going to be getting married to him."

"We haven't set a date yet," said Opal, bristling at Reva's judgmental tone. "Besides I don't have to tell Jordan everything."

"But this is important, Opal." Reva had the good sense to lower her voice. The two Leon sisters were hovering close by. Bridget and Carlotta Leon were known as the town criers around campus. When it came to the tightly knit African American community, both students and teachers, Bridget and Carlotta knew everybody's business and they were only too happy to share, usually some embarrassing information, with anyone who would listen. "This could be something serious, Opal."

Opal hated when Reva was so righteous. She would rear back like a preacher making a point on Sunday morning, and throw down judgment on whomever had earned her wrath. Still, with all that judgment, came a lot of kindness and good advice. She was a steadfast friend, and she didn't scare easily. She was loyal and loving, and in a tough situation, no one kept a cooler head than Reva, once she got through telling you what was wrong with you and your situation.

She would be the perfect girlfriend for some lucky man, but no one seemed to come Reva's way. She was a pretty girl, with beautiful brown skin, a perfectly oval face, and only slightly chubby cheeks. Reva was solidly built, and to Opal, Reva's round frame was a welcome change from the anorexic looking women that seemed to make up the majority of the student population at Middlehurst. Reva wore her hair in long, black cornrow braids pulled away from her face. To Opal, Reva looked like an African princess. What was wrong with the men that came over to the socials, as the dances at Middlehurst were called? Reva was a true gem. Opal felt that most men were intimidated by Reva's directness. She did not play games. She told you exactly what she thought, even when she was being kind about it.

"What are you going to do about this?" Reva asked, bringing Opal back to the problem at hand.

Opal cleared her throat and kept her voice low. "We don't know if it's serious. It could be or it could be nothing."

"Then you'll just have to go to a doctor to find out, won't you?" Reva asked.

Opal remained silent. She was going to go a doctor, but she wasn't ready yet. She couldn't explain this to Reva. Reva took the world on her own terms. She did not understand fear. Her constitution simply did not allow her to be anything less than absolutely confident.

"Opal, please tell me you're going to the doctor."

"Hey, ladies," Carlotta Leon sat down on the empty chair next to Opal. Bridget hovered close by her sister. "What are y'all talking about? Looks intense."

Opal had often wondered if Carlotta went out of her way to be disagreeable or if it came naturally to her. They had never gotten along. In freshman year, Opal had found out that Carlotta had pursued one of Opal's boyfriends, while he was still dating Opal. Carlotta was a good-looking woman. She was the better looking of the Leon sisters, but Carlotta's beauty was store bought. Blue contact lenses, wheat colored weave, a nose job and breast reduction had done wonders for Carlotta's looks, but nothing for her personality.

Opal watched as Reva arched one eyebrow and looked at Carlotta. "Not that it's any of your business, but Opal and I are having a private discussion. We'd appreciate it if you'd find someplace else to sit."

Straight and to the point. That was Reva. Carlotta rose, and if she took offense to Reva's words, she hid it behind a smooth smile.

"You don't have to tell me twice, Reva. You *know* I hate to intrude."

Opal watched as Carlotta walked across the Student Union with Bridget trailing nervously behind—off to get some information on yet another victim.

Reva shook her head. "Ain't nothing but the devil—those Leon sisters are enough to try the patience of a good woman and you know I am not that good."

Opal laughed. "I thought you were a little rude."

"Believe me," said Reva sipping her coffee. "I didn't tell Carlotta what I really thought about her trifling self."

"I think she got the hint."

Reva shifted in her seat. "When are we going to the doctor?"

"What do you mean we?" asked Opal, knowing even before she received her answer, that it was impossible trying to fight against Reva's wishes. She was like a force of nature. When Reva Nettingham set her mind to something, woe be unto those who stood in the way between her and her goal.

"I'm going with you, of course," said Reva.

"Reva, I can handle this on my own. I appreciate your help . . ."

Reva stood up. The conversation was fast coming to an end. Reva had apparently had enough. "Listen, sister girl—you've got until tomorrow morning to make a doctor's appointment. If you don't make an appointment by tomorrow morning, I will make the appointment and haul your behind to the doctor's office with me."

"Where are you going?" Opal asked, annoyed that Reva had backed her into a corner, but thankful that Reva would be with her when she got her examination. Reva could be a pain, but Reva was definitely the kind of soldier you wanted when you went into battle, and Opal could feel that there was a battle coming her way.

"Unlike you and your overly rich self, I've got to go earn my keep. I'm supposed to be working over at the library and as of five minutes ago, I'm late. Call me tonight and let me know what time your doctor's appointment is."

"You might not be available for the appointment."

"I'll be available. Count on that." Without a backward glance, Reva walked out of the Student Union. Opal had always admired how Reva carried herself—with her head held high and her shoulders thrown back like some warrior princess. Opal shook her head. What did she expect when she told Reva about her situation? She'd known that Reva would take care of business.

Opal stood up. It was time to make a phone call she probably should have made over a month ago.

Precious

When Reva, the most outspoken of her friends, would ask Precious, "What on earth do you see in those dry old ladies that come to those damn teas," Precious would smile. Those dry old ladies, the alumnae in the Boston area, would regularly come to the teas, week after week, no matter the weather or, in some circumstances personal drama, and had become Precious' friends. They were not in the same category as Reva, Faith and Opal, but she enjoyed their company and looked forward to talking with them about their lives, their past, their politics, their future and their stories. She enjoyed hearing the ladies talk about "the good old days." They were all, in their own individual way, trendsetters of their time. From the homemakers who raised children whose lives reflected their mothers' sacrifice, to the most hardened career overachiever, the alumnae were all interesting.

Her two favorite "blue-haired ladies," her personal name for the older women, were Miss Minniefield and Mrs. Hamlett. Miss Minniefield had been a principal for a school on an Indian reservation somewhere out west. She'd recently come back to the East, after living on the reservation for almost fifty years. Mrs. Hamlett was an eighty-two-year-old woman who had, in the face of considerable family finances and tradition, turned her back on her inheritance (which her parents promptly rescinded) for the unpardonable sin of marrying a black man. She had met and married a civil rights attorney. Mrs. Hamlett's family could be traced back to the Mayflower and they never reconciled that their daughter had married outside of her race. Mrs. Hamlett, who was recently widowed, still smiled that faraway smile of those who have known and welcomed unconditional love, when she talked about her beloved husband, Phillip Hamlett, a civil rights attorney who, despite his lucrative law practice, never forgot where he came from. Like Miss Minniefield, Mrs. Hamlett also had recently come back East.

In addition to the alumnae and various college professors who attended the teas, there was also a good amount of students who came, usually earnest freshmen who eventually stopped coming to the teas once they found out that other than good conversation, finger sandwiches, and strong English tea, there was no real benefit to attending them. Still, there was the faithful group of students, who like Precious, would come week after week to this "social ritual," Opal's derisive description of the teas.

The chapel bells pealed four times just as Precious walked across the Faculty House lawn. In front of her she could see that a small group of people had gathered under a stark white tent, which billowed in the soft September breeze. The usual suspects were there—some professors, Reverend Ward, a smattering of students, and the alumnae. Miss Minniefield and Mrs. Hamlett were there, but there was something odd with this very familiar picture. It took Precious a moment to figure it all out. There was someone new standing with the group—a young African American man with a hard, massive frame that betrayed an obsession with athletics, or more specifically, the weight machine. He was not much taller than she and Precious doubted if he was six feet. But his body, which even beneath an ill fitting navy blue suit was obviously tight and muscular, attracted her attention. He was standing near Mrs. Hamlett, but he was looking directly at her as if he had been waiting for her. Although there were a few male students at Middlehurst, exchange students who came from other colleges in the area and took courses at Middlehurst, until now, no male student had ever come to one of the weekly teas.

Mrs. Hamlett caught her stare and smiled at her. Waving her over to them, Mrs. Hamlett called out "Precious, come here. I'd like you to meet my nephew, Rory."

Precious had heard about Mrs. Hamlett's nephew, but she had assumed that he was white. Rory was obviously from Mr. Hamlett's side
of the family.

Precious was immediately self-conscious. She did not like the way this
man was staring at her. She couldn't quite place it, but she didn't like it.
In general, men did not look at her that way. In general, men did not
usually look in her direction at all. Precious did not consider herself to
be a raving beauty, but the way this man looked at her was as if he had
just discovered some rare jewel. She suddenly wished that she had worn
something other than the long black slacks and bright floral top, something her mother had bought her that did not in any way reflect
Precious' taste. *What is wrong with me?* Precious thought with a flash of
annoyance. *Why on earth should I care what this man thinks of my outfit?*

She walked over to Mrs. Hamlett and gave her a quick hug.
"How're you doing, Mrs. H?" Precious asked her friend.

Mrs. Hamlett replied in her typical fashion. "Splendid."

Then, Mrs. Hamlett turned towards the man standing next to her
and said, "This is Precious, and believe me she is aptly named."

Precious couldn't help smiling. Mrs. Hamlett was playing matchmaker. She was certain that Mrs. Hamlett had good intentions. She
had often talked to Precious about the importance of having someone special in her life. There were times that Precious wondered what
it would be like to be in a relationship with someone. She was twenty-
one years old, and apart from some short term hook ups, which could
not in any way be characterized as relationships, Precious had never
connected romantically with anyone. She'd apparently made the mistake of telling this to Mrs. Hamlett and that explained the presence of
Mrs. Hamlett's nephew at the tea.

He held his hand out towards her. "Rory Hamlett," he said, shaking
her hand.

Precious resisted the urge to pull away. There was something
strangely intimate about the handshake and she didn't like it. Besides,
Rory Hamlett was staring at her in an entirely too familiar way.

"Precious Averyheart," she replied, finally pulling her hand from his.

"Rory goes to Boston Union University. He's a football player," said
Mrs. Hamlett, as if this was the perfect explanation for this hulking
stranger to attend the weekly tea.

Precious nodded her head in Rory Hamlett's direction and gave
him a distant smile. The smile she received from Rory in return was
downright sunny.

"I've heard a lot about you, Miss Averyheart," said Rory. His voice
reminded her of rolling thunder, rich and deep.

Precious couldn't resist. "Have you now?"

"Indeed," said Rory, staring directly at her. His gaze was unwavering.

"I think I see Mrs. Atwell over by the punch bowl—I'll be back," said Mrs. Hamlett, rushing off in an obvious ploy to leave them alone.

He was not good-looking in the traditional sense. His features, while interesting, could not be construed as handsome. His chin was too pronounced, and his dark eyes were too wide apart, and his neck looked as if it belonged to a Russian wrestler or a prison convict who spent too much time lifting weights, but there was something arresting about Rory Hamlett. Precious couldn't quite figure it out. Perhaps it was the way he stared directly and unflinchingly into her eyes or perhaps it was his wide, easy smile. There was something almost appealing about Rory Hamlett.

"How did Mrs. H end up roping you into this?"

"I'm not sure what you mean, Miss Averyheart."

"Call me Precious, and I think you know what I mean. How did you get talked into coming to a Middlehurst tea?"

"Do you want the truth, Precious?"

"Always."

"Aunt Patti told me that she wanted me to meet a fascinating woman who had a charming name."

Precious laughed.

"I'm sorry about that," said Precious. "Mrs. H is determined to play the matchmaker when it comes to me."

"Don't be sorry, Precious," Rory replied. "I'm not."

Was this man flirting with her? This was new territory. Men did not flirt with her. They asked her directions. They asked her for advice. They asked her about her friends. But, they most definitely did not flirt with her.

At that particular moment, Reverend Ward announced that it was time for grace. As was the custom, the attendees all held hands. Rory Hamlett took her hand in his as if it were the most natural thing to do. Mrs. Hamlett walked over and took her other hand. Reverend Ward did not believe in simple prayers of thanks. Her prayers were exhortations to the Lord to not only bless the weekly teas, but to deal with whatever was on Reverend Ward's mind at that particular moment. The prayers were always interesting and by the time the prayers were over, Precious usually felt that she had been to church. This day, however, Reverend Ward's prayers were far away from her thoughts. Instead, Precious thought about Rory Hamlett and the feel of his calloused hand in hers.

Faith

Mulligan's Bar was not a nice place. It was dark, dirty and played loud rock music—but it was a place where Faith knew that she could have a drink without having to worry about running into anyone she knew. Her friends thought that she drank too much. In her heart she knew she had a drinking problem, but she would stop soon. The pressures of the senior year were alleviated with a drink. She would stop drinking at some point, just not now.

Faith had been drinking since she was seventeen years old. She'd discovered she liked her father's scotch. Back then, she'd sneak a drink, sometimes to calm her down or other times, just because she liked the taste. No one knew about her drinking then. After she started college, however, things changed. There were a few times when she'd gotten drunk and word had gotten back to her family. Last year, she'd passed out in the parking lot, then the DWI incident occured and the dean had gotten involved. She was forced to go to mandatory counseling and she took classes on alcohol abuse. She'd stopped drinking for a few months, but then over the summer, she'd begun drinking again.

Mulligan's Bar was located on the outskirts of the town of Middlehurst. Its clientele was strictly down and out, but no one bothered to card you when you asked for a drink and, except for the occasional curious patron who wanted to know why a young college woman was hanging out in a grubby bar, people left you alone. Faith took a sip of her drink, scotch and soda. Heavy on the scotch, easy on the soda. She took an index finger and stirred her drink absently. She was sitting at one end of the bar, watching the only working television monitor, which was permanently tuned to the sports channel.

Today had been a rough day. It had started with a phone call from her mother. Her sisters had apparently informed her about the wine bottle they'd found in her closet. Her mother had not been pleased. Then, she'd gotten another phone call. This one was more disturbing. Her ex-boyfriend, Alan, had announced that he was in town and he wanted to see her. She'd resisted the urge to accept his invitation for a date tonight, but it hadn't been easy. She wasn't in love with him anymore. He'd broken her heart on too many occasions, but she was lonely. She hadn't had a date in longer than she cared to remember and although she loved hanging out with her girls, she missed the companionship of a boyfriend.

Alan took her refusal to see him in good stride, which also bothered her. At least he could have had the good grace to act disappointed. But Alan had never really cared about her. She was a convenient relationship. He was an airline pilot who flew the New York–Boston route. Whenever he got to Boston he'd give her a call. Faith became inconvenient when she began pressing him for a more serious relationship. They'd met in a bar in Boston and for two years, whenever Alan came to Boston he would call. Looking back, they didn't do much more than drink. They hardly ever went anywhere other than Alan's hotel room, where usually a great deal of liquor was consumed. He was handsome, older and funny. She later found out that he was also engaged to a stewardess who showed up on campus looking for Faith. It took the intervention of her girlfriends and the help of the campus police to calm the stewardess down. They'd broken up six months ago and Faith had expected that Alan would have married his stewardess by now. When Faith had asked Alan about his fiancée he'd gotten suddenly uncommunicative.

"Gotta go," he'd chirped happily. "Maybe I'll see you around sometime."

Then, right before he hung up, he'd asked her a question. "Faith, are you still drinking like you used to?"

Faith had laughed, "Like *we* used to."

"I don't drink anymore," Alan had said quietly. "I've been sober for three months. I joined AA."

This statement had taken Faith aback.

"Faith, I'd like to send you some pamplets from AA."

"I don't need any pamplets," said Faith, annoyed that yet somebody else was bothering her about her drinking.

"Well, let me send them to you . . ."

"I don't need any pamplets," Faith interrupted Alan. "Listen, thanks for calling. 'Bye."

She'd hung up the phone quickly. Those AA people were like sinners who had found religion. They wanted to share the good news with everyone, but Faith didn't need this kind of help. Her drinking was under control. She liked to drink, there was nothing wrong with that. As she stirred her drink again, she caught a look at herself in the mirror across from the bar counter. She did not see an attractive black woman, with a short curly haircut. She did not see a student at Middlehurst College who was on her way to a masters degree in eduction. She did not see the eldest daughter of three beloved children. Instead, she saw a lonely woman with sad eyes.

Chapter 3

Reva

The black table was full. The table by the leaded glass windows in the cafeteria was known to everyone in Clifton Hall, Reva's dorm, as the black table, because it was the unofficial seating place of the African Americans in Clifton Hall. Reva was not sure exactly when this tradition started, but as long as she had been living in Clifton Hall, and this was now her fourth year, the big oval table by the window was where the majority of the African American students ate their meals. At first, the self-segregation of the dining room bothered Reva. She had initially refused to sit at the black table, but she had ended up sitting by herself at another table.

Middlehurst was a college where cliques thrived. There was the preppy clique, the artsy clique, the East Coast clique, not be outdone by the West Coast clique. People just seemed to gravitate to groups where they had something in common with the other members of the group. The African American students were no different. Reva, who did not grow up with the joy of having good girlfriends, had felt lonely and alienated when she first got to Middlehurst. The alienation was never more pronounced than at mealtimes, when there was no group to sit with. She did not know any of the African American students in Clifton and they, in turn, did not make any overtures to her. The other tables, with their specific cliques and pairings, similarly exhuded the "do not apply" air.

Reva was convinced that she was destined to eat alone until one day Precious had come over to her table, one Sunday evening. Reva had been sitting alone, eating particularly nasty meatloaf (the cooks at

Clifton were not known for their culinary talent) intent on a novel (her company) when Precious had walked over to her and said without any preamble, "My girls are wondering if you're shy or if you're just stuck up."

Reva had put down her book and looked at Precious. She had seen her before, and they had nodded to each other in the ways of folks who recognize each other but don't want to go much further than that. At that time, Precious, while not as plump as she was eventually going to become after four years of college food, was a healthy size. She had pretty brown skin, with long thick black hair, which she often wore in an untidy bun. She had large, piercing dark eyes, and a round face. Reva had noticed that she was fond of wearing jeans and oversize sweatshirts. She later came to learn that the times when Precious put on dresses were rare and noteworthy, usually signifying a celebration of some sort.

"So," Precious had continued, "are you stuck up or are you shy?"

"I don't fall into either of those categories," Reva replied.

Across the room she could see the two other young women who would become her dearest friends, Opal and Faith, looking over at them.

"So why do you eat alone?" asked Precious.

"I don't see how my eating habits concern you," said Reva, taking an instant dislike to Precious. She did not take kindly to people who tried to get into her business.

Precious laughed, apparently not taking any offense. "Actually, my girls and I thought you might like some company, seeing as how you eat all by yourself day after day."

It was on the tip, the very tip of her tongue, to tell Precious exactly where she could put her and her busybody friends' concern, but there was something in Precious' eyes that silenced her tongue. There was a warmth, an openness that she was unfamiliar with. She had been raised by a mother, Sugar, who had taught her to view other women with mistrust. The other girls that she grew up with were more interested in boys than books, and they, in turn, viewed Reva as if she were some sort of unexplained freak of nature. It had been easy therefore to grow up without the benefit of friendship. Her books were her friends. But something in Precious' eyes, something in the way of her teasing smile, made Reva instead ask, "Is this your way of asking me if I want to eat with y'all?"

"Absolutely. Why don't you join us?"

At that specific moment, Reva felt the familiar loneliness that she had become so accustomed to. She could stay in her seat, reading yet another book and eating yet another nasty meal by herself, or she could take a chance and meet some new people. Suddenly, it was no contest. She wasn't her mother. She was not in constant competition with other women. She would readily admit that there were women more beautiful than she, smarter than she, nicer than she and friendlier than she. She could hear Sugar's warning about "females" as her mother referred to other women: *"Can't trust not one of them."*

Reva stood up and picked up her tray. "I'd love to join you," she said. Looking back, that was the turning point in her life—the beginning of her friendship with Precious, Opal and Faith.

Over at the black table, the other African American students were eating and undoubtedly sharing new gossip. The black grapevine at Middlehurst was strong. She wondered where Opal was. She'd knocked on her door before coming down to eat, but had gotten no answer. She wondered if Opal was there and just avoiding her. The talk she'd had with Opal about going to the doctor had unnerved her. She was frightened, even if she didn't want Opal to see her fear. If anything happened to Opal, she didn't know how she would handle that. Opal, like the rest of her girlfriends, had crossed the line from friend to family a long time ago.

Reva shook those thoughts clear away. Where were Faith and Precious? Precious should have gotten home from her tea party a long time ago and Faith had disappeared again. She hoped that Faith wasn't off somewhere drinking. Faith had sworn to all of them that she had turned the corner after her last episode, as she euphemistically referred to the DWI—but lately it seemed that Faith had been spending more and more time away from them. Yesterday when Faith had come by her room, Reva thought she'd smelled alcohol, but she wasn't sure if she was being paranoid about the whole matter. Well, as Sugar would say, Faith was *grown*. She knew the consequences of her drinking.

Reva sighed—once again she was taking on the weight of other people's problems. She had plenty of practice with this. She'd been dealing with her mother's problems since she was a little girl. Her father had run away from them, from her mother's problems, when Reva was a little girl. Sometimes she wondered if things would have been different had her father stuck around. She didn't have much contact with him. He called her on her birthday last year and at Christmas she'd gotten an envelope with no return address with three hundred dollars in it. She thought that it was from her father, but she couldn't be sure who this anonymous benefactor was. Shaking off thoughts of her long gone father, and her friends' various problems, Reva walked over to a small table in the corner where she would eat her dinner alone, just as she had before that day that Precious had come over with the offer of friendship.

Precious

Precious sat on the wide, sloping lawn of the Faculty House with Rory Hamlett. The tea had ended hours ago, but Precious and Rory still sat on one of the wooden benches on the lawn. Mrs. Hamlett had left soon after introducing Precious and Rory. Instead of her usual talkative self, Mrs. Hamlett had made herself scarce during the tea, and she'd left without even saying good-bye. When she'd left, Precious could have sworn that she'd seen the flash of hope in the eyes of a determined matchmaker. In spite of her best intention, which was to get away from Rory, Precious found herself actually enjoying their conversation.

He was funny. He liked talking, and not just about himself. He told her about football and even though in general she had no interest in any sports, she found herself fascinated by his talk of strategy. Rory was a chess player and for him playing football was another form of chess. "Maybe you'll come and see me play sometime," he said, and although Precious had nodded yes, she had no intention of going to see a football game, no matter how interesting Rory Hamlett might be.

The bells in the clock tower chimed eight times. They had been talking to each other for four hours, and would probably have kept on talking if Precious hadn't remembered that she had a French test the next day and she hadn't begun studying. Madame Cherenfant was on the warpath again, and she was threatening to hand out some bad grades if she didn't see any improvement in what she termed her "apathetic charges."

"I've taken up too much of your time," said Rory, seeming embarassed.

"No, I've enjoyed talking with you." Precious was surprised that the words were true. With the exception of her father, she hadn't met many men who were either interesting or in any other way attractive to her. She hadn't grown up with parents who were in a reliable, solid relationship, and she had no point of reference on the subject of relationships. Her mother may have loved her and her father, but she loved the crack pipe even more. Her friends, particularly Opal, always seemed to have men buzzing around, but most of the men Precious came in contact with were as uninterested in her as she was in them.

"You should fix yourself up," said Opal. "You're a pretty girl; you just need to wear something other than sweatpants and jeans all the time."

Precious had listened to Opal's advice without any thought of heeding it. She did not want to "fix herself up." She had no interest in attracting members of the opposite sex. The few relationships she had been privy to, even those of the beautiful Opal, were filled with drama that she did not need. She had enough drama in her life without adding a man into the mix. Besides, she would rather just read a good book. Maybe one day she would meet someone who would change her mind. But for now, she was happy to be drama free.

"Can I walk you to wherever it is you're going?" Rory did not seem anxious to leave her.

"That really won't be necessary . . ." Precious suddenly felt ill at ease around Rory, although she had not felt any awkwardness during their conversation. She had no frame of reference in dealing with men who acted like they were interested in her. Rory Hamlett was a football player who, his aunt had told her often enough, was headed to an NFL team. He could have his pick of many more attractive women. She wasn't putting herself down, but she was no raving beauty and she had put on a few pounds on an already healthy frame—yet here he was acting like she was a candidate for Miss America.

"I know it's not necessary," said Rory. "But I'd like to walk the lady to her next appointment, wherever that might be . . . unless the lady would rather go alone."

Now, thought Precious, *if I refuse to go with him, that would be downright rude, but the lady in question needs to go and study for her French exam, and does not have time to discuss her preference that Rory go his way and she go hers.*

"I'm going back to the dorm and it's a hike from here."

"So, is that a yes? Can I walk you to the dorm?"

The word flew out of Precious' mouth before she had a chance to stop it. "Why?"

He looked at her as if she had suddenly grown three heads and all of them were spinning.

"Are you asking me why I would want to walk with you to your dorm?"

"Yes," said Precious. "Did your aunt put you up to this?"

Rory laughed. "I'm sure that my favorite aunt would love for us to get to know each other a little—no, a lot better—but the truth is that I'd like to walk you to your dorm. Plus, my mother raised a gentleman, if I do say so myself."

Precious raised one suspicious eyebrow, but remained silent. She was certain that his aunt had engineered his interest in her. Well, if this was a game, she'd play along with him at least until she got to the dormitory and then she'd politely tell him good-bye. Still, she wondered for the first time what it would be like to have someone special in her life, but then she shook those thoughts out of her mind. Roosevelt Averyheart was the only special man in her life and she was content to keep things that way.

"Are you ready, Precious?" Rory asked.

She found herself smiling at him. He was persistent. "Yes, Rory. I'm ready."

Opal

Opal's telephone rang five times before she answered it. She did not want to talk to anyone. She'd been in a deep slumber and was not ready to awaken. She wanted to lie in her bed and surround herself with the darkness that enveloped her room. The phone's ring was insistent.

"Hello," she said, in a voice that she hoped would convey to the caller that she was not interested in being interrupted by a phone call at this particular moment.

"Opal, it's me." It was Faith, and her words sounded slurred—as if her tongue had suddenly gotten thick.

"Faith, what's wrong? Where are you?"

"I'm at Mulligan's, Opal, I need you to come get me."

Opal closed her eyes for a moment and let that information sink in. Then, forcing herself not to scream, because she was tired of this scene that had been repeated all too often, she said, "Faith, what are you doing at Mulligan's? You said you had stopped drinking."

"I know, I know. . . ." Faith's words tumbled out, "but . . . had a bad, bad, bad day and I just, you know, had a couple of drinks. . . . Don't want to drive back to campus. I can't get another DWI . . . they put me in jail last time, Opal."

I know this, Opal thought silently. *I bailed you out that time, just like I'm going to have to bail you out now.*

"Faith, damn girl. You *promised*. You promised you'd stop drinking."

"No lectures . . . Opal, just come get me, O.K.?"

"I ought to leave you in that old nasty bar. I ought to just hang the phone up and leave you there until you learn your lesson. I ought to . . ."

"Opal, come get me."

"All right, Faith—but this is the last time. I swear . . ."

"Thanks . . . and Opal?"

"What?" she replied, wincing that her words came out sharper than she'd intended.

"Don't tell Reva and Precious . . . they're through with me."

"We're all through with you, Faith."

"Don't . . . Don't tell 'em."

Opal hung up the telephone and got out of bed. Turning on the light she wondered what it would take for Faith to understand that she had a problem and she needed to get help. They had all tried talking with her. They had yelled at her. They had cried with her. They had driven her to counseling sessions. They had even bailed her out of jail after she was caught driving drunk. Each time she would promise to get her life together, all the while saying that she didn't have a problem. Opal shook her head. She knew that going to pick Faith up now wasn't doing her any favors. She was acting as a partici- pant in this destructive dance that Faith insisted on doing—but she wasn't going to leave her friend now. Not when she needed her. She sighed. She was going to have to tell Reva and Precious, no matter what Faith wanted. She wasn't going to keep secrets.

Reva

"I am going to kill her." Reva did not let Opal finish talking to her about Faith's latest drama. She had heard it all before. "I am going to kill her."

"Not if she doesn't kill herself first," said Opal.

Reva and Opal walked quickly down the stairs, heading for the parking lot behind the dormitory, where Opal's car was parked.

"Have you called Precious?" Reva asked.

Opal shook her head. "Can't find the girl. Tried calling her, even knocked on the door to her dorm room and she wasn't there."

"Girlfriend is probably holed up in the library somewhere," Reva muttered. "What about Hope and Charity?"

Opal sighed. "Faith has enough drama in her life. They'd only add to the chaos."

"As if that's possible," said Reva. "I thought that she had put all this behind her!"

"Faith needs help," Opal replied.

"You're too soft on her," said Reva, "which is probably why she called you and not me."

They were walking across the lobby to the back doors, which opened up to the pathway to the parking lot. Around them, Reva could see the faces of other students, milling around the lobby. There were a few well dressed women, their faces perfectly made up—a sure sign that they were waiting for dates to pick them up. Others were in loosely formed groups, chatting with friends, undoubtedly talking about the latest happenings at Middlehurst.

"Reva! Opal! Where are you all going in such a hurry?" A voice called out from behind them.

Reva and Opal both turned around to see Precious walking quickly towards them.

"Where have you been?" Reva asked, realizing that her voice was unnecessarily sharp. A strange look crossed Precious' face and if Reva didn't know better, she'd think that Precious was embarrassed about something.

"Faith's in trouble," said Opal, when Precious walked to where they were standing. "She called me drunk from Mulligan's. We're on our way to pick her up."

Unlike Reva, Precious didn't ask any more questions. Instead, she said, "Let's go."

Chapter 4

Faith

Faith sat at the table in the rear of the bar. She had moved from the bar stools up front when her head started spinning. She wasn't sure if it were the room, or her head that was doing the spinning. She was drunk. This was nothing new. People got drunk. She got drunk, but when she'd gone to court for her DWI, she'd gotten a stern warning from the judge. *"The next time I see you here, Miss Maberley, you're going to jail."* Going to jail had less appeal to her than facing Opal. Of all her friends, Opal was the least judgmental. Reva and Precious were lost causes. They should have been born with gavels in their hands, but Opal, as self-absorbed as she might be, wasn't one to pass judgment on other people's weaknesses. Still, Opal was going to be upset that she'd gotten drunk again.

When Faith had first gotten to the bar she had set a limit. Two drinks. She could have two drinks and still drive. Three drinks were okay for her, but the third drink inevitably led to the fourth and the fifth and then all bets were off. She'd sat there sipping on a drink that even she in her intoxicated state knew was strong. She'd had one drink after another and then another. By the sixth drink, she'd stopped counting. It was nine o'clock and she needed to get back to the dorm. She was supposed to study for her History of Modern Civilization test tomorrow, but all she wanted to do now was crawl in bed and pull the covers over her head.

Where the hell was Opal? The bar was crowded now. Someone had put several quarters in the jukebox, which was playing Motown music—

her mother's kind of music. She thought about her mother briefly and the thoughts were not pleasant. She loved her mother, but neither party understood the other. Her mother blamed her drinking on her father's permissive nature. *"He's been spoiling you since the first time you cried."* Faith knew that her drinking had nothing to do with her father. Her drinking had nothing to do with her mother either. She loved to drink. End of story. The counselor she'd been forced to see after the DWI had told her that the drinking was to compensate for some family issues, but apart from a mother who needed to control everything about her life and sisters who were always underfoot, Faith could not point to anything in her childhood that led her to love the taste, smell and texture of alcohol.

Her grandfather's death from cirrhosis of the liver as a result of his own bout with alcoholism should have been enough to scare Faith away from the bottle. Faith had loved her grandfather with a deep and abiding love that she did not give to too many other people. She remembered the times she spent visiting her grandparents in Jamaica.

Her grandfather always smelled of rum and cigars—a smell that still made her long to hear the deep, gravely laugh of a man whose strong brown arms used to hold her tight. She remembered sitting down on her grandmother's back porch, listening to the night sounds of Jamaica—crickets, reggae music coming from a nearby disco and the honk of the truck horns rolling down the road just past her grandparents' home. She remembered sitting there with her grandfather, watching him pour rum slowly into a glass, talking all the while— telling her stories, most of which she was certain he made up. She remembered how she loved this old man. When he died, she'd been devastated, but in time, the memory of his voice, his laugh, dimmed and she was left with only a vague image of an old man who loved rum and cigars.

Just as she had worried about her grandfather's drinking, her family was worried about her. Her father had talked to her about her drinking a few weeks before she'd returned to school. He'd sat next to her on the couch while they watched a baseball game. *"About this drinking . . ."* he'd begun, but then his voice had trailed off. Faith had dismissed her father's words. He had his own drinking problem although few people in the family knew about her daddy's secret drinking.

"Faith, this place is a *dump!*" Opal walked over to where Faith was sitting, with Reva and Precious following closely behind. Faith's heart sank. Opal had brought the two judges, as Faith referred to Reva and Precious. She loved both of them, but they were both mother hens who loved to get right in the middle of her business.

Reva came in front of the table and stood there with her hands on her hips. Precious stood beside her. Faith faced three angry sets of eyes. She knew that she deserved their anger and more. They had all come to her alcohol abuse counseling sessions. They had come to court with her. They had spent countless hours talking to her about the evils of addiction, especially Precious, whose crack addicted mother taught her about the high cost of addiction at an early age. *I'm not an alcoholic,* Faith wanted to scream at them.

Faith turned to Opal, "I asked you not to talk to anyone about this."

"I'm sorry, Faith," Opal replied, "but I thought that Precious and Reva needed to be here. I need help to get you home."

"I'm sorry that I called you," Faith's words sounded slurred even to her own ears.

"Faith, I mean this in the most positive way . . . you are in no position to dictate terms to folks who are helping you." This pronouncement came from Reva.

"Leave me the hell alone," said Faith. "I love you, Reva, but I don't need this right now."

"Faith, you need Jesus," said Precious, her tone anything but charitable. "What is it going to take to stop you from doing this to yourself?"

Faith looked at Opal. *"This* is why I asked you to come alone."

"Y'all pretty ladies need some help?"

Four heads turned to see a nightmare dressed in red polyester, or more specifically, a man with a jherri curl reminiscent of Rick James in his "Superfreak" days. He was tall, and calling him skinny would be a sympathetic characterization. When he smiled at them, which he was doing just then, there was an impressive set of gold teeth winking back at them.

"Look, Cassanova Brown, we surely do not need your help," snapped Reva. "But if and when we do, we'll be sure to give you a holler."

"Ooooh, a feisty young thing. I likes my women feisty and young and you fit the bill on both counts."

Reva turned on him. "Don't make me forget that I am a church-going woman."

Mr. Red Polyester smiled some more. "Just like my dead mama, God rest her beautiful soul. She was a good church-going woman."

"Haven't I seen you somewhere?" asked Opal.

Red Polyester could not believe his good fortune. His eyes widened as he looked at the prettiest woman in the room. "I would have remembered a fine filly like you, that's for damn sure," said Red Polyester, "but I'd sure like to make your acquaintance tonight."

"It's not that kind of party," Opal said, quickly dismissing him. "But I know I've seen you . . ." Her eyes widened. "You were at the alcohol abuse counseling session in Boston last spring! Your hair was a little different . . . but I remember the gold teeth."

"Girl, you was at the meeting? I sure didn't see a fine sister like you . . . you feisty like your friend over here? Oh, I likes my women feisty!"

"So you've mentioned," said Precious. "Listen, we'd love to talk about the good old days in rehab, but my friends and I would like some privacy."

"Oh, so now y'all trying to *play* a brother, acting like y'all don't have time for Charlie."

"Charlie, we don't know you," said Precious, apparently trying to be reasonable.

"That pretty little filly over there remembers old Charlie, don't you now, Miss Lady?"

Reva looked over at Faith and said, "Girl, come on and let's get out of here before I forget that I was in church last Sunday and take care of this polyester-wearing fool."

"No need to be nasty, Miss Lady," said Charlie. "Looks like you might need some anger management classes in addition to coming to the AA meetings."

"You ought to be ashamed of yourself," huffed Precious. "You're a damn alcoholic hanging out in a bar!"

Once the words left her lips, she immediately realized what she had said. Faith looked up to see the eyes of her friends all trained on her.

"Help me get out of here," she said, embarrassed. Precious' words were directed at a buffoon, but they were equally applicable to her own situation.

"Can you get up?" asked Opal.

"Need some help," Faith admitted.

"Here, let me help you, pretty lady!" Charlie piped up.

"Charlie, if you don't go and find yourself someplace else to be, I will not be responsible for my actions," snapped Reva

Charlie sauntered away, but not before winking at Opal and licking his lips.

Faith tried to stand up, but her legs were unsteady. She felt the arms of her friends around her. Standing there, leaning on Reva, with Opal holding her around her waist and Precious standing behind her with both hands gently and firmly at her back, Faith did not know where she began and her friends ended. They were as entwined as if the four of them were part of one body.

Together they walked out of the bar into a brisk, cool night.

Opal

The drive back to the campus took longer than Opal had anticipated. A car accident up ahead had slowed traffic to almost a crawl. She switched on the classical music station and let the music wash over her. Her nerves were frayed, and usually classical music was a tried and true way to ease her tension, but tonight, the music, as beautiful as it was, did not do the trick. Beside her, Faith stared out of the window, unable or unwilling to talk to Opal. Opal glanced over at her friend and once again, fought the urge to yell at her. She knew that Faith had a problem—a serious problem—but arguments would not help. God knows that they had all argued with Faith more times than anyone would care to count.

There would be time enough for a discussion about Faith's lapse. Opal had suspected that Faith had started drinking again, but there was a part of her that did not want to believe it. After everything Faith had been through, after everything that Faith had put all of them through, it was difficult to understand how Faith could put a drink to her lips. If she lived to be an old and very wise woman, Opal would still not understand what would make a person as smart as Faith act so foolishly. Faith had been given every opportunity to get herself together. She had a supportive family and her friends were in her corner. She had the resources to fight this particular battle right at her fingertips. She had only to go to the alcohol recovery center in Cambridge. The counselors there knew her well. Everyone was rooting for her. Everyone except for Faith.

"I know you're angry." Faith's voice was quiet when she finally spoke.

Opal took a deep, steadying breath. She had to be careful about the words she chose. She did not want to push Faith any further down than she already was.

"I am angry," Opal admitted. "But I'm also concerned."

"Don't be," said Faith, her words louder now. "Don't be concerned about me."

"Faith, I love you. You're my friend. Of course, I'm concerned about you."

"It won't happen again," said Faith. "I'm through with this."

That's what you said the last time. Opal did not speak the words in her head, instead, she said, "I hope so, Faith, because you'll destroy yourself."

"I'm sorry." The words were said in a small voice. Opal wondered if she'd imagined the apology. Then, Faith spoke again. "Opal, I really am sorry."

Yes, you are sorry. "Faith, you need help," Opal said. "You need to go back to the recovery center."

"No."

Opal turned and looked at her friend. "What do you mean no?"

"I mean, I'm not going back to that place. Ever. I don't belong there Opal. Those folks are alcoholics . . . I am not an alcoholic."

Opal fought hard to keep her temper in check. "Girl, you have a problem. Call it whatever you feel like—you need to stop drinking, and apparently you can't do that. You need help."

"I can stop anytime I feel like it," Faith replied.

"Faith, for God's sake—you're drunk! You could barely walk out of there . . ."

"I need to hold my liquor better," said Faith. "I got a little carried away, but that doesn't mean I'm a damn alcoholic."

Opal shook her head. "Faith, the next time you get drunk, do me a favor and forget you know my number."

"There won't be a next time, Opal," said Faith. "I promise."

Opal wondered how long it would take Faith to break this particular promise. They drove the rest of the way to the campus in silence.

Precious

Precious lay in bed and closed her eyes. Trying to blot out the image of her drunk friend stumbling out of Opal's car was going to be difficult. Opal had driven ahead to the campus with Faith in her car. Reva had driven Faith's car with Precious keeping her company. During the entire drive Reva had railed about Faith. "What are we gonna do about her?" Reva had asked. Precious did not have any answers then, nor did she have any answers now. Precious knew that once someone's drug of choice got hold of them, there was little anyone else could do. Her own mother had taught her this hard lesson. They'd all helped Faith into her room. Reva decided to stay the night with Faith, sleeping on the sofa in the corner of Faith's bedroom. Opal and Precious had gone to their respective rooms, and as Precious said good night to Opal, she saw the same despair she felt, reflected in Opal's light brown eyes.

After she left her friends, Precious had tried to study for her French test, but her mind was elsewhere. After half an hour of trying to concentrate, Precious had closed the textbook. She knew the material anyway, and if she didn't know the material by now, she deserved to fail. She thought of her mother and the times she'd seen her high on crack. She had stumbled also. She remembered asking her father why her mother had left them. *"She's sick,"* her father had explained. *"She has a bad disease."* For years, Precious had believed that her mother was in the grip of some unexplained and terrifying disease that would ultimately attack her also. It wasn't until her seventh birthday that she understood, when one of her cousins had told her the truth, that her mother was on the crack pipe. *Crack baby, crack baby, crack baby.* The taunts hurt even now, years later. *Crack baby.*

Her mother had only one desire in the world now—to get high. Her father had tried to help her, but the only help that Evangeline Averyheart wanted was someone to point her in the direction of her next hit. She was a beautiful woman once, although by the time Precious was born, the beauty that had stolen many hearts on Lenox Avenue was long since gone. Her father kept pictures of her mother before she was a junkie. Pictures that showed a laughing, brown-skinned woman, with curly black hair and wide lips, always painted bright red. She was slim, even then, and wore clothes that accentuated a sleek shape. She looked like a movie star. *"This is the woman I fell in love with,"* her father would say wistfully, when he lay his eyes on those pictures. *"She was a beauty. Black beauty is what I used to call her. She loved that . . . Black beauty."*

No one in the family was certain about the exact time Evangeline Averyheart fell in love with the crack pipe, but everyone agrees that it was well before the birth of her only child, Precious. The knowledge that her mother smoked crack while Precious was in her belly was only one on the list of many grievances Precious held against her mother. Breaking her father's heart, stealing her father's money, walking out on them, not giving a damn if her child lived or died . . . the list of grievances was long. *"You need to forgive her; I have,"* her father had told her on numerous occasions. Roosevelt Averyheart believed in the power of forgiveness. *"Don't do nobody any good holding on to all that hurt, all that pain."*

Precious knew that his words made sense, but she had lived with the anger and the pain so long that it was as natural to her as the air she breathed. She hated her mother, and if her daddy's soft heart, and even softer head, made him look kindly towards her mother, then God bless him. As for Precious, any feeling that she might have had for Evangeline died when she walked out on her family.

The ringing of the telephone interrupted Precious' dark thoughts. It was eleven o'clock, and that usually meant that her father was calling. He worked late and the only time he would have to call her on weekdays was after eleven. She would be glad to hear his voice. She

wanted to tell him about Faith. There were no secrets between Precious
and her father. Precious reached out and picked up the telephone receiver.

"Hi, Daddy."

"I've been called many names before, but I've never had the pleasure of being called daddy." It was Rory Hamlett.

"How did you get my number?" Precious asked, taken aback. Rory
Hamlett was the last person she expected to hear from.

"My aunt gave it to me."

Lord spare me from any more matchmakers, thought Precious.

"I hope it's not too late to call—I just wanted to wish you good luck
on your test."

Precious sighed. He was laying this on a little too thick. She wasn't
putting herself down, but she knew that Rory was a football player.
His aunt had bragged that he was on his way to the NFL, and that
meant big contracts and beautiful women. She was not a beautiful
woman. She was pleasant looking, and overweight. She was not football star material. She didn't know what kind of game Rory was playing, but she was not going to play with him.

"Why exactly are you calling me, Rory?"

"I told you," he replied, "I wanted to wish you good luck on your
test."

"Why?"

"I'm not sure what your source of confusion is, but I thought it
would be nice to call you up and say good luck on your test."

"That's nice," said Precious, using the same tone of voice she was
used to hearing from the other students in her French tutorial class,
who just did not understand how to conjugate French verbs, let alone
pronounce them.

She heard Rory chuckle over the line. His voice was deep, and rich,
and brought to her mind, slow, lazy Sunday afternoons. "I'm a nice
guy, Precious."

"Oh, please!" said Precious, rolling her eyes in exasperation. "You're
a football player for God's sake!"

She didn't want to be rude, but she was tired and Faith's latest
lapse had gotten her down.

"Football players are nice guys too," said Rory, after he finished
laughing.

"Yes, I'm sure they are," said Precious, annoyed that he was apparently not taking her seriously. "But let's put it this way, I'm not your
typical groupie, cheerleader or any other type of woman that you guys
usually go after."

"Who said I'm going after you?"

Precious was mortified. He was right. He just called to wish her good luck and here she was acting like he was a Casanova out to seduce her.

Rory laughed. "I am after you, Precious—but not in the way you think that I am. I want to get to know you better. I know that we football players have a bad reputation, but surely you can't think all of us are *that* shallow."

"You can't tell me that you've never gone out with a groupie or a cheerleader," said Precious, refusing to give up her point.

"Yes, Precious, I have gone out with a groupie and I have gone out with a cheerleader, but I've gone out with other women—different kinds of women . . ."

Precious chuckled. "Are you telling me that you're an equal opportunity lover?"

"I don't know what that is," said Rory. "Why is it so hard for you to understand that I'm interested in getting to know you better?"

"Why do you want to go out with me, Rory? I'm not putting myself down. I know my benefits and my pluses. Hell, I think I'm a good catch. It's just that I don't think I'm your type."

"You want to know the truth?" asked Rory.

"Always," said Precious.

"You intrigue me," said Rory. "I like you. I like talking with you. I don't get to talk to a lot of women the way we talked today. Most women talk to me as if I'm this big, dumb football player. They don't talk to me about politics and philosophy. They don't talk to me about the Million Man March. They don't talk to me about sanctions in the Middle East. They don't talk to me about rap music and reggae dancehall."

"You make me sound like a science experiment," said Precious.

"Is that how you see yourself?" asked Rory.

This conversation was getting entirely too personal, Precious decided. Still, she answered him honestly. "I haven't had that much experience having conversations with men that are interested in what I have to say."

"Then you must know some foolish men."

Now, it was Precious' turn to chuckle.

"You should laugh more, Precious."

"Believe me, this has been a tough night for laughter," Precious replied.

"Tough night?" Rory asked.

"You don't know the half of it," Precious replied.

"Do you want to talk about it?" Rory asked.

"No," said Precious. "But thanks for the offer."

"Anytime," replied Rory.

"Goodnight, Rory."

"Goodnight, Precious."

Precious placed the telephone receiver back into the cradle, and stared at the ceiling. Thoughts of Faith, her mother, Rory Hamlett and her French exam competed for Precious' attention before she fell into a fitful sleep.

Chapter 5

Reva

Bonnie Spencer, Reva's roommate, was the only non-African
American student who regularly sat at the black table. Bonnie,
whose ancestors came over to America on ships that carried wealthy
English adventurers to the New World, had never interacted with
black people until she became Reva's roommate at Middlehurst. They
were from opposite ends of the financial and social spectrum. Bonnie
was raised in the privileged enclave of Scarsdale, New York. Her father was CEO of a financial services company and her mother was
known for her support of the arts as well as her tendency to donate
large sums of money to various charities.

Reva and Bonnie had formed an unlikely friendship in their freshman year. They had both initially viewed the other person with the
vague sense of mistrust that comes from being raised in different
worlds. Eventually, Reva and Bonnie had become friends.

From their first meeting Reva had recognized that despite their differences, Bonnie had a kind heart. She was constantly doing crazy
things for people as far as Reva was concerned. Bonnie would literally
give the shirt off her back if someone needed it. Reva remembered
going to Boston with Bonnie and encountering a homeless woman
with yet another hard luck story. The woman had related a tale of woe
that included an abusive husband and sick children—a story that
made the Harlem-raised Reva was more than a little suspicious. Yet,
Bonnie had opened her purse and given that woman every cent she
had. She also spent half the day trying to locate shelters in Boston
until she found someone who would take the woman in, and then she

had accompanied the woman to the shelter. Reva had grudgingly accompanied Bonnie and the woman to the shelter, wondering how Bonnie had gotten her into yet another adventure. Bonnie fasted every Friday for migrant workers in California. She worked in a soup kitchen. She mentored inner city school children in Roxboro. Reva had often teased Bonnie that she was working through some Protestant guilt ethic, but she knew the truth. Bonnie was a decent person, who despite all the wealth and privilege that easily came her way, cared about others.

Reva poured homemade maple syrup over a thick stack of wheat pancakes. Beside her, she watched Bonnie attack her raspberry yogurt and wheatgerm with gusto. In addition to being a chronic do-gooder, Bonnie was a poster child for healthy eating. They sat silently for a moment, each person seemingly lost in her own thoughts. It was early, not quite seven o'clock and the cafeteria had not yet come to life. Other than the cafeteria workers, they were the only people in the cafeteria.

Bonnie broke the silence. "So are you going to tell me where you were last night?"

"I spent the night in Faith's room," Reva replied.

Bonnie swallowed some more yogurt. "I was hoping that you'd met some wonderful man and had spent the night making passionate love."

Reva smiled. "You sound like my mother."

"What's going on with Faith?" Bonnie asked.

"She got drunk last night."

Bonnie shook her head. "I had hoped that she'd put that part of her life behind her." Reva had confided in Bonnie about Faith's drinking. Bonnie had been supportive and had even tried to accompany Faith to one of her alcoholic support groups, but Faith had not wanted her help. Faith viewed the friendship between Bonnie and Reva with mistrust. "I don't need her help, or her charity."

Reva wouldn't call Faith a racist, but she was close. Faith had no friends who did not share her racial background. She did not trust anyone who didn't look like her. "You might be ready to sing 'We Shall Overcome' with Bonnie, but count me out," she had declared to Reva on more than one occasion. Faith did not like Bonnie sitting at the black table, but she was too much of a friend to Reva to say anything about it. She tolerated Bonnie, albeit from a distance.

"I'll keep her in my prayers," said Bonnie, standing up.

They said their good-byes and Reva watched Bonnie leave. *She's on her way to save the world,* Reva thought. She wondered if you had to be born with such determined optimism. She was inclined to believe that Bonnie's unrelenting positivity was genetic, but Reva had met both of Bonnie's parents and while they were pleasant enough, they did not share their daughter's seemingly universal belief that all God's children were inherently good. Reva sighed. There were times that she wished she shared Bonnie's sense of good will, but then she knew better. She was Sugar's daughter and any sense that all was well with the world had been completely erased by her mother at an early age. Reva put another piece of bacon in her mouth and wondered what further drama was going to come her way.

Faith

Faith awoke with the sense that all was not well with her world. Her head was pounding and she felt bile rising in her throat. She was going to throw up and she knew distinctly that she did not want to throw up in her bed. She raised her head to look around but the sudden pain that accompanied that movement convinced her to lie back down. A fresh wave of nausea threatened to overcome her and she closed her eyes, willing herself not to vomit. *Never again.* She promised herself. *Never again.* But how many times had she said those words before? She opened her eyes and the bright sunlight streaming in was a fresh assault. There was a knock on the door. Faith pulled the covers over her head in a protective cocoon. *Go away,* she silently pleaded. The knocking continued. *Go away, go away, go away.*

"Faith, I know you're in there. Open this door!" It was Precious.

Just what I need, thought Faith, *Miss Holier-Than-Just-About-Everybody-Else, Precious.* She loved her like a sister, but Precious and her goody-two shoes routine could wear a body down. *Did I lock the door last night?* she wondered, but last night was blurry, indistinct. She remembered calling Opal and she remembered seeing her friends in the bar. The rest was lost to her.

The door opened and Precious walked inside. Like the avenging hand of the Lord, Precious pulled down the heavy quilt covering Faith. Faith opened her eyes and found herself staring into the troubled eyes of Precious.

"Faith, you know better," said Precious, getting straight to the point.

Faith shook her head. "Not now, Precious. I'm gonna be sick . . . not now."

"If not now, then when is the right time to deal with your problem, Faith, because you have a problem, a very real problem . . ."

Faith felt the nausea overwhelm her. She sat up slowly. "I'm gonna be sick . . ."

"Oh, for heaven's sake," said Precious crossly. "Why do you do this to yourself?"

"Help me get to the bathroom, Precious," Faith asked, knowing even as she spoke she would never make it there.

She threw up on her bed, her stomach heaving violently. She vomited even when there was nothing left in her stomach to give up. She was dimly aware that someone was sitting beside her, holding her. Precious. At last, the urge to vomit left, and she lay back down, her body spent with the effort. She closed her eyes. She did not want to see Precious. She was at her lowest and she did not want her friend's pity or her self-righteousness. She waited for Precious to say something but she remained silent. Then Faith heard the door close and soon thereafter, open again. She felt something warm on her face. Opening her eyes, she saw Precious wiping her face with a rag. She tried to say "thank you" but her throat was raw and even if she were inclined to talk, the shame that consumed her had robbed her of her voice.

She felt Precious lift her up to a sitting position. "Come on, Faith— let's get you to the shower. Let's get you cleaned up."

Opal

Opal sat next to Jordan in his latest sports car. If Jordan had one weakness, it was his love of flashy cars. It was a weakness that Opal shared, but Jordan took his love of cars to an extreme. Opal was content with her BMW, her latest black urban professional accessory. Her friends teased her about her car, but as European imports came, her midnight blue beamer was fairly conservative. Jordan's bright red Porsche was another matter entirely. The car screamed "look at me!" and it made Opal uncomfortable. She was used to getting attention from other folk—she was good looking and her family was well known—but her Volvo-family had instilled some conservative values in her. *"You can have it,"* her mother would caution, *"but you don't have to flaunt it."* As far as Opal was concerned, a bright red Porsche was the epitome of flaunting it. Although she had to admit that the distinction between her BMW and Jordan's Porsche was lost on most of her friends.

"You nervous about seeing Pastor McDonald?" Jordan's question cut through her thoughts.

Opal laughed. "You're the one who should be nervous," she replied. "He's been our family minister now for about twenty years."

They were on their way for their first pre-marital counseling session. Pastor McDonald, whose Episcopal church was one of the oldest in Boston, was not only their minister, he was a close family friend. Although Jordan belonged to a well established Baptist church, her family made it clear that if he wanted Opal's hand in marriage, he would have to convert to the Episcopalian way. Opal was, at best, an ambivalent Episcopalian. She secretly yearned to attend a church where it was okay to shout amen and clap your hands to the sound of righteous, gospel music, but her family would hear none of it. "Born Episcopalian, die Episcopalian," was her mother's comment and that was all there was to it.

"He'll love me for the good black man that I am," said Jordan. His good humor lifted her spirits. Last night had been difficult. After she'd gotten Faith home, she'd lain awake for most of the night. She was worried about Faith, and she was worried about herself. Although she'd promised Reva that she'd make an appointment to see a doctor about the lump, she still hadn't called the doctor. She was afraid of dying. There, it was out in the open—her fear. She'd been afraid of death for as long as she'd understood the concept. She'd lost her grandmother to breast cancer when she was eleven years old, and since that time, she had lived with a terror that the same disease that ravaged her grandmother would one day come for her. When she found the lump, there was almost a sense of relief—the disease had finally made its appearance. She didn't need a doctor to explain her fatigue. She didn't need a doctor to explain why she never felt well. She didn't need a doctor to explain the significance of the lump.

"Opal, what are you thinking about?" Jordan sounded worried.

"Nothing," Opal lied. "Nothing at all."

She felt a wave of guilt wash over her. This man was going to be her husband and she hadn't yet told him that she'd found a lump in her breast. She shook disturbing thoughts out of her head. She would deal with this later.

"Sometimes I wonder if I know you," said Jordan quietly.

Opal looked at him as he maneuvered his Porsche through the early morning Boston traffic. Jordan stared straight ahead. She had never seen him like this. His good humor was his trademark. This serious person sitting next to her was a stranger.

"Opal, I know that something has been bothering you. When are you going to tell me about it? We're going to be married in a few months—there should be no secrets between us."

Opal thought about his words. He was right. He was always right.

"No secrets, Opal."

Precious

Precious put her pen down. Her French exam was finally over. She had no doubt that she had made at least a B, but she was capable of getting A's. She should have studied more. She was tired and worried about Faith. She had gotten her cleaned up and then she'd called someone from campus housekeeping to clean up Faith's dorm room— the perks of attending a college used to catering to its elite student body. She'd left Faith curled up in her bed, sleeping off her hangover.

What gets into folks? Precious wondered. She would never understand people who did things that they knew good and well were self-destructive. Faith knew that her drinking was a problem. Hell, it had almost landed her in jail—if it wasn't for Opal's family and their connections. She could have gotten suspended from school, but everyone looked at Faith's lapse in judgment as a learning experience. Faith had gotten a get-out-of-jail card free and what had she done but started drinking again.

"Mademoiselle Averyheart, may I have a moment of your time?" Madame Cherenfant called out as she collected the test papers. "Please wait for me after class."

The rest of the advanced French Literature class seemed to breathe a silent and collective sigh of relief that they had not earned Madame Cherenfant's attention. Madame Cherenfant was not known for her good disposition. Any request to stay after class was certainly not a good thing.

"*Oui,* Madame," Precious replied, her heart sinking. *What now?*

After all the students cleared out of the classroom, Madame Cherenfant sat down on her desk, her arms folded across her chest in the universal sign of displeasure.

Clearing her throat, Madame Cherenfant began speaking. "Mademoiselle Averyheart, despite your recent lack of attention in my class, I think you are a very good student, who, with the proper tools, would become an excellent student."

Lack of attention? What was Madame Cherenfant talking about? Precious chose to remain silent. With Madame Cherenfant, it was much better not to engage her when she was about to get ready for one of her tirades, which Precious suspected was about to occur.

"You are without question one of my best French students, but lately it seems as if you no longer apply yourself with the same vigor that you did in years past."

Oh, thought Precious, that explains the B and B+ grades that Madame had started marking on her test papers.

"I just need to get back into the groove of things . . ." Precious began.

Madame Cherenfant waved her long, thin hands as if swatting away something disagreeable. "Into the groove of things," her lips, painted with an impossibly bright red shade of lipstick, which served to make her pale skin, paler still, sneered. "What is that?! You are blessed with a quick mind and what is more important, your accent is as good as someone born and grown in France. You have talent, Mademoiselle Averyheart, and I fear that you are throwing it away!"

Madame Cherenfant was a difficult teacher. She was also an odd person. That, in Precious' mind, was a bad combination. Still, she had managed to stay on reasonably good terms with this peculiar woman for the first three years at Middlehurst. Precious took considerable pride in the knowledge that while Madame Cherenfant flunked students with seeming relish, she regularly gave Precious high marks in each of her classes. Madame Cherenfant unapologetically lived up to the stereotype of an American-hating French woman. It wasn't that Madame Cherenfant hated Americans, she just thought herself better than them, better than most of the non-French speaking world.

She was a small, thin woman with jet black hair that tumbled in unruly curls around her shoulders. She was as stylish as a model, with her size six shape, tapered skirts, and clinging blouses. When she talked, she waved her hands in the air, inviting the listener in with her passionate nature. When she smiled, which was not often, Precious thought that she was beautiful. At sixty years of age, she looked at least two decades younger and she was proud of it.

"What do have to say for yourself?" Madame Cherenfant sneered. "I see you staring off into the distance . . . I have been called many things, Madamoiselle, but boring is not one of them. You are slipping, Mademoiselle Averyheart."

Precious sighed. Madame Cherenfant's assessment was accurate in every way. "I'll do better, Madame."

Madame Cherenfant sighed with the same dramatic relish that she did everything else. "I certainly hope so, Mademoiselle Averyheart, because I don't want to be disappointed. I have recommended you for a scholarship to study French Literature at the Sorbonne next year. I do not make my recommendations lightly."

The Sorbonne. The words rang out in her head. *The Sorbonne. Paris. Studying Literature.*

"Madame, I'm flattered . . . honored, but I'm planning to go to Law School next year. I'll be taking the LSAT exam this fall."

"Nonsense!" Madame Cherenfant's response was immediate. "You can go to Law School anytime. A chance to study at the Sorbonne is a once in a lifetime opportunity . . . a chance to get a scholarship to study at the Sorbonne is even rarer. I have the forms back in my office for you to fill out."

Precious found herself smiling. Damn it if Madame Cherenfant just shot her plans to attend Harvard Law School straight to hell. Precious was on her way to Paris. Later, when she would talk to Reva, who hotly demanded why Precious let that crazy French woman turn her life around, Precious would explain that going to France to study had been one of those impossible dreams when she was growing up in Harlem, that this was fate. But at that moment, when all her plans for next year had gone completely out of the window, Precious couldn't help but smile. She was going to Paris and crazy Madame Cherenfant was sending her on her way.

"I fail to see the humor in this," said Madame Cherenfant, one severely plucked eyebrow raised in disdain. "There is one thing," Madame Cherenfant continued, "B students do not go to the Sorbonne. Only A students. I suggest that you bring your grade point average back to its normal range."

Precious stood up from behind her seat. "I don't mean to sound ungrateful," she said. "But why did you choose me? There are other good students in your class."

Madame Cherenfant's reply was immediate. "It is true, Mademoiselle, that I have other good students. You, however, are better than them."

Madame Cherenfant had just given her a compliment. The world was surely coming to a fast end.

"Come along, Mademoiselle Averyheart, I don't have the time or the inclination to debate your good fortune. I believe you know where my office is. Come along, before I change my mind."

Reva

Reva heard the sirens in the background and cursed under her breath. A quick glance at her odometer confirmed that she was speeding. She ought to know better. Route 82 was a driver's nightmare. There were always policemen hiding behind speed traps. But she was late for an interview at the Free Health Clinic in Boston and she'd been trying to make up time. Being late for a first interview definitely did not make a good first impression.

Easing her car over to the shoulder of the road, Reva placed her hands on the steering wheel and waited. She'd already paid two speeding fines this year and her insurance rates were already too high. Another ticket would almost certainly raise her insurance fee. "Damn, damn and damn again," she cursed under her breath. Things were definitely not going her way.

He approached her from the driver's side of the car, one hand resting by the lowered front door window and the other hand resting reassuringly on his hip, no doubt cradling his gun, Reva thought without bothering to shake loose the bitterness. She noticed his hands first—strong, brown hands with long, graceful fingers. Then, she looked up into his face. Her immediate thought was that this po-

liceman had the kindest eyes she had ever encountered. He was
handsome, but she had encountered many handsome men in her
life. Her father was handsome, too, but he had broken her heart and
her mother's heart.

"Good morning, ma'am," his deep voice carried the distinct lilt of
the West Indies.

"Officer," Reva replied, unable to tear her gaze from those kind,
brown eyes.

"Do you realize that you were speeding?" He said, his lips curved in
the slightest smile.

Reva cleared her throat. She stared into the face of a man who felt
like home. There was something about him that immediately seemed
familiar, connected somehow. *Focus, Reva, focus!* She chided herself.
"Was I?" she asked.

He nodded his head. "Yes, indeed. You were going fifteen miles
above the speed limit."

Reva was a feminist. She did not believe in using her feminine
charms to get out of predicaments, but she was desperate—and this
officer had kind eyes.

"Look," she said. "I am late for an interview for a job that I really
need to get."

The officer raised one eyebrow.

Reva continued, "I've already gotten two speeding tickets."

"I'm not surprised."

"I can't get another speeding ticket."

"Well then, Mrs. . . . ."

"It's Miss," Reva corrected the officer. "And my last name is
Nettingham."

"Miss Nettingham, if you have an aversion to getting speeding tickets, perhaps you should drive within the speed limit."

Reva clenched her teeth. She ought to know better than to try to
talk her way out of this. She was wrong and he had caught her. Not
only would her insurance rates increase, but she probably lost any
chance to get the internship at the Free Clinic—a paid internship.
She'd be able to give up her work study job where she barely made
minimum wage. "Just give me the ticket."

He raised his eyebrow again. "You want the ticket?"

What kind of game was this man playing? She was not in the mood.
"Are you going to write me the ticket or aren't you?"

"I wasn't planning on writing you a ticket. I thought that under the circumstances, a warning would be sufficient, but if you want a ticket . . ."

"Look, I really appreciate it," the relief Reva felt was immediate.
She had dodged this particular bullet.

Reaching into his pocket, he pulled out a business card and gave it to her. "My name is Simon Bennett. Here's my card. Maybe you'll call me sometime."

Reva did not have much in common with her mother, but one of the traits they shared was being forthright.

"Why would I do that?" Reva asked.

Officer Simon Bennett smiled. "Oh, I don't know. Maybe you'll come up with a reason . . ."

Reva knew that she shouldn't be ungrateful, after all the man had just let her off without writing her a ticket—but she hated arrogance of any sort. If he thought that she was going to dial his number, he would have to think again. As her mother Sugar would say: *"I'd have to die and be born again!"*

Still, she held back on sharing her thoughts on that subject with him.

Instead, she said, "Thank you, Officer."

"Have a good day, Miss Nettingham," said Officer Bennett, with a smile. "Good luck on that interview and remember to drive safely."

Reva thought she heard him chuckling as he walked off, but she couldn't be sure. Throwing his business card onto the passenger seat, she started the ignition to her car. She still had an interview to get to, even though she was past late.

Chapter 6

Opal

Reverend McDonald's book-lined office was at the end of the hall-way on the first floor of the rectory. Opal had been here countless times and she felt at ease with her surroundings. Jordan, however, contrary to his earlier good humor, seemed uncharacteristically nervous. Reverend McDonald was sitting in the corner of the room on a wooden rocking chair. Jordan and Opal sat on the comfortable, floral motif couch with soft, oversize cushions that invited anyone lucky enough to sit on them to relax.

"Can I get you some coffee, tea?" Reverend McDonald's broad smile was inviting.

"Thank you," Opal replied, "but I had a large breakfast."

"I'm fine," said Jordan, although to Opal's eyes, he looked the opposite. She was not used to seeing Jordan sweat. As long as she had known him, he encountered adversity and good fortune with the same easy manner. He looked uncomfortable. He looked troubled.

Reverend McDonald leaned back in his rocking chair and began to slowly rock back and forth. "I just want to talk to you a little bit today. Later on, we'll start with the counseling sessions. I already know Opal but I don't know a lot about you, Jordan."

"He's wonderful," said Opal, in an attempt to get her nervous fiancé to smile. Her attempt failed.

"What do you want to know?" asked Jordan, staring directly at Reverend McDonald.

"Well," said Reverend McDonald, "What do you want me to know about yourself?"

Opal watched as Jordan shifted uneasily in his chair. "Only that I love Opal Breezewood and I'll be a good husband to her."

"Well now," said Reverend McDonald, continuing to rock back and forth slowly, "that's a good place to start. Love is definitely a good ingredient for a successful recipe for marriage . . . but there's more . . . a whole lot more than love that makes a successful marriage. There are a lot of folk running around in divorce court that loved one another and may still love one another."

Opal gave a nervous laugh. "Reverend McDonald, are you trying to scare my fiancé away?"

"I don't think he scares that easily, Opal," the Reverend replied.

"You're right," said Jordan. "I don't scare easily. Reverend McDonald, I know that love isn't the only thing needed for a successful marriage, but I think that Opal and I have what it takes to go the distance."

Reverend McDonald cleared his throat. "Well, I certainly hope that you're right, Jordan. Marriage is a wonderful institution, but it is not an easy one. Mrs. McDonald and I have come to know this after forty-three years of marriage—some years better than others, I might add. I'd like to see you young people at least once a month before the wedding—when is the wedding scheduled?"

"We haven't picked a date yet," said Opal.

"I was hoping that we'd have a summer wedding," Jordan spoke to Reverend McDonald, as if Opal had not spoken.

"What do you think, Opal?" asked Reverend McDonald.

"I don't know," Opal replied.

"I think that this is something that you both should discuss before we meet again," said the Reverend.

Opal glanced at her fiancé and did not like what she saw. The same stubborn determination that allowed her mother to make every decision was reflected in Jordan's face. Did she want to spend the rest of her life with another person who wanted to control her life? True, Jordan was a lot more pliant than her mother, he was in love with her after all, but was Jordan her mother in a man's clothing? She had rushed into this engagement with the hope that it would all sort itself out somehow.

The rest of the meeting with Reverend McDonald passed easily with the mood lightened by the reverend's jokes and Jordan's discussion about life at Harvard Business School. Opal smiled at the jokes and interjected herself into the conversation whenever appropriate, but her mind was far, far away.

There was a feeling of uneasiness that clung to her, a sense that all was not right with her world. Without thinking, her hand moved toward her left breast where the lump was located. Then, as she caught herself, she placed her hand back in her lap. She needed to go to the doctor. She needed to slow things down with Jordan. She needed to walk away from Jordan until she was certain that this was the right thing to do, but she didn't want to lose him. He was a good man, and in the circles she ran in, a good man was getting to be a rarer and rarer commodity. She was used to men who were more impressed with themselves, their education, their pedigree, their looks, their various Ivy League degrees, than the women who loved them. Jordan wasn't like that. He was faithful, kind, smart, well educated and he adored her—not for her outward looks, but for something that he saw inside of her. No man had ever talked about her or looked at her that way. They were either blinded by her light complexion and long hair or her family history. They were not interested in what she had to say. They were not interested in finding out who she was as a person, what her likes and dislikes were—what her challenges were. She did not want to walk away from Jordan, but she just wasn't sure she wanted to marry him.

"Opal," Reverend McDonald interrupted her thoughts, "you are just about a million miles away."

"No," smiled Opal, with the same smile she used to hide her unpleasant thoughts from the outside world. "I'm right here, Reverend McDonald."

Faith

Charity sat on the floor beside her sister's bed. Faith stared at her baby sister and faced yet another person who was disappointed in her. This was becoming a habit. She had spent most of the day in bed, asleep or trying to use sleep to keep away a wicked hangover. Charity had brought soup over for her to eat in the late afternoon. After this morning, Faith had lost all appetite for food. Her stomach still felt raw, and although her head was no longer pounding, there was still a dull ache just behind her eyes. Charity had learned about Faith's latest binge from Reva who, Faith thought bitterly, never met a secret she wanted to keep.

"Where's Hope?" asked Faith. "Aren't you two supposed to be a tag team or something?"

"That's not funny, Faith," Charity replied. "I haven't told Hope about this."

"Thanks," said Faith. She loved her sister Hope, but she already had three friends who were going to lecture her, and she didn't need Hope joining their crusade. Charity was just as hard on Faith as Hope was, but there were times when Charity would surprise her with unexpected acts of kindness.

"Don't thank me,"Charity said quietly. "I just don't have the heart to upset Hope about this."

Faith closed her eyes tight, as the pain behind her eyes sharpened suddenly. "I don't need another lecture about this," she said, when the pain finally subsided.

"What is it that you need, Faith?"

Faith opened her eyes and stared at her sister.

"I don't need you to shout at me, Charity. That, I definitely don't need."

"I'm sorry," Charity said immediately, then she said, "No Faith, I'm not sorry. You are destroying yourself with your drinking."

Faith sighed. "Tell me something I don't already know."

"I'm not going to sit here and be a part of this game anymore. You drink, you get hurt, then you're sorry, and then you drink again. You don't care who you hurt. You don't care if you hurt your family, or worse, if you hurt yourself."

Faith stared at her sister. Charity seemed surprised by her own words.

"Look, I'm sorry . . ." Faith began.

"Yes, you are sorry," said Charity, standing up. "I love you, Faith—but don't call me until you're ready to get help. Whatever Hope decides is up to her, but as far as I'm concerned, I will not be a witness to your destruction."

Faith watched as her sister left her room.

Opal

The ride back home from Reverend McDonald's office was quiet. Opal was lost in her own thoughts and Jordan was just as far away. After giving her a perfunctory kiss, with a brief "I'll call you later," Jordan drove away. Opal knew that she should be more concerned about her fiancé and his strange mood, but she had other things on her mind. It was past time to deal with the lump in her breast. Just last night she had silently lectured Faith for being irresponsible with her health, and she was doing the same thing. It wasn't that she was afraid of death. It was, after all, an inevitability. Still, the thought of yet another battle in her life was draining. It seemed to her that she was always fighting a battle, from other people's perceptions of her, to her family's expectations. Sometimes, she just wanted to be.

When Jordan had come into her life, she'd experienced a relative period of calm. She was even happy at times, but there lurked deep down a feeling that trouble was never too far away. She glanced at her watch, it was already four o'clock. After the meeting with Reverend

McDonald, Jordan had taken her to lunch. Neither of them had any appetite, and after going with him on a few errands, they had driven back to the campus. During the drive she had almost talked to him about the lump, but his far away silence dissuaded her from any conversation.

She needed to talk to someone. She needed to talk to Reva.

She walked over to the telephone in her dorm room and dialed Reva's extension.

"Hey," Reva answered the telephone on the first ring.

"Hey, Reva. It's me."

"What's up, Opal. You sound like you just lost your best friend."

Opal felt tears spring to her eyes. Then, composing herself, she said, "It's not that bad, but I do need someone to talk to."

"I'll be right up," said Reva, hanging up the telephone receiver.

In a few minutes, Reva was knocking on her door.

"Come on in," said Opal.

Reva entered the room and Opal wondered how anyone could have quite so much energy. Reva looked like she was moving even when she was standing still. She sat down on Opal's bed beside her and said, "Talk."

"I haven't called the doctor yet."

Reva's response was strong. "I knew I should have called the doctor myself!"

Opal couldn't help smiling. Reva was tough and tender at the same time. Even as she was lecturing her, she saw Reva's concern and, more importantly, she saw her love.

"I'm going to call the doctor, Reva," she said.

"When?" asked Reva. "I swear between Faith and her drunken self and your determination to ignore your health, I am getting old before my time. It's no wonder I'm going prematurely grey."

"Where's the grey hair?" Opal teased, knowing the story of Reva finding a strand of grey hair last week. It qualified as a natural disaster and had propelled Reva to the drug store to get an unnatural shade of black hair dye, which still stained her pillows.

"Don't you worry about my hair," said Reva. "When are you going to call the doctor?"

Opal sighed. "Today."

"No," Reva shook her head. "Right now. You are going to call the doctor right now, while I'm sitting here.

Opal sighed again. Then she reached over for the telephone and dialed the number of her family practitioner, Dr. Reed. She had been her doctor since high school and although she was close friends with her mother, she had no doubt that Dr. Reed would keep her confidence. She could have gone to another doctor, but she trusted Dr. Reed and she felt comfortable with her.

She dialed the number from memory and waited for Tia, Dr. Reed's receptionist to answer the telephone.

After the greetings were exchanged, Reva said, "I need to set up an appointment with Dr. Reed . . . the earliest available."

"The earliest available?" asked Tia, who had been with Dr. Reed as long as Opal had been going to the office. "Everything okay with you?"

"I hope so," said Opal, with a laugh that she did not feel.

"I can put you down for 11:30 tomorrow."

"Thanks, Tia."

Opal hung up the receiver, but instead of feeling relief, the feeling of disquiet only increased. It was as if she had set things in motion and she knew that once she started this journey things would not ever be the same.

Turning to Reva, Opal said "the appointment is tomorrow at 11:30."

"Good girl," said Reva. "Do you want me to come with you?"

"No," said Opal. Then she said, "Yes. I do want you to come with me."

"Have you told Jordan yet?" asked Reva.

Opal shook her head. "No, and I'm not going to tell him unless there's something to tell. I don't want to worry him."

"Opal, the man is going to be your husband."

"Don't remind me." The words slipped out of her mouth before she had a chance to stop them.

Reva looked her directly in the eye. "Opal, why are you marrying this man?"

"He's a good man," said Opal.

"I know this, but there are plenty of good men in this world. That's not a reason to marry someone."

"I can't deal with this right now," Opal replied. "I have to deal with one major life trauma at a time."

"Marriage shouldn't be considered a major life trauma," said Reva, "at least not before the wedding."

"What's up with Faith?" Opal asked, changing the subject.

Reva rolled her eyes. "The last I heard she was sleeping it off. I ran into Charity and talked to her about it. I think she's just about through with homegirl."

"I think we all are," said Opal.

"Are you hungry?" asked Reva. "I have had the day from hell, and I haven't eaten yet."

"What happened to you?"

"Well, I was stopped by this policeman for speeding . . ."

"Reva, not another ticket!"

"No, he let me go with a warning. But then I was late for the interview at the Free Clinic. They said they'd let me know soon, but I think I have as much chance of getting that position as O.J. Simpson has joining the Klan."

"Be positive, Reva. At least you didn't get a ticket," Opal replied. "Where do you want to eat?"

"Does Joe's Soul Shack sound in any way enticing?" Reva asked.

"It's not even dinner time!" Opal laughed.

"Good," said Reva. "We can beat the crowd. Besides we won't get to Roxbury until after five and Joe will open up the shop for me."

Opal shook her head. "Do you know everybody in Boston?"

"Just folk who cook good soul food," said Reva. "Come on, girl. Get the keys to that fancy car of yours, I feel a deep longing to be connected to some macaroni and cheese and smothered fried chicken."

"At least you didn't say chitterlings," Opal shuddered.

"Hmm," replied Reva. "Now, that's a thought!"

Precious

Rory Hamlett was sitting on the outside steps of Precious' dormitory. As she walked up the path from the library at dusk, Precious had thought that her eyes were playing tricks on her. He was dressed in a blue and white jacket, the collar turned up against the chill, and looked completely out of place with his surroundings. His wide smile greeted her as she walked up to him.

He stood up, and although at five feet ten, Precious considered herself to be tall, he towered over her. "I am not stalking you," he said.

"What are you doing here?" asked Precious, not quite grasping that he was here to see her—although today had been a day of surprises, starting with the surprising announcement that she might be on her way to France next year.

"I was here doing some stuff for my aunt—she wanted me to deliver some of her papers to the library. I thought while I was here I'd take a chance and see if you were around. I tried calling you, but I didn't get any answer."

Precious was suddenly self-conscious about her appearance. She was wearing sweats and sneakers, and her hair was in bad need of a combing after the New England wind had blown it in several different directions. She knew that she looked awful, but here he was, smiling at her as if she were Miss America, tiara and all.

Something in her expression caused him concern. "I'm sorry, I guess it's a bad time."

Precious shook her head. "I'm just surprised, that's all. I didn't expect to see you."

Rory smiled at her. "I didn't expect to be here either. I intended to just drop the papers at the library and go back to school. I've got a game coming up this Saturday and I need to study my playbook."

"What?" asked Precious. If he had spoken Ancient Greek it would have been just as incomprehensible. "Football players have to study books for games?"

Rory laughed and said, "Yes, we actually do study different plays but we'll talk about that later. I wanted to know if you'd like to go to one of my games—maybe this Saturday's game?" There was a note of hope in his voice.

"Did your aunt put you up to this?" Precious asked.

Rory laughed. "No, Precious. My aunt did not put me up to this. Will you come to a game?"

"I don't know anything about football," Precious replied truthfully.

"You can learn about it later. It'll be fun."

Precious doubted that there was anything fun about running around after a football, but she kept that opinion to herself. He was a nice guy, and it wasn't like he was inviting her out on a date.

"My friend Reva likes football, I'll see if she can come. I'll see if my other girlfriends want to come, too."

"Great," said Rory, who seemed relieved. "Let me know how many tickets you need. I'll leave them at the will call station at the stadium."

"I don't have your number," said Precious.

Rory handed her a slip of paper with his name and telephone number written on it. "I was hoping you'd ask," he said.

There was an awkward moment of silence after Precious took the slip of paper. She wondered if he wanted to say something else to her. He looked as if there was something else on his mind, but instead he just stood staring at her. For the first time, she wished that she looked like other girls who always seemed to have it all together, girls like Opal—even Faith with her crazy self still managed to be beautiful.

"I guess I'll see you Saturday," said Precious.

"Okay," said Rory. He looked pleased that she was coming.

He looked as if he wanted to hug her, instead he smiled at her. "Are you going to wish me luck?" he asked.

"Good luck," Precious said stiffly. He was making her nervous and she was uncertain why she felt so ill at ease with him. She watched as he walked away and wondered, yet again, why this handsome, apparently nice football player was so interested in her.

Chapter 7

Opal

Opal took a deep breath and released it slowly. She needed to calm down. She had been to the doctor's office several times, but as the hammering in her chest indicated, this was different. The doctor's office looked more like a cozy living room. Dr. Reed lived in a townhouse in downtown Boston. She had converted the first floor of the townhouse into an office where she saw her patients. The walls were painted a warm, deep russet color and had several prints from African American artists hanging on them. There were several comfortable chairs, artfully arranged around a kente cloth couch in the waiting area. The receptionist sat at a desk in the corner of the waiting room, by a bay window with green ferns hanging overhead.

The last few days had been difficult ones. Opal had avoided Jordan's calls and she was certain that he was either going to be suspicious or annoyed. He knew that there was something going on with her and he also knew that she was not talking to him about it. She wondered when his patience or his good nature would run out. She planned to tell him when the results came back, but she didn't want to talk to him about it before that occurred. She didn't need the added pressure of Jordan hovering around her and she knew that Jordan would hover. He would worry and he would be here at her side, instead of Reva. She didn't want the attention. She wanted the company, but she didn't want the conversation.

Reva touched her arm. "Are you nervous?"

"Yes," said Opal.

"You're doing the right thing," said Reva.

"So you keep telling me," Opal replied.

"Miss Breezewood, the doctor is ready to see you."

Opal stood up and took another deep breath. Reva looked up and gave her a small smile, but Opal could see that Reva was nervous.

"It's going to be all right," Opal said with more strength than she was feeling.

Reva nodded her head. "If you need me, I'll be right here."

Opal walked down the long hallway that connected the sitting room/reception area to the examination rooms in the back. The walls were painted a bright blue color that reminded Opal of the Mediterranean sea. There was a nurse waiting by an open door at the end of the hallway. She was small and thin and she looked as if she had only recently graduated from high school. She had a short curly afro that only made her look even more like a little girl. She smiled at Opal.

"Hi, I'm Patrice," she said, stretching out a long, thin brown arm

Opal shook her hand. "I'm Opal."

"Right this way," said Patrice, pointing to the room where Opal was going to be examined. "Take off your clothes, except for your underwear. You can put that robe on . . ."

"I know the routine," said Opal. Her voice was sharper than she intended.

Patrice nodded her head. "Once you're ready, let me know. I'll get the doctor."

"Thanks," said Opal, stepping into the examination room and shutting the door quickly. Her heart was hammering in her chest and her mouth was dry. Signs of nervousness. Signs of fear. Opal undressed with unsteady hands, and then she put on the pale green robe. Slipping her feet into paper sandals the same color of green as her robe, she called out "I'm ready."

A few minutes later, her friend and physician Dr. Reed knocked and then entered the room.

"Opal," she said, "it's always a pleasure. What brings you here today?"

Dr. Reed was a contemporary of her mother's, but she carried none of the "I'm-so-important" airs that seemed to cling to her mother and her friends like an expensive, yet unpleasant perfume.

"I've got a lump," said Opal. "A lump in my breast."

Faith

Another day, another dollar. The phrase kept coming back to Faith as she struggled to keep her eyes open during the lecture on Greek philosophy. She had no interest in Greek philosophy. She had only taken this course because Reva told her that it was an easy A. What Reva had neglected to tell her was that the professor was a good substitute for a strong sleeping pill. Faith looked around the room and counted at least three students who had apparently given up the good fight and were fast asleep. The classroom was large enough that the nodding off of a few students could go unnoticed by the professor, who seemed nothing short of enthralled by his own words.

The afternoon sun shone through the stained glass windows and cast the room in hues of deep red, blue and gold. The philosophy classes were all housed in one of the oldest buildings on campus, Merritt Hall, named after some long-forgotten benefactor. Faith had taken a few classes in the building and she had always admired the architecture. A three story, red brick building with stained glass windows, reminiscent of an old European church, Merritt Hall invoked a sense of serenity. Stepping into Merritt Hall, with its worn purple carpet in the hallways and wood-paneled walls, was like putting on an old, familiar sweater.

Faith felt her eyelids start to droop and she shook her head in a struggle to remain awake. Behind her she heard the soft snoring of Crazy Nellie Cooper. Crazy Nellie came by her nickname honestly. She walked around the campus talking to herself and she had several phobias, which she would happily detail to all who would listen. She was as sweet as she could be and she was brilliant—on her way to becoming a Phi Beta Kappa—but she was crazy. If Reva, Opal or Precious were here, she could write notes to them—that would surely keep her awake—but Reva had already taken the class, and neither Opal nor Precious had any interest in Greek philosophy, nor did they need to get an A to bring up their grade point averages. Faith had always been a good student, but the drinking had taken a toll on her grades, as it had with other things.

For the past few days she had not had a drink. After her last episode, and the lectures she got from her sisters, and her friends, she had made up her mind to stop drinking. *I am not an alcoholic. I can quit at any time.* She'd told them all these words, and she'd meant it. She was a recreational drinker—well, a recreational drinker that occasionally got out of hand. She had to admit that she still craved the alcohol. It wasn't like she had the shakes or anything like that, but she wanted a drink. But she didn't need a drink and she was going to prove it to everybody that was hollering about her going to Alcoholics Anonymous, or any other substance abuse program.

At four o'clock, the class ended and Faith breathed a sigh of relief. She had dozed off for a few minutes, but she had awakened to the sound of chairs scraping the wood floor, as the students in the Greek philosophy class made their collective hasty exit.

"Hey, Faith," Crazy Nellie walked beside her, smiling at some unknown joke.

"Hey, Nellie," said Faith, hoping to dodge Nellie as quickly as possible. Once Nellie started talking, it could be a while before she escaped—and nothing Nellie said would make any sense whatsoever.

"You ought to be careful, Faith," Nellie said. She was still smiling.

Faith stopped walking and looked at her. What was Nellie talking about? Did Nellie know about her drinking? The campus grapevine was strong, particularly in the small, tightly knit, African American community, but her friends were very protective of her and her business. She knew that her sisters wouldn't gossip about "the family shame," as Charity had referred to her drinking.

"What do you mean, Nellie?" Faith asked.

Nellie's smile faded. "Girl, there's forces out there just trying to suck you in, but you've got to fight, Faith. You've got to fight."

As usual, Nellie was talking crazy. "Okay, Nellie."

"I like you, Faith," said Nellie.

"I like you too, Nellie."

"So, you just have to be careful. Very careful. Don't slip up, now!" Nellie started laughing again.

Faith watched Crazy Nellie walk down the hallway to the front door, and wondered what the hell Nellie was talking about.

Opal

The test was over. She would get her results in a few days, but at least the test was behind her. She didn't feel relief, but she was glad that at least this part was finished. Now, the waiting would begin. She knew Dr. Reed well, and she knew that the good doctor was worried. She tried to conceal it with jokes about how big the diamond on Opal's engagement ring was, and a conversation about the latest gossip in her mother's social circle, but Opal could see worry in Dr. Reed's dark brown eyes.

Opal tried to block everything else out of her mind as she drove back to the campus. Reva had switched the radio on to a hip-hop station. Opal had tried to elevate Reva's musical tastes, but Reva was strictly an around the way girl who loved her rap music and her hip-hop songs. They hadn't spoken much after they left the doctor's office. Instead, Reva had sung various rap rhymes, all off-key. Opal shook her head as she wondered what she would do without Reva, without the rest of her friends. She couldn't imagine going to the doctor's office alone, or worse, driving back by herself—just her and her thoughts.

"Ooooh, this is my song!" Reva started bopping her head, turning up Funkadelic's "One Nation Under A Groove." "Talk about old school music!"

Opal smiled. "Girl, that song is so old! We were in diapers when this one came out!"

"There's nothing wrong with an oldie, but goodie—and this one is in my goodie bag," said Reva, as she sang, "One nation under a grooooove, gettin' down for the funk of it. . . ."

"You are truly insane," said Opal, finding laughter for the first time that day.

"Sometimes, girlfriend, life is like that," said Reva, bouncing on the seat of the car to the beat of the music.

Opal felt her spirits rise slightly. There was, unaccountably, joy in the car. She still was worried, but perhaps because of that worry, she was able to see joy in a very simple thing—joy in the songs of Funkadelic, joy in the company of a friend.

"I'm going to tell Jordan," Opal said. The words came from an unknown place, but as Opal spoke them, she knew that she was doing the right thing. He was going to be her husband and they needed to face this test together.

"What did you say?" Reva turned Funkadelic down slightly.

"I said I'm going to tell Jordan about what's going on with me."

"What brought this on?" asked Reva, clearly surprised.

"I don't know. Funkadelic. You. Me. Everything. He deserves to know. He's going to be my husband."

"Well, I don't know how the hell you arrived at the decision, but it's the right one. But, I'm curious—what made you decide to tell Jordan?"

"I can't explain it," said Opal, "but sometimes, girlfriend, life is like that."

Reva

Reva hit the play button on her answering machine for the second time. She wanted to be sure that she'd heard the message correctly.

"Ms. Nettingham, we'd like to offer you the internship position at the Free Clinic. The Committee was very impressed with you. We've already sent you a confirmatory letter in the mail, but we wanted to reach you as soon as possible. Could you call us at . . ."

Reva hit the stop button. Thank God, she'd gotten the position. As long as she could remember she'd always wanted to be a doctor. She thought of the countless times folks laughed about her dream to become a physician. From neighborhood kids to unimpressed teachers, folks had either looked at her as if she were a lunatic or merely delusional when the girl from Harlem told them that one day she'd be wearing a white coat and treating her very own patients. She had not attained that particular dream. Yet. But she was on her way. Working at the Free Clinic would be a step in the right direction.

She thought about calling her mother to tell her the good news, but Sugar would undoubtedly find a way to make her feel inadequate. She knew that her mother was proud of her, but there was a part of her that suspected that her mother was secretly resentful of her successes. Sugar had planned to go to medical school but she'd gotten pregnant with Reva. She'd settled in the very fine career of nursing, but for her mother, it was tough to give up her dream of becoming a physician. It wasn't what she'd wanted out of life.

Reva felt the familiar pangs of guilt when she thought about her mother. If she hadn't been born, her mother's life would have been different. Not necessarily better, but different. Maybe her father would not have run away from her mother. Her mother's story was that once her father found out she was pregnant he left the scene. Sugar's family, with its middle-class hoping-to-climb-a-little-bit-higher pretensions, had turned their back on a single mother. Sugar had relied on her looks, her guts and her sheer determination not to fail, to keep those who turned their backs on her from having the last word. She had provided for her daughter and made sure that although money was never in any great supply, Reva got an education, got music lessons, traveled, dressed well and, in general, did not embarrass her as Sugar had embarrassed the rest of her family.

She suppressed any urge to hear her mother's voice and, instead, she picked up the telephone to call Precious. Of all of her friends, Precious was the eternal optimist—the one you called when you wanted to be assured of getting unconditional support. Faith and Opal were also supportive, but there was no one like Precious when it came to sharing good news. She was always happy for you, even when her life wasn't exactly working out. She had a rare quality of being genuinely happy for others' good fortune. Reva dialed Precious' telephone number.

Precious picked up the telephone on the first ring. "Hello."

"I got the position at the Free Clinic," Reva said, without any preamble.

There was a squeal on the other line, then Precious yelled, "I'll be right down. Girl, we have to celebrate!"

Chapter 8

Precious

Precious sat in the stadium with Reva and Faith sitting on either side of her. She had convinced Rory to get her an extra ticket for Faith, who lately had been acting as though she was a long forgotten stepchild. She had invited Opal to come, but she was spending the day with Jordan. Precious was used to spending Saturday afternoons in the library, either studying or losing herself in yet another novel. She was not used to sitting in a stadium, with the cold wind blowing off the Charles River, screaming with a few thousand other people, while grown men hurled themselves at each other in a battle to get a football across the goal line.

She did not understand the game, although Reva, in between cheering and cursing, would explain what was going on. Faith was more interested in looking at all the good-looking men attending the game, but Precious found herself focused on one man in particular—number twelve, the running back, Rory Hamlett. She watched him get the ball and run through groups of men intent on doing him bodily harm. At one point he was knocked down, and she found herself rising to her feet, anxious, worried that he was hurt.

"Relax," Reva had said, laughing. "Your man is all right, although he did get the wind knocked out of him."

"He's not my man," Precious replied.

"Whatever he is," said Faith, "I hope he keeps giving you tickets—these men are fiiiine!"

Right before the game began, Rory had looked up at their seats from the field. He'd waved at her and she'd waved back, conscious that her girlfriends were staring at her. She'd been unaccountably happy to see him. She felt like a complete fool, grinning as soon as she saw him, but there was something about Rory Hamlett that made her feel different. She couldn't explain the feeling, but she knew that whatever this feeling was, it felt good. She was not used to getting male attention, and she had to admit she liked it, but it was more than the attention. There was a connection between them. She felt as if he looked beyond the exterior—he looked beyond what everybody else saw, and saw her for who she really was. He looked beyond the good grades, the overweight body, the shyness, the awkwardness, and saw her as herself. Precious.

"Touchdown!" screamed Reva, as Rory ran across the goal line, the football thrust triumphantly in the air. "Your man just made a touchdown!"

"He's not my man," Precious responded again, but her answer was lost in the celebration as Boston Union University moved ahead against the visiting football team, 14 to 7.

Opal

Cool Runnings was one of Opal's favorite restaurants. Located in one of Boston's used-to-be-too-urban-now-trendy neighborhoods, Opal and Jordan had come often to dine on the restaurant's upscale Jamaican cuisine. The owner, Charmaine, knew them both by name. She had greeted them both with a kiss on the cheek and a declaration that they were definitely the best looking couple in the room, if not in Boston. Opal had laughed at Charmaine's flattery, although secretly agreeing with Charmaine's assessment. Jordan had not responded, instead, he looked as if he were far away.

Opal had noticed his preoccupation. All day he had been distant and uncharacteristically silent. They'd spent the day looking for antiques and Opal wondered if he was tired. He'd wanted to stay home and order Chinese, but Opal had wanted to go out. Opal, as she always did, had won the battle. Although Jordan had given in easily, Opal felt a small pang of guilt. She promised herself that she'd work on being more accommodating with her future husband.

Charmaine seated them at their favorite table, in the back by the bay window, which looked out on a cobblestone street illuminated by gaslight lanterns. Opal watched as Jordan studied the menu. His face looked as though it had been carved out of mahogany. She had always felt that he was a perfect complement to her. Where she was light, he was dark with strong features—high cheekbones, full lips, large dark eyes with thick lashes that were so long they looked as if they should belong to a very pretty woman, and not this strong-featured man.

The waiter appeared as if he had been summoned. "What is the lady's pleasure?" he asked.

"Hmmm . . ." said Opal, turning her attention back to the menu. "I know I should be more adventurous, but I always get the same thing and I'm going to have it today. I'll have your curry shrimp dinner, with a side order of extra plantains."

"I'll have the escovich fish and a Red Stripe beer," said Jordan.

Opal looked at her fiancé with surprise. He hardly ever drank.

"And what drink will the beautiful lady have?" asked the waiter, his songlike Jamaican accent taking her away from a cold Boston night, transporting her down the Atlantic, to warmer climes.

"I'll have some water," Opal replied.

Around her, Opal could hear the hum of conversation in the restaurant. Saturday night was a busy night for Cool Runnings. Its diverse clientele included dreadlocked rastamen, hippies who looked as if they had escaped from a movie on the seventies, young African American urban professionals, and various Jamaican and other West Indian families. Cool Runnings was a lively place. Soft reggae music played in the background.

Opal took a deep breath. It was time to tell Jordan about her situation. She had tried to speak to him earlier, but he had seemed distracted. He still seemed distracted and she was starting to lose her nerve. She needed to tell him the truth. Besides, she didn't know anything definite, other than that she had a lump in her breast and she was waiting for test results.

She reached across the table and held his hand.

"I need to talk to you about something," she said.

He pulled his hand from hers and instead clasped his hands on the table.

"I need to talk to you," he said.

Something in his voice frightened her. She knew that she was going to get some very bad news from the man who was going to be her husband.

She took a deep breath and composed herself. Holding her head up, and staring directly in his eyes, she said, "Go ahead and tell me what you want to tell me, Jordan."

"I don't want to tell you this, Opal, but I need to tell you."

Opal nodded her head. "I'm listening."

Opal watched as Jordan took a deep breath and blew it slowly out of puffed cheeks. Clearing his throat, he said, "Remember when I told you that there should be no secrets between us?"

Opal nodded her head again. This time, she did not speak. She did not trust her voice.

"Well, I've been keeping a secret, Opal."

Bad news was coming her way. Opal sat up straight and stiffened her spine.

"Opal," Jordan's eyes dropped to the tablecloth. "I was with someone else . . . this past summer."

Opal blinked her eyes once. Twice. Then, she said, "I'm sorry, Jordan—but did I just hear you say that you were with someone else?"

"Yes," said Jordan, raising his eyes to meet hers.

"What exactly are you saying, Jordan?"

"I'm saying that I slept with someone else this summer . . . I'm sorry, Opal. I never meant for this to happen."

Opal repeated the words slowly. "You . . . never . . . meant . . . for . . . this . . . to . . . happen."

"No," said Jordan. "I didn't."

"Who is she?" Opal asked.

"No one important," Jordan replied.

"She's important to me," said Opal.

Jordan blew out another long breath. "An old girlfriend. I was in New York—I ran into her and one thing . . . led to another."

"One thing led to another."

"Yes."

"Not that it matters, but are you still seeing her?" asked Opal.

"No. It was only one time. It was before we got engaged."

"I'm curious, what made you decide to tell me now?"

"We're going to get married. I should have told you before, but I was afraid that I'd lose you. I knew when we sat in the minister's office that I needed to tell you . . . before the wedding."

Opal shook her head, slowly. "If you were afraid of losing me, you would never have done this, Jordan."

"It was a mistake," he said miserably.

Opal felt her heart hammering in her chest. Her head hurt—sudden, sharp pains. She was dangerously close to crying, although she wasn't sure exactly why she was crying. She wasn't even sure that she loved this man, but still, his betrayal hurt. Badly. She had expected this from her last boyfriend, Adrian. He had never been faithful to her, but he had been open with her. He'd told her that she wasn't the only one and she'd accepted it until she grew tired of sharing. Opal knew that Adrian would never be true to any one woman. Even so, Adrian's actions had hurt—but not like this.

She felt as if the ground she stood on was no longer solid. The world she lived in, believed in, was no longer the same. She knew if she looked in the mirror she would see the same face that she saw every day, but something was now fundamentally and irrevocably different. Jordan was her rock—the only man other than her father who she'd ever depended on. How could he have done this and how had she been so stupid to think that Jordan was different from Adrian?

"Opal . . . Opal . . . I'm so sorry," Jordan's hands reached for hers. She pulled her hands away as if she had burned them on a hot stove.

"Yes, you are," said Opal. "You are sorry."

She pulled the ring off her finger and placed it on the table.

"Opal," Jordan's eyes were filled with tears. "Don't throw us away." He was pleading.

"You threw us away this summer, Jordan—I just didn't know it."

Jordan kept shaking his head. "I was crazy. The whole situation was crazy. I wasn't sure how you felt about me . . ."

"So you slept with someone else."

"It was wrong. I was wrong. There's no excuse, Opal. None. I can't lose you, Opal. You mean everything to me. I can't lose you."

Opal stood up. "You already have."

"Opal, we can go to counseling. I'll do whatever it takes . . ."

Opal chose her words caefully. "Jordan, I want you to listen to me very carefully. I am going to walk out of this restaurant. I am going to have Charmaine call me a cab. You are not going to follow me. You are not going to try to stop me. You are not going to make a scene. You are going to leave me alone. You are not going to call me. Ever. You are going to forget that you ever knew me. If you see me on the street, or anywhere else, do me a favor—do not acknowledge me, because I will not acknowledge you."

He looked as if she'd just slapped him across the face. "What was it that you were going to tell me?" Jordan asked, his voice flat.

"Nothing," Opal replied. "Nothing at all."

He had shaken her, more than anyone else had ever done. For a terrible moment, she thought that she would burst into tears in front of him. But, in the end, she was her mother's daughter. She was taught, almost from the time of birth, that appearances meant *everything*. She would not create a scene. It was undignified, unladylike. She was a Breezewood, and Breezewoods were made of strong stuff. *"Breezewoods might bend,"* her mother would declare, *"but we'll be damned if we break."*

Opal walked out of the restaurant to the waiting area and did not look back.

Reva

"Ms. Nettingham, I didn't know that you were a football fan."

The voice was familiar, but Reva could not allocate it to a time, place or person. She looked at the crowd waiting outside the stadium for the players to emerge. Precious and Faith had gone to the restroom and were undoubtedly caught up in the line of folks who waited until after what had turned out to be an exciting game to go to the ladies room. Reva, who hated using public bathrooms unless absolute necessity compelled it, waited for them at the entrance of the stadium.

Turning in the direction of the familiar voice she could not place, Reva found herself facing the officer who had caught her speeding. At first, she couldn't place him because he was dressed in civilian clothing—blue jeans, black cowboy boots, navy blue turtleneck and a black bomber jacket. He looked more like a student than the serious, young officer who had given her the stern warning against speeding.

He grinned at her. "You don't recognize me, do you?"

Reva smiled back. "I guess you look a little different without a traffic ticket in your hand."

He threw his head back and let out a deep, rich rumble which passed as a laugh. "As I recall," he said, "I didn't give you a ticket, although you did deserve one. Did you get the job?"

Reva was surprised that he remembered this fact. She had been speeding on the way to her interview at the Free Clinic. "I did get the job—even though I was late for the interview."

"I'll bet you forgot my name," he said. "I remember yours—Reva Nettingham. Pretty name for a pretty lady."

Reva immediately felt herself grow cold. Another lame line even if it was said in a sexy West Indian accent. "You're right, I don't remember your name," she said, turning to see if she could find her friends.

"It's Simon," he said. "Simon Bennett."

There was something in his voice that made her turn back in his direction—a promise of more to come, of something indistinct yet almost palpable. Once again, the indefinable yet tangible connection to this man rose again, surprising her.

He stood in front of her and said in that formal way of Caribbean folk, "I would very much like to further our acquaintance, Miss Nettingham."

Simon Bennett handed her another business card. "I gave you one of these before, but I had the very distinct impression that you threw it away. I hope you keep this one and I hope that you'll call me sometime. Have a good day, Miss Nettingham."

She watched him walk away, eventually swallowed up by the swell of people leaving the stadium.

"Who is that?" Precious' voice drew her attention away from the intriguing Officer Simon Bennett.

"Nobody," Reva replied.

"Well," said Faith, who had now walked up to where Reva and Precious stood. "Nobody looks awfully good from where I'm standing."

Precious

Precious felt as if she were floating. Clouds were carrying her up the stairs. She had spent a day sitting in the cold, watching a football game, and she had been happier than she'd been in a very long time. She couldn't wait to get home to call her father. She hadn't spoken to him in a few days and she wanted to tell Roosevelt everything that had happened to her. She still hadn't gotten a chance to tell him about studying in France next year, although a part of her was afraid to tell him. She was all that Roosevelt had in the world, and she wasn't sure how he'd feel about his only child going to a foreign country.

She had told Rory about France tonight and he'd been excited. He looked as if he were impressed and if this was an act, he was damn good at it. After the game, he had taken her, Faith and Reva out for dinner at an Italian restaurant. They'd eaten good food and stayed away from alcohol in deference to Faith's problems. When Rory noticed that no one else ordered alcohol, he'd ordered a ginger ale. He had been attentive to her friends, and Precious had to admit that he held his own in the company of three loud, opinionated women.

Boston Union had won the game by a field goal, and Rory was as happy as if Santa Claus had just given him his favorite toy. After dinner he'd driven them back to the campus. He'd walked them to the dormitory door. Reva and Faith had disappeared inside as if on cue. There had been one uncomfortable moment when Precious thought that he might want to come up to her dorm room. She wasn't ready for that. He'd asked her permission to kiss her, which she'd granted, and he had kissed her lightly on the lips. Then, he said "I'll call you."

The kiss had taken her by surprise. She'd assumed he meant to kiss her on the cheek. It had been a while since anyone kissed her, and that quick, light kiss held the promise of more.

"Goodnight, Rory," she said. "I had a good time."

"Me too," he grinned. Then, he walked down the pathway to his car.

After that, she'd walked inside, lost in thoughts that were unfamiliarly scandalous. She placed her key in her dormitory room and stepped inside. Closing the door behind her, she switched on the light and almost screamed when she saw Opal sitting on the floor in the corner of her room.

"Opal, you scared the . . . well, you scared me," she said. She was making an effort to watch her language. Since she'd started Middlehurst, she'd started cursing like a sailor on leave, a by-product of hanging around Reva. Her father had gently mentioned that such language was unbecoming of his baby girl.

"What are you doing sitting in my room in the dark?" asked Precious.

"I had your extra key," said Opal in a small voice, as if this explained everything.

"Opal, what's wrong?" asked Precious, as a closer examination revealed a tear streaked face. In the three and a half years that she'd known Opal, she'd never seen her cry.

"Jordan slept with another woman," said Opal.

"Oh, Opal. I am so sorry," said Precious, immediately feeling her friend's pain. She walked over to Opal and sat down next to her.

"I'm sorry," Precious repeated, not knowing what else to say.

"Before we got engaged. He slept with another woman."

"I'm sorry."

"I expected this from Adrian. I didn't expect this from Jordan."

"Baby, I'm sorry."

"What is so wrong with me that every man I date cheats on me?"

"There's nothing wrong with you, Opal!" Precious felt her anger rise within her. How could Jordan do this to Opal? He practically begged Opal to date him and then he cheated on her.

She would never have expected Jordan to act this way. "This is Jordan's problem. It has nothing to do with you!"

Opal put her head in her hands and let the tears fall freely down her face. "I'm not crying over him. He's not worth my tears. I just feel like a complete fool."

Someone was banging on her door. Only Reva carried on like that. "Precious, are you in there?" Reva bellowed.

Precious looked at Opal. "Should I tell her to go away?"

"No," Opal shook her head, and wiped the tears away with a defiant hand.

"Come in," Precious called out.

Reva opened the door and walked into the room. Slamming the door behind her, she walked quickly over to Opal.

"Girl, I am so sorry," she said. "I could just kill Jordan!"

Both Opal and Precious looked at Reva. Bad news travels fast, Precious thought, but not that fast.

"Jordan called me," said Reva. "He's been trying to find you, Opal. He told me everything."

"I don't want to talk to him," said Opal. "Ever."

"Amen," said Reva. "I told him not to call me again, either."

"Is that all you told him?" asked Precious. That was a subdued response from Reva.

"Hell, no," said Reva. "I cursed him out! I don't play that mess—folks know where they stand when they mess with me and mine."

Opal looked up at Reva and started laughing. Then, she stopped and said, "How could I laugh at a time like this?"

"You ought to laugh at his trifling . . ." Reva began.

Precious held her hands up. "Reva, I don't see how this is helpful to Opal."

"Oh, you don't?" asked Reva, eyebrows arched in displeasure.

"Okay," said Opal, wiping her eyes again. "The good news is you all don't have to worry about wearing ugly bridesmaids' dresses."

"Oh, Opal. I am sorry." Precious said, as she saw that the smile on Opal's lips fell far short of reaching her eyes.

"Don't be sorry," Opal replied, as Precious watched the familiar composure descend on Opal like a shroud. "I'll be fine."

"Of course you will," said Reva. "The hell . . . oh, Precious, I said hell all right . . . the hell with him."

"Yes," said Opal, her face completely free of tears. "The hell with him."

Opal

Her mother's voice over the telephone was clipped. "Don't waste any time on him," she said. "He is not the man we thought he was. You're a beautiful woman, Opal. You can do better."

Jordan had obviously called her mother.

"Mother, I don't want to talk about it.

There was a moment of silence, then her mother said, "Of course you don't, Opal—I just wanted to let you know that I'm here if you need me."

Her mother was a wonderful woman but she had never been like other mothers. She was not the one that Opal ran to when she was hurt. Opal would go to her father to soothe all hurts. Her mother's advice was always to put things, whether they be hurts or unpleasant events, behind her. Opal's mother did not believe in tears and she did not believe in self-pity. If any of her children got hurt while playing, she would tend to their injuries and send them on their way with a quick air kiss and an admonition that crying never solved anything. Most people thought that Lola Breezewood was a cold woman, but Opal knew better. Her mother was taught by her own mother that giving in to emotions was a sign of weakness, and she ruled her own family the same way she had been brought up.

"Don't look back, Opal," her mother said before hanging up the telephone.

Opal lay in her bed and stared up at the ceiling. Don't look back. It sounded like good advice.

Chapter 9

Faith

She stared at the bottle of vodka for a long time. The ice in the crystal cut glass had long since turned to water as she talked to herself about her desire to take a drink. It wasn't a need, she reasoned. She certainly didn't need the drink, but Lord, did she want a drink. She needed to calm down. It had been a rough day. Things had not gone well. Starting with the D she received on her Art History test and continuing with the lecture she received from her professor about not living up to her potential, she had been thinking about having a drink, just a small one, all day. The phone call from her mother hadn't helped and a letter from the Dean of Students about her low grade point average had all contributed to the bottle of vodka that she was now cradling.

The letter from the Dean came with a warning. She would not be able to graduate with a degree in Art History with a D average. The department only awarded degrees if a student had a C average or higher. Her grades had begun suffering in her sophomore year, the year her drinking began to spiral out of control. She had gone from being an A student to a C student with frightening ease. Now she was in danger of getting worse grades. Her mother was going to kill her. At the thought of her mother, Faith's hands tightened around the vodka bottle. Parents' Day was a week away and she was not in the mood to face her mother.

From her earliest memories, her relationship with her mother had always been difficult. Her mother was a strong, loving, domineering woman who held all those she loved tightly, too tightly. Unlike her sisters, who thrived from the overwhelming attention and affection that her mother lavished on her offspring, Faith had resisted all attempts by her mother to run her life. Her mother was a self-made woman, a woman who had arrived in this country from the Caribbean with very little money, but very big dreams. Winsome Phipps Maberley was a force to be reckoned with, and that force propelled her from a tough Caribbean background, which she never spoke about, to becoming the proprietor of several beauty salons, all called Winsome's, in Shaker Heights, Ohio. Faith was not close to her father. He was a kind man, but he was a man who seemed overwhelmed and bemused by his wife's strong character. He was content to stay out of Winsome's way and he treated his three daughters as if they were very interesting visitors in his home. He was polite, but vaguely distant. He ran a small insurance business, played golf and secretly drank when he thought no one was watching, but Faith watched.

The first time she'd seen her father drunk, she'd been repulsed. She was eleven years old and she'd gone into his study to hide from her mother. The study was her father's sanctuary, and even her mother respected this fact. He'd tried to push the bottle of amber liquid away when Faith burst through the study, but Faith saw the bottle and smelled the alcohol on her father's breath. He'd tried to stand up, but ended up falling back in the seat of his worn brown leather chair.

"Faith, what're you doing here?" he asked her, his words slurring.

He was drunk. Whatever little respect she had had for her father up until that point had disappeared in that moment.

"Nothing," said Faith.

"Don't you know you should knock before you come barging into a room?"

He couldn't look at her. Instead, he nervously studied his hands, the books on his desk, the family pictures on the wall—anything, except her.

"Yes, Daddy, I know."

He waved one hand at her, dismissing her. "Well, then, I've got some work to do. . . ."

When her family had discovered that she had begun drinking, her father had tried to lecture her about the evils of alcohol. She knew that her father still drank, and his hypocrisy had enraged her, but he was still her father. He had never hurt her like her mother did. He had never looked at her with overwhelming disappointment as her mother had. He had really done nothing to her, positive or negative. She'd held her tongue. In his own way, she supposed he was trying to show her that he cared about her, but by that time, he was nineteen years too late.

She did not want to become a drunk like her daddy, or her grandfather. She took a deep breath and stood up. Carrying the vodka bottle in her hand, she threw it in her wastebasket. I want a drink, her mind screamed, but the thoughts of her grandfather and her father stopped her.

Opal

"Opal, please call me, I need to talk to you. . . ."

Opal erased Jordan's message from her answering machine. Over the past several days, Jordan had called her repeatedly. She'd kept her answering machine on for most of the time, but there had been one occasion when she'd absently answered the telephone without waiting first to screen her call. It had been Jordan. As soon as she had heard his voice, she'd hung up the telephone. There was nothing more that he needed to say and she did not want to speak to him. After the first night of tears, she'd made a pact with herself not to shed another tear, not over someone who had betrayed her. Still, his unfaithfulness hurt. She was surprised by this.

"Opal, this is Jordan. I guess you're not going to return any of my calls, not that I blame you. I deserve what I get. I just wanted to make sure that you're all right. I know that I hurt you and I've got to live with that for the rest of my life. I can't make this right. Opal, I love you. I will always love you. And I'm sorry for any pain that I've caused you. . . ."

There was a small part of her that wanted an explanation. She wanted to understand how someone could claim that they love you, yet still lie down with someone else. For Opal, this was unfathomable. Her other boyfriends had not loved her. She was clear about that. They were caught up with the Opal Breezewood trophy—the looks, the money, the name—but Jordan had loved her, or he had pretended to. He was unimpressed with the Breezewood pedigree. His own family had just as much money and probably more connections. He thought she was beautiful, but his compliments were always about something else—things she said, things she did. She remembered times when he would silently wrap his arms around her. For the first time in her life, she'd felt safe. She'd felt cherished. Now, it turned out that Jordan had apparently given a performance worthy of Sidney Poitier and Denzel Washington.

What's wrong with me? Opal asked herself. She wasn't even sure that she loved Jordan and here she was, acting like a drama mama, just because Jordan had done what countless other men had done. She had always trusted her instincts, and her instincts told her that Jordan was an honorable man. His betrayal turned her world upside down and the thought that something she believed in, something she had intended to build her life on and around, was false, hurt—worse, it made her look stupid.

The light was still blinking on her answering machine, indicating another message. She hit the play button, expecting another sorry plea from Jordan. Instead, she heard her doctor's voice.

"Hi, Opal. This is Doctor Reed. Could you give me a call when you get this message? If you get this message after office hours, please have my answering service page me. Thanks. Bye."

Reva

Reva loved her mother, but there were times when her mother drove her completely crazy, as she was doing now. There were times when she and her mother would have normal conversations—they would talk about school, what was happening in her mother's love life, what wasn't happening in Reva's love life, church gossip, normal things. But there were other times when the conversations would veer on topics that either made no sense, completely enraged her, or both. This was one of those times.

"After all this time, now your father wants to come into your life!" her mother railed over the telephone.

"He's my father, Sugar." Reva never called her mother Ma, Mom, Mommy, Mama or any other usual names that folks used for their mothers. She called her mother by her first name, a habit encouraged by her mother who at the time thought that maternal appellations applied to women who were considerably older, and less attractive, than she. "He should want to be in my life."

"I know who that sorry bastard is," Sugar hissed.

"Sugar, please. Have some respect."

"He walked out on us," said Sugar, her anger making her words come out in a clipped, abnormal manner.

"Sugar, let it go already," said Reva, reverting back to her most familiar role, the sane one in this mother-daughter relationship.

"That's easy for you to say," said Sugar. "He didn't leave you while you were pregnant, now did he?"

Reva sighed. Her mother was a good woman, even if she were a little different from other mothers. But her mother was always caught up in her own drama. She was not someone who could see, or empathize with, another's pain—if that pain involved her.

"He didn't just walk out on you, Sugar," said Reva. "He walked out on us."

Sugar moved on. "Tell him that you don't want him to come to Parents' Day."

"It's my last Parents' Day," said Reva. "Maybe he should come at least to one of them."

Sugar's voice raised with indignation, and Reva could imagine that one slender hand was now firmly on her mother's hip while the other clutched the telephone. "If he comes, I will NOT be there."

"Sugar . . ."

"I mean it, Reva. *I* am the one who raised you. *I* am the one who sacrificed for you, while he was God knows where, doing God knows what with whom, and now after telling me that he wasn't the marrying kind, he's found some woman, gotten married and now he wants to be a part of your life! Where was he for the past twenty-one years!"

So that was the problem. Her father had gotten married and her mother, even after all this time, was upset.

"He's married?" asked Reva, surprised at the new development. Her father had called her sporadically over the past few years, but he had never mentioned any woman in his life, not that Reva cared. When she was little, her father's disappearing act had hurt her, but she'd grown up with a wild woman-child who made her life interesting, or at least unconventional, and along the way, she'd turned out all right. She hadn't forgiven her father, nor had she made peace with him. She just didn't hate him anymore. It took too much energy.

"Yes, he's married!" Sugar spat out the words. "And he and that hussy want to come to your Parents' Day. He told me he's going to call you, but I wanted to get to you first, to make sure that old soft heart of yours didn't fall for his daddy dearest act."

"Sugar, you don't know that his wife is a hussy and if he wants to come to Parents' Day, I'm not going to stop him."

Reva knew that her mother would hang up the telephone. The conversation was not going her way. She also knew her mother would call back later. Sugar was predictable with her craziness. Reva was also surprised by her father's marriage. When did all of this occur? She wondered what kind of woman would marry her father. It would have to be a woman with a strong constitution. Her father was a wanderer. He'd lived all over the world. Sugar said he made his living selling freelance stories to magazines. She'd seen him a few times; the last time was several years ago, when he'd shown up at her high school. They'd talked for a few minutes and he'd shoved some money in her hand, then he'd left, promising to keep in touch. She didn't hear from him again for years. He sent her mother child support regularly, but apart from the payments, he had no real interaction with Reva, or her mother.

The telephone rang again and Reva picked up the receiver.

"Hello," said Reva.

There was a moment of silence, then she heard her father's voice, tentative as it always was. "Reva, is that you?"

"Hello," Reva said again, not sure what to call him. She'd never called him daddy. Calling him by his first name seemed odd, but calling him by his last name seemed odder.

He cleared his throat. "Your mother gave me your number."

"So she told me," said Reva, feeling uncomfortable. This man was a stranger to her, although she looked more like him than her mother.

Her father cleared his throat again. "I'd like to come up to see you this Parents' Day," he said.

"Why?" Reva asked. *Why after all this time are you showing interest in anything that involves me?*

"I want to see you."

"Why?"

"You're my daughter, Reva."

"I've always been your daughter." Although Reva fought to keep the bitterness out of her voice, she failed.

"There are a lot of things that I can't explain. I can't make up for the past, Reva, and I'm not going to try. But I'd like to get to know you a little better."

"I heard you got married," Reva said, turning the conversation to another direction. Although she didn't have Sugar's almost pathological hatred towards her father, the memory of childhood pain inflicted by an absent father was not that far removed and she had no wish to engage in a conversation with her father about his absentee status.

"Yes, her name is Belle. We got married six months ago. She wants to meet you."

Reva felt a flash of anger. He only wanted to see her to appease his new wife. Well, at least that explained his sudden interest in her. When Sugar had told her that her father wanted to come to Parents' Day, she had been secretly pleased. There was a small part of her that still wanted to believe that her father cared about her. She'd thought that Parents' Day might be a beginning of sorts for them, but now she saw that he was the same selfish person that her mother had always proclaimed him to be.

"I don't want you to come to Parents' Day," said Reva.

"Did your mother put you up to this?"

"Leave my mother out of this, I don't want you to come."

"Reva, please . . ."

Reva shook her head. The old familiar pain returned. Her father didn't want her. He had never wanted her. He had left her mother when he found out that she was pregnant with Reva. Now, in some effort to make himself look good in front of his new wife, he was going to pretend to be the father he never was.

"I don't want you to come. Don't call me again." Reva hung up the telephone with the knowledge that her mother's day was just about to get a whole lot better.

Chapter 10

Opal

Opal sat in Dr. Reed's office, waiting for her to finish seeing her patients. She had instructed the receptionist to have Opal come at the end of the day. Opal was certain that whatever news the doctor was bringing was certainly not good. She had delayed her call back to Dr. Reed for two days. During those two days she had gotten several messages from Jordan and from Dr. Reed. She'd erased all the messages and had gone on with her life as if everything were normal. She hadn't told her friends about Dr. Reed's calls and no one asked her about Jordan. It was as if he had never been a part of her life. Instead, her friends surrounded her, hovering like mother hens on alert for any signs of distress. She had acted as if everything was all right. Only Reva, who had cornered her yesterday, demanding to know what was going on with her, guessed that the smile plastered on her lips was as much an accessory as the rhinestone barrette in her hair. She'd lied to Reva, just as she lied to herself. "There's nothing wrong with me."

Jordan had called every day with the same message, imploring her to call him back. Dr. Reed was blunt. "If you don't call me," she said in her last message, "I'm going to come to Middlehurst to find you myself." In the end, Opal had done what she knew she was going to do anyway. She'd called back Dr. Reed's office and made an appointment to see her. As for Jordan, she'd continued to ignore his calls. The letters he sent her, she'd thrown in the garbage, without bothering to read them.

The door opened and Dr. Reed walked in. Her eyes confirmed

what Opal knew she was going to say. Dr. Reed pulled a chair next to where Opal sat and looked directly into her eyes. She had always liked Dr. Reed. She was a doctor who was ruled primarily by compassion for her patients. Most of the doctors she had come in contact with were more impressed with themselves than their patients, and their bedside manner was often abrupt. Dr. Reed was the kind of doctor who knew about the lives of her patients, and although it often annoyed Opal that the doctor was invariably late for appointments because of her habit of chatting with her patients, Opal kept returning to Dr. Reed for that very reason, the compassion that she now saw in Dr. Reed's eyes.

"Opal, your test results are back and they indicate the presence of cancerous cells in your left breast."

The room did not swim. The ground did not shake, and except for the rapid beating of Opal's heart, nothing changed with the utterance of those words. Then, the weight of the words came down and she realized their significance.

"Am I going to die?" Opal asked.

"I'm not God," Dr. Reed replied. "We're going to have to schedule you for some more tests to make sure the cancer hasn't spread, but our preliminary tests show that you have what is commonly referred to as Stage I breast cancer. We don't believe that the cancer has spread."

"You don't believe that the cancer has spread," Opal repeated, trying to make this more real to her. She understood that her fears had now been confirmed, but there was a part of her that did not grasp that this diagnosis applied to her. It was as if she were talking about another person who shared her same characteristics, but still, was not Opal Breezewood. Some other person who looked like her, acted like her, talked and walked like her, but wasn't Opal.

"No," replied Dr. Reed. "But we need to take more tests. I have the name of an oncologist for you. Of course, you should feel free to do your own research in terms of finding an oncologist that you'd be comfortable with, but Dr. Rusov is quite simply, in my opinion, the best. We trained together at Columbia . . ."

"Am I going to die, Dr. Reed?" Opal asked again.

The doctor reached out and held Opal's hand. Until then, Opal did not realize that her hands were shaking. Dr. Reed did not answer that question, instead she said, "Opal, you are fortunate that you found the cancer in what appears to be its early stages. As I said before, we don't believe that the cancer has spread, but we need to do more tests to verify that."

"What do I need to do?" Opal asked. "What do I need to do to get this taken care of?"

"That's something you and your oncologist will decide, but typically, in these types of cases, your doctor might recommend surgery to remove the cancer and some of the surrounding breast tissue. Surgery is usually followed with some form of radiation therapy . . ."

"Do I have to leave school?" Opal asked.

"I don't know," said Dr. Reed. "It really depends on how you respond to the treatment. Have you talked with your parents yet?"

Opal shook her head.

"Well, I suggest that you talk to them. Have them call me also. I'm going to give you my home phone number. You can call me there anytime, Opal. Your mother already has the number. Tell her that she should feel free to use it as often as she needs to."

Dr. Reed was silent for a moment, then she asked "What about Jordan? Have you told him?"

"We're no longer together," Opal replied. "There's nothing about me that he needs to know."

Dr. Reed nodded her head, but she did not say a word.

"I need to talk to my parents," Opal said, standing up.

"Of course," replied Dr. Reed. "Would you like me to come with you?"

"No," said Opal. "I need to do this alone. But I know that my mother is going to need you."

"Your mother is one of my dearest friends," said Dr. Reed. "Any support she needs from me, she'll get, unconditionally."

"Thank you."

"We're going to need to schedule you for some more tests, the sooner the better—can you come in tomorrow afternoon?"

"Yes."

"Opal, do you need me to give you a lift somewhere?"

"I'm all right," Opal lied. "I just need to talk with my parents. I'll come in tomorrow afternoon."

Opal walked out of Dr. Reed's office, walked out of the townhouse, and walked the half block to where her car was parked. She got inside the car and turned on the ignition, without knowing how she got her feet to move, her hands to raise themselves and clutch the steering wheel and to turn on the ignition. She had cancer. Her life had irrevocably changed. She had the same disease that took her grandmother away from her.

She needed to talk with her parents, but first she wanted to speak to her father. Together they would face her mother. Her father would know the right words to say, the right things to do, the best way to approach this with her mother. Even though she had her differences with her mother, she knew that her mother loved her and would be devastated by this, just as her mother was devastated when her own mother was diagnosed with cancer.

Opal drove down narrow streets, taking well-known shortcuts through Boston neighborhoods until she reached downtown Boston. Turning on Charles Street, she drove a few blocks until she reached the building where her father's law firm was located. She maneuvered her car into the underground parking lot, calling out a greeting to Patrick, the parking lot attendant.

"Little Miss Breezewood!" He called out with his familiar appellation, "Sure is good to see you!"

"Hi, Patrick" Opal smiled. "Is Daddy's car here?"

Patrick nodded his head in the direction of her father's parking space where his silver Jaguar was parked.

"Thanks, Patrick. Have a good day!"

"My day just got better seeing you, Miss Breezewood."

She parked her car in a parking space close to the elevator and got out. Her legs were now shaking. She was afraid. She was afraid of hurting her father. She was afraid of her mother's reaction. She was afraid of dying. Opal took several deep, gulping breaths and then walked quickly towards the elevator, afraid that she'd lose the nerve to do what she needed to do.

The elevator opened and Opal pressed the button for the fortieth floor where the offices of Breezewood & Watkins was located. As she rode up in the elevator she tried to rehearse what she was going to say, but the words that kept coming into her head were jumbled and disjointed. The elevator opened and she was thrust into the plush world of Breezewood & Watkins. Her father was the founding partner of this successful, midsize law firm. Some of the best litigators and power brokers in Boston were in this firm.

The receptionist, whose name she had forgotten, smiled in greeting. "Miss Breezewood, is your father expecting you?"

"No," Opal replied.

"Why don't you have a seat and I'll see if I can locate him?"

"Thank you, I'll stand."

After a few minutes on the telephone, the receptionist said, "He was in the North Conference Room, but he'll meet you in his office."

"Thank you," Opal replied automatically, her mind focused on the immediate task at hand—telling her father about her diagnosis.

Opal walked down the hallway towards her father's corner office. His secretary, Lorraine, who sat directly outside his office, was on the telephone, but she waved Opal into the office. Opal walked into her father's office. He had not yet returned from the conference room. She walked over to the large windows with their view of downtown Boston. As a child, she used to love coming into this office, sitting at her father's large mahogany desk, pretending that she was the famous lawyer her father was. Around the office were several mementos of his successes. Letters from Presidents, Senators and other important people framed and hanging on the cream-colored walls, various awards and honorary citations all vied for space with the many pictures of the Breezewood family. As proud as her father was of his accomplishments, he was prouder of his family.

"Well, this is a distinct pleasure," Opal's father's deep voice greeted her. She turned around to look at her father. Osmond Breezewood was an imposing figure. His six-foot-five frame, kept in shape by biweekly tennis matches and weekend golf, was clad in its usual dark, tailored suit. Unlike the rest of her family, her father had a rich, dark complexion. With his prominent chin, large, sleepy eyes and solitary dimple, Osmond Breezewood was still a good-looking man. His salt and pepper hair only seemed to enhance his good looks, but it was the good-natured air with which he carried himself that Opal was certain accounted for his almost universal appeal. Everybody loved her father.

Something in her face made her father's smile immediately disappear. In quick strides, he was soon standing in front of her. Placing both hands on her shoulders, he looked down at her. "Opal, what's wrong?"

"I have cancer, Daddy."

Chapter 11

Reva

Step singing was a tradition at Middlehurst College. At first, Reva had thought the sight of women dressed in their class colors, standing on the steps of the college chapel, looked nothing short of ridiculous, but after four years of gatherings at the chapel, Reva had actually begun to look forward to the monthly spectacle. She supposed that she was getting nostalgic in her senior year. Nothing else would explain the tight lump in her throat at the thought that next year neither she nor her friends would be out in the cold, as they were now, singing as if their lives depended on it. The tradition of step singing dated back to the origins of Middlehurst, when for some still unknown reason, the forty-five young women who graduated from the first class at Middlehurst would get together on the same chapel steps to sing songs.

Unlike Precious, Reva was not big on traditions, but she enjoyed the sense of camaraderie that came along with this particular activity, and she loved to sing. Reva never had to coerce Precious into going step singing with her, but Faith and Opal only came when they were bullied or cajoled. Reva had tried to get Faith to come today, but Faith was writing a paper that was due the next morning. As for Opal, she was nowhere to be found. Only Precious decided to come and join in with the rest of the hardy souls who minded neither the cold, nor the songs.

Reva looked around the chapel steps and saw that apart from herself and Precious, there were not many other women who looked like her. The choral group was overwhelmingly homogeneous, but still good-natured. This was one place where the people involved were unified in their love of this particular tradition despite their various backgrounds. Reva's class all wore yellow. Each woman wore clothes representative of their particular class. The freshmen wore blue, the sophomores wore red and the juniors wore purple. The seniors wore yellow. Reva knew that she looked ridiculous in her yellow turtleneck and yellow pants, but she was not going to buck tradition. Some more fashion conscious women skipped the colored pants and stuck with khakis or jeans, but Reva and Precious went all the way in their get-up. The temperature dipped to the fifties, but the bright sunshine brought warmth to the group, which was smaller now that the weather had cooled. About eighty young women stood on the steps waiting for the choral master to arrive.

"Have you seen Opal today?" Precious asked. Like Reva, she was dressed completely in yellow—a long yellow knit skirt, yellow sweater, yellow tights and yellow sneakers.

"No," Reva replied, "and I'm worried about her."

Reva hadn't told anyone about Opal's breast exam, and she was not going to betray her friend's confidence.

"I think all this stuff with Jordan has really hit her hard," said Precious.

"I didn't think she was in love with him," Reva responded. "I thought she was marrying him because she thought that he was good husband material."

"What exactly does that mean?" Precious asked.

"Damned if I know," replied Reva. "But she's used that phrase often enough."

"Well, I'm worried about her," said Precious. "However she felt about Jordan, he hurt her."

Reva sighed. "Jordan was just about the last person I would ever expect to do something crazy like that. I know that he loves Opal."

Jordan's actions undoubtedly hurt Opal, but Reva knew that Opal was facing an even greater issue. After she had accompanied Opal to the doctor for her examination, Opal had steadfastly refused to talk to her about it. Every time Reva tried to bring up the subject of her breast examination, Opal would either change the subject or ignore her. Reva had known Opal long enough to know that she was scared. She also knew that Opal was not someone who would share her fears with anyone. She had inherited that Breezewood pride that seemed to be ingrained in all the members of her family. Still, as tough as Opal appeared on the outside, Reva was certain that Opal was frightened. She was going to need support and Opal was not a person who accepted help willingly.

The choral leader, a professor in the music department, arrived at the chapel out of breath, and carrying an armful of music sheets.

"Sorry I'm late," the choral leader called out. "I hope you all are ready for an hour filled with good music."

"He must be tone deaf," Precious whispered.

As the choral leader handed out music sheets to the assembled women, Reva thought again of her friend Opal and said a short prayer that she would be able to handle all that came her way, no matter how difficult things got.

Faith

Faith sat at one of the oak desks in the library. It was her favorite place to study or write papers. Unlike Reva or Precious, who could sit in their dorm rooms and study, Faith needed the structure of an organized study setting, and Merriweather Library had been the place for her since freshman year. She stared at her computer screen, which was still blank. The paper was due tomorrow and she hadn't formulated much more than a first sentence. The paper was for her Black Studies class and was supposed to be about the black Nationalist Marcus Garvey. Beside the computer was a stack of books and articles on Garvey that she'd compiled through her research, but she had only given them all a cursory look this morning. As usual, she'd waited until the last minute to get the assignment together.

She'd had a bad night last night. She'd wanted a drink. Still, she'd done everything, including going jogging, watching television, talking on the telephone, anything to put the thought of drinking out of her mind. Glancing at her watch she saw that it almost five o'clock. Time for dinner. Dinnertime, like everything else at Middlehurst, was regimented. Dinner was served from five to six-thirty. If students missed dinner, they were relegated to getting dinner from the student center, which specialized in greasy, fried foods.

"Faith," an unfamiliar voice called to her from behind. "I haven't seen you for a while."

Faith turned to see Jill Hall. Jill had roomed in the same dorm as Faith their freshman year, and although Faith found her to be loud and usually inappropriate, she had been a good drinking buddy. They had drifted apart sophomore year, although they occasionally saw each other in various classes or at the different parties on campus.

Jill sat down next to her. She smelled of cigarettes and coffee. Back in freshman year, Jill had been known as one of the prettiest girls on campus. She was an exotic mix of East Indian and African American, with smooth caramel colored skin, long jet black hair, and a face that looked as if it could grace a magazine cover. There had been many folks who were envious of her. Years of alcohol and cigarettes had taken a toll on Jill's looks, and her disposition. She had become bitter and catty.

"Thought you dropped out of school," said Jill. "I never see you anymore."

"I've been busy," Faith replied, silently hoping that Jill would not linger too long.

"What're you working on?" Jill asked, apparently in no hurry to leave.

"A paper on Marcus Garvey," Faith replied.

Jill rolled her eyes. "I don't know why you keep taking those Black Studies courses. No one takes them seriously anyway."

"I do," said Faith, her voice tight.

Jill looked at the blank screen. "Hmm. I can tell."

I really need a drink. The words came crashing down on her. What was wrong with her? Why was she letting Jill get to her? Everyone knew that Jill had an evil streak in her. To call her nasty was being charitable. Faith wondered how she'd ever enjoyed spending time with her, but she knew that whatever alliance they had formed was formed over a bottle.

"I can't wait to get the hell out of here," Jill continued talking. "Do you know what you're going to do next year?"

"I'm hoping to get my masters at a teacher's college."

"You want to be a teacher?" Jill's voice was incredulous.

Faith nodded her head. "I plan on teaching elementary school—I want to do the Urban Fellows Project, where teachers go back to schools in the community."

Jill rolled her eyes. "I forgot what a do-gooder you are," she said.

Go away! She wanted to scream out those words, but instead she kept silent, hoping that Jill would take the hint.

"Listen," Jill said, "I'm hungry. D'you want to go over to O'Donnell's Bar to get a burger or something?"

O'Donnell's was a bar not too far from the campus. The last thing Faith wanted to do was spend more time with Jill, but the thought of having a drink, away from judgmental eyes, had strong appeal. A drink could go a long way in settling her nerves. As trifling as Jill was, she was one person who would drink with her. Jill had her own problems with alcohol, and she was in no position to judge Faith.

"I've got to finish this paper," Faith said, even as any resolve she had started to weaken.

"We can have a quick bite to eat, and then you can come back and finish the paper."

One drink. A burger and a drink. Then, she would finish the paper.

"Come on," said Jill. "I'll drive. My car is parked outside the library."

Faith turned off her computer. She wasn't getting much done, maybe a change in scenery would get her creative juices flowing.

"All right, Jill . . . but I can't stay too long," said Faith, as she quieted the clear and very sane voice that told her that the last thing she needed to do was go to a bar with Jill. Shrugging those thoughts away, Faith closed her computer and stood up. "A burger sounds real good."

Chapter 12

Opal

Opal sat on the pale peach couch in her parents' livingroom and watched her mother pace around the room. Lola Breezewood was trying to regain her composure. Her mother was frightened. The news about Opal's cancer had literally knocked her mother off her feet. Lola had collapsed into her husband's waiting arms when he quietly told her what was happening to their youngest child. Opal had rushed to her mother's side and with her father they had helped her mother to the couch. "How could this happen?" her mother had repeated over and over again. "Cancer took Mama, and now it's coming for you."

"Mother, I'm going to be fine," said Opal, even though she had no firm belief in her own words. She did not have any feelings of reassurance that things would turn out better for her than they had for her grandmother.

"Lola, you're hysterical," Opal's father said quietly. His own eyes were red from unshed tears. "You have to pull yourself together. Opal needs you. She needs us now."

The words seemed to have some sort of magical effect on her mother who nodded her head quickly. Patting her daughter's hand, she said in a hollow voice, "Yes, yes, of course she needs us. We're a strong family. We've faced crises before and we'll face this one."

Opal wondered if those words reassured her mother, because they sounded flat and insincere to her. Still, she understood that her mother was doing the best she could. Her mother was a person who could not abide weakness in anyone, from her offspring or from herself. The fear she saw in her mother's eyes would undoubtedly be considered a weakness by her mother.

She'd watched as a transformation came over her mother, and she once again became the woman who ruled her family with a loving but iron hand.

"We need to find you the best oncologist . . ." said her mother.

"Dr. Reed has made some suggestions. . . ." Opal replied.

"Yes, yes," said her mother. "Laura will be able to help us with this."

Opal had sat down silently while her parents made plans about her future—discussing her as if she weren't in the room. She was not angry with them. They loved her, and they would be there to support her. This was their way. They were people who made plans. They were people who did not let circumstances get them down for too long. They were going to see that she got the best of everything.

"You'll have to pull out of Middlehurst," said her mother, pacing back and forth over an antique Indian carpet she had purchased on one of her many trips to the Southwest.

Opal finally spoke up. She'd let her parents run her life long enough. They'd done a decent job of things, but this was her own life, literally, that they were now planning without asking for any input from her.

"I'm not dropping out of school, Mother."

Both of her parents stared at her as if she'd lost her mind.

Her mother shook her head quickly. "Of course you're going to leave, Opal. You've got to concentrate all of your energy into getting better. Cancer is a very serious thing, Opal."

Opal was tempted to smile, but thought better of it. Her mother had obviously thought that her daughter had taken leave of her senses and as a result, she was explaining the gravity of her situation to her.

"I know that it's serious, Mother," Opal replied. "But I am not going to give up on graduating next year. I've worked hard for this and I won't put this aside—not unless a doctor tells me that it's necessary."

Opal's mother looked over at her father, her eyes wide with exasperation. "Osmond, help me talk some sense into your child."

Opal was always her father's child whenever her mother had a problem with her.

Opal's father walked over from the corner of the room where he'd stood. He sat next to Opal and held her hand. His hands shook. He was scared, just as she was. Opal looked over at his face and she could see the fear in his eyes. Her father was not afraid of anything, or anyone. She'd watched him regularly slay dragons all her life—from domineering judges, to political opponents—she'd even seen her father take on a hate group, who'd objected to their family moving into a predominantly white neighborhood. They had placed a burning cross on the family's lawn; they had called her family's home, spewing anonymous hate; they had threatened her family and although her mother had declared that "no house is worth this much trouble," her father had remained, working with the police to finally catch the culprits and thereafter, to prosecute them. "I'm not running," her father had declared. "If I start running from folks now, there's no telling when I'll stop." This man, Osmond Breezewood, who stood so tall in her eyes, now looked like a frail, old man in a matter of hours.

He cleared his throat. "Lola, we are going to support our daughter. If she wants to stay in school and if the doctors say that she is able to do so without compromising her health, then we are going to support her."

Opal squeezed his hand. "Thank you, Daddy," she said, wishing that she was young enough to crawl into the safe harbor of his arms, as she had when she was a child.

Faith

The alarm clock awakened Faith. She sat up in her bed, a familiar sour taste in her mouth. It was nine o'clock and her paper was due at 11:00 A.M. on her teacher's desk. She cursed herself again for going out last night with Jill. One drink had turned into a lot more drinks and by the time Jill had dropped her off back at her dormitory, she was drunk. *I'll write the damn paper in the morning,* she had told herself and she'd fallen asleep. Now she had two hours to write a paper that she still hadn't finished researching. *I'm not going to drink again,* Faith promised herself, but the words, now so familiar, sounded as false as she knew them to be.

Opal

Opal drove back to Middlehurst the next day. Her father had wanted to drive her back but after spending the night at her parents' house, Opal just wanted to get back to school. She wanted to talk to her girls. More specifically, she wanted to talk to Reva. She loved all of her girlfriends equally, but she had always been able to talk to Reva about anything. Faith had good intentions, but she was often impatient with other people's problems. Besides, Faith had her own issues. Precious was sweet, but she was too sensitive to others' problems. She was the kind of friend that took empathy to a whole other level. Opal remembered times when she attempted to tell Precious about a particular incident and Precious burst into tears, genuinely distressed by Opal's predicament. Opal had ended up consoling Precious.

Opal switched on the radio and absently listened to a news station while she drove along the interstate. Her thoughts turned briefly to Jordan. If he had been in her life, he would have been another rock to lean on. She had always admired how Jordan rose to the occasion whenever times were rough. He shared that quality with her father. She pushed Jordan out of her mind, just as she pushed the thought of cancer away. She would deal with those issues later. She needed to get back to school. She needed to talk with Reva.

The foliage had already turned and the traditional New England autumn bounty was in full bloom. Trees blazoned with leaves of varying shades of bright orange, red, and yellow flanked the road on which she drove. She had always loved autumn. It was her favorite time of year. She loved the cool weather, the fall foliage, the promise of winter around the corner. She wondered, without drama, whether she was in the autumn of her own life.

Her cell phone rang and she answered automatically. "Hello."

It was Jordan. "Opal, don't hang up."

She wanted to hang up the telephone, but there was another part of her that wanted to talk with him, wanted the normalcy of a telephone conversation, wanted to turn the clock back to a time when she still believed that he was her Prince Charming, or at least a good friend. She wanted to turn the clock back to a time when she did not have this disease.

"What do you want, Jordan?" she asked.

"I want you," he replied. "I want you to forgive me."

"I can't do that."

"Opal, I need to talk to you," said Jordan. There was the sound of desperation in his voice.

"Leave me alone," Opal said.

"I deserve this," Jordan said.

"We don't always get what we deserve," said Opal. "But it doesn't matter. Not anymore."

"I love you, Opal."

He was a good man. He was a good man who had done a terrible thing. Maybe if she'd loved him more she could have forgiven him, but it was a waste of time trying to sort this out. She'd rushed into the relationship with him, just as she'd rushed into getting engaged. They'd come together for the wrong reasons. He had come to her out of some childhood infatuation, which hadn't withstood the reality of his infidelity. She'd come to him out of a need for security with the hope that true love would follow. They'd both made a mistake.

"You don't love me, Jordan," she said. "You don't even know me."

"That's where you're wrong, Opal. I made a mistake, Opal. A stupid mistake, and I deserve to pay for it—if that payment means losing you, then so be it. But I know now just as I've known since my twelfth birthday that I love you, and I will always love you."

She felt a longing for him, for the safety of his strong arms that she knew would hold her and guide her through this terrible time. It was an ache that both surprised and frightened her. She did not love him, she told herself. She'd gotten caught up in the happily ever after story of Jordan and Opal, that was all. She did not love him. Still, she couldn't explain this pain she felt with the knowledge that what they shared was finished.

"Don't ever call me again, Jordan," she said, and then she hung up the telephone.

She dialed Reva's telephone number. After three rings, Reva answered. "Hello."

Opal began crying. For the first time since she'd been diagnosed with cancer she cried.

"I'm scared, Reva," she said. "I'm so scared."

Admitting her fear brought a release to her. Her life, which had seemed completely on course just a month ago, had now dramatically changed. She'd lost a man whom she believed was meant to be her life partner and she'd gotten a potential death sentence.

"I have cancer," Opal said.

"Where are you?" Reva asked.

"I'm somewhere on Route 16. I think I just passed the exit for Framingham."

"Pull over," said Reva. "I'm coming to get you."

"I can't just pull over on the highway," said Opal.

"Yes, you can," said Reva. "And you will. You're in no condition to be driving that car. You're only about ten minutes away. I'll be there soon."

Reva hung up the telephone without listening to another word of protest from Opal.

Reva

Reva drove twenty miles over the speed limit and prayed that none of the Massachusetts state police were out with their radar guns. Beside her sat a worried and apparently hungover Faith. After her telephone call with Opal, she had run to Faith's room. The girl looked like hell and Reva strongly suspected that Faith had been drinking again, but she only had time for one crisis and at the time Opal's crisis took a clear priority. "Opal needs us to come get her," said Reva. She didn't explain the particulars of Opal's problems. She'd let Opal tell Faith in her own time. "She's in trouble," was Reva's only explanation.

Faith had not asked for an explanation. Together they'd hurried to the student parking lot and got in Reva's car. While she drove, Reva explained that she was going to drive Opal's car and Faith would follow them. This seemed to be a pattern with them, thought Reva, remembering an almost similar scenario when they'd gone to pick up Faith when she was drunk in the bar some weeks ago.

Reva felt relief when she saw Opal's car at the side of the road, its emergency blinkers on. They drove to the next exit and then turned around, finally parking the car behind Opal's. Handing Faith the keys, she told her, "Just drive it back to the campus. I'll explain later."

Faith nodded. "Let her know that I love her and I'm here if she needs me."

Reva got out of the car. Slamming the car door behind her, she walked quickly over to Opal's car. Opening the driver's side door, she told Opal as gently as she could. "Slide over, girlfriend."

Opal moved over to the passenger seat and Reva got inside.

Reva turned and looked at her friend. Her heart twisted with the fear that she was going to lose Opal. In her heart, she'd had a feeling that her friend had cancer. Reva was afraid but she knew that she could not give in to her fear. Opal needed her.

Reaching over she took Opal's hands in hers.

"The cavalry's here," she said.

Chapter 13

Precious

"I shouldn't be doing this," said Precious.

Rory Hamlett grinned at her. "Eating Chinese food on a Wednesday night is not my definition of sinful activity."

Precious could not resist smiling at him. She'd been smiling since his call this afternoon, inviting her out to dinner at his favorite Chinese restaurant. At first she'd been reluctant, giving him the usual excuse—it was a weeknight and she had work to do. "I'll pick you up early," he'd promised "and then I'll get you back by eight o'clock—in time to do any assignments that you have to do. Besides," he reasoned, "you have to eat."

No, I don't have to eat, thought Precious, knowing that just this morning she had vowed to start yet another diet. She was a size fourteen and she was inching closer to a sixteen—this was not the kind of movement she'd hoped for—she was still trying to get to a size ten, or twelve by Christmas, which was two months away. Her weight had always been an issue for her. She had never been obese, but she'd been chubby most of her life and she'd been teased about it as a child. She'd lost count of the people who would comment about her pretty face, always followed with another comment about her weight. Losing herself in books had helped. Books had provided a world of acceptance for her—a world in which she was not constantly judged by her appearance. Still, she couldn't live in her fantasy world forever—eventually, reality had to intrude.

"I'm on a diet," she'd told Rory, explaining her reason for declining his dinner invitation.

"Diets don't work," he responded. "Besides, you look good."

He was either blind or a very good liar, but his words sounded good.

"Nobody wants a bone but a dog," Rory continued. "I like my women to have a little bit of meat on them. I happen to like curves."

Either she had died and gone to heaven, or she was hallucinating. "Most men aren't like you," Precious told him.

"I can't answer what most men are like," Rory replied, "but if you want to get healthier—maybe we can start jogging together."

"Rory, you're in Boston and I'm in Middlehurst—a good twenty-three miles away. You're not going to have time to go jogging with me."

"I'll make the time," said Rory. "Now, what do I have to do to get you to come to dinner with me? Do I have to beg?"

No, she said silently, *you don't have to beg at all.* "I'll take the five o'clock bus to Cambridge. I'll meet you at Harvard Square."

Wong's Place was a popular Chinese restaurant in Cambridge and it was one of Precious' favorite places to eat. The food was good, plentiful and cheap. Students got a ten percent discount and free refills on their beverages. She'd been there several times with her friends. It wasn't exactly a romantic spot, but she did not know whether Rory had romance on his mind. She knew that he enjoyed her company and he seemed attentive—but she had a faint but stubborn perception that his aunt had put him up to this. Whatever his reasons for coming into her life, she was grateful. She was having fun and if that was all this was—fun—then she was just fine with it. She wasn't looking for a relationship, but a little male attention definitely did not hurt.

She'd spent the afternoon trying to figure out what she was going to wear. She didn't want to send the wrong message to him—that she was desperate, or easy—but she wanted him to know that she was interested. It was the first time she'd admitted this to herself—she was interested in Rory Hamlett. She didn't fool herself that this was any great romance. He was a college football star on his way to the NFL. Football stars do not end up with plain, overweight, although brilliant women. She finally settled on a pair of black slacks—slimming—and a deep purple turtleneck sweater that hugged her hips in the right places. Putting on a trace of lip gloss, she'd brushed her thick black hair off her face, clipping it back into a neat chignon. Precious was not a vain person, but she was often convinced that her thick black hair was her best asset.

She'd looked for Faith, Opal and Reva to ask them their advice on her outfit. She wasn't the kind of person who paid too much attention to her wardrobe, but her friends were, all in their own way, divas who believed in looking good, especially when it came to members of the opposite sex. Usually, she could locate at least one of her friends, but today, she'd been out of luck. Giving herself one more look in the mirror, she'd deemed herself presentable and hurried to catch the five o'clock bus.

As the bus had pulled up to the stop in Harvard Square, her heart had done a little dance when she saw Rory waiting for her, his hands jammed in the pockets of his black leather jacket, his collar turned up against the chilly New England weather. His face broke into a wide smile when he saw her get off the bus and for one crazy moment she thought that he was going to grab her and kiss her. Instead, he grinned at her and said "I wasn't sure if you were going to stand me up."

"You don't know me well," Precious had replied, "but I always keep my word."

"Good," Rory said, taking her hand in his, "I like that in a woman."

It felt natural, strolling down Harvard Square, holding Rory's hand. They talked easily as if they were old friends. Once they got to Wong's Place, the waiter seated them at a small table in the corner. Placing an aromatic votive candle in the center of the table, he took their orders and disappeared.

It was just past six-fifteen in the evening and the restaurant was not yet crowded, but Precious knew that in the next half an hour, the place would be buzzing with activity. She had never gone out to dinner on a weeknight. She was far too practical for that. Precious had lived a life where she did what she was supposed to do. Unlike her mother, who'd lived her life without regard to the consequences of her actions, Precious always wanted to do the right thing.

As if he read her thoughts, Rory said, "Having dinner on a weeknight is not going to send you to eternal damnation, you know."

Precious lost the battle in suppressing her smile. "I'm a scholarship student—which means I have to keep my grade point average up. Usually, I'm locked down in the library on week nights."

"I'll make sure you'll get home by eight."

"I think that I can make the seven-fifteen bus back," said Precious. Rory shook his head. "I'm driving you back to the campus."

Precious protested. "It's not necessary. It's too far."

Rory raised both hands in mock protest. "Precious, I enjoy your company. The time in the car will just prolong my enjoyment."

The food was delivered to their table as if on cue. Precious dug into her dish of steamed shrimp and broccoli. She'd ordered plum wine, one of her favorite drinks. It was too sweet for most people, but she loved the thick, sweet nectar. She was not a person who drank often. Faith had given her enough reasons to be cautious where drinking was concerned, but she enjoyed an occasional glass of wine. Rory ordered scallops with black bean sauce. He drank water.

"I'm curious about something," Precious said, the plum wine, good food and candlelight relaxing her. "Is there someone special in your life?"

She'd wanted to ask him this question from their first meeting, but she'd thought that was too forward. Besides, it was none of her business. His aunt had told her that he wasn't dating anyone, but she wanted to make sure.

Rory took a sip of water and looked at her. "Not yet."

She wasn't sure if it was the wine or the way he stared directly into her eyes that made her heart start racing in her chest. Clearing her throat, she said, "I'm surprised that you're not dating anyone."

"I didn't say that," Rory replied.

Precious choked on her plum wine, and then struggled to regain her composure. "I thought you said that there was no one special," she said, hoping that her voice had not even a trace of a whine.

"There's no one special yet," said Rory, "but I do date occasionally."

"Oh." Precious could taste the disappointment. What did she expect, she thought, fighting with herself to keep any bitterness away. He was smart, good looking, funny and on his way to signing a lucrative football contract. He probably had to beat the women off him with clubs.

He looked at her directly. "There's no one special in my life, Precious. If you're asking me do I spend time with other women, then the answer is yes. I do go out occasionally. But I do not sleep around. The last serious relationship I had was two years ago."

"What happened?" Precious asked, cursing herself for being so curious. Any attempts at being cool tonight had hopelessly failed.

"She cheated on me," he said.

"I never think of women cheating," said Precious. "Whenever infidelity is involved, I always assume it's the man in the relationship."

"Well, I'm sorry to be the one who disappointed those assumptions, but men get cheated on and men get dumped. Both of those things happened to me."

Precious reached out and touched his hand, genuinely sorry for any pain he might have felt. "I'm sorry," she said.

"Don't be," Rory grinned at her. "She did me a favor—on both accounts. She found someone who was already playing for the NFL."

"She's crazy," Precious said, with more feeling than she intended. "To let a good man like you go, she had to be out of her mind."

Rory laughed. "You think I'm a good man, Precious?"

Precious took another sip of the wine. "You appear to be."

"I've never met anyone like you," he said quietly. "Someone who wants to see the best in everybody. I wish I had that quality, Precious.

"I'm not a saint," Precious replied.

"Precious, I want you to get to know me. I want to get to know you. Do you think we'll be able to do that?"

"You're asking me to be your friend?" Precious asked.

"I'd like to be your friend. Yes."

Friendship. That was not a bad thing, thought Precious, but why was she so disappointed?

"I'd like for us to get to know each other better. I'm not a perfect man, Precious. If you were to get involved with me, you'd have to understand that."

"Get involved?" asked Precious. "As in get involved in a relationship?"

"Yes. I want us to be friends and if that leads us somewhere else, we'll see. Like I said, I'm not perfect. I've done some things that I'm not proud of, but I believe in second chances, Precious. Do you?"

She had no idea what Rory was talking about, but she liked him and she felt comfortable with him—and she trusted him.

"Yes, Rory," she replied. "I believe in second chances."

"Eat up," Rory Hamlett said, grinning like a schoolboy. "Your food is getting cold."

Reva

The boathouse at Middlehurst was the place Reva went when life got particularly difficult. Located at the lake's edge, the small cottage, which housed the crew boats and equipment, also had a room with a few wooden chairs, throw pillows and a comfortable leather couch, which had seen better days. There were two large windows in the corner of the room, which looked directly out to the lake. On the wooden floor was a rug that once might have been red but was now a faded brown color. There was a large fireplace, which someone usually stocked with wood once a week during the winter months. Reva had lit the fire when the chill of the late fall afternoon got to be more than she could stand.

One of the advantages of being on the crew team was unlimited access to the boathouse, and Reva often found herself in this room, sorting out problems or seeking solitude. She'd taken Faith and Opal to the boathouse where they'd stayed for most of the day, talking, crying, trying to wrap their arms around a problem that seemed too big for any of them to conquer, or even understand. Opal had cancer. Opal could die. Those were the thoughts that refused to leave Reva, even as she tried her best to look for a silver lining in a dark cloud.

"My mother wants me to leave school," Opal said. She was sitting on a large pillow on the floor. The light from the descending sun bathed the room with a warm, golden glow and framed Opal with an almost ethereal look.

"What are you going to do?" asked Faith.

Reva had been surprised at how strong Faith had been. Faith was not known for being someone you could turn to when life got difficult. Reva knew how fragile she was—the drinking confirmed that fact—but once Opal told her about her breast cancer, it was as if Faith became transformed. Although Opal and Reva had cried throughout the day, Faith had remained clear-eyed and focused. She'd talked to Opal about treatment options. She'd told her stories about women she knew who beat breast cancer. She'd held Opal when the tears threatened to overwhelm her. She had been the woman that Reva always suspected, but wasn't too certain, she was.

"I told her that I don't want to leave school, not if I don't have to," Opal replied.

"It's going to be difficult with the chemotherapy," said Faith, "but if anyone can pull it off, Opal, you can."

Opal's smile carried a lot of sadness in it. "I wouldn't be so sure," she replied.

"You have to be sure," Reva said. "This is a fight that you have to be certain that you'll win."

If Opal gave up, if she became insecure, frightened—it would be harder to beat back the enemy. Cancer.

"Whatever you do from here on in," said Reva, "you have to be sure that you are going to beat this . . . this thing."

"I think the word is cancer, Reva," Opal said quietly.

I know what the word is, Reva replied silently. *But if I say the word, I give it power and I will not give it any more power than it already has.*

"I think we should pray," said Faith.

Reva and Opal both looked at Faith with unconcealed surprise. Faith was not a religious person and despite her given name, Reva could not remember the last time Faith had gone to church.

"Don't y'all look at me like that," said Faith, a sly grin turning up the corners of her mouth. "Even sinners like me know how to pray."

"All I can say to that is amen," said Reva, as she joined her two friends in a circle of prayer.

Chapter 14

Faith

Dean Hambrick's office was a clear reflection of her personality, dark and humorless. The room was small and although it contained windows that looked out on to the academic quadrangle courtyard, or the Quad as it was known to everyone who had spent more than a day at Middlehurst, the floral print shades were perpetually closed. It was rumored that Dean Hambrick had an aversion to sunlight. There were a few pictures of European cities on the wall, as well as Dean Hambrick's academic credentials, all encased in gilded gold frames. The office was dominated by Dean Hambrick's oak desk and chair, with four uncomfortable wooden chairs scattered haphazardly around the desk. Faith was sitting in one of the uncomfortable chairs.

As she waited for Dean Hambrick to begin what was undoubtedly going to be a difficult conversation, Faith thought about the past few days. After learning about Opal's cancer, it was as if instead of time standing still, it seemed to travel at warp speed. Assignments, classes, talks about Opal's treatment options, preparation for graduate school exams all jumbled together and Faith often found herself in an effort to remember exactly where it was she needed to be at a particular time. Through it all, the longing to have a drink continued, but for now, she resisted. Going to the bar with Jill was a mistake that she did not intend to repeat.

"Faith, you are not a dumb woman."

Dean Hambrick often began conversations in this manner—jumping right into the subject without any pleasantries or preamble.

Faith nodded her head. She was inclined to agree with the Dean's assessment.

"What I would like to know is why a smart woman would act in such a dumb manner." Dean Hambrick leaned back in her chair and waited for a response.

What had she done now, Faith wondered. Dean Hambrick was the academic dean for the senior class. In addition, she had been Faith's African History teacher. Faith wasn't sure whether or not it was because Dean Hambrick was one of the few African American deans at Middlehurst that she seemed to take an unusual interest in Faith and her studies. Although she remembered a comment by Reva that seemed to contradict any thoughts of African American solidarity where Dean Hambrick was concerned. *"I, too, belong to the African American race," Reva said, "and she barely looks in my direction, even when I say hello to her."*

Faith stalled for time. "I'm not sure I know what you mean Dean Hambrick."

Dean Hambrick was a beautiful woman. Even in her late fifties, she had dark brown skin that Faith swore actually glowed from apparent good health. Her short afro was now almost completely gray, but the gray hair was in contrast with an unlined face. Dean Hambrick had a disconcerting way of staring at Faith with a direct, unblinking stare as she was doing now.

Dean Hambrick opened a pale yellow file on her desk, pushed her glasses down her nose and began to read, "Missing classes . . . low grades . . . assignments not turned in . . . need I go further?"

Faith had been the recipient of many lectures from Dean Hambrick, and she knew from experience that silence, in this case, was the more prudent way to go.

Dean Hambrick continued. "Faith, you've been given chances . . . many chances. If you were a cat, I'd say that your nine lives are just about over. Do you still intend to graduate on time?"

Faith sighed. She deserved this lecture, which made it even more difficult to listen to.

"Yes, Dean Hambrick."

"Then, my dear, you have a great deal of work to do. You are currently running a D average in Contemporary Social Theory and the rest of your classes are not much better—I am told that you are in danger of failing your Philosophy of Law class. You can do better, Faith. Have you been drinking again?"

There were two people in the world that Faith could not be dishonest with. One was her mother. The other person was Dean Hambrick.

"It hasn't been as bad as it's been in the past," said Faith. "But, yes, I have been drinking recently."

When Faith had gotten arrested for driving under the influence, the school had wanted to suspend her, but Dean Hambrick had supported her. She had arranged for Faith to complete a sobriety program in conjunction with the court's order, and she had been placed on a semester's probation, which she had completed without incident.

Dean Hambrick sighed. "It's a tough road, Faith. My husband is a recovering alcoholic—and it really is one day at a time in terms of recovery, but you've got to want to get better. I don't think you want to get better, Faith. I don't think you feel that you have a problem."

"I know that I have a problem," Faith replied. "But I can handle it on my own."

"Can you?" Dean Hambrick asked, two severely plucked black eyebrows raised in disbelief. "My husband has the name of a good therapist—he still sees her. She's been very helpful. Her specialty is addictive personalities . . ."

Faith stopped the Dean before she went much further down this road. "Dean Hambrick, could we talk about my academic problems?"

The dean cleared her throat. "I believe the two are interrelated."

"I know I have a problem with drinking and I'm handling it. Now I know that you want to talk to me about my classes . . ."

"Faith, at some point you are going to have to deal with your drinking problem and I hope that this day comes sooner than either of us anticipate that it will . . . but you're right, this is about academics. I've spoken with your professors and each of them have agreed to consider raising your grades if you do some extra work . . ."

"Extra work?" Faith asked, feeling overwhelmed by the work that was currently due that she hadn't started yet.

"Yes," said Dean Hambrick. "You need to go to each of your professors to find out what the specific assignments are. Some may involve research, or taking tests over, or writing papers. I went to each of your professors and found them all in agreement that you are an intelligent person who is letting something else sidetrack you. I believe that you and I know what that is. . . . In any event, you have been given another opportunity to make things right so you can graduate with the rest of the members of your class."

Faith knew that she should be grateful but she felt an anger rise within her, which she knew was unreasonable. She was tired of everyone in her life doing what they thought was best for her, and then hoping she'd follow along. Still, she knew that without Dean Hambrick's help, she might not graduate.

"Thank you," Faith said through tight lips.

Dean Hambrick did not reply, instead she stared at Faith with those unblinking eyes until Faith left the office.

Opal

The waiting room in the oncologist's office was crowded. Located in a medical office building in Cambridge, behind Harvard Square, Dr. Rusov's practice was thriving. The waiting room was filled with patients. Opal tried not to look at them. She did not want to see their sickness. It frightened her. There were some patients who had lost their hair; many appeared gaunt and frail. *Is this my future?* Opal asked herself. She had gone to Dr. Rusov's office last week to have a CAT scan taken of her body, and further tests were done to see whether or not the cancer had spread from her breast. Taking those tests had made Opal feel as if she were walking into her own funeral. She had not given up hope, but the realization that she was closer to death than she had ever been before, frightened her. Her parents sat beside her, each one flanking her as if providing her with silent protection. They had met her at the doctor's office, although they had wanted to drive her there. There would be time enough to lean on them, Opal thought, but at this time she wanted to remain as independent as she had always been.

When the nurse called her name, she waited a moment before standing. She wanted to stop her heart from hammering. Fear was an unfamiliar emotion for her. She was going to need time to get used to the feeling—the sinking of her stomach, the hammering of her heart, the dryness of her mouth. She was going to have to take some time getting familiar with fear. Her parents stood up and looked down at her, their own eyes reflecting her own silent terror. Her mother moved her mouth but no words came from them. She saw her father's eyes water. *Be strong,* a voice from somewhere deep inside her, cautioned, *or at least pretend to be strong.*

She stood up and followed her parents, who followed the nurse to Dr. Rusov's office. They sat down and waited for the doctor. They did not have to wait long. Opal's first impression of Dr. Rusov was that she was the tallest woman she had ever seen. She was easily over six feet, and she wore black pumps making her long legs look like they belonged in a basketball court, and not sheathed in sheer black stockings. This was their second meeting. During the first meeting, before she'd taken the tests, Dr. Rusov had gone over in detail the different treatment options that were available to her depending on the results of the tests. Her mother had asked a lot of questions, and Dr. Rusov had patiently answered all of them. Opal had liked her immediately, and under different circumstances she would have enjoyed talking to Dr. Rusov. She was funny, direct and seemed to have a wealth of information on cancer, and interesting things to do in Boston.

"I have some good news," said Dr. Rusov, sitting on the chair by her desk.

Opal took a deep breath to steady her nerves, and her voice. "Good news is always welcome," she said.

"What is it?" Opal's mother asked, her voice sharp.

"The tests indicate that the cancer has not spread—which is wonderful news. That makes our treatment options simpler."

Opal let her breath out slowly. The cancer had not spread.

"Thank you, Jesus" said Opal's mother, who despite her regular appearance at church on Sundays, was not particularly religious.

"What's next?" Opal's father asked.

"We begin the treatment plan we talked about the last time I saw you. Surgery, followed by chemotherapy treatments. As we discussed, we won't be doing the radical mastectomy. We'll be able to keep the breast—but we do have to get at that tumor. We'll do that and evaluate how things go. The good news is that we've caught this relatively early and the cancer hasn't spread."

"But the bad news is that I have cancer." The words left Opal's mouth before she had a chance to catch them.

Her mother looked at her sharply, but said nothing. Her father coughed.

"Yes, Opal," Dr. Rusov replied, "that is bad news."

"This may not be the right time to discuss this, but I think this subject needs to be discussed," Opal's mother spoke up.

"Yes, Mrs. Breezewood?" Dr. Rusov turned to face Opal's mother.

"Opal wants to continue her schooling this year. I think she needs to take some time off to use her energy to fight this thing," said Opal's mother.

"I don't want to quit school, Mother," said Opal. "I intend on graduating with the rest of my class."

"Oh, for heaven's sake, Opal." Her mother had clearly lost all patience on this subject. "What difference does it make when you graduate?"

"It makes all the difference to me," said Opal.

Dr. Rusov cleared her throat. "Why don't we see how the treatment progresses? You'll need to take a few weeks off after the surgery—but once you begin feeling a little better, then maybe you'll be able to resume your studies."

"While she's having chemo treatments?" Opal's mother did not bother to keep the sarcasm out of her voice.

"Perhaps," replied Dr. Rusov. "We'll see how things go."

The only folks less committal than lawyers, Opal was certain, were doctors.

"I've scheduled your surgery for next week Friday," said Dr. Rusov.

"That's the day after Parents' Day," said Opal.

Opal's parents looked at each other.

"Are you guys still coming?" Opal asked. Parents' Day was usually Opal's definition of a nightmare, but she wanted her parents to come this year. For them not to come would be a tacit understanding that life had changed because of her cancer. Opal was not ready to wave the white flag of surrender to cancer—not just yet—even if it meant having to suffer through another Parents' Day.

"We'll be there," Opal's father replied.

Chapter 15

Reva

The luncheon at Imani House was usually the only part of Parents' Day that Reva looked forward to. Imani House was a pale yellow Victorian that served as the cultural center for African American students at Middlehurst. Imani House was once a sorority house, but when Middlehurst abolished all private sororities on campus, the Victorian was abandoned until the seventies, when a handful of African American students convinced the college that, like other ethnic groups on campus, they needed a place where they could congregate, make meals, have parties or host different events. The Parents' Day luncheon, which was usually catered by a soul food restaurant in Boston, was always a success. The food was good, the conversation pleasant, and Molly, the Imani housemother and Director of Cultural Affairs and Diversity at the college, always made sure that Marvin Gaye or some other Motown legend was singing on the stereo system in the background.

Imani House was too small to host a sit-down luncheon, so the luncheon was always buffet style. Folks who were lucky enough to get a chair were usually few in number, so most people either stood around with plates in hand, or sat on throw pillows on the meticulously shined wood floor. It was an informal break from all the events the college put on to impress parents.

Reva sat on the floor beside her mother, Sugar, who was licking rib sauce off her fingers in a way that Reva could best describe as borderline pornographic. Her mother was in a class by herself. As a child, Sugar's tight clothes and loud voice used to embarrass Reva, but she'd made her peace with her mother. Sugar was never going to be the bread-baking PTA mother that Reva had hoped she'd be. She was a good mother in her own way. She'd raised Reva without much help from anyone else, including her father. Sugar had made a lot of sacrifices for her only child, and she was quick to remind Reva of this when she perceived that her offspring was getting out of hand.

Sugar looked at Reva's plate. "Reva girl, do you think you should have quite so much on your plate?"

Reva's weight was a source of constant friction between herself and Sugar. Sugar was a woman who kept her slight physique despite her legendarily voracious appetite. Reva had always been slightly overweight. Lately she had moved from the slightly overweight category to the confirmed overweight group.

"Don't start, Sugar."

"Well, if you lost a little weight maybe you could meet a nice young man. . . ."

Reva put her fork down long enough to glare at her mother. Then, because even though Sugar was crazy, she was still her mother, Reva kept her voice at a well-modulated tone although she was quite close to yelling. "Sugar, having a man in my life is not a high priority."

Unbidden, an image of Simon Bennett was conjured up like some old black magic spell. She pushed the image away. She hadn't thought of him much since their encounter at the football game, but from time to time, in the most unlikely of circumstances, like sitting in Organic Chemistry class, or eating lunch at the black table, thoughts of Simon Bennett would come her way.

Sugar licked the rib sauce off her pinky finger before she answered. "Maybe it should be a priority, honey. You are not getting any younger."

Reva understood that her mother was not being mean. She was just being Sugar. Sugar was a good-looking woman who invested a lot of time in making sure that her best asset, her looks, did not fade. Sugar thrived on the attention of men. She was not a loose woman—Reva could only remember her mother actually dating a handful of men. Still, her mother loved male attention. It did something for her when a man noticed her—an inner light seem to shine a little brighter, her step got quicker, her smile got wider and her hips swayed a little more than their usual hypnotic way. Her father's rejection of her mother only made Sugar more intent on culling male attention—but Reva saw through her mother's flirtatious ways. She was scared of men, even as she beckoned their attention. Whenever a man got too close—whenever her feelings got involved—she'd back away.

Reva put her plate down on the floor. Her appetite had now vanished. Sugar could do that to a person.

Satisfied that she had gotten her point across, Sugar moved on to a new topic. "Have you heard from that no good man who is perpetrating as your biological father?"

Reva looked at her mother. Sugar's placid expression did not change, but there was something about the way Sugar gripped her glass of punch that made Reva know that her mother was still upset about her father's marriage.

"Not after I hung up on him," said Reva, anxious to change the subject. She didn't want to talk about her father. Even after all of these years, his rejection still hurt.

"He's got some nerve, I tell you, trying to come here with his . . . woman . . . trying to act like a father after all these many years . . ."

"Let it go, Sugar," Reva said, her head suddenly throbbing.

Her mother smiled at her. "I just want to let you know that I support you, baby—in your decision not to see him."

"Can we change the subject?" Reva asked.

"I don't blame you one bit," said Sugar, taking a barbequed rib from Sugar's plate. "Talking about that disagreeable man upsets me too."

Reva loved her mother, but sometimes it was difficult liking a person even though you loved them. She watched her mother, squeezed into a two sizes too small leopard print dress, her short afro now dyed a bright shade of red, large round hoop earrings dangling from her ears, nibble on a barbequed rib. Her mother had always embarrassed her with her loud ways. Sugar had often angered her with her seemingly effortless, and thoughtless insults. Reva couldn't ever remember her mother giving her praise in one hand without taking it back with a criticism—that was her mother. Reva sighed. *Another Parents' Day.* Her only consolation was that God-willing, this was her last one.

Precious

"Come on, Daddy," Precious said, "Let's go rescue Reva."

Roosevelt Averyheart's rich bass laugh came from somewhere deep inside his belly. "She does look like she's been sucking on a lemon."

"Lord knows what her mother said to her now," Precious muttered. She was familiar with Sugar. Sugar was a nice woman, but she kept on hurting her daughter, even though Precious was sure that the hurt was not intentional, but a by-product of a strong and abrasive personality.

Imani House was filled with people. Marvin Gaye was on the sound system singing "Let's Get it On." Molly, the housemother for Imani House, was a Marvin Gaye fanatic. Once, when she'd had too much to drink, she had told Precious, *"Girl, I saw him shortly before he died . . . it was at a concert and he was so fine, I threw my panties at him!"* Precious had been shocked. Conservative, fiercely independent and feminist were the words that came to mind when Precious thought of Molly— panty-throwing groupie did not come close to any description that Precious would have used in relation to Molly. *"I wasn't actually wearing the panties!"* Molly had explained, which only served to confuse Precious more, *"I brought them with me!"*

Precious and her father walked over to where Reva and her mother sat. Sugar was talking to Reva and Reva was ignoring her. From the looks of things, Precious got there just in time. Roosevelt sat down next to Sugar and Precious sat across from them, next to Reva.

"Roosevelt!" Sugar purred, fixing a bright smile on Roosevelt.

Precious watched as he leaned over and kissed Sugar on the cheek. "Aren't I the lucky one, sitting next to three beautiful young ladies! How's life, Reva?"

"Life's pretty good, Mr. Averyheart," Reva replied, a smile breaking through.

Precious suppressed her own smile. Her father knew how to work a room, and he knew how to work women. With the one exception of her mother, Roosevelt knew how to make women feel good. Although he was close to sixty, plenty of good living and regular church going had taken years off Roosevelt Averyheart's face and body. He was still good-looking, but Precious was convinced that ultimately it was not his looks that impressed women—although his good looks helped— but it was a good heart and a genuine interest in others that made women fight for his attention. Precious smiled to herself because she knew that no matter what women came his way, she would always be number one in her father's life.

"What's this I hear about Precious' new boyfriend?" Sugar asked.

Precious thought that her father's smile faltered, but it happened so quickly she couldn't be sure. "That's news to me. You got a boyfriend, Precious?"

Precious glared at Reva. She'd thought that Faith was the one with the big mouth.

Reva had the good grace to avoid Precious' glare, but she couldn't hide her grin.

"I don't have a boyfriend," Precious said stiffly.

"That's not what I hear," Sugar chirped. "I hear he's some big football star."

"Is that the guy you told me about—the one from Boston Union?" Roosevelt asked.

Precious had casually mentioned to her father that she'd met a friend named Rory, but she'd been vague in the details. She didn't want to get her father's hopes up. Every random man she met had brought dreams of a future son-in-law to her father.

"He's just a friend, Daddy," said Precious.

"A good-looking friend," said Reva, now laughing.

Precious glared at Reva.

"Oooh, Molly is playing my song!" said Sugar, turning her attention to Molly who was now dancing with somebody's father to "I Heard It Through the Grapevine."

"That's one of my favorites," said Roosevelt.

"Well, what are we waiting for?" asked Sugar.

Precious couldn't be entirely certain, but was Sugar flirting with her father? Before she could answer that question, Precious watched as Sugar and her father joined Molly and her partner.

Precious shook her head and said to Reva, "I swear Reva Nettingham—I don't know which is more distressing—watching your mother dance with my father or hearing about a so-called boyfriend that I do not have."

"My vote goes to Sugar dancing with your daddy," Reva replied. "I wish I knew what my mother's secret is. No man is safe around her."

Faith

Charity and Hope were not talking to her. That made family togetherness a little tough. They talked to each other and to their parents, but they ignored Faith. Her parents knew that something was wrong with their offspring and tried to get to the bottom of the situation. "What is wrong with you girls?" her mother had roared. "You're acting like you're not even related." But Charity and Hope had refused to let their mother bait them into answering. Finally, their father, who after living for the past twenty years in a house populated solely by women, had come to understand moodiness when he saw it said, "Leave it be; they're all grown."

Faith wasn't ready to say that her family drove her to drink, but drinking surely helped her deal with them. She knew that her drinking was the cause of Charity and Hope's refusal to acknowledge her presence. She had hurt them and they'd had enough. Still, she hated their sanctimonious attitude—although she supposed it couldn't be helped—they'd inherited and improved upon this trait from their mother. Faith was in a funk. She'd been working at bringing her grades up—late nights and early mornings in the pursuit of her college degree did very little to improve her disposition, and Opal's health situation further helped her mood deteriorate.

Opal was not supposed to be sick. She was too young. They were all too young to face something like cancer. She'd hardly seen Opal these past few weeks. Faith had been playing catch-up with all the work she was supposed to have done during these past few months that she had fallen off the wagon. The few times she'd seen Opal, she'd gotten the clear impression that Opal did not want to talk to her about anything. Faith did not blame her. She was sure that Opal was scared. She needed time to understand and make peace with her situation. But how does one make peace with the specter of death?

"Ma, are you sure you don't want to go the luncheon at Imani House?" Charity asked as they walked down the narrow path to the school canteen. "The lunch at the canteen is usually pretty nasty."

"That's right, Ma," Hope chimed in. "All they serve are hamburgers and hot dogs, and you know that I don't eat flesh."

Hope was a reformed vegetarian. Before coming to college, Hope ate pork and any other meat she could get her hands on, but after a semester at Middlehurst, Hope had made the switch to becoming a vegetarian. Faith was not sure what precipitated this radical change, but knowing Hope there was probably a man involved.

"Your eating habits, thankfully, no longer concern me," replied Faith's mother. "We are going to the canteen. At least we can find a place to sit and eat there—besides, I told you that I don't like all that high cholesterol food that they always serve over at Imani House."

Faith knew that it wasn't the food that was keeping her mother away from Imani House—it was her philosophy that African Americans should not segregate themselves that prevented her from going to any function at Imani House. It didn't matter to her mother that there were houses on campus for Asian American students, Hispanic students, Foreign students, the French and Latin Club and other groups. Her mother saw Imani House as the last bastion of segregation and her mother most definitely did not approve.

When they reached the canteen, her mother told her sisters and her father, "You all go on in, Faith and I need to talk about something."

Faith felt her heart move south toward her stomach. She did not want to talk with her mother.

Her father shot her a sympathetic smile and walked inside the canteen. Her sisters ignored her and followed their father.

Her mother turned and stared at her. Hard. "What's going on with you and your sisters?"

Faith shrugged her shoulders. "You need to ask them."

"I'm asking you," said Faith's mother.

"I don't know what's going on with them, Ma," said Faith, suddenly feeling like she was five years old.

"Have you been drinking again?" her mother asked.

Faith didn't answer.

"Maybe there was too much pressure here at Middlehurst," her mother continued, not bothering to acknowledge Faith's silence. "I know that at first you didn't want to come here, but I thought that Middlehurst would be good for you."

Faith had wanted to go to Spelman, but her mother had refused to send her to a historically black college. Faith had given in to her mother's wishes.

"It doesn't matter, Ma," said Faith. "It's all water under the bridge. I'm graduating in June."

"I just thought that this was the best place for you," said Faith's mother. "I thought you'd be happy here . . . but this is where the drinking began."

"It doesn't matter, Ma," Faith replied, and it didn't. Spelman College had been a long forgotten dream. She'd met a woman from Spelman many years ago. She'd been impressed by her and her stories about Spelman—with its rich history and tradition of educating African American women. But, she'd come to Middlehurst and gotten a good education. Middlehurst would not have been her choice, but it had all worked out for the best. She'd met her friends here. She'd gotten a great education. It made no sense to blame Middlehurst for her drinking. Just as it made no sense to wonder if her life would have been different if she'd attended Spelman.

"Let's go on inside and eat," said Faith, fighting back the urge to cry. "I'm hungry."

Chapter 16

Opal

Opal sat in the college chapel and waited for lightning to strike her, or, at the very least, for the walls of the chapel to fall down around her. For most of her life she had gone to church without feeling in any way connected to God. Church was an obligation. It was by no means a compulsion. Yet, here she was in the chapel bargaining with God for her life. She was not a hypocrite and she was not going to become one now. She wanted God's help. Whatever it was she was facing was bigger than her. Still, in her heart she knew that she didn't deserve any intervention from the Lord, but according to what most preachers said, God gave even the undeserving a break.

When she'd first discovered that she had cancer, she'd run away from the possibility of death. But the ugly reality of a shortened life span was never too far away. These past few days Opal had thrown herself back into her life with a renewed passion. She'd started reading poetry again and calling people she hadn't talked to in a while. She'd almost called Jordan, but self pity only went so far. She was not about to call a man who made a fool out of her.

She missed him. She still wasn't sure if she loved him. But she missed him. She missed his calm reassurance. She missed talking to him. She knew that if he were still in her life, she'd have some strong arms to hold her right now and she missed that. For the first time in her life, she couldn't lean on her parents. Her parents were scared and their open and obvious fear for her made it impossible for her to confide in them. She did not want to hurt them any more than they had already been hurt. She did not want to scare them any more than they already were scared. She put on a facade whenever she was around them. She appeared outwardly calm, while her insides were in turmoil. She'd even joked with them, tried to cajole the terror from their faces. With Jordan, somehow she knew that she wouldn't have to put on a mask for him. She could just be. Be scared. Be angry. Be confused. Just be.

There had been a few times when she had picked up the telephone and dialed his number. She'd always hung up before he answered. She knew that to hear his voice now would be her undoing. She would run back to him. It was easy. She could forgive him. Forget about what he did to her. After all, she could reason that because of her cancer, all bets were off. All was forgiven. "Just help me get through this," she would say. "Help me get through, get over, and get around this." But pride, or something else that made her backbone tighten whenever she thought about what Jordan did, prevented her from running right back to him.

There was no one else around in the chapel. The Parents' Day activities were in full swing this afternoon. Although Opal's mother had not wanted to come to Parents' Day, she had given in, apparently under pressure from Opal's father. Her three brothers had also accompanied her parents to the school. Since finding out about her cancer, and Jordan's betrayal, her brothers had rallied around her. Opal hated pity from anyone, but it was particularly difficult when the pity came from blood relations. Her brothers looked at her as if she were a wounded bird. She'd escaped from her family, telling them that she had to run a quick errand. They had been attending a reception at the President's House, but her parents' fear and her brothers' pity had been too much to handle and Opal had retreated to the only place where she knew for certain that she'd be alone, the college chapel.

At first she had come to the chapel to escape, but now she wanted to pray—but prayer was difficult. She wasn't sure if the God to whom she prayed would answer her prayers. People die. People get cancer. Why should God answer her prayer request? There were a lot more people out there with better connections to the Lord. Still, the knowledge that tomorrow she would be operated on, brought her to her knees on the cold, stone chapel floor. Even if God didn't listen, she was going to pray for the strength to get through this—to get through cancer.

She remembered a conversation she'd had with her grandmother years ago. Her grandmother was a woman who believed in getting down on her knees when it was time for prayer. It didn't matter where her grandmother was, whenever it was time to pray, she would kneel down. Opal had once seen her grandmother kneel down in prayer in a crowded mall. *"Grandma, why do you kneel when you talk to Jesus?"* Opal had asked. Her grandmother had replied, *"Opal, sometimes you have to let yourself get out the way, and let God do the work—that's what prayer is about, asking God to do the work that needs to be done—and if God is going to do my work, then it's all right for me to kneel down to him. I know that you're proud, Opal—but you must never be too proud to humble yourself before God, honey—that's why I kneel when I talk to God."* God had taken her grandmother away and she'd been angry at God for years because of that. Yet, this was the same God she was going to ask to spare her life.

Humble yourself. The words came from another time and place, yet their familiarity made it easy to kneel down on the cold floor.

Reva

Reva lay on her narrow twin bed and waited for sleep to come. It was past midnight and the activities of Parents' Day had exhausted her. Sugar had embarrassed her carrying on with Precious' daddy. She had flirted with him openly, and just before she left for New York, Reva had witnessed her mother slip him her number. *God help him,* Reva thought, shaking her head. Behaving appropriately was never a concern for her mother. Sugar lived her life the way she saw fit, and there was nothing Reva could do to change her mother's ways. Still, it was not her mother's conduct that kept Reva from sleeping, it was Opal.

She had tried to talk with Opal today about the operation, but Opal had been surrounded by a protective phalanx of parents and brothers. The few times Opal had been away from her family, she had made it clear that the discussion of her upcoming operation was not going to happen. Reva understood that this was Opal's way of dealing with pain. She retreated until she came to terms with whatever trouble she was facing. But cancer was not something that Opal could deal with by herself. Reva knew that Opal would understand this, and when she did, Reva would be there to help her in any way that she could.

"Reva, what's the problem?"

Reva had thought that her roommate, Bonnie, was sleeping. She switched on the lamp by her bed. "I'm worried about Opal."

Her roommate sat up in the bed across the room. She was dressed in her usual red flannel pajamas, her curly red hair pulled back from her face. "Is tomorrow the operation?" Bonnie asked.

Reva nodded her head. "I wanted to go to the hospital with her, but Opal wouldn't hear of it. Sometimes that girl is so stubborn."

"Don't be so hard on her, Reva," Bonnie replied. "It's easy to say what we'd do when we're faced with a tough situation, but until you've been where Opal is now, you can't judge her."

"I'm not judging her," said Reva, although she knew that she had already judged Opal, just as she judged everyone else.

"Yes, you are," said Bonnie.

"You're lucky I like you," said Reva, feeling her temper rise.

"Yes, I am," Bonnie replied.

There were times when Reva forgot about the differences between their backgrounds. Although she considered Bonnie as a friend, Reva was very well aware that they were more dissimilar than alike. It wasn't just their economic differences, but their outlook on life. Bonnie's outlook was almost universally sunny and Reva just expected bad things to happen, and they usually did. But there were times when Reva realized that their differences were inconsequential. They were, after all was said and done, two young women trying to find their way. Bonnie had rescued her, once again, from drowning in a sea of pessimism. Bonnie had also, without getting into an argument or preaching, quietly shown her that her reaction to Opal's cancer was selfish. Reva was not thinking about Opal, but instead she was focusing on how Opal should have reacted to her cancer with her friends or, more specifically, with her. She was frightened for Opal, but she realized that she was also frightened for herself. Frightened that the lives of her and her friends would change in the face of this unseen enemy, cancer. She wanted reassurance from Opal, when she should have been concerned about reassuring Opal. She had done what most frightened folk do—she had condemned Opal for not being who Reva wanted her to be. Going to the hospital was solace for Reva—she wanted to be there so she would not have to spend the day wondering and worrying. True, she did want to support her friend, but Opal did not want, or apparently need, that support.

As if reading Reva's thoughts, Bonnie said, "Opal will call you when she needs your support."

"What if she doesn't call," Reva replied. "What if she decides that she doesn't want me in her life anymore. Cancer changes things—perspectives, friendships, feelings. What if I lose my friend?"

Reva had secretly thought these things after hearing about Opal's diagnosis, but the sheer selfishness of those feelings had prevented her from sharing them with her friends, yet she found herself talking openly with Bonnie. She did not talk as much to Bonnie as she did with her other friends. She did not hang out with Bonnie. Bonnie's save-the-earth-and-don't-eat-meat group was not exactly her set, but Bonnie was a true friend in the deepest sense of the word. She was always there when Reva needed her. Reva wondered if Opal could say the same about her.

"Opal loves you," Bonnie said. "Cancer won't change that."

Reva turned off the light and waited for sleep to come to her.

Winter
Session

Chapter 17

Faith

A gay man had just made a pass at her, although she couldn't be entirely certain since the five White Russians she had just consumed made rational thinking difficult at this particular moment. Faith knew that she had no business being in the bar at the Boston Regency Hotel, but she had agreed to meet her friend Ty for drinks. Ty was a friend from her high school days at Shaker High and he was staying at the Boston Regency for the weekend. He'd come to Boston for an interview at Harvard Medical School and he'd decided to make a weekend out of it. Ty had always been open about his sexuality, and this made it difficult to understand why a confirmed gay man had just asked her to sleep with him.

"Excuse me?" Faith asked, not sure that she had either heard or understood Ty correctly.

"I said would you like to sleep with me?"

The bar at the Boston Regency was an upscale affair—wood panels, crystal chandeliers, antique furniture, all spoke of a grander time and place. The room was almost empty; it was one o'clock in the morning and almost time for closing. Faith had been sitting in the bar for almost three hours, drinking and eating peanuts and pretzels and listening to the jazz music playing in the background. Ty had regaled her with stories of mutual friends and her nostalgia for Shaker Heights, and all things Cleveland related, was strong. But Ty's question drove all thoughts of home out of her head.

"Ty," she said, taking care not to slur her words—she was drunk, but she didn't have to sound that way—"you're a gay man."

He nodded his head. "I know this."

Ty had broken many hearts at Shaker High. He was good looking, smart, funny, athletic and destined to be successful at anything he chose to do. But he made it clear to the several girls who wanted to get to know him better that it was not that kind of party. There were a few girls at school who were convinced that they could "change" him—get him to "see the light." But Ty would swiftly, though always kindly and respectfully, reject them all.

"Then why are you asking me to sleep with you?"

Ty smiled at her and a weaker person might have been tempted. Ty was uncommonly beautiful. "I'm giving heterosexuality a try."

Faith began a coughing fit as the White Russian went down the wrong way. When she'd regained her composure, she said, "I hate to break it to you, but you're going to have to give heterosexuality a try with someone else. I may be drunk, but I'm not drunk enough to agree to be someone's guinea pig."

"You are drunk," Ty agreed, "but you wouldn't be a guinea pig. We've always been good together, Faith."

"We're friends, Ty, that's all."

"We could be more," Ty replied.

"No, we can't," Faith said, standing up, wondering how her life, in such a short time had come down to this. It had been a while since anyone had shown any interest in taking her out on a date, let alone sleep with her, but there was a desperation in Ty that she recognized as an old friend. He was lonely. So was she. But they would both regret this, not just in the morning, but forever after. "I need to get back to school; it's late."

"I'll call you a cab," said Ty. "And Faith, if you ever change your mind . . . give me a call."

She'd begun drinking again when she went home for the holidays. She'd made it through the fall semester without failing any of her subjects, but her decidedly mediocre academic performance had not pleased her family. Her parents had been vocal in their disappointment. Christmas had not been a happy time in her household, but the spiked eggnog helped. For a short while. The hidden vodka helped. For a time. The gin and tonics helped. For a bit. At least this time she didn't fool herself as she usually did. She knew that she was not going to stop drinking anytime soon. She would just try to control it, so that it didn't control her. She liked her drinks and she was not going to give them up. She just had to learn how to avoid drinking in excess. That was the trick.

"Ty, you're gay and I'm not a man. I don't think either of those things is going to change. I don't want to sleep with you, and I'm certain that had you not just broken up with Mr. Wonderful, you would not be trying to sleep with me. We're friends. Now, and hopefully, forever."

Ty stood up. "You can't blame a man for trying, Faith. You're a good-looking woman. Even a confirmed gay man can see that."

"I think I need to get back to school," said Faith, anxious to leave this conversation behind.

Opal

Although her mother had urged her to wear a wig, Opal wore her newly shaved head with pride. She'd begun losing her hair shortly after the chemo treatments began. Her hair, which she had always lovingly cared for, had fallen out in clumps, leaving bald patches. One day, after getting tired of seeing the bald spots, Opal had taken her father's razor and shaved her entire head. After she'd gotten used to the look, she'd determined that it didn't look that bad. Usually, she'd wear a baseball cap but there were times when she went cap-free. Her bald head was her way of telling cancer that she was not robbed of her pride. She didn't wait until the chemo treatments took away all of her hair, instead, she shaved her own head. Precious had offered to shave her hair off in solidarity. Reva and Faith both proclaimed their love for Opal, but as Reva said often enough, "love only goes so far." Opal had been touched by Precious' offer, but she had declined.

Her friends had helped her get through the past few months. The operation had been tough on her body. It had taken her longer to heal than the doctors had originally predicted. A few weeks after the operation, the chemotherapy treatments had begun. They had been as awful as the doctor had warned her they would be. After a treatment, she would be sick for at least a week—days spent throwing up, feeling as if she had a perpetual flu. She had spent most of the time commuting to school from her parents' home in Boston. Her parents had insisted that if she were determined to stay at school, she would have to live with them, so that they could keep a watchful eye on her. Her friends took turns picking her up for classes and driving her back home. Sometimes they would stay over, but more often than not, they would drive back to school after dropping her off. Her parents had offered to take her to school, but the arrangement with her friends was working, and Opal stood her ground on this particular issue.

Middlehurst had allowed her to miss many of her classes, and her professors had all given her take home exams. She'd passed every single one of her exams, and she'd managed to keep her grades up to a respectful B range, although she was used to getting A's. In light of her current circumstances, she'd settled on a B. She was taking one Winter Session class in Art History. Her three friends had all signed up for Winter Session and Opal was grateful for the company. Middle-hurst's winter break lasted from the middle of December to the middle of February. She didn't know what she would have done if her friends were not around during this time. They kept her laughing. They helped her study. They listened to her. They rubbed her back while she vomited. Her family had also provided her with support, but they were dealing with their own fear of losing her. With her friends, the pressure of not hurting folks, not making them feel bad, was not there. Her friends were scared, but they were determined to help her fight this battle, and she was grateful.

The doorbell to her family's Boston home rang and Opal went to open the front door. She was expecting Precious to pick her up for her afternoon Art History class. She opened the door without looking through the peephole and found herself staring at Jordan. Looking at him was like standing face-to-face with a ghost. He was thinner and there were faint tension lines around his mouth.

Opal was suddenly self-conscious about her bald head. Jordan had always complimented Opal on her looks and she was acutely aware that she did not look like the same woman who had been engaged to him. She had lost weight and her normally slender frame now looked gaunt. The jeans and sweater that she wore hung from her body. She was also not wearing any makeup. Although she no longer felt the need to impress him, she didn't want him to see her like this. She looked like a defeated woman.

He didn't say hello. Instead, he said, "You look beautiful."

His words were so absurd that Opal laughed, a hollow sound coming from an unknown place.

When the laughter died, Opal asked, "What do you want, Jordan?"

He took a deep breath. "Can I come in, Opal? It's cold out here. I won't stay long."

For a moment she hesitated, then she moved back from the door, allowing him to enter. She didn't know why she let him come in. The anger and the hurt caused by his actions, though weakened, re-mained with her. He was the last person that she wanted to talk to, but there was something in the way his eyes lit up, even seeing her look-ing and feeling her worst, that softened her resolve—slightly.

Opal walked over to the couch in the living room. Jordan remained standing by the door—as if he feared approaching her. They stared at each other in silence, and in those moments, Opal felt a longing for him that she had not acknowledged before. She missed him.

Jordan spoke first. "I heard that you . . ." His voice trailed off.

Opal finished his sentence. "Have cancer. . . . I guess bad news travels."

"I wanted to come to you, but I waited for you to call me. Then today I woke up and I decided that I was tired of waiting. I was going to come to you."

"Why?" Opal asked.

"Because I love you," Jordan replied. "I have always loved you and I always will. It doesn't matter how long we've been apart. It doesn't even matter if you love me . . . I'm sure after what I did to you, you couldn't love me, but it doesn't matter. I love you and I know you need me. You'll never admit that and I don't want you to. But you need me, Opal."

Opal stood up. "Get out!" she screamed. "How dare you come in here after what you did? How dare you pretend to care about me! How dare you? I don't need you! I don't love you! I never did!"

She felt rage, hot spite. She wanted to hurt him. She wanted to hurt him as badly as he had hurt her. "I never loved you!" she screamed over and over again, until the nausea overtook her. She ran, stumbling to the bathroom in the hallway adjacent to the living room. Pushing the door open, she threw up before she reached the toilet bowl. She bent over, retching even though there was nothing left in her. Her stomach heaved with a violence she had become familiar with by now.

She felt Jordan's arms holding her. She heard his voice, soothing, comforting her as her body shook with the effort it took to stop the vomiting. Finally, when her body had released all it had to release, he carried her to the upstairs bathroom, where he undressed her and bathed her. She didn't resist. She was too sick to care. She was too sick to tell him to leave her the hell alone. Somewhere he found a clean T-shirt and he dressed her, carrying her to her bed and tucking her in.

Opal closed her eyes, relieved to be in her bed. She was not going to be able to make it to class today. "I don't love you," she said to Jordan, her voice weak.

"It doesn't matter," he replied.

"I don't need you," she said, not caring that she hurt him. If he thought that she was some mercy patient because of her cancer—if he thought he could work through his guilt for what he had done to her—he was wrong. He was dead wrong. "I don't need you," she repeated, opening her eyes.

He sat on her bed. "It doesn't matter," he said. "I need you."

Precious

Precious sat in Opal's living room and spoke with Jordan. She had been surprised to find him at Opal's house. She had always liked him, but he had hurt Opal badly. Now that Opal was sick, the magnitude of Jordan's actions loomed even larger.

"Now that I'm here, maybe you should leave," said Precious. "Opal will call you if she needs you."

Jordan nodded his head. "I should leave," he said. Yet, he remained, standing still like a solitary ebony statue, in the corner of the room, his fists jammed in his pockets. Then, he slowly knelt to the floor, covering his face as he began to cry.

Precious walked over to him without hesitation. His sorrow touched her and echoed her own feelings about Opal's sickness. Forgetting all thoughts of Jordan's betrayal, she knelt beside him and wrapped her arms around him. No matter what he had done to Opal, it was clear that he felt remorse. It was even clearer that he still loved her.

"It's going to be all right," Precious said, although the words sounded false and empty, even to her.

"She can't die," he said, between sobs. "She can't die."

She held him tight until his cries subsided.

Chapter 18

Reva

R eva stared at the man standing in the dormitory lobby.
"Hello, Reva," said her father.

"What are you doing here?" Reva asked, feeling her heart start to hammer against her chest. After his telephone call, when she'd told him that she didn't want to see him, she hadn't heard from him again. Although she hadn't seen him in years, he looked the same. Tall and slender, Reva wondered where she had inherited her heavy genes. Both of her parents were slim.

The last time she saw him was shortly before her high school graduation when he showed up on the sidewalk outside her school. Her father's infrequent visits were always unannounced and unanticipated.

"I think that should be obvious," her father replied. "I wanted to see you."

Reva was acutely aware that there were other people in the lobby and they were staring at them. Only about thirty percent of Middlehurst students took advantage of Winter Session—most students relished the time away and chose to stay home—but it seemed to Reva that most of the students were here in her dormitory lobby. She had no wish for her family drama to be played out before curious eyes.

Her father seemed to feel the same way. "Is there somewhere we can go where we can talk?" he asked.

Reva nodded her head.

Opal

"He's got his nerve coming here," Opal said, as she lay against the pillows in her bed.

Precious sighed. "How are you feeling? Jordan told me you had a bad time."

Opal shrugged her shoulders. Leave it to Jordan to try to play the hero. She'd been fooled by his act before. She didn't want Precious to be fooled too. "I've got breast cancer," she said, her voice tight. "What did he expect?"

"Opal, I know it's tough . . ." Precious began, but Opal stopped her before those hated words of empathy crossed Precious' lips.

"No, you don't," Opal snapped. "You don't know what it feels like. You don't have cancer. You haven't been handed a possible death sentence. You don't have to stare at the fear in everyone's eyes when they come in contact with you. You don't have to have poison pumped in your veins so that another poison can be eradicated from your body. You don't have to get mouth sores. You don't have to feel sick every single day. You don't have to worry about throwing up in public. You don't have to worry about your hair falling out. You don't know, Precious."

Opal watched the hurt immediately cloud Precious' eyes and she was sorry. Precious did not deserve that tirade. No matter how sick or how evil she felt, Opal knew that it was wrong to hurt a hand trying to help and that's what she was doing.

She closed her eyes and took a deep breath. Then, she said, "I'm sorry, Precious. I could blame it on my sickness, but I think sometimes I'm just plain old evil as a rattlesnake."

The hurt in Precious' eyes was quickly replaced by concern. "No, don't apologize, Opal. You're right. I don't know how you're feeling and it was wrong of me to presume."

Opal shook her head, "Why do you have to be so damn agreeable? At least, let me feel bad for how I just treated you."

Precious sat on Opal's bed and took her hand in hers. "I don't want you to feel bad, Opal."

Too late, Opal thought, but she kept that comment to herself. She had been nasty enough for one day.

"Jordan just brings out the worst in me, I guess."

Precious didn't reply.

"I wish he would just leave me alone!"

Precious looked at her as if she were trying to read an indecipherable map. "Are you sure, Opal?" she asked. "I mean, are you absolutely sure that you want him to leave you alone?"

"Yes," said Opal, "I'm certain." Her words did not have the ring of conviction in them, and Opal knew that Precious was not fooled.

"I know that what he did was wrong . . . downright unforgiveable, but under the circumstances . . ."

Opal raised one thin hand in warning. "Precious, do not go *there.*"

Precious did not back down. "I'm not suggesting that you go back to him, Opal. Only you can decide that. What I am suggesting is that you forgive him. Whatever he did hurt him almost as much as it hurt you. He turned his back on everything that he knew was right and good and he lost you in the process. *That* should be punishment enough. You don't have to try to hurt him."

"I'm not trying to hurt him! I didn't call him up and ask him to come up here, now did I?"

"No, you didn't," said Precious. "But it seems to me that you have enough on your plate to deal with right now; maybe you should release some of the bad feelings you have towards Jordan."

"That's easy for you to say; he didn't cheat on you and make a fool of you."

"That's right," said Precious. "He didn't cheat on me, but he cheated on someone who is very dear to me. I don't hurt the same as you, but his actions hurt me, too. I know a little bit about holding on to resentment a little too long. I've held on to my resentment for my mother leaving me and my father for so long, that I just don't know how to live without the resentment—it's become an old, familiar friend. I don't want to see that happen to you, Opal."

Opal leaned back on her pillows. She hated when Precious got righteous. She also hated when Precious made sense. Damn, she was having a bad day.

Reva

Reva sat on the worn sofa in the boathouse and watched the man who stood across the room from her, his hands jammed in his pockets. She pulled her heavy wool coat around her shoulders against the chill in the room. The heating system was temperamental at best. She wondered what normal people felt when they looked at their father. She envied Precious and Opal their hero worship of their daddies. The best emotions she could muster for her father were mild curiosity mixed with a strong feeling of distrust. He had let her down on too many occasions before.

"Reva, I would like us to start over."

"Start over?" asked Reva. "When did we ever start?"

Her father sighed. His eyes looked tired. "I know you hate me," he said quietly.

Reva shook her head. "I don't hate you."

Her father gave her a crooked smile, and in that smile, that moment, she saw in him the sadness that had been a part of her own life for as long as she could remember. She was good at hiding it. As a child, she learned to smile when she felt tears close by. She learned to push the sadness away, but even as that feeling was submerged, she knew that it was never too far away, like an unpleasant acquaintance that showed up when it was least expected or wanted.

"You should hate me," he said.

"That's what Sugar says," Reva replied. "Do you want me to hate you?"

Her father shook his head. "I want us to start over . . . or start. I'm ready to be the father I should have been."

Too late, a loud and very clear voice screamed in her head. *It's too late for that.*

"What brought all this on?" asked Reva. "Did your wife put you up to this?"

Her father looked directly into her eyes. "Belle did have a part in this, yes. But she only confirmed what I already knew was right in my heart."

He cleared his throat and then said, "Your mother and I had problems. I let those problems keep me away from you. It's no excuse, but there it is."

"And I'm supposed to open my arms and let you in?" Reva asked, as she could hear her mother's words come to her: *"One thing that man ain't lacking is nerve."*

Her father flashed the same crooked smile at her again. "I was hoping."

"Tell me something," Reva asked, "where do you live? I've never known exactly where you live."

"I live in New York City."

Reva felt the air leave the room slowly. For a terrible moment she thought that the tears she felt when she heard this information would roll shamefully down her face. She had always heard that her father traveled around the world and she'd reasoned that his travels took him so far away he couldn't see her when the truth was that they lived in the same city.

"How long have you lived in New York?" she asked, her voice steady.

"I've been there the last ten years—I travel a lot, but my home base is in New York."

Reva felt her temper rise, before she had a chance to do anything about it. "You lived in the same city and never came to see me."

Her father raised his hands. "That's not fair, Reva. I did try . . ."

Reva interrupted him. "If you're talking about those few times that you showed up . . ."

"I tried, Reva. Honest to God, I tried."

"You've been out of my life for the past twenty-two years. Is that your definition of trying?"

"This is not going anywhere, Reva."

Reva stood up. "You're right. It isn't."

She watched as regret, her other familiar friend, descended on her father. "Maybe I should go," he said.

"Yes," Reva agreed. "Maybe you should."

"Good-bye, Reva."

She didn't respond, instead, she watched as her father left the boathouse, closing the door behind him. The tears that she'd held at bay ran unchecked down her face. She jammed her hands into her pocket and felt something in her left hand. She pulled out her hand and stared at Simon Bennett's business card. She stared at it for a long time.

Chapter 19

Precious

Rory's apartment did not look like any other college student's apartment that Precious had seen. He lived three blocks away from his college, but it was a world away from the college dormitories that most students live in. Located on the thirty-third floor of a high rise building, its floor to ceiling windows afforded a spectacular view of Boston. The furniture was strictly bachelor pad with the black leather couches and black and white checkered leather chairs, large screen television set, state-of-the-art stereo system and obligatory white shag rug.

"Would you like something to drink?" Rory asked.

Precious shook her head. She had to steady her nerves. This was the first time that she'd been to his apartment. He'd invited her several times before, but she'd always declined. In her mind, a trip to a man's apartment was an invitation to fall deep into debauchery. She'd said as much to Faith, who'd countered with, *"nothing wrong with a little bit of debauchery . . ."* Despite Faith's flippant reply, Precious knew that she wasn't going to go down that road with any man unless she heard the word commitment first, and although they'd been seeing each other now for a few months, she had yet to hear that word. It took her awhile to recognize that they were dating. Neither she nor Rory had used that word either—but the calls, dinners, movies, long talks all led up to that inevitable conclusion.

Rory walked over to where she stood and wrapped his arms around her, drawing her into his warmth. Lowering his mouth over hers, he kissed her. She lost herself for one long, sweet moment in his kiss before he pulled slowly away. Precious felt her nervousness slide away. They'd spent the evening having dinner at their favorite Chinese restaurant followed by a movie that she'd picked—a romantic comedy, which they'd mostly missed having spent most of the movie necking like two high school students.

It hadn't taken much convincing to get her back to his apartment, but now that she was here, she wasn't sure if she was ready for the inevitable next step. As Reva had assured her, "You can only eat appetizers for so long, then there comes a time for the main course." She just wasn't sure she was ready for the main course. She liked things the way they were.

"Remind me to send my aunt a dozen roses," Rory murmured in Precious' ear.

Precious pulled away from his embrace and sat down on the sofa. She needed to put some distance between them. If she didn't, she'd end up in his bed and that wasn't where she wanted to be. Not yet.

"Is she still asking you about me?" Precious asked.

Rory walked over to the sofa and sat next to her. "Every chance she gets she reminds me that I better be good to you."

Precious smiled. "I always liked her."

"Apparently," said Rory, pulling her close to his side, "the feeling is mutual."

There were not many times that Precious felt safe. Having a mother who was a crack addict did not tend to lead to feelings of security. Even with a father who loved and cared for her, who would lay down his life for her, the instability and chaos that came whenever her mother came back into their lives, as she often did when her money or her luck ran out, had taught Precious to always be on guard. She lived her life waiting for the next bad thing to happen, the next drama to unfold. Tonight, in the arms of a man she was beginning to learn to love, she felt protected . . . as if she were in a warm cocoon. There was a part of her that wished that she could stay in this cocoon forever, but she knew that eventually reality would rear its head. Rory was on his way to an NFL contract and some unknown team in God knew which part of the country, and she was headed to the Sorbonne for a year in Paris.

Life would pull them apart. For now, however, she was going to let herself believe in this fairy tale, where the handsome prince woos the sister that everyone else overlooked.

"Precious, don't leave tonight . . . I'll take you back to your dorm tomorrow."

Precious took a deep breath. The feeling of well-being left just as suddenly as it had come. She knew that eventually they would have to come to this conversation. They were both attracted to each other and Rory made it clear that he wanted their relationship to progress. In the past, she'd been able to evade this conversation, but tonight, Rory was not going to be put off again.

"Rory, I'm a virgin."

She waited for him to laugh. She expected some indication of surprise. A twenty-two-year-old virgin was not exactly the norm. Instead, he just looked at her silently, his expression inscrutable.

"Say something," Precious said, suddenly nervous. What did he think of her? His opinion mattered.

"What do you want me to say?" Rory asked.

"I don't know. Why are you staring at me?"

"Because I think you're beautiful. You're a beautiful person, Precious. I care about you, Precious, and at this moment, I would like nothing better than to make love to you, but if you're not ready, that's O.K."

"You don't have a problem with this?" Precious asked, surprised that he wasn't going to try to convince her, as other men had, that she should change her mind.

"I didn't say that. I'd be lying if I said that I didn't want you. But, when that day comes, and it will come, Precious—I want you to want me just as much as I want you."

"Thank you," Precious whispered.

"Why are you thanking me?" Rory asked.

"For not making me feel bad about this."

"Somehow," Rory said, the corners of his mouth turned up into a smile, "I don't think I could do that, even if I tried."

Precious smiled in return, "You're probably right about that."

"I still want you to spend the night," said Rory. "But I'll take the couch. You can have my bed."

Precious glanced at the neon clock in the corner of the living room. It was almost eleven o'clock. "It is getting late."

Rory pulled her back into his arms. "I'm really not all that concerned with the lateness of the hour," he said, still smiling. "Right now, I'm interested in kissing some full, ruby-colored lips; that's what I'm concerned about . . ."

"Rory . . ." Precious began to protest—kissing might lead to something more, something she was dangerously close to doing, despite their previous conversation on the subject.

"You said that you weren't ready to make love," said Rory. "I accept that. You didn't say anything about kissing me . . . something you and I both know that we enjoy."

Precious had one clear thought before she felt his lips touch hers, *Lord, have mercy.*

Faith

"So did you give it up?" Faith asked. She was sprawled on Precious' bed, waiting, like Reva and Opal, who were sitting on the floor in Precious' dorm room, for details on Precious' date with Rory. Precious had gone out for what was supposed to be dinner and a movie three days before, but for three days she had not come home. She'd stayed with Rory for three days while her friends had delighted in talking and laughing about Precious' scandalous behavior. Of all of the friends, Precious was the least likely to find herself hanging out in a man's apartment for three days of what Faith hoped was wild sex.

"Faith, you are the true definition of a hussy," said Opal.

Faith's heart twisted when she looked at her friend. Opal was now past thin. Still, there was a fire in Opal's eyes that had not been extinguished. No matter what Opal was going through, she was still a fighter. Opal was far from waving the white flag of surrender to cancer. She was on campus today for the only class she was taking during the Winter Session.

"I might have used another word," Reva commented.

Faith laughed, refusing to let her friends deter her from finding out information that was none of her business, but was nonetheless intriguing. Who would have thought that Precious would be having a heavy romance with a sexy football player? Still, she was glad for her friend. Precious was beautiful, kind and smart, and it was about time that men started noticing. This hang up that folks had about being heavy was yesterday's news. You didn't have to be a size six to be beautiful and both Precious and Reva proved that point.

Precious was sitting cross-legged on her window seat, looking happy and relaxed. A definite sign in Faith's mind that good sex was had. With her hair pulled back from her face, and not wearing a stitch of makeup, she still looked beautiful.

"We didn't do anything," she said with a broad smile.

"Don't lie to us, Precious," said Faith. "You don't stay in a man's apartment for three days without there being some serious sex going on."

Precious laughed. "Sorry to disappoint you, but he slept on the couch the whole time."

"You spent three days, or more specifically, three nights with a man and you didn't give it up?" Faith asked.

"Faith, just because you believe in sharing your love freely, doesn't mean that Precious is the same way," said Reva.

For a moment, Faith's good humor slipped away. Her sex life was a sensitive subject for her. She had slept with more men than her friends, but that didn't mean she was loose. She knew that her friends disapproved of her sex life, but it was her own business. It wasn't that she slept around—usually the men she slept with were men that she was in a relationship with. There had been a few times where alcohol had led her into situations where, upon reflection, usually the next day, she wondered what the hell she had done, or how the hell she could have done what she had done. She had never gotten pregnant or gotten a disease. She'd been lucky, but she wasn't stupid. She couldn't keep putting herself in that situation. Someday, her luck would run out.

Precious, the dependable peacemaker, quickly steered the conversation into a safer direction, and Faith was grateful. "We didn't have sex but I can say without any equivocation whatsoever, that the man's lips should be registered as a public weapon."

Laughter erupted in the small dorm room, as the sun streamed in through the lead glass windows.

"Precious, you've been hanging around Faith too long. You're starting to sound like her," said Reva.

This time, Faith refused to let Reva bait her into losing her good humor. "You all should be so lucky!" said Faith. Then, turning to Precious, she said with a wicked smile, "You make a sister proud! I'll have you and that football player swinging from the chandeliers before I'm through with you! I've got some toys that you can share with him—"

"Faith!" Precious voice rose in a high pitched squeak. "I'm a Baptist. We don't use sex toys!"

"Shoot," said Faith, "Baptists got to have fun too!"

Chapter 20

Opal

Opal lay back in the chair in the hospital room and stared at the television set. The I.V. needle in her arm felt uncomfortable but she forced herself not to think about it. It was chemo day, as she referred to the visits to the hospital for her chemotherapy treatment. She was in a large, sunny yellow room with chairs containing other patients who were also getting their chemo treatments. Over the past few weeks, she'd gotten to know some of the other chemotherapy patients. Like her, they were facing the same battle. Cancer.

Most of the patients were friendly, too friendly, thought Opal, who just wanted to be left alone. She wanted to get her treatment and leave. But, in spite of her best efforts, she was unable to escape the camaraderie of folk who were sharing the same struggle. She had become close to two patients, in particular—Max, a twelve-year-old leukemia patient, and Mrs. Firenze, an eighty-year-old seamstress, who despite sixty years in this country, still spoke English with a beautiful Italian accent.

Mrs. Firenze was sitting in the chair next to her. Max was coming in the afternoon. Opal missed him. Before Max, Opal had viewed kids as necessary nuisances—necessary simply to keep the human race going. It wasn't that she disliked children, she just had no patience for their needs or their wants. Max, with his sense of humor, goodwill and curiosity, despite facing his disease, was a source of inspiration for Opal. When she was tempted to shake her fists at God for giving her this disease, she thought of Max and the courage and the grace with which he faced his leukemia. Each time she came for treatment she

looked for him first. As always, if she didn't see him, an almost un-
controllable fear would grip her as thoughts of where he might be
would surface. In the months since she'd started treatment, there
were a few patients who had died. Miss Mack, the nurse that was usually on duty on her treatment days, accurately reading the fear in her
eyes, would assure her that "the little one was all right." Today, even
before she had a chance to enter the room, Nurse Mack had greeted
her with the news that "the little one" was not going to come in until
the afternoon.

"So have you heard from your young man?" Mrs. Firenze's voice interrupted Opal's thoughts.

During one of her weaker moments, Opal had confided in Mrs.
Firenze about her relationship with Jordan. An innocent conversation about a long lost love in Italy had led to Opal's true confession
about Jordan. At that time, Mrs. Firenze had shook her head when
Opal declared that she would never return to a man who was unfaith-
ful to her. "You're young," Mrs. Firenze had told her. "You don't know
the importance of forgiveness and the role it plays in love. Time is too
precious to waste on grudges . . . you should know even this now."

"Don't tell me that you're one of those women who believes that all
men cheat," Opal had told her, weary of that line of reasoning, which
had been thrown at her far too often for her liking.

"No," Mrs. Firenze had replied. "I don't believe that all men cheat.
My Giovanni, God rest his beautiful soul, was married to me for forty-
two years, and I would lay my hand on all that is holy that Giovanni
was faithful to me, as I was to him."

"What about the long lost love?" Opal had asked. "The one you left
behind in Italy."

"Aldo . . ." Her eyes had misted over some long ago memory. "He
died soon after I left Italy . . . a broken heart, I'm sure. He was true
to me, also, Aldo. But infidelity isn't the only way that a man can hurt
a woman. Both Aldo and Giovanni hurt me. Aldo chose to stay with
his family when I wanted him to come to America with me. And
Giovanni was not an easy man . . . Still, I chose to forgive. As they say,
and I know now at eighty years old, life is short. Too short for
grudges."

Opal was not ready to forgive. She was not ready to let go of the
hurt. Jordan caused her pain and she was not the kind of woman who
did not want retribution. Still, she envied Mrs. Firenze's ability to let
go of the desire to get even, just as she envied Mrs. Firenze's certainty,
her knowledge that the men she gave her heart to cherished her
enough to forego temptation. Sometimes it was easier to think that
men are by nature untrue, even as Opal would bristle at this
thought—if men were natural cheats then it wasn't her fault that

Jordan cheated on her. The fact that there were men who did not be-
have in that manner only made the pain a little more personal.

"Have you heard from your young man?" Mrs. Firenze repeated
her question.

"He's not my young man," Opal replied. Mrs. Firenze was one of
those women who was blessed with love and she couldn't understand
why Opal should not belong in this club.

Mrs. Firenze shook her head. "Whose fault is that, Opal?"

It was time to change the subject. Any other person would have gotten a curt remark, but Opal had come to care about the old lady, and
she did not want to hurt her feelings. Mrs. Firenze had liver cancer.
"The doctors tell me I'm gonna die. What the hell do they know?
Only God knows that."

The door opened and Max bounced into the room. There was no
other word for it. Max did not walk. He bounced. Opal wondered
where he got his boundless energy from. The chemotherapy made
her feel constantly tired.

Max had red hair, although she had never seen his hair. He had
told her how he'd hated his red hair. "I wanted blond hair, or black
hair, or brown hair. Everyone makes fun of red hair," Max had told
her. "Now that I'm bald, I want my red hair back." He was tall and
skinny, and his face was covered with freckles, which only increased
his already considerable appeal. "You're going to be a hunk when you
grow up," Opal had assured him. "Opal, I'm a geek," Max had retorted. "Girls treat me like I'm the plague." "Those same girls will be
chasing you down," said Opal.

"Hey, Opal!" Max called out.

His mother walked behind him. Opal could see the fear in her
eyes—the same fear she saw in her own parents' eyes. Max was her
only child and he was the world to her. She was a single mother who
had devoted her life to helping her son beat leukemia. She had the
same flaming red hair that Opal was certain that her son had.

"Hi, Opal," Max's mother's smile fell far short of her eyes. "Mrs.
Firenze."

"Hello, Miss Monaghan," Opal replied.

"Hey, Miss Lady,"said Mrs. Firenze. "We were wondering where you
two were!"

Opal watched as Max walked over and gave Mrs. Firenze a quick
hug. "I got something for you," Mrs. Firenze told Max as he sat down
in his chair and Nurse Mack prepared to give him the I.V.

Max's eyes lit up. "That book on Italy you were telling me about?
You got it for me!"

Mrs. Firenze laughed. "I got you the book. It's got great pictures
too . . . pictures of the town where I was born."

Opal heard Max's quick intake of breath as Nurse Mack stuck the needle carrying the chemo into Max's arm.

In the corner of the room Max's mother began to tremble. Mrs. Firenze noticed it also. "Miss Lady," said Mrs. Firenze, "you go on down to the cafeteria and get yourself something to eat. We'll watch your guy for you."

Max's mother shook her head. "It's all right. I want to stay here with Max."

"Ma, go eat!" Max issued an order. "You haven't eaten anything all day."

"Miss Monaghan, we'll take good care of Max," said Opal. "Please go and eat something."

Max's mother gave them a wan smile. "I guess I'm defeated here— three against one."

"Make that four," Nurse Mack entered the conversation. "Go and get yourself some food."

"I'll come right back," said Max's mother. Giving her son one last pained glance, she left the room.

Mrs. Firenze looked over at Opal and shook her head. "Like I said, Opal—time is a precious thing . . . too precious to waste over grudges."

Reva

The Free Clinic had become a second home to Reva. In the short time since she'd begun working at the clinic, her conviction that medicine was the right career for her became even stronger. She felt an instant sense of belonging around the patients, medicines, machines and everything else that came along with working in a clinic in one of Boston's poorest neighborhoods. The doctors were still idealistic and the patients were, most of the time, appreciative. In addition to her clerical work, answering the telephone, sweeping out the reception area and doing anything else that needed to be done, Reva was now allowed to shadow some of the doctors.

"I don't understand why you can't do work at one of those big time hospitals in Boston," Sugar had complained, when Reva first told her about her job with the Free Clinic. "With your grades, you could do something better than work with ghetto folk."

"Sugar," Reva had replied to her mother, biting back the familiar disappointment in her mother's stubborn refusal to be happy with any decision she made. "We're ghetto folks, remember?"

"Don't use that sassy mouth on me, Reva. I know where we live, and where we come from . . . but that doesn't mean that you can't aspire to get up out of that type of situation. All those folks will do is drag you down to their level and God knows I sacrificed enough for you that you ought to want better . . ."

What did she expect, Reva thought as she placed the medical files of patients who were supposed to be seen today in order. Sugar never agreed with anything she did. Reva's decision to become a doctor had been greeted with similar disapproval. Reva was living her mother's dream and her mother never seemed to make peace with that. While other mothers might have been proud of their daughters' accomplishments, Sugar only seemed to become more resentful with each honor that Reva achieved. "Medicine is a tough profession, Reva. Do you think you have what it takes to be a doctor?"

What would it be like to have a mother who smiled with benign approval when Reva shared her dreams and accomplishments with her? What would it be like to have had a father who cared, who gave even a small damn? Reva quickly pushed all thoughts of her parents out of her mind. Those thoughts brought pain, and she was not going to give either of her parents any more time than was necessary. The latest information that her father had lived so close to her and yet had failed to become a part of her life, hurt. She'd always thought that his travels had kept him away from her. Now, she realized that Sugar was right. He just hadn't wanted her. He hadn't cared enough to take the subway a few blocks north to Harlem to see his daughter, his flesh and blood.

The door opened to the reception area, bringing in a blast of January, New England air. Reva looked up and saw two women walk inside. The reception area had been filled with people from early that morning. Usually, by the time the clinic opened at nine o'clock, there was a line waiting. Good health care for people who did not have insurance was still a possibility at the Free Clinic and word had gotten out. Reva did not recognize the women who had just entered the clinic. After two months, she'd begun to recognize the regulars. There was an air of desperation that clung to the two women, like old clothes that that they refused to throw away.

As they walked over to Reva's desk, she saw that one of the women was in reality a young girl, a teenager. The other woman was of an indeterminable age. She could have been thirty or she could have been fifty. Her face was unlined, but her eyes were the eyes of someone who had been here too long and had seen too much. The woman's stride was purposeful and she grasped the girl's hand in a tight grip.

"I want y'all to fix her," the woman said, her raspy voice carrying across the room, turning patients' head in her direction.

"Excuse me?" Reva asked, putting the files down on her desk.

"I want y'all to fix my girl!"

"Mama, please!" The girl hissed. "Please. . . ."

"I don't understand," said Reva, looking into the eyes of the woman who, she had now come to the conclusion, was a lunatic. "What is it that you want exactly?"

The woman sneered at Reva. Throwing one dismissive hand in the air, she said, "You ain't no doctor. I needs to see a doctor about fixing my girl."

Reva cleared her throat, trying to quell the panic rising in the base of her stomach. This woman had clearly stepped over the edge a while ago, and although Reva had taken her share of psychology courses, she had no point of reference in dealing with the truly insane.

The woman placed both hands on the reception desk and moved her face within inches of Reva. Reva did not back up, even as this woman screamed at her. "I need to have my girl fixed. I got nine kids at home. My Mama didn't fix me, you see? So, I need to fix her. She's fifteen now, same age that I was when I had her. I ain't gonna make the same mistake with her that my Mama made . . ."

Reva reached her left hand underneath the desk and pressed the black knob that was referred to as the panic button by the clinic staff. She had been told about the panic button on her first day at the clinic. This knob was to be pressed in situations of imminent danger. Reva was certain that this situation qualified. Once this button was pressed, the alarm light in the doctors' offices in back would notify all concerned that trouble was brewing.

"Do you have an appointment?" Reva asked, stalling for time.

"No, I don't have a damn appointment!" The woman reared back as if she wanted to slap Reva, but still Reva held her composure.

"Ain't no need to carry on like that," an older man sitting in the corner called out. Reva recognized Phillip Johnson, one of the regular patients.

The woman turned around and shouted, "Mind your business, old man!"

Phillip stood up. "Who you calling old? I ain't too old to whup your . . ."

Annie McLachlan, the head physician at the clinic, walked in to the waiting room with all of the confidence of Daniel heading into the lion's den.

The woman turned around and faced Annie. "I'm trying to get my daughter fixed and I'm getting the runaround."

Reva waited for Annie to tell the woman where to go and how to get there, but instead, Annie walked over to her. Annie wasn't more than five foot one, and the joke was that Annie weighed ninety pounds when she was wet. Still, Annie did not show any fear or hesitancy when she stood in front of the woman. She put her hand on the woman's arm and said, "Why don't you and your daughter come back into my office. I can see you."

"Who the hell are you?" asked the woman.

"My name is Dr. McLachlan, but you can call me Annie. I run the clinic."

Reva watched as the woman and her daughter followed Annie towards the hallway that led to the doctors' offices in the back of the reception area. Annie turned and said to Reva, "Could you bring me two cups of that raspberry tea I made this morning?"

Reva nodded her head mutely. She had always respected Annie McLachlan, but her respect for the doctor had grown tenfold in the few short moments she'd seen Annie calm the woman.

Later that day, just before Reva left the clinic, she walked into Annie's office.

"Annie, can I talk to you for a minute?" Reva asked. It had taken a while for Reva to get used to calling Annie by her first name. Annie felt that the title "doctor" put unnecessary space and stress between her and her patients.

"Sure, Reva, come on in."

Reva walked into Annie's small, cluttered office and sat down on one of the few chairs that did not have piles of paper on them.

"What happened with that woman who came in today—the one that caused a scene?"

Annie's smile was sad. "She just wanted someone to listen to her. She's a very scared lady who, believe it or not, loves her daughter. She doesn't want her daughter to end up being like her—so she came here and asked me to do something that would prevent her daughter from getting pregnant. I talked with her and she calmed down. I've referred her and her daughter to a friend of mine who does counseling. He won't charge them."

Reva asked, "Do you think that they'll go?"

Annie shrugged her shoulders. "Who knows? We can always hope, now can't we?"

"That woman needs a lot more than hope," said Reva. "She's a lunatic."

Annie took off her glasses and stared at Reva. "I think that maybe it's time for you to learn your first real lesson in medicine. Reva, if you can't give your patients hope, then you're just taking up space."

"What if there is no hope?" Reva asked.

"There's always hope, Reva," Annie replied. "That's why you wear this white coat. I'll grant you that sometimes hope is hard to come by, but on those days I remember what Martin Luther King, Jr. said about hope—it's one of my favorite quotes, 'Everything that is done in the world is done by hope.' Remember that, Reva."

Chapter 21

Faith

Faith pulled her car into the hospital parking lot and searched around for a parking space. The parking lot was always full and Faith was annoyed. She was supposed to pick up Opal from her chemotherapy treatment and she was late. On a good day Opal didn't tolerate lateness, on a day that she'd undergone chemotherapy treatment, Opal would be downright ugly. Thanking the Lord for mercy, she spotted a parking lot at the end of the row in which she was driving. If she hurried she'd still be late, but not as late as she thought she'd be. She'd overslept after a night of hanging out with vodka, kahlua and cream. She'd spent the day sleeping until the incessant ringing of her alarm clock and the guilt that she'd be beyond late by the time she got to Opal had propelled her out of bed.

She'd joined the rest of the notoriously crazy Boston drivers, and driven her car at breakneck speed until she'd gotten to the hospital. She'd tried calling the oncology department on her cell phone, but the nurse who answered appeared singularly noncommittal in response to Faith's request that she give Opal a message that she was running late. Reva was originally scheduled to meet Opal at the hospital and drive her to her home, but she'd been called in to the Free Clinic because they were short-staffed. "Can I count on you?" Reva had asked, and Faith had been offended. "Of course you can count on me," she'd replied. "How selfish do you think I am?" Faith had asked. That was before her night of White Russians. Damn, damn and damn again, she thought as she hurried through the front door of the hospital and looked around for the elevators.

Finding the elevators just as the doors were about to close she jumped in and pressed the button for the third floor. Following the directions that Reva had given her last night, she eventually ended up at the oncology department. "I'm looking for Opal Breezewood," Faith addressed the nurse standing at one of the nurse's stations.

"She's in the waiting room over there," the nurse nodded her head in the direction of the waiting room.

Faith walked into the waiting room and saw Opal sitting on one of the sofas. She was leaning back and her eyes were closed. In that moment the gravity of Opal's disease grabbed hold of her. Opal really could die.

Opal opened her eyes and looked in Faith's direction.

"I'm sorry I'm late," she said.

Opal opened her mouth to say something, then snapped it shut.

"She's had a rough time," said the little boy sitting next to Opal. "My name's Max. I'm a friend of Opal's."

"I'm fine," said Opal, but her voice betrayed a physical frailty that Faith had heretofore refused to acknowledge. "Max, this is my friend Faith."

Faith stared at the young boy. Like Opal, he was bald. He had the thinness that often came hand in hand with cancer.

"I'm gonna need your help," Opal said to Faith. "I'm feeling a little dizzy."

"Maybe we should stay here until you feel better," Faith replied, afraid for her friend and afraid of not knowing the right thing to do at this time.

Opal's voice remained weak, but she was emphatic. "I want to go home, Faith. I just need your help in getting up."

Faith walked over to her, and helped her to stand up.

"O.K., just hold my arm . . . my legs are strong enough to get me out of here, but sometimes I stumble . . ."

"I'll walk with you, Opal," said Max.

Opal turned to him, and Faith could see the smile that was the downfall of many a good man. "I'm fine, Max, but thanks just the same. I'll see you in about two weeks."

"Take it easy, Opal."

Opal and Faith walked out of the waiting room and down the hospital corridor towards the elevator.

"Where's his family?" Faith asked, referring to Max.

"All he's got is his mother," Opal replied. "She was talking to the doctor and he was waiting for her."

Faith shook her head. "Damn, that's tough."

Opal looked at her and said, "Life is tough, Faith."

Faith held on to her friend's arm. "Don't I know it," she said.

Opal stopped walking and turned to face Faith. "Drinking doesn't make it any less tough, Faith. That's all I'm going to say on the subject."

Faith did not respond. Instead, she took her friend's arm again and together they walked towards the elevator.

Reva

Reva sat in a café in downtown Boston and stared outside at the falling snow; then she stared across the table at Officer Simon Bennett.

After her day at the Free Clinic, she'd been unnerved. Truth be told, since her father's surprise visit, she'd been decidedly off-kilter. She'd thought about Simon Bennett often in the weeks after she'd seen him at the football game. There had been an undeniable attraction between them, but it had taken a bad day at the Free Clinic, some discussions with Faith and Precious, and a spur of the moment decision to make her pull out the business card that she'd been carrying around in her bag and call his number. He'd suggested that they meet, and she suggested the café. It was a safe, public place.

Simon took a sip of his tea and said, "I'd given up hope that you would ever call me."

"If you'd wanted to get in touch with me, you could have asked me for my number when you saw me," Reva retorted.

"I got the impression that you weren't interested—the business card was a last ditch effort on my part. I never expected you to call. I thought maybe you'd be a missed opportunity."

Reva took a sip of her blackberry tea and said, "A missed opportunity?"

"I have these feelings about people, and when I met you I just felt that you would be a part of my life—or at least I hoped so."

His rap was as smooth as his West Indian accent, but Reva wasn't buying it. She knew a line when she heard one.

"Don't tell me you're like Miss Cleo . . . or the rest of those psychic hotline people?"

"Not quite," Simon stared directly into her eyes.

"Are you going to tell me that when you saw me it was love at first sight?" Reva raised one skeptical eyebrow.

Officer Simon Bennett laughed. "It was more like attraction . . . very strong attraction, I might add, at first sight."

"Ah," said Reva. "Are we talking lust here?"

"No," said Simon. "I just hoped that I would have the chance to get to know you better."

"You're wondering why I called you?" Reva asked.

Simon nodded his head. "I tend not to look a gift horse in the mouth and all that, but it did surprise me to hear your lovely voice . . . what is it, months, after I last saw you. So why did you call?"

Reva decided to tell him the truth. She was never good at games. "I had a very bad day and I kept thinking of you. So, I called you."

Simon leaned back in his chair as if to get comfortable and said, "Why don't you tell me about it?"

Spring
Semester

Chapter 22

Faith

"Faith, I don't do parties."

Faith looked over at Precious and shook her head. "What do you mean, you don't *do* parties?"

"I mean exactly what I said. I don't have fun at parties."

Faith lay down on the wide sloping lawn in front of the dormitory and stared up at the sky. It was one of the warmest March days that she had encountered in a long while. New England winters often seemed interminable for the folks who had to suffer through the months of cold that challenged even the most hardy soul. Middlehurst had awakened to warm temperatures and brilliant sunshine—an early beacon of upcoming spring. Faith looked around at a campus filled with people coming to life, as if awakened from a long slumber—people jogging, riding bikes, sitting outside, letting the warmth of the sun caress them like a long lost friend.

"This party is different," said Faith to her friend. "Rory invited you—at least you know that you'll be guaranteed a good time—plus, the way that brother moves on the football field, you know he can dance. You all are going to have a good time."

Precious sighed, and lay down on the lawn next to Faith. "That's not the point—his dancing skills are not at issue here."

"Isn't that what you always complain about?" Faith asked. "You're always saying that no one asks you to dance."

"I remember freshman year when I went to that party over at Harvard Yard. I hugged the wall the whole night," said Precious.

"Girl, that was years ago. Get over it."

"That's easy for you to say, Miss Life of the Party. You and Opal always have men fighting all over themselves to ask you to dance. Reva can't be bothered with the phony folk that go to these parties. That leaves me out there alone."

Faith looked over at her friend. The words carried something unspoken and distasteful to her attention. It wasn't spite or jealousy . . . but something just as insidious. Insecurity. She could not understand how Precious couldn't quite see how fabulous she was. Faith knew that her weight was an issue for Precious, but she couldn't understand why Precious failed to see how beautiful she was when she looked in the mirror. Precious had a pretty face, but she had something deeper than that. There was an inner spirit—something just plain old good— that came through when you looked at Precious. There were so many people in this world with beautiful faces but hearts that held so much loneliness, hurt and bitterness that their beauty was often diminished. Precious' innate goodness came shining through. Faith wondered what it would take for Precious to finally embrace herself for who she truly was, a beautiful, black woman in every sense of the word.

"Precious, what is really going on here? Tell me why you don't want to go to the party."

"I told you . . ."

Faith interrupted her. "I know what you told me, but I want to know the truth. What's going on?"

Precious lowered her eyes as if she were afraid that they would betray her secret.

"Precious, tell me why you really don't want to go to the party."

Precious let out a long breath and then said in a voice so low that Faith had to lean closer to hear her. "All those people there . . . they're going to be expecting Rory's woman to be fine. They're all going to be mighty disappointed when they see me."

"First of all, that's crazy. If anything, they'll congratulate Rory on having the good sense, and the good fortune to have you in his life. Second, and this is much more important—what do you care what folks say about you? Few things in life are certain, Precious, but one thing's for damn sure—there's always somebody who's going to think that you don't deserve what you have, whether it's good grades, a good man—whatever. Giving these folks any of your time is truly a waste."

"What if Rory starts listening to them?"

Faith didn't hesitate before she answered Precious' question. "Then he isn't worth your time."

Precious laughed. "Have you ever thought about writing an advice column for lonely hearts?"

"The last time I checked, Mr. Rory was making sure that you're not

a member of that particular club. Enough talk about this party—
you're going and I'll go with you. Your man is too fine and too nice to
let him get around these barracudas that are sure to be swimming
around at the party—they need to know that, yes, he does have a
woman and she has a crazy friend!"

"That's what Opal said," Precious replied. "She told me that I need
to be there with my man. I wish she were coming with us."

Opal was back in the hospital for the second time this month.

"I went to see her yesterday, she seemed . . . weak." Precious continued.

"Opal is going to be fine," said Faith, with an assurance she did not
feel.

Precious nodded her head, but she did not look convinced.

Opal

Opal opened her eyes and saw Jordan standing next to her hospital
bed. She closed her eyes and opened them again. Licking dry lips,
she said, "I thought that maybe you were a figment of my imagina-
tion."

"No, Opal—it's the real thing," he replied. He looked thinner than
when she'd last seen him. Dark circles under eyes that were still beautiful spoke of nights when sleep was hard to come by. "Can I sit
down?"

Opal shrugged her shoulders. She wanted him to stay. She was
lonely here in this hospital room. She was scared. But she would not
admit this to him. Since the last time she'd seen him, when he'd
helped her while she was sick, she'd thought about him often. She had
been hard on him then—said some things that were harsh and guaranteed to hurt him. At times, she'd wondered if she'd gone too far.
She'd even picked up the telephone a few times to dial his number,
but she'd never followed through. *Let sleeping dogs lie,* a voice inside of
her would caution. But she missed him, and she knew that made her
something she despised, a weak person—but she missed him.

"Suit yourself."

Jordan pulled a chair close to her bed and sat down.

Opal closed her eyes and tried to fight another wave of nausea.
Since last week she'd been unable to keep anything down, and was
now suffering from dehydration. The fluids that were pumped into
her veins helped quell her nausea, but there were times when a wave
of sickness would come over her and it was all she could do to hold on
while the nausea passed. After a few moments, when she was certain
that she would not vomit, she opened her eyes and looked at her ex-

fiancé. Her heart twisted when she looked at a face that she had planned to see for the rest of her life. Once again, the bitterness that was never too far away when she thought of his betrayal came to the surface.

"Don't get too comfortable," she said. "You're not staying long."

The hospital door opened and Max walked in. After a cursory look at Jordan, Max walked over to Opal's bed and sat down.

He had been coming to see Opal every day since she'd been admitted to the hospital. She'd looked forward to his visits. He'd become very dear to her in a relatively short time. Unlike Precious, who warmed too quickly to folks, Opal was very reserved about letting new people come into her circle of friends and family—Max had firmly entered that sphere and Opal was glad for it.

"So is he the bum?" Max asked, staring directly at Jordan.

Opal nodded her head, trying hard not to smile. "Yes, this is the bum. Jordan, this is my friend Max. Max, this is Jordan."

Mrs. Firenze and Max had spent countless hours with her discussing "the bum" as Max referred to Jordan. Mrs. Firenze was of the firm opinion that a second chance was in order. Max wasn't so sure.

Jordan leaned over and offered his hand to Max, who shook his hand with all the formality of a British butler.

"You don't look like a bum," Max said to Jordan. "You look like a pretty nice guy to me . . . not the kind of guy who would hurt a good person like Opal."

Opal looked at Jordan, curious to see what his reaction would be. If Max's words upset him, he did not show it.

"Looks can be deceiving," said Jordan, with a rueful smile.

"That's a cliché," said Max. "Opal deserved better. If you didn't want to be with her, you should have just told her straight."

"You're right," Jordan replied. "But I always wanted to be with her. I made a mistake."

"A big one," said Max. "What are you doing here?"

"I wanted to see her," said Jordan. "I thought she might need a friend."

Max squinted his eyes as if he were a prosecutor grilling a witness. "Oh, so you want to be friends, now? Seems to me that you weren't too friendly to her when you hurt her . . ."

Opal suppressed a laugh. "Max, honey. It's O.K."

Max's mother entered through the door left open by Max's entrance. "The nurses told me you were here," she said to Max. "But I should have known that anyway."

"Hi, Miss Monaghan," Opal greeted Max's mother.

"Hiya, Opal." Miss Monaghan walked over to her son and put her arms around his shoulders. "I hope Maxi here wasn't bothering you too much."

"Not at all," Opal said quickly. "Anytime he wants to visit is fine . . . although I hope I won't be in here much longer."

Max's mother stared at Jordan, as if noticing him for the first time.

"Hi," said Jordan. "I'm Jordan."

"The bum," said Max, by way of explanation.

"Oh," said Miss Monaghan, who had heard the story of Jordan. "Well, Max—it's time for us to go. It's a short visit, I'm sorry, but Max has a doctor's appointment this afternoon. Opal, we'll stop by tomorrow."

"Call the hospital first," said Opal. "I might be home by tomorrow."

"I'll say a prayer," said Miss Monaghan.

Max stood up and held his mother's hand. "I'll call you tonight, Opal."

Opal smiled at him. "I'll be waiting."

Max turned to Jordan and said. "You hurt her again and you'll have to answer to me, got that?"

Jordan nodded his head. "Loud and clear."

"That's a cliché, too," said Max. "You need to work on getting some more original vocabulary."

Opal let out the laugh that she had been trying to suppress.

Max's mother shook her head. "Let's go, Max."

Opal watched them walk out of her room.

"It's good to hear you laugh." said Jordan.

Opal sighed. "It beats the alternative . . . "

She looked into his eyes and saw love there. She had missed him, more than she cared to admit. They had been friends once. Good friends. At this very moment she realized that was what she missed the most about Jordan. His friendship. He hurt her. That was an inescapable fact. It would always be a part of the fabric of whatever she felt for him, but Precious' words came floating back to her.

"I just don't know how to live without the resentment . . . I don't want to see that happen to you."

She had cancer. It was no exaggeration that she was in a fight for her life, a fight in which she needed all her resources to help her to win. Hating Jordan suddenly seemed much less significant than the battle she was now facing.

"Why are you here, Jordan?"

He answered without hesitation. "I love you, Opal. That hasn't changed. I don't want you to face this . . . without me being by your side. I don't want anything else, Opal. I don't deserve anything else. I'm not asking for a second chance. Not anymore. I understand all that stuff about reaping what you sow . . . yeah, I know, that's a cliché . . . I know it's over between us. I just want to be here with you to help you in any way I can. I'm not even asking you for friendship. I don't deserve that either."

Opal watched as tears fell freely down Jordan's face.

"I know I said all that stuff about being your friend, but I know that . . . that I haven't been a friend to you . . . in a while. Just give me the chance to be with you while you fight this . . ."

"Cancer," said Opal.

"Cancer," Jordan repeated. "Let me be here with you. Please."

He held out his hand to her, and Opal hesitated for a moment. She was still angry. She was still hurt. But she had looked into her heart today and she had found that there was still a place for him there. She loved him. What kind of person did that make her? A person who loved someone who had caused her so much pain? All this time she had wondered if she loved Jordan or his resume, his credentials, his pedigree—she loved him—and as she realized this with certainty, she also realized that the pain that he had caused her would never allow her to admit this love to him. She had found him and she had lost him all in the same moment.

She took his hand and held it tightly.

Chapter 23

Precious took a deep breath and walked into the party, which was in full swing. It had been a while since she'd gone to a college party, but immediately all the reasons why she disliked these parties came rushing back to her. The mating ritual of men standing around deciding which woman to bestow their favor on bored her. She hated the desperation she saw on women's faces, the sly cockiness of the men who were certain that their college pedigree and universal goals for a fat bank account bestowed the King of the World crown on them. She hated the feeling of being invisible that descended upon her almost immediately when she was at a party.

The color game, one that should have ended way back at the plantation, flourished at these parties. There was a definite caste system in those who were selected for the dance floor. The lighter skinned women with long hair were usually the first to be chosen as dance partners, then women with long hair were chosen thereafter, with the darker skinned sisters with their hair short usually being the last to be asked. Although this party would be different for her—she was coming as Rory's date and, therefore, for one night she would be an honorary "in" person, the whole ordeal left a bad taste in her mouth.

"Girl, what are you thinking about?"

Faith's voice drew Precious back to the present.

"Nothing," Precious lied.

The party was being held in the basement of a fraternity house on Boston Union's campus. There was not much room in the basement, and it was already jammed with people. Precious tried hard not to think of how many fire codes were broken by this soiree. She felt awkward looking at the women in their skintight outfits, high heels and impeccable hairstyles. She felt positively underdressed with her black slacks, white turtleneck and sensible black boots. She'd pulled back her thick hair into what she hoped was a sleek ponytail, but she could feel stray strands of hair blowing about her face from the constant breeze that was emitted by the fans placed throughout the room. Precious envied Faith her ability to look good seemingly without any effort. Faith was dressed in a black mini skirt that accentuated a small waist and slender hips. Her red silk shirt with its low neckline and black four inch stiletto heels screamed "come hither, all who dare," while Precious was equally certain that her own outfit screamed "librarian." Faith fit in with the rest of the women at the party; Precious stood out like a cherry in a bowl of milk.

Almost as soon as Faith walked in, she was invited to the dance floor. "I'll be back," Faith said to Precious, nodding her head to the music. Precious nodded back at her, feeling unaccountably abandoned. Then she walked over to the wall and let the dark room envelop her.

A flurry of excitement drew her attention to the entrance of the basement. She watched as Rory walked in with another man, whom she'd never seen before. He was taller than Rory, with smooth, dark skin. Even from this distance, Precious could see that this was an extraordinarily handsome man with perfectly chiseled features, dressed in a cream colored shirt and black pants; he made an arresting picture. Precious fought the urge to run over to Rory. She was glad that he was here, but still, she held back—she was not used to seeing Rory in this environment and she felt awkward.

Rory scanned the party and Precious hoped that he was looking for her. Still, Precious remained in the shadows. She wanted to watch him a while longer before she revealed herself. There was a shyness that crept over her, a sense of hesitation. This was a different venue for them. She had never seen Rory in these circumstances, in a place where he was publicly revered as the college football star. Their relationship had been relatively private, and now Precious felt as if this were a coming out for both of them.

Precious watched as the man standing next to Rory bent and said something in his ear and Rory laughed. Then, she watched as three women, each in a dress tighter than common sense would have dictated, walked over to them, surrounding Rory and his friend. A wave of insecurity gripped her and Precious took a deep breath, blowing the air out slowly through her nostrils. She fought the urge to turn and run—anywhere, out of the party, to the bathroom, out of the party, anywhere but where she was standing. As if Rory sensed her panic, he looked in her direction. The strobe light flashed and revealed her and Rory greeted her from across the room with a wide smile and a wave.

He said something to the group and walked over towards her, and Precious felt her heart soar in that moment. This was Rory. Her man. Her boyfriend. Judging from the wide smile on his face, he was happy, very happy to see her. It didn't matter how many women were there who were prettier than her, wore sexier clothes than she did, all this didn't matter. He was her man, and he was coming over to get her. In the background, Phyllis Hyman began to sing "Meet Me on the Moon."

Phyllis's unmistakable contralto soared and for one perfect moment, Precious felt her spirits rise with Phyllis's voice, and all her fears slipped quietly away. Rory walked over to her and pulled her close to him. Leaning his head towards her, he kissed her lightly on the lips.

Reva

Reva opened the door to her dormitory room with music still floating in her head. She had just come back from a date with Simon—a jazz concert in Boston. She had never been appreciative of jazz music, but Simon had opened her eyes to its beauty, as he had opened her eyes in other ways. In the few short weeks since they had begun seeing each other, Simon had introduced her to jazz music, West Indian food, Bruce Lee movies and soccer games, which were played by a group of expatriates, Africans, West Indians, Irish and Italian, every Saturday in a park in Roxbury even in the frigid New England winter. Closing the door behind her, she walked quietly over to her bed. It was late and she didn't want to awaken Bonnie.

A lamp light was switched on and Reva found herself staring at her roommate, who was grinning at her.

"I didn't mean to wake you," said Reva.

Bonnie sat up in bed and brushed her light brown hair out of her eyes. "Are you kidding? I've been waiting for you. I want to hear *all* the dirt."

Reva smiled. "There's not much to tell. We went to dinner and then we went to a concert. Then he brought me back home."

Bonnie laughed. "Since when did you of all people consider Middlehurst home? You've been counting the days till graduation since freshman year."

"That's true," said Reva, "but after four years, this place just might be growing on me."

"Maybe it's Simon that's growing on you," said Bonnie.

"Maybe," Reva replied, unwilling to admit to herself or to her roommate how much Simon had come to mean to her in such a short time. She wasn't sure that she was in love with him; she had no point of reference for being in love. She had been infatuated with many guys but this feeling was different. She felt comfortable with him, happy with him. It was as if she found a long lost friend who saw her for exactly what she was, and even with all her faults, he accepted her. Was this love? She wasn't sure—but she was going to ride this train as long as the journey lasted.

"Reva, this is a good thing. You deserve to be happy," said Bonnie.

Reva lay down in her bed, too tired to undress. Pulling the covers up to her chin, she turned to face her roommate and replied, "Yes, I do. I deserve to be happy."

Bonnie let out a shriek of laughter. "Your mother is going to *freak out* when she finds out that her baby is in love."

Oh, Lord, thought Reva. Sugar. Sugar had called her two days ago and she had forgotten to return the call. There would be hell to pay. She'd have to call her tomorrow. As for letting her mother know about Simon, she was not in any rush for that to happen. She didn't want to hear Sugar's mouth when she found out her daughter was dating a policeman and not the doctor, lawyer or other high salaried person that Sugar felt was right for her offspring. She pushed Sugar firmly out of her mind and let the music that was in her head continue playing.

Precious

Rory's handsome friend pushed his way through the crowd, followed by the three women in their tight dresses. They were headed in Precious and Rory's direction, and Precious felt a familiar shyness creep over her. Her shyness had plagued her throughout her childhood, and was something she had never quite overcome. Rory's friend moved with almost feline grace, but as Precious watched his approach she saw that there was something self-conscious about his movements, as if he knew that several pairs of approving eyes were turned in his direction. Rory put his hand in hers and held it tight, giving her a reassuring squeeze. Precious wondered if he could sense her apprehension.

"Rory, aren't you going to introduce me to the lovely lady?"

Rory's friend stood in front of her, with his accompanying trio hovering close behind.

Precious stared at his face and felt a chill come over her. If she were a superstitious woman, she would have made the sign of the cross over her heart three times, just like her grandmother used do in an effort to ward off impending bad luck. This man was very handsome, a close examination confirmed, but there was something cold and disconnected in his eyes.

"This is Precious," said Rory, making introductions. "Precious, this is my boy Everton. Everton Rhodes."

Why hadn't she recognized him, thought Precious. Everton played on the football team with Rory, and he got even more press than Rory did. He was one of the few African American quarterbacks in college, and he had caught the attention of several football teams. She'd seen him on the field a few times and in newspaper articles, but she'd never paid much attention to him. Rory was the only football player she had any real interest in. Still, even she, a football novice, knew who Everton Rhodes was. His football exploits were downright legendary, and according to the gossip in the tight-knit African American college community in Boston, he had a healthy appetite for the ladies.

"Hello," said Precious, with a smile she did not feel like giving.

Everton took her hand and kissed it lightly. Precious fought the urge to wipe her hands on her slacks. His gallant gesture repulsed her. It seemed contrived, designed to elicit a specific response. This was a man who knew that he was attractive and this was a man who had no qualms about using whatever it took, whether it be his athletic prowess or his looks to take him where he needed to go. His smile was wide, but Precious had the very distinct impression that this man was well acquainted with being cruel.

"So, *this* is who you've been spending your time with, Rory," said one of the women accompanying Everton. She was tall, thin and carried with her the bored air of someone who had been used to getting her own way for a long time. The tight black lace dress that hovered above a pair of lean brown legs was molded to her body as if it were a sheath. Fat, shiny curls framed her face and tumbled around her shoulders. Her light green eyes glittered with a malice undisguised by the party's dim lights.

The woman walked over to Rory and kissed him lightly on the lips.

Precious pulled her hand away from Rory. She had never been jealous of anyone in her life, but the heat that covered her face, this sudden urge to wrap her hands around this woman's neck, this rapid beating of her heart, this unaccountable flash of anger towards Rory could only be diagnosed as jealousy.

She watched as the woman placed a thin and possessive hand on Rory's arm, clearly indicating to all concerned, that she and Rory were more than friends.

Rory extricated himself from her with a move just as smooth as when he evaded tackles on the football field. "Candace, this is Precious. Precious, this is Candace."

Candace did not bother to smile. "I've never seen you around before," she said.

"No, you haven't," Precious replied.

Candace turned her attention back to Rory. "How about a dance with an old friend. I remember how you used to love this song."

Rory put his arm around Precious' waist. "I'm sorry, Candace, but my dance card is full. Precious has promised to save all her dances for me."

He moved Precious towards the dance floor as a slow Isley Brothers song came on. Pulling her body closer to his, he began to move with her in perfect time with the music. As he pulled her closer, Precious felt her body stiffen. Who was this woman and what was going on between her and Rory?

Rory put his lips close to her ear and said, "What's wrong?"

"Nothing," Precious replied in a tone of voice that she was certain would let Rory know that there was plenty wrong.

"I'm going to ask you one more time, Precious—what's wrong, and don't tell me nothing."

Aware that at least four pairs of eyes were on them, Precious forced herself to remain calm, even though she felt like shouting. It was as if the temperamental, overly dramatic spirit of some long gone ancestor had descended on her.

"Are you and Candace lovers?" Precious asked, expecting a quick denial.

"We were," Rory replied.

Precious pulled her body away from him instantly, as if she had been burned by a hot stove. Rory held her tight and pulled her back towards him.

"Is it over?" Precious asked.

"Yes," Rory replied. "It was over before I met you."

"Apparently she doesn't think so," said Precious, unable to keep the waspishness out of her voice.

"What she thinks right now is just about the last thing on my mind," said Rory.

"That sounds cold," Precious replied.

"It's life, Precious," said Rory. "I know that you want to see the good in everything, but sometimes things—situations—just aren't good for us. Candace is not a nice person, Precious—and it took me a while to find that out. Once I did, it was over. I've made that clear to her. She knows it. It's been over for a long time."

Precious digested this information in silence as the Isley Brothers kept crooning.

"Precious, let me ask you something," said Rory. "Would you date me if I didn't play football?"

"Of course," Precious replied instantly, annoyed that he would ask her this idiotic question. "I didn't even like football before I met you."

"Would you date me if you didn't think I was going to get a big contract with some football team?"

"I am going to law school," replied Precious. "I think I'll be able to take care of myself. Where is this conversation going, Rory. It's beginning to wear thin."

"What do you see in me, Precious? Why are you with me?"

"I see an honorable, funny, handsome, smart man who used to date a she-devil," Precious replied.

Rory's laughter covered her like a warm blanket, and she felt herself wrapped tightly in his arms. This time, she did not resist.

Chapter 24

Faith

Faith looked around for Precious but could not find her in the crowd. She was hot, with sweat from her dancing making her red silk blouse cling to her like a damp, second skin. She wanted a drink. There was a bar set up in the corner and it took a great deal more willpower than she thought she possessed, and the fear of Precious' lectures to make her turn away. She walked towards the spot where she'd last left Precious and bumped into someone's chest. She felt as if she'd run into a brick wall.

Looking up, she found herself facing a tall man with blond hair that was almost white and the bluest eyes she'd ever seen. She looked as if she'd seen a ghost. Like everything else in her college experience, college parties were usually segregated. Black folk partied with their own kind, and the same could be said for all the other races. She had never seen a white person at any of the black parties.

He smiled down at her. He was well over six feet, and the top of Faith's head, even in her heels, came up to his chest.

"I've been hoping you'd bump into me. I guess the Lord does answer prayers." he said.

I know *this boy is not flirting with me,* Faith thought, as she tried to think of a reply that would sufficiently put him in his place. She knew the stereotypes of oversexed, easy black women and she was not going to let him entertain this fantasy, not even for a moment. Reva had often accused her of being a racist, but Faith would protest this label. It wasn't that she didn't like people who were different from her, it was just that she had no real point of reference and she never went out of her way to meet people who did not share her common background. She had had only one white friend before—when she was six years old. Janae Miller had been her best friend in first grade, but she'd moved away to another neighborhood when school was over. Faith had seen her a few years later in the mall with some of her friends. When Faith had walked over to her, Janae had pretended she didn't recognize her. After that, Faith had adhered to her mother's caution to "stick to your own kind."

"My name is Kevin Davies," he raised his voice over the music. "Would you like to dance?"

"No," replied Faith. "My feet hurt."

Kevin nodded his head. "I understand," he said, and for a moment Faith felt bad. She'd rejected him for the same reason that Janae had rejected her—because of his race.

"Maybe another time," Kevin said, still looking down at her. His eyes told her that he understood her reasons. There was no malice in those eyes, no hurt—he understood and he did not hold grudges. He stepped aside and let her pass.

She walked toward the spot where she'd last seen Precious, near the entrance of the party. She did indeed spot Precious, but not before she spotted one of the most handsome men she'd ever seen, and Precious and Rory were standing and talking with him.

Precious saw her and waved to her to come over. Glancing at the man who was now staring at her, Faith knew that her evening was about to get interesting.

Opal

Opal lay in the hospital bed and watched Jordan as he slept in the chair next to her bed. He had been there most of the day, and although visiting hours were over a long time ago, the nurse on duty allowed him to stay with her in her room. They had talked to each other, each one filling the other with information about the months they had been apart. It was still awkward. There were topics that were not discussed. They discussed neutral topics—school, the state of the economy, family gossip, friend gossip. They did not talk about cancer, nor did they talk about the subject that led to their breakup.

Opal was glad for the company. Jordan knew when to talk, when to be silent, and when to just hold her hand. They watched television— CNN, the Sports Channel and the classical movies. He helped feed her when dinner was brought in. She'd been embarrassed by the way her hands shook when she tried to lift the fork to her mouth, but Jordan had taken the fork from her without a word and fed her, all the while talking about his favorite basketball team, the New York Knicks, as if feeding her was the most natural thing in the world. He'd left her only for a few minutes, when she'd convinced him to go down to the hospital cafeteria to get something to eat.

Around nine o'clock she'd started drifting off to sleep, but she'd asked him to remain with her awhile. Since finding out that she had cancer, going to sleep was difficult. Before she could fall asleep she would always have to conquer her fear that she was not going to wake up. She'd talked to Reva about this, who assured her that while this was probably normal, it was still an unrealistic fear. Still, even though she knew she was being unrealistic, she always kept a lamp light on when she went to sleep—it was her way of telling herself that she had to get up at some point, to turn off that lamp—although the lamp would always remain on. Tonight, Jordan was her lamp.

"Just stay here for a few minutes until I go to sleep," she'd asked him.

She'd awakened just past midnight to find him still there, sleeping in the chair next to the bed. He looked peaceful, with his head cradled in the armrest of the chair. His long legs were stretched out on another chair, which served as an ottoman. She thought about waking him up, but decided against it. She knew that she was being selfish, but she wanted his company. She wasn't ready to let him go just yet.

Pulling back her blanket, she stepped out of the hospital bed. Taking one of the pillows from her bed, she shifted his body until she could get the pillow under his head. He murmured in his sleep, but he did not awaken. Opal walked over to the closet in the corner of the room and took out one of the blankets that were folded there. Taking the blanket, she walked over to Jordan and covered him with it.

Opal got back into bed and, for the first time since her diagnosis, she turned off her lamp and let darkness envelop the room. Pulling her blanket around her shoulders, she felt a feeling of peace come over her. As she lay in the darkness, she heard Jordan's voice—quiet and heartfelt.

"Thank you," he said.

Faith

Everton Rhodes was certainly not the most handsome man that Faith had ever seen, but he was close. Tall, dark and handsome with a few other favorable adjectives thrown in, including charming, Everton Rhodes was an intriguing prospect. It had been a while since she'd met anyone who'd interested her, but the good-looking football player had just made an otherwise ordinary party get a lot more exciting.

He took her hand and kissed it lightly. "It's nice to meet you, Faith."

Precious cleared her throat and Faith looked over at her. Precious looked as if she had seen a ghost. What in the world was wrong with her, Faith wondered.

"Faith . . ." Precious stammered her words. "I just saw Winnie Flood over there . . . you remember Winnie?"

"Yes," said Faith, wondering why Precious was interested in Winnie. Winnie dropped out of Middlehurst two years ago to pursue her dream of becoming an actress. The last they'd heard of Winnie, she'd been working in a strip joint. "I remember Winnie."

"Well, let's say hello to her," Precious said brightly. Turning to Rory, she said, "We'll be right back."

What was the deal with Precious? It wasn't as if it were Winnie Mandela at the party. It was Winnie Flood, who on her good days was not the most pleasant person. Faith was certain that her new occupation wouldn't make her any friendlier.

"Come on," Precious said, grabbing Faith's hand. "I remember how close you two were."

Before Faith could ask Precious what herb she had smoked lately, Precious pulled Faith behind her, like a mother pulling a recalcitrant child.

"What in the world is wrong with you?" asked Faith, when they had walked away from Rory and Everton. "You know I can't stand Winnie Flood."

"Neither can I," Precious hissed. "I needed to talk to you about Everton."

"Lord, that man is fine," Faith replied. "You never told me that you knew him! You've been keeping secrets, Precious!"

"Faith, I don't know the man, nor do I want to. Stay away from him, Faith. He's bad news."

"What has Everton Rhodes done to you?" Faith asked, now confused. Precious was acting as if Everton was the devil's offspring.

"He hasn't done anything to me, but there's something not right about him," Precious replied.

"Is this one of your sixth sense things?" Faith asked. Precious was known to have premonitions about things, usually bad things, and so far, she'd been accurate with all her warnings.

"Don't joke about this, Faith," said Precious. "That man has the coldest eyes I've ever seen."

"Precious, don't be ridiculous," Faith spoke quickly, but there was a small voice inside her that warned that Precious was usually right when she had these kinds of feelings. "You're being a drama queen."

"Faith, please . . ."

Faith interrupted her, looking over at the woman Precious had thought was Winnie. "Precious, that woman is not Winnie Flood. I've never seen that woman before."

Precious appeared distracted. "Faith, forget about Winnie Flood. Just please listen to what I've told you about Everton."

"I'm a big girl," said Faith. "I think I can handle Everton. Besides, why should you be the only one to have fun with a football player."

"Rory's different . . ." Precious began.

"Is he?" said Faith, not resisting the urge to be cruel. Precious had hit a raw nerve with her warning about Everton. She knew that all her friends, Precious included, thought that she was a royal screwup. She loved her girlfriends, but their perfect little worlds and their perfect little ways tended to get on her last nerve. Precious meant well, but it was time that she and the rest of her girlfriends figured out that Faith could take care of her own business. "All these men are the same, honey, and the sooner you figure that little fact out, the better for all concerned."

Faith watched, without any satisfaction, as her words took their desired effect on Precious, who had now clamped her lips together in a clear sign of disapproval.

Then, shaking her head, Precious said, "Faith, I've done the best I can do—I've warned you about this man. I'm through with this."

"So am I," Faith replied, as she turned her back on her friend and walked over to where Everton and Rory stood waiting for them.

As she approached them, Everton walked over to meet her.

"Would you like to dance?" he asked.

"Absolutely," said Faith, fixing a big smile in Everton's direction.

Precious

"What was that all about?" Rory asked Precious, as they watched Faith and Everton get swallowed by a crowd of people that had taken to the dance floor after the disc jockey put on a popular song.

"Do you really want to know?" Precious asked, turning to face him. The good feelings that she had felt a short time ago had disappeared. Everton Rhodes troubled her, but Faith's cruelty troubled her even more. Her comments about the nature of men hurt. It was as if Faith were mocking her. It was true that she hadn't had much experience with men, certainly nothing compared with Faith's numerous conquests—but she was a good judge of character and she knew that Rory was different from most men she had encountered. He wasn't perfect, but like her father, Rory was a good man.

"Precious, I want to know what has gotten you so upset."

"I'm just worried about Faith," said Precious.

"From what I know about Faith," Rory countered, "she can take care of herself. She doesn't need you to worry about her."

No she can't, Precious replied silently. Faith had proven on too many occasions to count that she could not take care of herself. She was the queen of bad choices and Precious had a strong feeling that Faith was about to walk into a situation that she was not equipped to handle.

"I hope you're right," said Precious.

Rory turned her around to face him. Placing his hands gently on both shoulders, he said, "You don't like Everton, do you?"

"No," Precious replied honestly.

"You're the first person that I've met who hasn't been bowled over by the famous Everton charm."

"It takes a lot to bowl me over," said Precious.

"So I've noticed," said Rory, drawing her closer to him. Lowering his lips to hers, he kissed her and for the first time, Rory's kisses were not enough to chase away her disquieting thoughts.

Chapter 25

Faith

There had been many times in Faith's life where she asked the question: "How did I get here?" Tonight was no exception. The transition from the dance floor to Everton Rhodes's dormitory room had been too smooth. At first, Faith had demurred. Although her friends were all of the general opinion that she was easy, as a general rule, she did not fall into bed with men with whom she had just become acquainted. As fine as Everton was, she was not interested in having a one night stand. She'd already had too many of those—but Everton's offer of a nightcap in his room, although lacking in originality, proved to be appealing.

"We can just go up to my room and have a few drinks—listen to some music, get to know each other," Everton had said. "My room is upstairs."

Faith had not envisioned that Everton stayed in a fraternity. She thought that he'd have a funky apartment like Rory.

"I thought you football superstars had fancier digs," said Faith, stalling for time before she gave him an answer to his request to go to his room.

"You mean like my man, Rory?" Everton asked, with a crooked grin that only increased his already high appeal. "I don't come from money like Rory."

Precious had never mentioned that Rory's family was well-off financially. Faith had just assumed that the school gave all the football players fancy apartments. Leave it to Precious to be closemouthed about her man. At the thought of Precious, she had felt a flash of annoyance. Precious meant well, but she was always trying to save folks and Faith did not need saving from Precious or anyone else.

"So, how about that nightcap? I have a magarita mix and I make a mean margarita."

The lure of sipping a margarita with a handsome man was an irresistible combination and Faith had thrown caution and all good sense to the wind. She'd agreed to go up to Everton's room. Everton's dorm room was pleasant, but there was nothing particularly special about it. It was small, even by basic dorm room standards. There were a couple of posters on the wall, pictures of football players that she did not recognize. The room was dominated by a waterbed, which left very little room for the television, refrigerator, and desk and chair. There were some throw pillows on the floor, one of which Faith was sitting on.

She was beginning to feel uncomfortable. She had already had three magaritas and Everton was coming on strong. He had tried to kiss her neck, but she had pushed him away. She was not interested in sleeping with him. She'd come upstairs for a drink, and maybe some conversation. She had not come upstairs to play football groupie.

"Look," she'd said. "You need to slow down. I don't even know you."

She sounded like Precious the prude, thought Faith, moving Everton's hands away from the hem of her skirt.

Everton poured out another drink. "You need to relax," he said.

Faith took the glass from Everton and took a sip. Everton was right, he did make a mean margarita. She drank the margarita and listened to the music playing on Everton's stereo. He had terrible taste in music. So far, she had listened to two teenybopper groups where the lead singer was off-key.

"Here," said Everton, pouring her another drink. She noticed then, that after his first margarita glass, Everton had not had another drink.

Faith giggled, as she felt a familiar buzz overtake her. She was drunk. "Are you trying to ply me with alcohol?" she asked.

Everton did not reply, instead he kept looking at her, his expression serious.

"Hey," said Faith, suddenly looking at the clock. It was almost one o'clock. "I need to get back to Precious. She's probably wondering where I am."

"Don't worry about that fat bitch," Everton replied. "She's probably getting laid right about now, but what the hell Rory sees in that cow I don't know. He could have any bitch he wants and he chooses that piece of pork."

Faith was drunk, but not drunk enough to let those words go unattended.

"The hell with you," Faith yelled. "Precious is probably the best thing that could ever happen to Rory!"

Faith rose unsteadily to get up. She was going to get the hell away from this idiot. Precious was right about him.

What happened next was so sudden and unexpected that it took Faith a moment to catch her breath. Everton pushed her and she found herself lying on the dirty grey carpet, her drink knocked from her hand.

"Stop playing games," he said, as he tugged at her skirt.

"Stop it!" Faith shouted, more angry than afraid. "What the hell is wrong with you!"

"You know you want this!" Rory said, his breath hot and stale on her face. "Hell, I like a tease as much as the next guy, but there comes a time when enough is more than enough. We both know why you came here tonight, so stop playing games."

The charming man who had joked with her, teased her, danced slowly with her had turned into a monster. His face was contorted with a rage that Faith did not understand. Then she saw clearly what Precious had glimpsed—cold eyes that glittered with undisguised malice.

Struggling to sit up, Faith said, "Get away from me!"

Pushing one hand over her mouth, Everton pushed her back to the ground with his other hand.

"Shut up, bitch, and spread your legs."

How did I get here? How did I get here? How did I get here? The words swam around her head, as her anger gave way to fear. He was going to rape her.

She struggled to get away from his grip, but his weight was crushing her. She felt him push her skirt up above her legs with his free hand. The other hand remained clamped firmly on her mouth.

"Keep stuggling, baby," Everton said, his breath now coming out in ragged bursts. "It only makes it sweeter. I love it when you bitches struggle, I swear I do!"

He was pushing her panties down below her knees, cursing at her in an incomprehensible language—it was as if he were in a desperate trance—he could not stop himself, even if he were so inclined. His eyes were focused on her face, and for one moment, she thought that he might kill her.

She bit his hand and he cursed, pulling his hand away. He slapped her across the face and she tasted the bitterness of blood on her lips. Then, she opened her mouth and screamed.

"Shut up, you bitch!" he yelled, trying to put the hand that was not bloody over her mouth, as she twisted her head, still screaming. There were no words coming out of her mouth, only a sound of primal need, distress, a call for help.

"Shut up, bitch!" Everton kept yelling. "Shut up!"

She heard banging on the door, and the sound of a man yelling, but she could not make out what he was saying. Everton turned towards the door and cursed. "Help me!" she screamed.

"Go away!" Everton yelled towards the door. "Me and my lady are just having some fun in here!"

"Help me!" Faith yelled again. "Help me!"

There was the sound of wood splintering, coming apart. Then, Everton jumped off her, adjusting his clothes. "What the hell did you do to my door?" he asked.

"Forget about your door," said a male voice that sounded vaguely familiar. "What the hell is going on in here?"

Faith scrambled to her feet. "He tried to rape me!" she screamed, crying. She recognized the white man who had asked her for a dance earlier that evening. She tried to run to him, but she took a step and fell.

"I'm calling the police," he said to Everton.

"We were just having some fun in here, that's all. Ain't no need to overreact," said Everton.

Faith was aware that there were more people now standing at the doorway, but she didn't care. With her clothes ripped, and her skirt torn away from her body, she could only think that someone had come to help her. Everton would not hurt her now.

"I'm going to take you to the hospital," the man said to her. "He won't hurt you again. Don't worry."

She tried to tell him to go and get Precious, but her mouth was full of blood and her words came out with a soft gargle.

"Precious," she said, when she could form the words.

"What is it?" he asked.

Taking a hand and wiping the blood away, she said, as steadily as she could. "My friend, Precious. I need Precious."

"Look, man," said Everton. "Get out of here before I kick your ass."

The man turned around and faced Everton. "Try it," he said, his words soft, but the force behind them was unmistakable. "Try it."

A woman came in the room and knelt down next to Faith. "It's all right," she said. "We're going to get you some help. I've called an ambulance, and I've called campus security."

The woman then turned to the group gathered at the open doorway and told them to get back. "The show's over!" she shouted with authority. Faith turned her attention from the onlookers to the man who had saved her. Faith grabbed his hand. She tried to remember his name. Ken. Karl. What the hell was his name?

"My friend, Precious," she said. "At the party. Need her."

He nodded his head. "The woman I saw you standing with—the woman with Rory?" he asked.

Faith nodded her head. "Yes," she whispered.

"I'll stay with her, Kevin," the woman said to Faith's rescuer. "Go get her friend."

"Fuck this!" Everton screamed. Faith watched as he pushed his way through the crowd that was still gathered at the door.

"Don't worry about him," said Kevin Davies. "He can't hurt you anymore."

Precious

Precious followed Kevin Davies to the elevator. She could feel her frightened heartbeat pounding in her chest. He had been brief in his description about Faith's condition. "Your friend was attacked," he said. "She needs you."

"Was Everton with her?" Precious had asked and Kevin had nodded his head and replied, "He was the one who did it to her." After that, he wouldn't answer any other questions. He was intent on getting her to Faith's side as fast as possible. Rory was holding her hand tightly. The feeling of dread that she had been unable to shake earlier this evening had come full circle to a tight fist of terror lodged in the middle of her stomach.

The elevator door opened and Kevin, Rory and Precious stepped in. Kevin pressed the button for the twelfth floor and the door closed quickly. Everton Rhodes had hurt her friend. She should have done more to convince Faith to stay away from him. She had seen something in the depths of Everton's light brown eyes that had assured her that he was capable of cruelty. She should have tried harder to keep Faith away from this man.

The elevator door opened and Precious saw a crowd by an open door.

"Right this way," Kevin said, walking in the direction of the crowd of people.

Precious felt the ground underneath her feet, but there was a buzz in her ears that she could not explain—a sound that blocked out voices, the sound of her footsteps on the tile floor, and the sound of Rory's voice. She could see that he was talking to her, but she could not hear his words. It was as if Rory were starring in a movie with the sound turned completely off.

Kevin said something to the people gathered at the open door and they parted to give way.

Precious could see Faith lying on the floor, her head cradled in a the lap of a woman she did not recognize. There was a campus policeman kneeling next to Faith, holding her hand and talking to her.

Faith's lip was swollen and her hair, usually in its smart, immaculate short cut, was disheveled. Her red silk blouse was torn and her panty-hose were ripped.

Precious broke free from Rory's hold and ran towards her friend. Kneeling across from the policeman, Precious took Faith's free hand and held it tightly. She tried to say something, to offer some comfort, but her throat was filled with tears.

Rory knelt beside her. "Faith, baby," he said, as if he didn't believe Kevin Davies's words. "Did Everton do this to you?"

Faith closed her eyes and nodded her head. "Yes," she whispered.

Precious heard Rory curse for the first time since she'd met him. "I'm going to kill him."

Faith turned her face towards Precious and said, "I'm sorry." The words came out slowly.

"No need to be sorry, Faith," Precious said, trying to use her I'm-in-control voice, although she felt that whatever grasp she had on self-control was tenuous at best.

"Should have listened to you," Faith said.

There was a commotion at the doorway and Precious saw that there were two emergency medical services workers coming to the room.

Precious stood up, along with the few people who had knelt on the floor, offering Faith whatever support they were able to give.

Precious stood up and said, "I'm coming with her to the hospital."

The EMS workers grunted a reply, which Precious surmised meant that they had no objections. Faith was trying to say something to Precious, but either the pain or the blood in her mouth was making it difficult for Faith to talk. Precious leaned down to hear what Faith was saying.

"No more," Faith said, looking directly into Precious' eyes.

"Faith, tell me what you're talking about," Precious replied.

"No more," Faith said, her voice now stronger. "I won't be drinking anymore."

Chapter 26

Opal

Opal woke up with the sun shining directly into her eyes. She had slept soundly last night for the first time in many weeks. It was a dreamless sleep and for that she was thankful. Since her diagnosis she had been plagued by dreams, often disturbing ones. Her dreams could not be considered nightmares, rather they were random, confusing scenes and vignettes from various times in her life. People, both dead and alive, came in and out of her dreams with messages she did not understand. In her dreams, her grandmother would issue vague warnings, her brothers would pass her from one set of arms to another, her mother would rock an empty cradle, and people whom she had long since forgotten would occupy a troubled world with her. Glancing over at the chair next to her, she saw that Jordan was gone.

The clock on the wall informed her that it was seven o'clock. She wondered when he'd left and whether he would come back. She knew that Jordan would not leave her for long and she felt relief and fear at the same time. Relief that her friend, her love, was still in her life and fear that the hurt that accompanied him would occur again. It had taken awhile to acknowledge the hurt. There was a stubborn part of her that had refused to believe that she had let Jordan get so close that he could hurt her. She had always kept him at arm's length and now she knew the reason why, the reason that she had refused to acknowledge that he meant so much to her was now apparent. She had grown up with the fear and admonition that vulnerability was a weakness and with Jordan, she was vulnerable. She just hadn't known it. It took his betrayal to force her to confront her true feelings.

The door opened and Dr. Rusov walked into Opal's hospital room. "I have good news," she said with a wide smile.

"How can you possibly be so cheerful so early in the morning?" asked Opal, returning the doctor's smile.

"It's a beautiful day," Dr. Rusov replied. "The sun is shining in Boston and I'm about to sign your release papers."

Opal sat up in her bed. "Please don't tell me you're joking."

Dr. Rusov walked over and sat on Opal's bed. "I'm crushed that you want to leave us," she said, "but yes, I looked at your charts from last night and I don't see any reason to keep you any longer. We'll start back on the chemo next week."

The doctor examined Opal and then stayed for a few minutes chatting about the upcoming baseball season and the doctor's beloved Red Sox team. Opal was a Yankee fan, but she kept her sentiments about her team to herself while the doctor dreamed about a Red Sox pennant race.

After Dr. Rusov left, Opal called her father with the good news. "Your mother and I will be right over to come get you," her father had said, with a lift in his voice. Her father had probably taken her cancer the hardest of all in the family. He had been used to being the man in charge, head of his household, head of his business, protector of all those within his domain. He had not been able to protect his own daughter from cancer and his frustration had taken a toll on him. Her mother had a hard time coping with Opal's cancer, but there was something in her, some maternal device that would allow her to only go so far in the fear and depression that was engulfing her. A mother has to be strong for her offspring and Opal's mother prided herself on her ability to be the rock that her children leaned on, whether they wanted to or not.

After Opal called her father, she dialed Reva's number, but no one answered. *Where could Reva be,* she wondered. Reva was not an early riser.

There was a knock on the hospital door, and in stepped Nurse Lucien, the Haitian nurse who took care of her on the night shift.

"I thought you'd be gone by now," Opal said, greeting Nurse Lucien, who had spent more time than she should regaling her with stories about the small town she was from, Fort Liberte.

"I heard you were leaving us, so I came to say good-bye," said Nurse Lucien.

Opal sighed, "I'm sure you'll see me again."

Nurse Lucien put her hands on her wide hips. Shaking her head she said, "You must have faith, Opal. As good as medicine is, faith will get you through."

"Faith is hard to come by right now," Opal admitted honestly.

Nurse Lucien said, "I saw a sign in front of a church once, and it made so much sense. The sign said 'Feed your faith and you'll starve your fears.' "

Reva

Reva sat in Precious' dorm room and tried to stop her hands from shaking. Precious had awakened her at five in the morning with news of Everton Rhodes's assault on Faith. Precious, Rory and the man who had rescued Faith, Kevin Davies had spent the night in a Boston hospital, while Faith was first examined by the doctors, and then questioned by the police. Charity and Hope, whom Precious had called, had also come to the hospital.

"She's going to press charges against Everton," said Precious.

Reva pushed her braids out of her face. "Damn right, she's going to press charges."

Precious shook her head. "I warned Faith about that guy. There was just something about him that wasn't right."

Reva felt her temper rise and she struggled to keep it in check. Precious had been through the fire last night. She had been there with Faith in the ambulance and at the hospital. She had stood by her friend as she should, Reva reasoned, but it sounded as if she were blaming Faith for what happened to her.

"Faith didn't deserve what that bastard did," said Reva.

"I know," Precious sighed. "I just wish she had listened to me, that's all. I feel that I should have tried harder to reason with her."

"You didn't cause this and neither did Faith. Faith might have been foolish to go to his room, but she wasn't bargaining for a rape. That wasn't part of the deal."

"Poor Faith," said Precious.

Reva felt her temper break. "Precious, Faith doesn't need your pity! She needs your support!"

Precious put her face in her hands and started to cry.

Reva's anger melted at the sight of Precious' tears. "Don't cry, Precious," she said. "I shouldn't be coming down on you like this . . . I know that you did your best."

"Did I?" Precious asked. "Did I do my best?"

"I know you did," said Reva, giving her a quick hug. "What happened to Faith was not your fault. It was the fault of a psychopath . . . a psychopath who is going to pay for his actions. I'm not certain of much in this life, but I'm damn certain of that."

Precious wiped the tears from her face with her hands. "I wish I could be as strong as you, Reva."

Reva did not answer. Instead, she tried to stop her hands from shaking.

Faith

Faith lay in her bed with her sisters lying on either side of her. They both held her while she dozed off, but sleep was hard to come by. Instead, she would drift off for a few minutes, only to be awakened by a nightmare that in fact was a reality. Scenes from last night kept turning over and over and over in her head, as though they were part of a movie that kept replaying itself. When she opened her eyes she saw Everton. When she closed her eyes, he was there also.

Even now, she saw herself lying on the ground, her clothes torn away from her body. She saw the pity on the faces of the ambulance attendants. She saw the shame on her own face. She remembered the sirens on the ambulance ride. She remembered Precious holding her hand tightly, her face stricken and tear stained. She remembered the examination by the doctor in the emergency room. She had insisted on a woman doing the examination. She could not bear the touch of a man, not then, not now. The doctor had talked to her about many things, including her drinking. "Your blood alcohol level is high," the doctor had said bluntly. "Excessive alcohol impairs judgment," the doctor had said.

She wanted to shut it out. Shut it all out.

Charity's arms held her close. They had not spoken in weeks, except for the cursory greetings they would give each other when they encountered each other walking across campus. The Maberley pride was legendary. The Maberleys were known to keep grudges. Faith's mother had refused to talk to her sister for thirty years for a slight that neither woman ever discussed. It took imminent death to bring the sisters together, and even at the sister's deathbed, her mother had been aloof and cold. Faith recognized, much later, that her mother's distance from her sister was born of hurt, but at the time, Faith could not understand her mother's coldness, her refusal to yield even in the face of death.

Coldhearted was how she had condemned her mother at the time, never realizing that there would come a point when she and her own sisters were similarly estranged. Thank God, it had not taken death to bring them back to one another, but it had taken something terrible.

"Are you hungry," Hope asked softly.

"No," Faith shook her head. Her throat hurt and her head pounded.

"You've got to eat something," Charity said.

"I just want to lie here," said Faith. "I don't want to eat."

Charity sat up, "I'm going to make you some tea . . . something herbal to soothe your nerves."

It was going to take much more than herbal tea to calm her nerves, thought Faith.

"Thank you," Faith said. "Both of you, thank you. Thank you for not giving up on me."

"Shoot," said Charity. "We're family. You can't get rid of us."

Chapter 27

Precious

Precious sat across from Rory in the coffee shop on the Middle-hurst campus. Since the night of the party, they had barely spoken. Precious' attention was focused on Faith. She was not sure where Rory's attention was placed. During their few telephone calls over the past two weeks, he had been distant and preoccupied. Precious had been angry. She knew that her anger was misplaced. Rory was not guilty for the actions of his friend, but there was a small yet insistent and nagging feeling that Rory could have somehow warned her about Everton. They had stayed away from the topic of Everton, except to discuss what was going on with him in vague and very general terms. Precious knew that Boston Union had launched an investigation into his actions and the police were also involved.

Rory had called her early this morning. "We have to talk," he'd said, and she'd agreed. They'd tiptoed around this particular subject long enough. "What are you doing this morning?" Rory had asked.

"I've got a French class at eleven—but we can have breakfast before that."

"I'll meet you at nine."

It was another short conversation without the usual loving terms they had started to call each other. It was as if there was now a chasm between them that neither side wanted to breach. Precious had gotten dressed without her usual sense of joy at the prospect of seeing Rory. She had avoided this conversation for a reason. She knew that the battle lines had been firmly drawn and she suspected that just as she stood behind Faith, Rory had chosen to support Everton.

They'd arranged to meet at the coffee shop on campus, and as Precious would have predicted, Rory was on time. He was sitting at a table in the back and he rose from his seat when she entered the shop. His good manners had always intrigued and secretly pleased her. Other than Roosevelt, Precious had never known a man who would stand up when she walked into a room. He held doors for her, he gave up seats whenever there was a woman standing, whether she was in close proximity or not. She thought as she walked towards him that she was going to miss him. She knew good-bye when she saw it.

She kissed him lightly on the cheek and sat down across from him. Rory sat down and stared out of the window. They let the silence envelop them, as each one struggled with his or her own thoughts. Precious could see that this was not going to be an easy task for either party.

Precious sighed. "Rory, let's not drag this out."

Rory turned and faced her. Nodding his head, he said, "You're right, as always, Precious."

"Am I?" Precious asked, feeling a surge of anger rise at his distant tone. She understood loyalty to friends, but Everton had violated another person, he had violated her friend. She could not understand how Rory could support him.

"Look, I know you're upset. What went down was just . . . unbelievable . . ." Rory began talking.

"Unbelievable!" Precious' voice rose. "Unbelievable?"

"Precious, I've known Everton for four years and I have to tell you, your girl's story doesn't fit the person that I know. I confronted him and he denied Faith's story."

Precious counted to ten three times before she answered. Her anger, which she was certain came from her mother's side of the family, was not something she wanted to give in to, not just yet.

"Are you saying that you think that Faith made this up? You saw her after Everton was finished with her."

"I know that it looks bad . . . Everton said that things got a little rough . . ."

"A little rough!" Precious didn't bother to lower her voice.

Rory took a deep breath and then said, "Precious, I am not the enemy."

"You're sounding like you're in the enemy camp, Rory."

Rory shrugged. "It just doesn't add up. What was she doing in his room if she wasn't interested in getting busy . . . I know things might have gotten out of control with them, but when a girl goes to a guy's apartment late at night, she shouldn't be shocked if a guy tries to sleep with her."

"Getting busy?" Precious asked. "Let's call what Everton does by it's proper name: attempted rape."

"Precious, Everton's career can be ruined through all this . . . I mean, he's not stupid. Why would he try to force himself on anybody? He's got too much to lose. Hell, he was the lead story on ESPN for three nights in a row. What football team is going to touch him now?"

Precious rose from the table. She had heard enough. "So this is about his football career?" she asked.

"No," said Rory. "Precious, you know me better than that! I'm just saying that there are a lot of women who cry rape when things don't exactly go as planned."

"You think that Faith made this up?"

"Look, I don't want to trash your friend . . ." said Rory.

"Too late!" Precious snapped.

"It's just that she was mighty impressed when she met him," Rory continued. "And she went to his room. No one forced her to do that. You wouldn't do that, Precious."

"You're right," Precious replied. "I wouldn't do that. But it's not me we're talking about; we're talking about Faith. Rory, since when does entering a man's room become an invitation for rape?"

"It's not an invitation for rape," said Rory. "I know Everton and I know that he's not capable of raping anyone. Everton can have just about any woman he wants . . . he doesn't have to rape anybody."

"Why don't you tell *him* that," said Precious. "Apparently the point is lost on him."

Rory shook his head again. "I can't get through to you when you're like this."

"Damn right you can't!" Precious snapped.

"Look, I had a long talk with Everton. He swore to me that he didn't do this. If I thought that Everton had raped that girl, I would be the first in line to kick his ass. But I trust Everton's word and if tells me that he didn't try to force himself on her, then his word is good enough for me."

"Well, I guess that's it then," said Precious. "Nothing more to discuss, is there?"

"Precious, where does this situation leave us?" Rory asked.

"Rory, I respect you, but I can't sit here and say that your opinions about what happened to Faith don't matter."

"You *respect* me!" Now it was Rory's turn to shout. "I *love* you, Precious, and this is killing me that I am going to lose the woman I love because of some groupie bullshit."

"Well, you'll get over me," said Precious, "just as I'll get over you."

She knew she was being cruel, but Rory's words stung her. Precious, the ultimate goody-two-shoes, the ultimate good sport, was tired. She was tired of spending her life trying not to hurt people, trying to get along, trying to make people like her. She was tired. She walked out of the coffee shop without looking back.

Opal

Opal took a deep breath as the towers of the Middlehurst quadrangle came into view. She was dreading this journey, but despite her stubborn denials, she had known that this day would come once her diagnosis of cancer had been confirmed. The toll of the chemotherapy treatments, and the disease itself proved to be too much for her body. She could not complete her final semester as she had planned. She had missed too many days of classes, and the effort it took to fight her disease didn't leave her any energy left over for studies. She was withdrawing from Middlehurst.

She had discussed her decision with her family, her friends and the Dean of Students. All were in agreement that she was doing the right thing. Still, for Opal, the withdrawal from school felt too much like a surrender, a giving in to a disease that she had vowed to fight and win. Opal had never run away from a fight and leaving school was like running away.

"You're doing the right thing," said Jordan.

He had volunteered to drive her back to the campus to help her get some of her clothes and a few personal items. Her friends had already packed up most of her room and her family had arranged for a moving van to carry her items back to her parents' home.

"I know," said Opal, "but it still hurts."

Jordan didn't respond and for that Opal was grateful. She didn't want to hear any platitudes designed to make her feel better about her situation.

"How's Faith?" Jordan asked. "Have you talked to her yet?"

Opal shook her head. "She won't take my calls, but Precious says that she's hanging in there, whatever that means."

Jordan turned his car into the main entrance to the campus. "Has she decided what she's going to do about all this?"

"Well, I think it's out of her hands now. The prosecutor is deciding whether to bring assault and attempted rape charges against him." Although Opal got some information from Reva and Precious, Opal got most of her information from the newspapers. The combination of a star football player, attempted rape and college coed seemed to be irresistible to the local news. Faith was not identified in the papers, but the Boston college community was small enough and bad news traveled fast enough that most folks knew who all the parties were in this drama.

"Where's Faith staying now?" Jordan asked. Faith had been hounded by reporters trying to get her side of the story and as a result, she'd had to leave campus.

"She's staying at Dean Hambrick's house." Dean Hambrick lived in nearby Wellesley, another picturesque New England town populated by professors and the Boston elite that still longed for a small, college town atmosphere.

Jordan chuckled. "Not Hambrick the Hammer." Dean Hambrick's tough reputation was legendary at Middlehurst. "I remember how you used to talk about her."

"The Hammer is about as tough as they come, but apparently underneath that hard exterior, beats a very kind heart. She offered her home to Faith for as long as she needs it."

"It's going to be a long, tough road back for Faith. I just hope she'll be able to get past this," said Jordan.

"If anyone will get past this, it'll be Faith," Opal replied. "She is a very strong woman—I just wonder when she'll realize that fact."

"Seems to me that I know another strong woman," said Jordan.

"I wouldn't be too sure about that," said Opal. "If I were so strong, I wouldn't . . ." Opal stopped the words before it was too late.

Jordan finished the sentence for her. "You wouldn't be sitting here in a car with me. That's what you were going to say."

"Yes," said Opal, not bothering to lie.

"When are you going to forgive me, Opal?" he asked. "What do I have to do to show you how sorry I am? Do you want me to admit that I made a mistake. I made a mistake. A huge mistake. I let you down. I let your family down. I let myself down. If I could go back and change that moment, I would. But, I can't. All I can say is that I'm sorry. All I can do is show you that I'll never let you down again. Never."

"I understand that you're sorry," said Opal. "So am I, Jordan. I'm sorry, too."

Jordan parked the car in the circular driveway in front of her dormitory. Turning off the engine, he turned to Opal and said, "Tell me what I can do to earn your forgiveness. Anything. Just, please, tell me, Opal. Tell me what I need to do."

His plea touched a place inside her that she had thought was closed to him. She knew in her heart that he was sorry. She knew that every day he tasted the bitter taste of regret for his actions. She also knew that she needed to forgive him for her own sake as well as his. The refusal to forgive only kept her chained to her bitterness.

"I wish I knew the answer to your questions," Opal said. "I want to forgive you. I don't want to hold anything hard in my heart anymore. This whole forgiveness thing . . . this concept of letting go of anger when someone has wronged you . . . I don't understand it. I never have. The best I can do is try to figure out what it means. I'm willing to do that, Jordan. I just don't know that even if I find out what forgiveness means . . . even after that, whether I'll be able to truly forgive you for hurting me. I'm sorry, but it's the best that I can do."

Jordan reached over and held her hand for a moment. Then, he let go. "I understand, Opal. I don't like it, but I understand it. I have only myself to blame, and I've got to live with that."

Opal did not reply.

Faith

Dean Hambrick's cheerful yellow colonial was the haven that Faith needed. In direct contrast with her small, dark office, Dean Hambrick's home was filled with sounds of laughter from the Dean's three good-natured children. Ever present classical music piped through the speaker system in the house. Smells of something delicious always seemed to be cooking in the kitchen, no matter what time of day. There were moments, albeit fleeting, that Faith did not think about Everton Rhodes.

The horror of that Saturday evening was undiminished. If anything, the events seemed magnified as time went on. Often, she would push the memories quickly from her head before they would have a chance to settle in, punishing her over and over again for her stupidity. She blamed herself. She knew that she did not cause Everton to become a beast, but she had put herself in a position where she could not protect herself and she would have to live with the consequences of her actions for the rest of her life.

Dean Hambrick had taken her to a therapist and that had provided a release. Faith had tried to talk about what happened to her with her friends and with her sisters—but her shame, her regret and her pain at allowing Everton to hurt her, prevented her from engaging in any real discussion with them. Her parents had come to school and had spent a few days with her, but while their unshakeable support of her, which included several trips to the District Attorney's Office, helped, she needed more than any of her family or friends were capable of giving. The encouragement of the therapist, a short, balding man with a goatee, who bore an uncanny resemblance to W.E.B. DuBois, to open up, to share her feelings, to cry, to scream, to vent, helped her sort through the conflicting emotions that often threatened to strangle her whenever her thoughts would run in the direction of Everton Rhodes.

"You've got company," said Dean Hambrick's nanny, Syleena. A short, Hispanic woman with a flawless olive complexion, curly dark hair, and eyes surrounded by laugh lines, Syleena had spent many hours with Faith and the Hambrick children.

Faith was sitting in her favorite room in the Hambrick household, the library. It was a small room, crammed with books—on the bookshelves, the floor and the desk pushed in the corner of the room. The room was dominated by an oversize sofa with a faded floral print. French doors opened to a small patio which overlooked Dean Hambrick's backyard.

"Who is it?" Faith asked, hoping it wasn't yet another stubborn reporter who didn't understand the meaning of the relatively simple term: "No interviews."

"His name is Kevin Davies. He said that Precious told him where he could find you. If you'd rather not talk to him . . ."

"No, no," Faith said quickly. "Please tell him to come in."

She had wanted to talk to him, to thank him for all that he had done. If he hadn't come to Everton's room, a bad situation would have turned out even worse. At first, she'd tried to contact him at his school, but once she realized that she had become a minor celebrity as a result of Everton's actions, she had gone into hiding.

"Are you sure?" Syleena asked.

Faith nodded her head, "Absolutely."

Syleena disappeared with a small smile, then in a few moments reappeared at the open door to the library with Kevin Davies standing directly behind her.

"Thanks, Syleena," Faith said, as Kevin walked into the library and faced her. Syleena lingered in the doorway for a moment, like a protective lioness watching over one of her cubs, then she turned and walked back in the direction of the voices of the Hambrick children.

Kevin sighed. "Listen, I don't want to bother you. I just wanted to see for myself how you're doing."

"Have a seat," said Faith. "Please."

Kevin sat on the couch and Faith sat on a chair by the French doors.

"I'm glad you came," said Faith, "I've wanted to thank you for everything you did that night."

"I wish I could have done more," said Kevin. "I've already given my statement to the school, and to the police. I told the police that I'll be a witness if the D.A. needs me."

Faith felt tears spring to her eyes. The kindness of a stranger was her undoing. "Thank you," she said again.

"I know this is a stupid question, but how are you, really?" asked Kevin.

"Terrible," Faith replied, without any hesitation. "Terrible. I keep running through what happened over and over and over again. I guess I'm hoping for a different outcome each time I replay the scene. The thing is the end result is always the same."

"Are you seeing anyone?" Kevin asked. "Like a therapist?"

"Yes," replied Faith, tasting the salt from her tears on her upper lip. "That helps a little bit. But I've got so much more to do to get my life back together. It's been off track for a while now. I guess I always felt like a train wreck waiting to happen and then when I met Everton . . . well, you know the rest."

"It sounds as if you're taking the right steps to get things back together," Kevin commented. "You're seeing a therapist. That's a good start."

"Yeah, but I have a long way to go," said Faith. "All my life, I've gotten away with stuff. I was this smart kid, so I could get away with not studying. I was always able to talk my way out of trouble, whether at school, or at home. I got away with driving while I was drunk, and what did I do? I kept on drinking. So, I just kept pushing, and pushing, until finally something happened. I ran into a Mack truck named Everton Rhodes."

"Is that how you see Everton?" asked Kevin. "Like he's some kind of immovable, invincible object?"

"Come on," said Faith. "You watch the news. The papers are portraying me like some gold digging, loose groupie. Everton comes off like a wronged man."

"I don't read that crap," said Kevin. "And neither should you."

"It's hard to ignore it," said Faith. "Especially when it's about you. I think Boston Union is more concerned about losing their star quarterback than addressing what Everton did to me."

"I wish I could disagree with you, but you're right on all counts. Football is king at Boston Union, and you know how people are about their false gods. They want to keep worshipping them, no matter how blatant their flaws are."

"I didn't go to the room because he was a football player," said Faith. Suddenly it seemed important to her that she should explain her reasons for being with Everton that night. She had read so many lies about her intentions, that she was starting to doubt herself.

"I didn't go to the room because I wanted to have sex with him," Faith continued. "I went to his room because I wanted to have a drink," said Faith, "and I thought that I could drink there without the prying eyes of my girlfriend. No one will believe me. They'll all think that I was asking for it, and I ought to know better, and the bottom line is that Everton is going to be this rich, first round draft football player and he won't be held accountable for his actions. He will get away with it."

"Are you still drinking, Faith?" Kevin asked.

"I haven't had a drink in two weeks, " Faith replied. "But I know that I need to stop drinking permanently, and I haven't yet figured out how to do that."

"Are you doing anything around six-thirty tonight?" Kevin asked. "How about going to an Alcoholics Anonymous meeting with me? My church hosts these meetings every Tuesday and Thursday evening."

Faith did not reply right away. She was grateful for Kevin's help that night, but she didn't know him. After her last experience with a stranger, she was not about to get into a car with anyone, man or woman, she did not know.

"You want to stop drinking, don't you?" Kevin asked.

"Yes," Faith nodded her head.

"Well, here's your chance, Faith," said Kevin. "Are you going to go for it? Or are you going to wait for the 'right time.' "

This time, Faith did not hesitate. She felt, for the first time in a long time, that someone had thrown her a lifeline to keep her from drowning, and she was going to grab hold of the rope. And she was not going to let go.

"Where is your church?" Faith asked.

"It's at 1103 Beacon Street, near the intersection of Marbury. The church is called St. Mark's Episcopalian Church. The meeting is going to be in the church basement."

"I'll meet you there," said Faith.

"Are you sure?" Kevin Davies asked her.

"I'm sure," Faith replied.

"The meeting begins at six-thirty," said Kevin, getting up from his seat.

"I'll be there," said Faith. "Count on it."

Reva

Reva stared at Opal as if she had seen an apparition. It was no exaggeration to say that Opal was a shadow of her former self. Already slim, Opal's weight loss made her look like a victim of starvation. Her pale skin seemed to stretch over her bones—just barely covering them. Her bald head was covered with a bright red scarf, which only highlighted her pale skin. Opal smiled at Reva. "I look like hell don't I?" she asked.

Reva stood in Opal's dormitory room, which was now filled with boxes. She had spent the majority of the last two days with Precious placing Opal's belongings in boxes.

"You look great to me," Reva replied. It was the truth. Opal was still beautiful, although it took Reva a while to get adjusted to this new version of her friend.

"And to me," said Jordan.

Reva surveyed him with cool eyes. Apparently Opal had decided to give her cheating boyfriend another chance. If so, that was Opal's business, but Reva didn't have to welcome him back with open arms. "Hello, Jordan."

"Hi, Reva," Jordan replied. His eyes told her that he understood her animosity. If he were in her shoes, he would probably feel the same way. Reva was a loyal friend and her last comments to him made it clear that she did not appreciate the way he had treated her friend.

Reva turned to Opal. "Most of your stuff is packed. Precious and I have a few more things to put in the boxes, but that should be done by the end of the day. When are the movers coming?"

"Tomorrow," Opal replied.

"Well, we're on target then," said Reva. "I put away the stuff you asked for in the blue duffel bag in the corner."

"Thanks," said Opal, walking slowly over to her bed. She looked tired, and worse, the fight that had always been in Opal's eyes was now absent. "Where's Precious?"

"In the library studying for a test. She'll be here in about an hour."

Jordan cleared his throat. "Look, I've got some errands to run. You guys probably have a lot you want to discuss, so . . ."

"Can you come back later on this afternoon?" asked Opal. "About five o'clock?"

"I'll be here," said Jordan. "I'll meet you out front."

"Thanks," Opal replied. Reva could see that there was an awkwardness between them. If they were back together, it was clear that there were still unresolved issues between them.

Jordan kissed Opal on the cheek, nodded at Reva, and then left the room, closing the door softly behind him.

Reva got to the point quickly. "What's going on between you two? Are you guys back together?"

Opal sighed. "No, we're not together."

"So what's going on?"

"I don't know. He showed up at a time when I needed a friend."

"You already have friends," Reva replied. "We're your friends."

Opal remained silent. Her eyes refused to meet Reva's face.

"So, it's more than friendship, then?" Reva asked.

"Yes," Opal looked miserable.

"Opal, I don't want to see you get hurt again," said Reva. "He's already hurt you once. Why would you give him another chance to hurt you again?"

"I don't know if I'll be here in six months," Opal said, now looking directly at Reva. "I don't know if I'll be here in six weeks. As my oncologist always tells me, in life there are no guarantees. Maybe Jordan will hurt me again. Maybe he won't. Right now, I have other more pressing priorities and if he wants to be here in a time when I'm scared, then I'm going to let him."

"I'm sorry."

Opal smiled. "Don't be. I'm not offended. You shouldn't be either. I know you love me and you want the best for me and I accept that."

Reva walked over to Opal's bed and sat next to her. "You are too damn good to me."

"Don't I know it," Opal replied with a grin.

Chapter 28

Precious

Precious walked down the stairs of Harrison Library and almost ran into Mrs. Hamlett, Rory's aunt. She had avoided the weekly teas since her breakup with Rory. She had not wanted to give any explanations to Mrs. Hamlett. She was not ready to answer any questions. The breakup hurt too much and Precious suspected that this hurt was going to hang around for a while.

"Precious Averyheart!" Mrs. Hamlett let out a yell. "I have been looking for you!"

"Hi, Mrs. H," Precious tried to muster up a smile without much success.

"Listen, where are you going?" Mrs. Hamlett asked.

"Well, I was on my way to meet my friends . . ." Precious began.

"That can wait!" said Mrs. Hamlett, taking her by the arm. "I need to talk to you."

"I don't mean to be rude, Mrs. H, but I'm actually busy right now . . ."

"Nonsense!" Mrs. Hamlett declared. "My car is parked just behind the library. I'll give you a ride to wherever it is you need to go."

There was no use arguing with Mrs. Hamlett. Precious had seen that stubborn look before on her father's face. It was time to raise the white flag of surrender. She walked silently with Mrs. Hamlett to the library parking lot and got into her 1968 sky blue Mercedes Benz. Mrs. Hamlett slid into the driver's seat with more agility than her years merited.

Turning to Precious she said, "Now what is going on with you and my nephew? I asked him about you the other day and he mumbled something about having differences. I asked him what he meant by that vague phrase and he wouldn't give me any information other than to say that you had broken up with him. Now, I don't mean to pry . . . well hell, I am prying but I love you both, what is going on? You both look positively miserable."

Precious looked down at her hands. She didn't want to hurt Mrs. Hamlett's feelings. She knew that Mrs. H had high hopes for her and Rory. There was a part of her that felt that she had somehow let Mrs. H down. "Rory's right," Precious replied. "We are different people."

"Well, of course you are, my dear. That's what makes the world go round for heaven's sake. My husband was as different from me as right was from rain . . . whatever that means, but we loved each other. Precious, Rory loves you. Surely, you both can work out these differences, whatever they may be."

Precious shook her head. Praying that the tears that were welling up in her eyes would not roll down her cheek and betray her misery, she answered, "Some differences are insurmountable."

"Is it another woman?" Mrs. Hamlett asked. "Lord knows that these young women today don't respect the fact that a man is taken. Some of those women take it as a personal challenge to take your man away from you."

"It's not another woman," said Precious.

Mrs. Hamlett was silent for a moment, then she said, with a dramatic sigh "Another man, perhaps? These things have been known to happen. I mean, I didn't think that Rory . . . well, you know what I mean."

Precious smiled at Mrs. Hamlett. "It's not another man, not the way you're thinking. Rory has a friend who hurt a good friend of mine. He doesn't understand my loyalty to my friend."

"Is this that Everton Rhodes mess?"

Precious nodded her head.

"Your friend is the young woman who is accusing Everton of assaulting her?"

"Yes," Precious replied.

"I take it that Rory doesn't believe your friend?"

"I'm not sure," said Precious. "He almost seems to think that somehow my friend deserved what Everton did. Everton Rhodes tried to rape my friend. I don't know how Rory could take his side."

"You believe your friend, don't you?" Mrs. Hamlett asked.

"Yes."

"And what is that belief based on?"

"It's based on four years of friendship. It's based on knowing the kind of person she is."

Mrs. Hamlett stared into Precious' eyes. "Could Rory's difficulty in seeing Everton as he really is be based on the same things?"

"Everton Rhodes is a snake. I don't understand how Rory can't see that."

Mrs. Hamlett sighed, "Personally, I have never been fond of Everton myself. But, he is one of Rory's closest friends. Rory thinks the world of him."

"Apparently so," Precious replied.

"Well, this is a tough dilemma, Precious," said Mrs. Hamlett. "I see both of your points of view. If only it were as simple as another woman—I could help you with that. But, I'm afraid that I'm at a loss."

Precious opened the door. "I hope you don't take offense, Mrs. H, but I think I'll walk back to the dorm."

"Of course, dear child," Mrs. Hamlett reached over and patted Precious' hand. "Just know that whatever you two decide, I still love you, Precious."

"Thank you," Precious replied, fighting back the urge to cry.

Faith

Faith turned on the jazz music station in her car. She needed to calm down. Usually when she felt like this she would reach for a drink, but those days were over. She'd had enough. Finally. She couldn't lie to herself, she thought about having a drink, but then Everton's face would stop her. Dean Hambrick's house had been a haven for her—a warm cocoon, filled with children's laughter, good food, and space when she needed it. She had been protected, but she knew that she couldn't live that life forever. It was time to come back to the real world, whatever that was. Kevin's invitation to Alcoholics Anonymous was an invitation to start over again.

She had thought about Kevin Davies a lot. When Everton's face would haunt her, Kevin's face would come into view. She remembered how she'd blown him off at the party and she felt embarrassed and ashamed. After her friend Janae's rebuff, she had stayed away from people who did not look like her. But the tables had turned in a direction that she could never have anticipated. A black man had tried to rape her and a white man had come to her aid. She had never understood Reva's friendship with Bonnie. Bonnie came from a different race, a different culture and a different social background. They had nothing in common, yet they loved each other. She still didn't understand it. Race relations were not something that she gave much thought to. She was content with each group staying in their own comfort zone. Thank God Kevin had stepped out of his comfort zone and come to her aid. If he hadn't come to help her, Everton would have raped her. *Don't think about it, girl,* she warned herself. *Don't think about it.*

She had gotten a telephone call from the District Attorney's Office after Kevin had left. The prosecutor was still interviewing potential witnesses. She called to find out how Faith was holding up. Her kindness touched Faith, just as Kevin's kindness had done the same. During the last few weeks, she had seen cruelty and she had seen kindness. She had read articles where male reporters pondered the prevalence of groupies, casual sex and false accusations of rape that *plagued* athletes. She had seen women on television say with great authority, *"any woman that goes to a man's apartment is asking for whatever it is she gets."* Or, as another female reporter on a popular sports radio talk show asked, *"who goes on a midnight run to some guy's place and then is surprised that the guy makes a move?"* Everton's attorney had been in the news, working overtime, declaring his client's innocence and promising information on "certain aspects" of the accusers background that would shed light on the accuser's "spurious allegations."

Dean Hambrick had tried to stop her from listening to the radio and television. "Don't pay attention to that mess." But Faith had paid attention. She wanted to hear every terrible thing that was being said about her. It was as if she were trying to punish herself for being so stupid.

The nastiness of folks who didn't even know her surprised her and hurt her. But there were also voices, not as strong or as prevalent as the opposition, as she called the reporters and the pundits who disparaged her—there were other voices that declared, "rape is rape" and "no means no" even if someone willingly goes to a man's apartment—even if that man is an athlete, politician, mailman, etc.

She turned her car off the exit for Beacon street and made a left in the direction of Kevin's church. She had passed that church many times and admired its architecture, never thinking that one day she would be going inside that same church to save her life. As dramatic as it sounded, she was going to save her life. She was going to stop drinking. No casual drinks. No dabbling. This was it. Everton was her wake up call and as Hope and Charity had both cautioned her, it was time to heed that call.

Other folks had invited her to Alcoholics Anonymous and other groups designed to help alcoholics, but it had taken a stranger to finally get through. The irony of that fact was not lost on Faith, although in light of her present circumstances, it was high time that she accepted her own personal truth. She was an alcoholic and she needed to get help before her life spun further out of control.

As she drove towards St. Marks she saw a solitary figure standing outside. Kevin Davies was waiting for her. Parking her car across the street from the church, she got out of her car and felt something in the pit of her stomach. She was nervous. She knew that once she walked through those doors, she would not be the same. She might not be a better person, or a worse person, but she knew that she would be a different person.

She walked across the street towards Kevin, who greeted her with a wide smile.

Faith found herself smiling back. Any feeling of awkwardness disappeared with Kevin's welcoming smile.

"I bet you thought I wouldn't show up," said Faith.

"The thought had crossed my mind," he responded. "We can use the side door to get in."

She followed Kevin through an open red door, down a brightly lit corridor. There was a room at the end of the corridor where Kevin stopped. "Are you ready to go in?" Kevin asked.

"Yes," said Faith, although the fear that she thought she would feel had now made its appearance. She thought about what it would feel like to stand up in front of a group of strangers, confessing to them what she had only just acknowledged to herself, that she was an alcoholic.

"How did you know about this group?" Faith asked, stalling for time.

"My mother is a recovering alcoholic," Kevin replied. "Fourteen years. She runs the group. Ready to go in?"

Recovering alcoholic. The next step for her. Recovering alcoholic. Recovering life. Recovering. The word gave her hope.

"I'm ready," said Faith, and this time, she meant it.

Chapter 29

Opal looked around the dining room table at her parents' house and felt the tears well in her eyes. In the center of the table, her father had placed a carrot cake, which was resplendent with twenty-two candles. Apart from the dimmed lights from the dining room chandelier, the light from her cake provided the only illumination in the room. Birthdays used to be a time of dread for her, a sign that she was getting older, that youth was slipping away and responsibility was approaching. This birthday, however, was different. She had longed for this birthday, for confirmation that her life had indeed continued.

A solitary tear rolled down her cheek. She had heard the expression, "tears of joy," but she had not understood it until tonight, as she stared at the people around the table, people who had loved and supported her, unconditionally, even when she was at her lowest point, the times when she was sick from the chemotherapy and she would wonder what kind of God had punished her. She had started going to church regularly and that was no surprise. Folks often got close to God when death became a reality, but that was not Opal's reason for going. She went to church to find a way to make peace with a God with whom she was angry. She did not want to die angry.

She looked across the table at Max and his mother, whom she'd invited in addition to Jordan, her girlfriends, her brothers and her parents. Max's condition was deteriorating. His frail body had taken a beating and he could no longer travel without a portable oxygen tank. From time to time he covered his nose and mouth with the oxygen mask. Still, his brown eyes were bright and Opal saw that Max had not given up. His courage made her want to be that strong, but she was convinced that Max was born that way, whereas she was not naturally inclined to such bravery.

There was a time, before cancer, when she had regarded tears as a sure and certain sign of weakness. Since her diagnosis she had learned how to cry. She cried often and she had learned not to be ashamed of the tears that now ran freely down her face. She had often wondered whether she would live to see her twenty-second birthday. Although her doctors had been encouraged by the way in which her cancer was responding to treatment, there was always a part of her that would not take for granted any of the very ordinary milestones in her life— a birthday, Easter Sunday, her next appointment with her oncologist, her weekly dry cleaning run—she would not take another day for granted, no matter how many years God bestowed on her.

"Blow out the candles!" Opal's mother ordered with a smile on her face.

"Yeah, Opal, before it explodes!" Faith called out.

Opal laughed at her crazy friend and Faith laughed in return. It was good to hear Faith's laughter. There was a time, weeks ago, after the incident as everyone now referred to Everton's assault, that Opal had wondered if laughter would ever come back to Faith again.

Faith had spent a month at Dean Hambrick's home, and then had come back to the campus to finish her studies. She was determined to graduate, and she was focused in a way she had not been for the past three years—the way she was before the drinking began. Opal knew that things were still difficult for Faith, despite her smiles. The initial media frenzy had waned and she was no longer the biggest story in Boston, but there was still plenty of unwanted media attention. The school had gone to the unprecedented measure of having a campus police officer escort her to her classes, after a reporter had approached her on campus. Opal was not sure whether she could withstand such scrutiny, but Faith was pushing ahead. She attended Alcoholics Anonymous meetings twice a week, and she was developing a friendship with Kevin Davies, who accompanied her to all her AA meetings. Faith had denied that anything more than friendship was occurring with Kevin, and Opal suspected that after everything Faith had been through, romance was the last thing on her mind.

"Opal, please blow out the candles!" Jordan's voice jolted her out of her thoughts of Faith. This was the first time that he'd had to face her parents and her brothers. Although her family knew that Jordan was now a part of her life, they had kept their comments to themselves if they had any misgivings. It had been uncomfortable, Jordan arriving at the door with two sets of pale yellow roses, one set for her mother and one set for Opal, but Opal's father had broken the ice with a strong handshake and a discussion about the latest business school theories. Her family loved her and if she wanted Jordan in her life, they would accept it, whether or not they had any misgivings.

"Make a wish!" Precious sang.

Opal closed her eyes, but instead of making a wish, she offered a silent prayer for Max and she also offered her thanks to the Creator. She had cancer, but she still had life, and she still had love. She was a lucky woman and she hoped that she would not make the mistake of ever forgetting that fact. If the little boy sitting across the table could smile, after everything he'd been through, she could smile also, in spite of her cancer.

She blew out all of her candles on three tries.

"That's what you get for being so old!" said Reva. "Too many candles to blow out!"

Opal laughed. "Your time is coming, my sister. You're not that far behind me."

After the cake had been eaten and the dishes cleared, the party migrated to the living room, where sparkling apple cider and cookies were the after dinner treats. Max and his mother left despite his assurances that he was feeling a little better. He'd had a rough time the night before and his mother had almost kept him away from the party, but his entreaties had worn her down.

"Thanks for coming," Opal said, after she had walked the pair to the door.

"Thanks for having me," said Max. "By the way, the bum seems to be a pretty decent guy. Maybe he learned from his mistakes."

"I refuse to talk about my love life with a twelve-year-old," Opal replied with a smile. She watched them walk together to their car parked at the curb. She did not leave the doorway until their car pulled away.

Opal went back into the living room. Her father had put Marvin Gaye on the stereo and Opal watched as her parents did a spirited dance to "I Heard It Through the Grapevine." They looked like two teenagers. Opal wondered what it would be like to have someone love her the way her father loved her mother.

"Excuse me, ma'am, but may I have this dance?"

Jordan held out his hand and Opal clasped it. Marvin was now singing "Distant Lover," a smooth, haunting song about a love gone wrong. Opal stood up and moved easily in his arms. She was aware that several pairs of curious, and some disapproving, eyes were fixed on them, but she didn't care. Jordan's arms felt like coming into a warm, safe place.

"Opal, you're beautiful," said Jordan.

Opal smiled in response to the compliment, but she knew that Jordan was looking at her through biased eyes. She had moved past thin into the gaunt category, and she was bald. Tonight, in deference to the party, she had covered her head with a multi-colored African head wrap inspired by Erykah Badu, but the head wrap had been uncomfortable, and she had taken it off between dinner and dessert. Her size two black dress hung about her body like a sack. Her good looks were a distant memory.

"I look like someone who's fighting cancer," said Opal.

"You look beautiful to me," Jordan replied.

The music on the stereo switched from Marvin Gaye, to the heavy thumping bass of Funkadelic's "Knee Deep," one of her favorites. Opal pulled away from his arms, and threw her arms in the air.

"Ooooh, that's my jam!" Opal spun around and started shimmying to Funkadelic. Her brothers joined her in a circle, then her friends started dancing too.

Opal sang along with Funkadelic. Several months ago she'd thought she'd been handed a death sentence. Now, she knew differently. She'd been handed the chance to truly live.

Chapter 30

Reva

R eva sat on the park bench and watched the waning sunlight form brightly colored diamonds on the Charles River. She had always loved this place and she'd come here often to watch the crew boats glide seemingly effortlessly down the Charles. Beside her, Simon sat holding her hand and gazing out at the scene in front of them. Reva watched the joggers as they ran by, mothers with children happy to be able to play outside, and lovers strolling by—all taking advantage of the warmer weather. She watched a man dressed like Abraham Lincoln juggle brightly colored balls. Spring had come to Boston and not a moment too soon.

"I'll be hearing from the medical schools soon," said Reva. Medical school had now become a reality to her. As a child, that had been her dream—to become a doctor. At first, she hadn't been sure if it had been her mother's dream or her own. Sugar had never gotten over not becoming a doctor. She still watched every medical drama on television with wistful eyes. Reva used to think that her father was the lost love of her mother's life, but she'd come to realize that Sugar's decision not to attend medical school when she became pregnant with Reva was her greatest regret. Reva knew that her mother's love of medicine had influenced her own career decision, as well as her guilt for being the cause of her mother having to give up that dream—but somewhere along the line, Reva had fallen in love with medicine.

"We're going to have to celebrate," Simon said, with a sly smile.
Reva thought about the last celebration they had and grinned at

him. Turning to face him, she asked, "And how do you plan to celebrate this time?"

"I'm sure that we'll think of something," Simon replied, and they
both laughed.

Simon had become an important part of her life. She was in love
with him. Simon had made it easy for her. He cherished her, which
for Reva had been a new experience. She knew that she was dear to
him. He was proud of her and would openly brag about his girlfriend
to all who would listen. They would talk to each other—hours and
hours of conversations about anything, from music to world affairs to
her girlfriends' problems. All the other men she'd been with had tried
to change her into their vision of what a perfect girlfriend should be.
Her men had all fallen into the category of "I'll love you if . . ."—"I'll
love you if you lose weight," "I'll love you if you sleep with me," "I'll
love you if you do this, that or the other for me." Simon loved her just
as she was. He was patient with her. He was kind to her. He laughed
with her.

"What if I don't get into school in Boston?" Reva asked.

"Then you'll get into school somewhere else—but I have a feeling
that you'll get in anywhere you want to go," said Simon.

Reva wrapped her arms around his shoulders and whispered in his
ear, "You're saying this because you love me."

"I do love you," said Simon. "But I also know how smart you are,
and how compassionate you are—two necessary ingredients for becoming a doctor, in my opinion, and I'm sure those qualities will
open any door to any medical school that you want to attend. Believe
me, those schools will be lucky to have you."

"Simon, if I don't get into a school here in Boston, I'm still going to
go to whatever school will have me. I might end up in California, or
Atlanta, or D.C.—what will happen to us?"

"That," said Simon, "depends entirely on you. If you want me to wait
here in Boston—that's fine. But if you want us to be in the same city, we'll
work it out. Boston is not my home. It's where I work. I can find another
position in another police department. I can't find another you."

Reva untangled herself from his arms, then she asked, before she
lost her nerve, "Simon Jon Bennett, will you marry me?"

Simon threw back his head and let out a whoop. Then he grinned,
"I thought you'd never ask me!"

Faith

The prosecutor's words had frightened her. "We're going to indict
Everton Rhodes for attempted rape."

This was what Faith wanted. This, for her, represented justice. Still, she was afraid. There was going to be a trial, and she knew that not only would Everton be on trial, but she would be as well. That was the reality. The interest generated by this case would flare up again—visions of reporters shoving microphones in her face, her personal life, her drinking—all of it would come out. And the end result might still be acquittal.

She'd thanked the prosecutor and for the first time in months, she'd wanted to have a drink. Badly. After hanging up the telephone, she'd gotten out of her dormitory room quickly. The walls were closing in on her and she needed to breathe. The therapist had warned her that she was still an alcoholic—she would be fighting the addiction for the rest of her life—but the past few months, she had not craved alcohol. No matter how tough things had gotten, and they had gotten tough, her determination not to put herself in a vulnerable position again had driven away any desire to drink. But the prosecutor's decision to indict Everton had brought back thoughts she had struggled with and had thought she'd buried—thoughts of what Everton had done to her, thoughts of having her business splashed over the networks, thoughts of the shame this would bring to her family—all of this pushed her to drive her car to Peabody's Bar.

Faith sat in the bar's parking lot, her hands gripping the steering wheel. She prayed. She cried. She thought of everyone she would hurt, including herself. She lost track of the time she sat in her car, but by the time she decided to drive away from the bar, to drive away from putting herself back on the road to self-destruction, night had fallen.

She drove towards Boston. She drove towards Kevin. He had moved from the frat house and was now living in a studio apartment in Beacon Hill. She had come to lean on his friendship more and more. They spoke on the telephone every day and saw each other several times a week. She'd opened up with Kevin in a way she'd never done with anyone else. She told him about her one night stands and her drinking binges. She told him about passing out in a hotel bar after drinking too much. She told him about her own father's drinking. She told him everything with the certainty that he would not judge her. He never did.

Their cultural differences just didn't seem all that different anymore. He was her friend. It didn't matter what color he was. He was her friend. There were times when she would walk down the street with Kevin and face hostile stares from people. Boston, like many cities in America, was still very racially divided. Faith didn't care. Kevin was her friend, and if her friendship offended anyone's sensibilities, then that was just life. Kevin, for his part, seemed oblivious to any hostility directed their way. His hippie upbringing—he had lived on a commune in New Mexico for the first ten years of his life—his love of learning about other cultures, his struggle with his mother's alcoholism had taught him not to waste time on things that were unimportant, and for Kevin, disapproval of their friendship was unimportant.

Faith pulled her car into a parking space in front of Kevin's apartment building. Looking up to his third floor apartment, she saw that the light was on. Thank God. She got out of the car and walked quickly towards the front door. The doorman, a recent émigré from Ireland, recognized her.

"Good evening to you, Miss Faith," he said, with his thick Irish brogue.

"Good evening, Seamus," Faith replied.

"Go right on up," said Seamus.

Faith took the stairs and soon found herself in front of Kevin's front door. She rang the doorbell and Kevin opened the door as if he were expecting her.

"I'm sorry that I didn't call you," the words tumbled out of her mouth. "I'm sorry . . ."

"Come in," said Kevin, opening the door wider to let her pass. "I'm glad you're here."

Faith walked past him and sat down on the couch. His television was on. Kevin walked over and turned off the television. Then, he sat down beside her on the couch.

"The prosecutor is going to indict Everton," said Faith.

Kevin nodded his head, "I know. I saw it on tonight's news."

The circus had started.

"I went to Peabody's Bar today," said Faith.

Kevin nodded his head again, but his placid expression did not change. His blue eyes stared directly at her. "Did you have a drink?"

"No," said Faith. "But I wanted to."

"Are you O.K.?" Kevin asked.

Faith shook her head. "No. I'm afraid."

"What are you afraid of?"

"I'm afraid of what this trial is going to do to me. I'm afraid that it's going to drive me back to a place I don't belong. I'm afraid that it's going to make me start drinking again."

"When my dad died it was really tough," said Kevin. "Losing him was tough, but thinking about whether his death would make my mom start drinking again—that was tough, too. There were times that I know she wanted something to drink—anything to stop the pain."

"Did she slip?" Faith asked.

"Not that I know of," Kevin replied. "She told me that she was tempted to drink, many times . . . but she realized that after the drink was finished, my dad would still be gone. Faith, I can't make you stop drinking. Only you can do that—but I just want you to remember, after that drink is finished, you're still going to have to deal with your demons. Drinking doesn't make them go away."

Chapter 31

Opal

The telephone rang at six o'clock in the morning. Opal reached out and grabbed the receiver. "Hello," she answered, still in that place between sleep and consciousness.

It was Max's mother. "Opal, Max is in the hospital. He's . . . he's not doing too good . . . could you come?"

Max's mother's voice started to crack.

"I'll be there in half an hour," Opal said, now fully awake. She had been both expecting and dreading this call. Max had gone downhill at an alarmingly fast rate from the time of her birthday. She'd spoken to him every day since then, and she'd visit him at least three times a week. Sometimes, they would sit silently in his bedroom watching television, usually cartoons. Other times, she would read to him from his favorite Spiderman comic books, or they would have long discussions—discussions about death, cancer, the father he never met and whom even now refused to see him. Max was fully aware that he was going to die, but he was not afraid. She was twenty-two and the thought of dying at this age struck her with fear, yet Max seemed almost philosophical about it. "We're all going to die at some point, Opal," he had explained, as if he were the adult and she were the child. "I just know that my time will be a little sooner. I wouldn't have minded living a little bit longer, but I don't have a say in that. The only thing that's hard is leaving my mom alone. She doesn't have anybody. She's not that close to her family, and after she left my father he just cut us both off. She doesn't have too many friends either."

Opal had wondered what she would have done without her girl-friends. They literally carried her through this fight, this process. She remembered the countless times Precious would read the Bible to her and the times that Faith would come and pick her up after chemo-therapy, cracking jokes that were often inappropriate. She remem-bered Reva coming to rescue her when she first found out that she had cancer. Her family had been supportive, but she couldn't be as open with her family as she was with her girlfriends. She was always afraid of hurting her family—the fear that she was going to die was a clear and present foe in their lives. But her friends, despite their fears and their weaknesses, they had been there to lift her up every time she fell down.

"Would you do me a favor?" Max had asked Opal two weeks ago.

"Absolutely," Opal replied without hesitation.

"Would you look out for my mother when I'm gone? Would you be her friend?"

"Yes," said Opal.

"Please God, don't let him die," Opal prayed as she hurriedly got dressed. She'd awakened her father who quickly said that he would drive her to the hospital. Her mother also got dressed. "I'll go with you, too, Opal."

"Please God, don't let him die. Not yet."

Looking back, Opal forgot any specific details about the drive to the hospital, except that her father drove very fast and her mother sat in the back seat with her holding her hand. Her parents had walked with her to the Intensive Care Unit and then left, planting a kiss on her cheek.

"We'll be in the waiting room . . ." her father's voice faltered.

Opal nodded her head. She knew how difficult this must be for her parents. She knew that they loved Max and she knew that they were undoubtedly wondering if they would ever be in the same position as Max's mother.

"Maybe you guys should go home," Opal said. "There's really noth-ing you can do here."

Opal's mother interrupted her. "Our place is with our daughter," she said. "We'll be in the waiting room.

Opal kissed her parents and silently thanked God for them. She was going to need their strength and their love to get her through what she knew was coming. Taking a deep breath, she turned and walked through the open doors of the room the head nurse had indi-cated was Max's. His mother was sitting next to him reading aloud from her Bible. Max appeared to be sleeping, but Opal could see that his breathing was labored. An oxygen mask covered the lower part of his face and an I.V. was sticking out of his arm.

Max's mother looked up. "The priest has already been here this morning," she said.

"The priest?" Opal asked, confused.

Max's mother cleared her throat. "He administered last rights for Max."

Opal felt as if someone had punched her in the stomach. She had known that Max was going to die. She had lived with that reality from the time she met him and grew to love him. Still, in her mind, she had always expected some kind of miracle, a previously undiscovered cure, a laying of hands, something, anything to save her friend. Max lay with his eyes closed. She had never noticed what beautiful lashes he had—long, thick, and a color somewhere between brown and red.

Open your eyes, Max, she silently pleaded, but his eyes remained closed. Opal walked over to Max's mother and sat down beside her.

Max's mother turned to Opal. "How am I going to live without my baby?" she asked.

Opal shook her head. She did not have an answer for that. She could not imagine a world without her friend. She had only known Max for a few months, but in those months she had come to realize what his mother undoubtedly already knew—Max was special. He was different. Her mother had described him as an old soul in a very young body and Opal was inclined to agree.

Opal sat silently while Max's mother continued reading Psalm 23 to her son. "The Lord is my shepherd, I shall not want . . ."

How could God take away Max? "Not yet!" she wanted to scream. Don't take him away yet. There are still things left unsaid, more discussions, more laughter, more cartoons to watch, more arguments about the Red Sox and the Yankees. Much more.

Max's mother closed her Bible. Turning to Opal, she said, "You know, when my husband and I broke up, I thought I was going to die. It was almost indescribable pain. Max was three. I remember lying in bed crying and this little voice saying, 'Don't cry, Mommy. You still have me.' No matter how hard times got, I always remember my baby saying, 'You still have me.' "

Opal reached out and held her hand.

"You are very special to him, Opal. I was a little jealous, because he had fallen in love with you. Before he met you, we were sort of a team. We still are. But for the first time, my Max noticed a woman who was not his mother. You should hear how he used to go on and on about you . . . about how beautiful you are, how kind, how smart. Thank you for being so good to my boy, Opal. Thank you."

Opal started to cry, silent wails that tore her heart. *Don't take him yet,* she pleaded to God. *A few more days, a few more hours, don't take him just yet.*

Just then Max opened his eyes and looked at her. He tried to open his mouth to say something, but he was hindered by the oxygen mask. He motioned for his mother to remove the mask. His mother's hands shook when she took the mask from Max's face.

"I love you, Maxi," his mother crooned to her son. "I love you so very much."

Max smiled at her. "I know," he whispered, and Opal could see the effort it took for him to speak those words. He looked over at Opal and said, "I'm . . . gonna . . . be . . . O.K."

Max died just before eight o'clock in the morning. His mother was holding one hand and Opal was holding the other. It was peaceful, and for that Opal was grateful. He simply stopped breathing. When the doctor pronounced him dead, with a clinical "I'm so sorry," Opal wanted to hit him. Undoubtedly, the doctor was used to death, even the death of the young, but his perfunctory manner was offensive.

Max's mother did not cry. Instead, she leaned over and kissed his forehead. "Good-bye, my beloved," she said. "Until we meet again."

Faith

Dean Hambrick sat in her office with a wide smile on her face. "Faith, you look wonderful! How are you?"

"I'm not sure," Faith replied, honestly. "There are times when I feel optimistic, and then, there are other times . . . when optimism is hard to come by."

"Ah," said Dean Hambick, pushing her glasses even further down her nose. "How familiar that sounds."

Faith settled into her seat. "Dean Hambrick, is something wrong?"

Dean Hambrick's laughter made her look like a little girl. "Now, why would you say that, Faith?"

"Well, usually the only times you summon me to your office is when you have bad news."

"True," said Dean Hambrick, nodding her head. "That has been my habit, but habits are made to be broken. It so happens, Faith, that I have very good news for you."

Good news, thought Faith. *This I can definitely use.* The past few days had come close to her definition of hell. A newspaper had leaked her name and she was now no longer euphemistically referred to as "the victim." Reporters had gone as far as Ohio to interview her parents and yesterday a story about her drinking had made front page of the local newspaper in an article that suggested that anyone struggling with alcoholism could not be trusted to tell the truth.

"Are you still interested in teaching?" Dean Hambrick asked.

"Yes," said Faith. "But with everything that's happening to me . . . I don't know anymore."

"What exactly do you mean?" Dean Hambrick asked mildly, but Faith was not fooled. She knew that beneath that placid exterior was a volcano that was liable to erupt at any time.

"The reporters . . . the trial, I just think that maybe I should put off teaching until I get my life under more control."

"And when do you suppose that will happen?" Dean Hambrick asked.

"I don't know," Faith replied.

"So you are going to put your dreams on hold until life gets perfect . . . or a little better."

Leave it to Dean Hambrick to get her on the defensive. "I know that sounds crazy," said Faith.

"Not crazy," Dean Hambrick replied. "Just ill-advised. Some opportunities don't come around again. At the time I was accepted to Columbia University my grandmother, the woman who raised me, was murdered. I went to Columbia, Faith. It was hard, but I didn't know if that opportunity would come my way again."

Faith sighed. "You're a stronger woman than I."

"No, I'm not," said Dean Hambrick. "I was just lucky enough to have someone in my life to talk some sense into me—just as I am, hopefully, going to talk some sense into you."

"I'm listening," said Faith, with the certain knowledge that she would not be allowed to escape until she listened to what Dean Hambrick intended to say.

"Your GRE scores were excellent, Faith—as you already know. There's an education program at Fisk University for which you'd be perfect. I know the director, although I didn't pull any strings or do you any favors, except to talk to the folks at Fisk about you. Based on your scores and my recommendation, Fisk is prepared to offer you a full scholarship for the education program. This scholarship includes a generous living stipend, as well as a stipend for books and other incidentals. Now, you'll have to fill out the application and there are a few formalities . . . but if you want to go to Fisk, the door is wide open. It's a great program, Faith, and it would offer you the opportunity to start over somewhere new. Faith, I hope that you think about it."

Faith was overwhelmed. "Dean Hambrick, why are you doing this for me?"

"Because I see something in you that someone else saw in me—potential. Now, I hope that you give the program serious consideration. I know that Everton's trial is scheduled for sometime later on this summer and that you have a lot on your plate right now, but if I were you, I would be good and damned if I let someone like Everton Rhodes stop me from achieving my goals."

"O.K.," said Faith.

"O.K., what?" asked Dean Hambrick.

"O.K., I'll go to Fisk," Faith replied, feeling her spirits rise the way they did on those infrequent occasions when she made a good decision. "Thank you, Dean Hambrick."

Dean Hambrick took her glasses off and laid them on her desk. "I'm proud of you, Faith. Throughout this ordeal you've conducted yourself with a lot more guts and class than I've encountered in anyone in a while. You're going to go far, Faith—just give yourself a chance to shine."

Opal

Opal walked out of Max's hospital room. His mother remained with him and Opal wanted to give her time to say good-bye to her son. The reality of Max's death had not settled in and Opal knew that it would be some time before she could truly accept that her friend was gone. She wanted to cry, but the tears would not come. Around her, the nurses and doctors went about their business as if nothing out of the ordinary had happened. Harried resident doctors pushed past her, their lack of sleep making them irritable. Groups of families hovered by hospital doors, their faces reflecting their worry about their loved ones. "Max is gone!" she wanted to shout. Instead, she walked with her eyes fixed on the elevator down the hall. She wanted to get out of this place.

Her parents were in the waiting room, but she couldn't face them. Not yet. She needed to wrap her mind around Max's death. She needed to somehow come to a place of acceptance, although she knew that she would never accept that the world would continue without her friend.

"Opal," someone grabbed her arm, preventing her escape.

She turned around and found herself facing Jordan.

"How did you know?" she whispered.

"Your mother called me. I got here a little after you did. I just wanted to be here . . . in case, in case you needed me."

The last vestige of resentment left her at that precise moment. The animosity, the hurt, the bitterness, everything drifted away. At that moment, she chose forgiveness. She forgave Jordan. The lock that held her emotions, her love, her feelings for Jordan turned and she decided to let him in.

"He's gone, Jordan. Max is gone."

"I know, baby. I know."

She began to cry then, wails that came from somewhere deep inside her. She sounded like a wounded animal. Jordan held her while she cried, rocking her back and forth and when her tears subsided, he still held her tight.

Chapter 32

Reva

Reva placed the unopened letter from Harvard Medical School on her bed and stared at it. This was the first letter she had received from a medical school, and it was also her first choice.

"Reva, for goodness' sake, open the letter!" her roommate, Bonnie, pleaded.

"I can't," said Reva. She couldn't put her feelings into words. She was excited. She was scared. She was overwhelmed. She knew that she could be rejected and she knew that she would deal with it, but from her tenth birthday, when she met Dr. Sawyer, the doctor at her neighborhood clinic, who had assured her that she was going to go to Harvard Medical School, she had been fixed on attending medical school at that university. Dr. Sawyer had long since gone on to glory but Reva felt his presence as strongly as if he were in her dormitory room with her.

"Give me the letter then," said Bonnie. "I'll open it."

"Here," said Reva, handing over the letter to her roommate.

Reva closed her eyes and waited. She heard Bonnie rip the envelope, then she heard Bonnie's sharp intake of breath.

Reva opened her eyes. "Well?"

Bonnie smiled. "Congratulations, roomie. Or should I say, Doctor Roomie. You're on your way to Hah-vahd!"

"No!" screamed Reva, jumping up from her bed. "No way!"

Although she'd scored high on the MCATs and she was an honors student, Harvard was very competitive and many of her professors had cautioned her not to put all her eggs in the Harvard basket. At first, she'd ignored them, just as she ignored everyone else in her life that didn't support her dreams, but the caution of her professors had unnerved her. But, eventually their cautionary words had seeped somewhere they didn't belong, in that place where her confidence lived. As a result, she'd applied to several medical schools, most of which she did not want to attend, but her dream was to become a doctor and if Harvard didn't beckon, she was sure that some other school would. Still, when she saw herself in medical school, she saw herself at Harvard.

"Yes! Yes! Yes, again! We're on our way to Harvard!"

"We?" Reva asked, confused.

"I was accepted to the business school last week, but I didn't want to say anything until you heard from med school. I knew how nervous you were," said Bonnie.

"Business school?" asked Reva. "I didn't know you were planning to attend business school. I thought you were applying to the School of Public Health."

"Well, the evil empire beckoned," Bonnie joked. "I've been thinking about B school for a while. I still have time to get a degree in public health, but right now I want to approach health care issues from the business side."

"I am so proud of you," said Reva. "You are an amazing woman."

"What can I say," Bonnie replied, "except that you're right! Go call your mom."

After Bonnie left the dorm room, Reva picked up the telephone and dialed her mother's phone number. They'd had words last week when Reva had discussed getting married to Simon. Her mother was not pleased with her choice of a spouse, even though she'd never met Simon. Her litany included the fact that he had a dangerous profession, was a foreigner, and would ultimately get her pregnant and force her to give up her dreams. Reva had hung up the telephone on her mother, and then refused to take any of her mother's calls. She was happy with Simon. She was happy with her life, and for once, Reva was not going to let her mother steal her joy.

Sugar answered the telephone on the second ring. "Hello," her mother purred as if expecting a male caller.

"Hey, Sugar," said Reva.

"Oh, it's you," said Sugar. "I guess you finally remembered that you have a mother."

Reva sighed. "Sugar, I'm not going to join in your drama . . . not today."

"Don't sass me, Reva. A person is entitled to her own opinion. If you saw me rushing headlong down a path of ruination, I hope you would try to stop me. I'm not saying that you should never get married, but you're too young and what do you really know about this man. . . . he's probably marrying you for a green card . . ."

"Sugar!" Reva struggled to maintain her composure. Her mother could try the patience of a saint crossed with an angel.

"All right, I guess I can't talk sense into you, although God knows that I'm going to die trying . . ."

"Sugar, I got into medical school. I got into Harvard."

There was silence on the other line.

"Sugar?"

There was no response.

"Sugar, are you O.K.?" Reva asked again.

"I've got to go," Sugar choked out the words. "I'll call you back."

Her mother hung up the telephone, leaving Reva listening to the dial tone. Once again, the disappointment she felt whenever her mother refused to, or was unable to be happy for her, crept over her. *No*, Reva shook her head, *I will not allow Sugar to hurt me.*

The telephone rang and Reva picked up the receiver. "Hello."

It was Sugar. "I'm proud of you, baby."

Now it was Reva's turn to be silent. Her mother had never said those words to her. When she'd gotten good grades, awards, academic scholarships, her mother had expected no less. "That's what I'm making all these sacrifices for," Sugar would say, robbing Reva of any pride for her good grades. For as always, the unspoken guilt factor would be brought up by Sugar—the unspoken lament behind her words: "I gave up my dreams for you."

"I'm so proud of you, Reva," Sugar whispered.

Reva cleared her throat, "I'm still waiting to hear from other schools . . ."

Her mother cut her off immediately. "Of course you're going to Harvard!" she declared. Then a wicked giggle escaped her mother's lips, "I can't wait to tell your father!"

"Sugar . . ." Reva cautioned, but it was too late. Her mother had already hung up the telephone.

Precious

"Precious Averyheart, you have a caller at the front desk," a disinterested voice coming from the dormitory public address system bellowed.

Precious put down her pen. She was in the midst of writing a French history paper for Madame Breton that was due tomorrow. She'd waited until the last minute to start the paper and she hated the feeling of being rushed. She had been having an uncharacteristically hard time concentrating on her studies. There had been a lot of distractions pulling her attention away from her classes. Her impending graduation, her French thesis, which she had to defend before all the professors in the French department, the fact that she would be leaving the relative safety and comfort of her college campus to go to a foreign country where she knew not a soul—all of this was troubling. When she was being honest with herself she knew that the biggest distraction was that she missed Rory. They had not spoken since their conversation about Everton and Faith. In time, her anger towards him had subsided. He was supporting a friend, just as she was supporting Faith. Still, she could not understand how Rory could fail to see Everton's true nature. She had been tempted many times to call Rory, but she viewed any overture to Rory as a betrayal of her friendship with Faith. Rory was in Everton's camp and she was firmly in Faith's corner, and never the twain would meet.

"Precious Averyheart, you have a caller at the front desk."

The designation of caller versus visitor had always amused Precious. A caller was code for a man, and a visitor meant, "don't worry about getting yourself together, there's a woman at the front desk."

Precious was expecting Professor Olade, her African Studies teacher. He had promised her that he would drop off a book of African poetry for her to review for the school newspaper. The review, like everything else lately, was late. Professor Olade was one of her favorite people. An elderly man who had taught at Oxford for many years, he had come to Middlehurst to head the African Studies Department. They would spend hours discussing life and politics in Africa, and Precious was a frequent visitor to the home of the professor and his wife.

Putting on some tennis shoes to complement her serious study wardrobe of white T-shirt with the obligatory coffee stain and grey sweatpants, Precious walked out of her dormitory room. She thought about putting on some makeup; she didn't want to scare Professor Olade, but she didn't want to keep him waiting any longer than she already had. She ran down the stairs to the lobby and looked around for Professor Olade. He was not there. Instead, Rory stood by the front desk.

He walked over to her. "We need to talk."

It was on the very tip of her tongue to tell him to go away, that there was nothing to talk about. She also had the urge to throw her arms around him singing the Rodney King refrain—"Can't we all just get along." She settled for the more sedate, "Yes, I think we should talk."

She was suddenly self-conscious. She had no makeup on and she looked like yesterday's leftover supper. Her hair was an undisciplined bush, pushed back by a headband, and there was a giant pimple strategically placed in the middle of her forehead. Rory looked perfect to her, as always. He was dressed in black jeans and an Oakland Raiders jersey. He looked as if he had stepped off the cover of a college brochure.

"Where can we go to talk?" he asked.

Precious pointed to the sitting room in the back of the foyer. Rory followed her as she walked into the sitting room, which thankfully was free of any curious onlookers. Closing the door behind them, Precious sat down on one of the four oversize stuffed chairs. Rory remained standing.

"I got drafted by the Raiders," said Rory.

"The Raiders?" she asked. "The Oakland Raiders?"

Rory nodded his head. "I'll be competing for a running back position . . . there's no guarantee that I'll make the team."

Oakland. The word made Precious' heart sink. Oakland as in California, as in the other side of the world. Oakland. She'd never see him again. If he were on the East Coast, maybe once she got back from Paris, and if all the craziness between them had subsided, then they would have a chance to perhaps pick up from where they left off, but Oakland . . . when was she ever going to get to California? *Stop it,* she chided herself. *You two are no longer together. You are no longer a couple. His address or future address is no longer your concern. Stop it, stop it, stop it.*

Precious cleared her throat. "I'm sure you'll make the team, Rory," she said quietly.

"I'll be leaving right after graduation," said Rory.

Precious nodded her head. She wasn't sure what kind of response he was expecting from her. He kept staring at her as if he were waiting for something, although she had no idea what he was waiting for.

"That's good, Rory," Precious said.

"Is it?" Rory asked.

Precious stood up, "I'm happy for you . . . Look, I have a lot of studying to do . . . I'm in the middle of writing a paper . . ."

"I know, Precious. You're busy," he sounded angry.

"Rory, what is it you want from me?" Precious asked.

He walked over and put his hands on her shoulders. "I want things to be the way they used to be. I want you back, Precious. I got my dream, you know. I got drafted by an NFL team. There's a good chance that I'm going to make a lot of money. I'm going to do something that I love, have always loved. I am going to play football and all I can think of is that I want you to be a part of this. I want you to be with me, Precious. I know you blame me for what happened with Faith but I didn't know who Everton really was—I know some stuff about Everton now that I didn't know then. I keep playing everything back in my head, and if there were any way I could have stopped Everton I would have . . . I just can't figure out a way to make this right. Can you tell me how to make it right between us, Precious?"

Precious shook her head. "I don't know, Rory. Faith is my friend, just as Everton was your friend. I just saw us . . . see us as being in enemy camps . . . it almost seemed like you stood up for Everton."

"That's not fair," said Rory.

"That may be so," Precious replied. "But that's how I feel. I need to feel that you put me first. I feel that you valued Everton more than you valued me. I don't fault you for standing by your friend, but you didn't try to see my point of view . . ."

Rory interrupted her. "Did you put me first, Precious? Did you try to understand my point of view? Did you try to understand that in all the time I'd known Everton he was a stand-up guy? Did you try to understand that had I known Everton was capable of what he did to your friend I would never have brought him around you, let alone viewed him as a friend? Did you try to understand that?"

"No," said Precious. "I didn't put you first, Rory."

"Precious, I'm leaving for California. You're on your way to Paris. Our lives are going to take us far from each other. . . . Can't we work this thing out?"

"Rory, I want to work things out, but right now things are confused. Right now I have to focus on helping Faith, graduating . . . getting myself ready for living in a new place, a new country . . ."

"In other words, you have a lot of things to do before you get to me," said Rory.

"That's not what I meant," said Precious.

"That's what you said."

"Rory, maybe in a few months . . ."

"In a few months, you'll be in another country and I'll be in California, Precious."

She didn't want him to be angry. She wanted to make things right between them, but she couldn't see how that would happen. Everton had brought something ugly and unpleasant between them, something that Precious did not know if she could get past.

"Good-bye, Precious," Rory said, and walked out of the room.

Chapter 33

Opal

Max's funeral was held on a sunny day. The chapel was filled with people of varying ages, all carrying yellow balloons. Yellow was Max's favorite color, and Max's mother had requested that all of the mourners wear something yellow in tribute to her son. Opal had never been to a funeral where black or purple, the colors of mourning, were not predominant. There was something uplifting about the sun streaming in through the stained glass windows of the chapel, bathing the mourners clutching their yellow balloons in a golden, almost ethereal glow. Max's coffin was draped in a bright yellow cloth, covered with gold, red and blue baseballs. Beside the coffin there were several pictures of Max. His mother had assembled several of his valued possessions and placed them around the coffin, including a bat signed by several Red Sox players, his favorite music CD's, books, and a stuffed brown teddy bear wearing a baseball cap. The bear was missing one ear. The sight of the stuffed toy robbed Opal of her voice. She wanted to fling herself down on the cold floor of the chapel. She wanted to scream. She wanted to beg God to bring Max back. Instead, she leaned on Jordan, whose arm was around her shoulders.

Max's mother sat in the front row, surrounded by relatives that Opal had never once seen either at Max's house or at the hospital. She sat erect, staring at her son's coffin. There were a few times when she would wipe her eyes, but she was holding up with tremendous grace. Opal envied Max's mother her grace and her composure. Opal had started crying from the moment she saw Max's coffin, and continued during the procession led by his mother and his priest, and throughout most of the ceremony.

This was not a solemn funeral, filled with dirges and sad music. Instead, Max's mother had arranged a funeral that celebrated her son's life. There were fond recollections from Max's little league coach, his best friend Caleb, his English teacher, his oncologist, and his priest. There were also two musical selections, a spirited rendition of "Amazing Grace," sung off-key but with gusto by Max's upstairs neighbor, Mr. Gonzales, and the Lord's Prayer, which was sung by the choir from Max's school. Mrs. Firenze recited a love poem in Italian and in English, "for my little Max, my little bambino." Max's mother had asked Opal if she wanted to say a few words, but Opal had declined. She would be too emotional to speak. "My heart is broken," Opal had told her, and his mother had understood. Still, with all the pain that accompanied funerals, particularly when it was a funeral for a child, the ceremony was beautiful. Opal couldn't help thinking that Max would have loved it all: the balloons, the songs, the music, the poetry and the laughter that would erupt from time to time during the service as the speakers recalled the quirky, off-beat things that made Max the unforgettable person who had come into all their lives, albeit too briefly.

Beside her, Reva reached over and held Opal's hand. Reva, Precious, Faith, Jordan and Opal's parents had all come to the funeral and Opal was grateful for their support. Although there were times that she could almost forget that this was a funeral, the coffin in the front of the church was a stark reminder. Her beloved friend was gone. Jordan had once told her that most people cry for themselves when they go to funerals, and Opal was no exception to this rule. She cried for all the times she would no longer get to talk to her friend. She would miss his voice, the way his eyes would sparkle when he was excited, which was often. She would miss the telephone calls, the discussions about the Red Sox, the arguments about movies, music and sports. She would miss, most of all, seeing that wide gap-toothed smile.

Max's mother stood up and walked beside the coffin. Placing one hand on the coffin, as if she were caressing her child, she began to speak. "My beloved Max," she said. "You have brought me so much joy. You have been the greatest achievement in my life—nothing I have done, or will ever do, will be as important as being your mom. When I first saw you, I remember how scared I was—scared that I wouldn't be able to take care of such a precious gift—because you were God's gift to me. I knew then, as I know now, that I could not hold on to you forever, although I tried, Max. The Lord knows I tried to hold on to you, but someone in heaven wants you more than I, and

I have to let you go. I remember, Max, how once you were afraid . . .
when you were going to your first day of nursery school. I remember
how you wouldn't let me leave until I sang your song . . . our song. I
know that up in heaven, you'll be well taken care of, my darling, but I
want to sing your song for you again, my darling . . . and if you ever
are afraid, come to me, Max, in my dreams, in my thoughts, in my
memories, come to me, my darling, and I'll sing your song for you . . .
just as I'll sing now: 'Somewhere over the rainbow, way . . . way . . . way
up high, there's a land that I heard of . . . once in a lullaby . . .' "

Max's mother faltered, and she started to cry. Looking back, Opal
was not sure where her strength came from. She was not sure what
made her tears stop, what made her get up from the second row and
walk up to where Max's mother stood crying, although she was certain that somewhere, somehow and some way, Max had his hand in all
of this. Opal held Max's mother's hand and sang, in a clear, strong
contralto: "Somewhere over the rainbow, clouds are blue, and the
dreams that we dare to dream really do come true." They finished the
song together, Opal and Max's mother, hand in hand, and as they
walked behind the coffin, for the beginning of Max's last journey, the
words from the song wrapped themselves around Opal's heart and
gave her the courage to say good-bye.

Faith

Faith sat on the couch in Kevin's apartment and fought the urge to
sleep. They were both studying for their final examinations and it was
almost two o'clock in the morning. Faith had her first final exam in
two days and Kevin's exams were set to begin in two weeks. Faith had
been feeling like a prisoner on campus. Everton had been indicted
for attempted rape, and as Faith had predicted, her life had become
something very close to a media circus. Although Middlehurst provided a warm cocoon where she was protected from the press and gossip, she still had to deal with the looks people gave her. Most of the
stares were curious, as if people were wondering what was going on in
her life now that all hell was about to break loose. There were a few
hostile stares, which came from those who thought that Everton had
gotten a raw deal. Once, a student had approached her and asked her
how could she turn against a "brother." The incident had unnerved
her.

Reva had been with her at that time, and had used some choice,
profanity-laced words to get her point across, but that wasn't the answer either. Faith didn't want anyone to protect her. She wanted to be
left alone, to be anonymous. She wanted her old life back, without

the drinking. She wanted to just be plain old Faith again, but those days were over. Whether she liked it or not, she would always be linked in some way to Everton. She would always be the girl who cried rape.

"What are you thinking about?" Kevin asked. He was sitting across the room at his desk.

"My life," Faith said, looking over at her friend. Sometimes it worried Faith that she'd let Kevin have access to a place that even her girlfriends did not know about. She could talk to Kevin about her mistakes in a way she never could with Reva, Opal or Precious. They loved her, but they would judge her. Kevin did not judge her. Sometimes he would ask questions, but usually he would just listen. He let her be herself. It didn't matter if she were in a bad mood, he let her be in her moods. He did not try to cajole her into feeling better. He did not try to bring sunshine on a cloudy day. He understood that there were some days, no matter how hard you tried, when the sun was just not going to shine.

Kevin provided a good balance for her. Kevin's moods could best be described as even. He was generally good-natured, but there were times when he was just quiet. Faith, whose moods varied wildly from day to day, sometimes moment to moment, had a hard time getting used to the unflappable Kevin. But there were times, like tonight, when the demons were chasing her—the fear about the upcoming trial, the doubt about her future, her concern about relapsing—these were the times when she thanked God for Kevin's friendship. He was the shelter from her storm. He was a warm place, a safe place.

"What about your life?" Kevin asked, getting up from his desk.

"I'm thinking about the mess I've made . . ."

Kevin walked over and sat next to her. His eyes, which Faith had long ago decided were his best feature, were kind. "The mess *you* made?"

"You know," said Faith, attempting to make light of a heavy situation, "the drinking, the attempted rape, the trial . . ."

Kevin leaned forward and kissed her lightly. His action surprised both of them.

Faith drew back quickly. Where did this come from? Kevin was her friend. Her buddy. The person she talked to when she had problems. Kevin hadn't been anointed as a saint yet, but he was close. What was Saint Kevin, her buddy, doing kissing her.

"I'm sorry, I should have asked . . ." Kevin began. "I shouldn't have done that, I mean I've wanted to do that for a long time, but I shouldn't have forced myself . . . Oh, God . . ."

Kevin pushed his hand through his hair, then he stood up. He was agitated. Faith had never seen him in this state. "Faith, I can't do this," he said.

"Do what?" Faith asked.

"I can't just be your friend. I want more. I know that this isn't the right time, but I don't know when the right time is ever going to be. I don't think you can ever see past my color . . . I don't think you can ever just see me as a man . . . a man who is in love with you."

In love with her?

"Kevin, I . . ."

"Look, let me take you back to the campus. It's late."

The way Kevin spoke, it was as if he were saying good-bye. "Kevin, is our friendship over?'

"No," said Kevin. "I just think that maybe we need to put a little space between us . . . until I can get my feelings under control."

"Are you saying that if this doesn't go beyond friendship . . . then you won't be around?" Faith asked, surprised that her heart was now clearly moving up to her throat. She didn't want to lose Kevin. She had come to depend on him, his friendship, his advice.

"I'll always be there for you if you need me, Faith."

"I need you, Kevin."

The words surprised her just as much as his kiss had surprised her. She had never said those words to any man. "I need you."

He walked over to the stereo and turned on the radio. A slow jazz tune was playing. Turning to Faith, he asked, "Would you dance with me?"

She had refused the first time he'd asked her to dance. She wasn't going to make that mistake again.

"Yes, Kevin. I'll dance with you."

Faith rose and walked over to where Kevin stood waiting. She hesitated for a moment—she understood that this invitation to dance represented much more—it represented a crossing over from their familiar boundaries of friendship into a new, different place. She was attracted to Kevin and had been for some time—but the craziness in her life had made it easy to push that attraction somewhere else . . . somewhere far away, somewhere where she did not have to deal with her growing feelings for him.

All her life she had made wrong decisions. Decisions based out of fear, boredom, addiction. She had chosen the wrong men. She had chosen alcohol. With the exception of her girlfriends, she had chosen to have people in her life who were not good for her. Kevin was the right person at the wrong time. She needed to have her life be in order before she began any new relationship. She was on her way to Fisk University. He would be staying in Boston to attend Seminary

School. They came from different backgrounds. Her life, with all its warts, was about to be exposed. This was definitely the wrong time, but this time, she examined all her excuses for not having someone like Kevin in her life, and she found them wanting. There would never be a good time. Life would always intrude with the problems, joy and pain that came with living. Kevin was a good man. She deserved to have a good man in her life. She moved into his arms, and discovered, to her delight and surprise, that they fit together perfectly.

Kevin's arms tightened around her. "I'm not going anywhere, Faith. I'm not going to leave you."

"Don't make promises you can't keep, Kevin," Faith replied. "The ride is about to get very bumpy. The District Attorney has been honest with me . . . this is going to be a tough trial to win. Everton is a football star, the proverbial all-American guy. I went to his room voluntarily . . . at one o'clock in the morning. There's a good chance that a jury might determine that I asked for exactly what I got. The next few months are going to be rough."

Kevin leaned down and kissed her on the cheek. Then, he said, "I am a man of my word, Faith. I'm not leaving you. We're going to get through this together."

"How are you so certain?" she asked.

She looked up to see Kevin smile.

"I'm certain," he said, "because I have Faith."

Chapter 34

Reva

Despite her better judgment, Reva sat patiently in the booth at
Shim's Chinese Restaurant in Roxbury and waited for all hell to
break loose. Her fiancé—she had to get used to that word—sat on
one side of her, and her mother sat on the other side. Her father and
his new wife were due at any moment. Simon had talked Reva into
this madness. "We are getting married," he reasoned. "I want to get to
know your family and I want them to get to know me." At first, her
mother had refused to come to Boston. "I don't condone this marriage, Reva. You need to finish your schooling before you even *think*
about marriage." Simon had sent Sugar a first class airplane ticket,
and after a two hour telephone call, which neither Sugar nor Simon
would discuss, Sugar had agreed to this meeting, although she knew
that Reva's father and his wife would also be present.

Simon had also called Reva's father to invite him to the dinner.
Reva would have been content to let things stay the way they had been
all her life . . . with her father someplace comfortably far away, where
she didn't have to deal with his rejection of her. Simon was adamant
that he wanted to meet Reva's father. "He's part of you, Reva. I want
to know him and I want him to know me." Simon had convinced her
mother to give him her father's telephone number. Reva was surprised that her mother agreed. After all these years, Sugar was not
ready to let go of Reva's father. She was not ready to let go of her bitterness, and she was not ready to let go of the pain he had caused her
when he walked away from her life.

Sugar was dressed conservatively tonight. She had traded in her usual leopard-print motif for a long, close-fitting black skirt and a black turtleneck. In her ears, two silver hoops dangled, and Reva thought she looked as if she were a little girl—even her makeup was muted. Gone was the bright red lipstick and in its place her mother had on pale peach lip gloss. Sugar was nervous. She kept tapping her glass of ice tea with her index finger. Simon tried to make conversation with her mother, but Sugar either refused to answer or offered curt monosyllables in response to Simon's questions.

A sharp intake of Sugar's breath announced the arrival of Reva's father and his wife. Her father looked directly at their table. He looked as if he were a death row convict taking a last walk to the electric chair. Beside him was a very short dark-skinned woman in a long kente cloth skirt and a white peasant style blouse. Her hair was pulled back into a thick French braid and she was smiling. She walked beside Reva's father as they made their way towards the booth.

Reva watched as her mother rolled her eyes at her father, and she placed a restraining hand on Sugar's knees. "Easy, Sugar," she said under her breath, "we don't want any bloodshed tonight."

Turning to Simon, Reva whispered, "This was a very bad idea."

Simon smiled, and stood up as the pair approached their table. Holding out his hand, Simon said, "Hello, Mr. Nettingham. Mrs. Nettingham. Pleased to meet you both. I'm Simon."

Reva watched as her father shook Simon's hand awkwardly. Her stepmother offered a cheek to Simon. Once again, three words sprang to Reva's mind: "Very bad idea."

"Hello, Sugar," her father said warily, as if he expected Reva's mother to lob a dinner plate at his head at any moment.

Sugar stiffened her spine and smiled at Reva's father. "Hello, Coleman."

Reva realized that she had been holding her breath during the exchange. She watched as Simon grinned at her family. "Can't you see that this is madness," she wanted to shout at her fiancé, but instead, she said a quick prayer that the Lord would end this dinner in whatever manner He deemed appropriate. At that moment, a minor earthquake would have been a welcome proposition.

"Hi, Reva," said her father.

"Hello," Reva responded, wondering when the Almighty was going to do his thing and bring this impending disaster to a quick close.

Her father and his wife sat down in the two empty seats in the booth, then Simon sat down again. He held her hand, but he looked directly at Reva's father and his wife, Belle.

"Reva, Sugar . . . er, Simon, this is my wife, Belle." Coleman Nettingham looked as if he would have gladly taken a bullet instead of sitting at the same table with Sugar and his wife.

"I'm pleased to meet you, Belle," Sugar said softly.

Reva whipped her head around and stared openly at her mother. Who was this woman who calmly and politely spoke to her father's wife? Reva had expected a cold, terse greeting. Sugar was acting as if she had just met this woman at an afternoon tea.

"I'm so happy to meet you all," said Belle. "Particularly you, Reva. Your father talks about you often. I feel as if I know you."

The devil jumped on Reva's back. "Does he talk about me?" Reva asked. "That's surprising."

Reva watched with satisfaction as her words found their mark. Her father looked as if she'd just slapped him.

Belle continued talking as if she did not notice Reva's rudeness. "Yes, indeed, your Daddy talks about you all the time. He tells me how smart you are, how pretty you are. He's very proud of you."

Before Reva could get a chance to respond to that bit of news, Sugar jumped in.

"My baby's going to Harvard Medical School," she said.

"So I hear," said Belle, with a wide smile.

Coleman Nettingham cleared his throat. "I think that Reva gets her brains from her mother," he said.

Sugar took a sip from her glass of iced tea. "That's true," she said mildly.

Simon spoke up. "I'm glad you're all here. I've wanted to meet Reva's family for a long time now."

A waitress appeared as if on cue and took their orders. Reva struggled to keep her anger from rising. Watching her father sit across from her, being so attentive to his wife, in a way he had never been with her or her mother, made Reva want to spit. "Why weren't we good enough for you?" she wanted to scream. "What is so special about a kente cloth wearing, aging hippie?" What did Belle have that Sugar and Reva lacked. Belle was attractive, but she did not possess Sugar's dramatic beauty. "I'm your blood," Reva wanted to scream. "I'm your blood!"

"You look just like your father," the waitress said to Reva.

The devil jumped on Reva's back again. "That's about all we have in common," Reva replied.

Sugar grabbed her daughter's hand. "Excuse us," she said, before Reva could protest.

Reva stood up and followed her mother. Her heart went out to her mother. Now, she saw her mother's hurt because of her father's actions. Sugar and Reva were in this together. Her mother had raised her. Her mother had sacrificed for her. Her mother had been both mother and father to her. Now, that her father had met his hippie goddess, he had apparently realized the error of his ways and now he wanted a welcome with open arms. Well, Coleman Nettingham had another thing coming. She was Sugar's daughter and as they said down south, fruit don't fall too far from the tree. She was her mother's child and she would be good and damned before she let her father into her life, no matter how good Simon's intentions were.

The ladies room was empty, although Sugar didn't check before she put her hands on her daughter's arms and shook her.

"Reva, what in the hell is wrong with you?" she asked. "I didn't raise you to be mean to people."

"Sugar, this is Coleman we're talking about. The man whom you despise, remember? The man you said was lower than a pregnant snake's belly. The man who ruined your life . . . those are your words, Sugar. The man who walked out on you when you were pregnant."

Sugar sat down on the sink and put her head in her hands and started to cry.

"Mama, what's wrong?" Reva had not used that word since she was a little girl. She had given in to Sugar's request to use her given name, but as a child, she'd always thought of Sugar as "Mama." Eventually, she stopped thinking of the word "Mama" in conjunction with the woman who gave her life. Tonight, watching her mother cry, she felt like the little girl she once was, the little girl who wanted her Mama to be all right.

Sugar wiped her eyes. "Your father didn't leave us, Reva," she whispered. "I left him."

Reva tried to speak, but no words came out of her mouth.

"I never wanted you to know this, baby, and I hope you forgive me," Sugar said.

This time, Reva found her voice. "Forgive you for what?"

"For lying to you, baby. For not wanting you to know the truth about your mother."

"What truth, Sugar?"

"I knew your daddy for years before we got together. He grew up in my neighborhood . . . even then, I could tell that he was different. He was going places and I wanted to be with him. He was my ticket out. I learned to love your daddy and we were happy those first few years we dated. We were both in school. I was going to go into medicine and he wanted to teach. Those were good years, Reva. But I did something that I'm not proud of . . . I cheated on your dad. When he found out I was pregnant with you, even though he didn't know if you were his, he wanted to stand by you and by me. I was ashamed of what I had done, and I was scared, and I thought that I was in love with the man that I . . . cheated with on your dad. Your dad stood by me, even though I told him I wanted to be with somebody else . . ."

Reva felt the room start swimming around her. "Coleman is not my father?"

Sugar shook her head. "He's your father. Coleman took a test, but Reva . . . even without the test, he still wanted you. He didn't want to know who the father was . . . I was the one who made him take that test. Anyway, the guy I thought I was so in love with was fooling around with a whole lot of other people, but by the time I found out, I had hurt your dad so badly. Your dad still wanted to try, but I couldn't be with him knowing how much I'd hurt him. I was the one who told him that I wanted something else."

"Why didn't you tell me the truth, Sugar?"

"Because I didn't want you to hate me." Sugar whispered. "It was easier to make up this story about what your dad did to me, because I knew as long as I kept you two apart, then the truth would never come out."

Reva shook her head. "What about med school? You said that you didn't go to med school because you were a single mother . . ."

"I made a choice, Reva," said Sugar. "I could have gone to medical school. Other single mothers have done that and more. The truth was that after I left your dad, my life fell apart for a very long time. I knew that I had made a mistake . . . a terrible mistake, but I also knew that I could never go back to your dad. I was too ashamed. He would try, from time to time, to get to know you but I was afraid that he would take you away . . . that you would love him more . . . that when you found out the truth about who your mother really was, you wouldn't want me. I was the one who kept your father away from you, baby . . . and there are no excuses, no amount of 'I'm sorry's' that will ever make that better, Reva."

"So you pushed my father away because you were ashamed of what you did?" Reva asked.

"Yes," her mother stared directly into her eyes. "Yes."

Reva walked over to her mother and put her arms around her. "I'm not going to let you push me out of your life, Sugar. We'll have to work through all of this . . . but I'm not letting you push me away. You're my mother and I love you."

Sugar grabbed her daughter and started to cry. There was a knock on the bathroom door, and Belle walked in.

"I'm sorry," she said. "We were worried about you guys . . ."

Sugar pulled away and wiped her eyes. "It's all right," she said to Belle. "We'll be right out."

Belle smiled at them. "Take as much time as you need. Just don't get too upset if we start eating without you."

Belle walked out of the bathroom.

"She's a good woman," said Sugar. "She'll make Coleman happy. He deserves some happiness."

"What about you, Sugar?" Reva asked. "Don't you deserve happiness?"

Sugar took Reva's hand. "I don't think I could be happier than I am at this very moment, Reva."

Reva and Sugar walked out of the bathroom hand in hand. Just before they got to their table, Sugar said to Reva, "Do you think that you could start calling me Mama? I would like that, Reva."

"Yes, Mama," Reva replied.

Her father and her future husband both stood up when they got to the table.

"Is everything all right?" Simon asked.

Reva smiled at the man who had helped her put the pieces of her family back together again. "It's better than all right."

When they sat down and started eating, Reva was surprised at how easy conversation came to them all. They laughed and talked as if they had all known each other for a long time, and when dinner was finished, Simon invited everyone back to his apartment for dessert, Jamaican black cake.

As they walked out of the restaurant, Reva said to her father, "My graduation is next week. I'd love for you and Belle to come if you're not too busy . . ."

Her father's smile gave her the answer. "We'll be there," he said simply. Behind her, Reva could hear her mother and Simon laughing. *Family*, she thought. *Family*.

Chapter 35

Faith

Precious and Faith walked down the path that led from the library
to their dormitory. In their arms, they carried their black graduation caps and gowns. Although graduation was less than two days
away, it still did not seem real to Faith. The thought that in two days
she would be saying good-bye to Middlehurst had not quite taken
root. Unlike Precious, who had fallen irrevocably in love with
Middlehurst, it had taken Faith a while to learn to appreciate Middlehurst's charms. She'd spent most of her college years anticipating getting out and moving to the next phase—independence, adulthood,
responsibility—and now that those concepts were about to become a
reality, she wanted a little more time. The familiarity of life at
Middlehurst suddenly appealed to her. She was going to a new city, a
city without her friends, a city without Kevin. "Friendship has no
boundaries," Precious told her last night. "No matter where we all
end up, our bond will continue." Faith was certain of that, just as she
knew that Kevin would still be a part of her life—even if they were not
in the same city. She had finally admitted to herself what her friends
had apparently known all along—she cared for Kevin.

She thought about what her life would be like in a few months,
when the trial began. She was still afraid—afraid that it would be her
life, her choices that would be on trial, and not Everton. Still, she was
not turning back now. She knew in her heart that the trial and everything that came with it would be tough. She knew that her dirty laun-
dry was about to be washed in public, but she had her friends, her
family, and Kevin in her corner. Her new life, a life of sobriety, a life of

facing hurt, pain, fear, anger without alcohol, was not going be destroyed by Everton or the trial. She had fought hard for this life and no one was going to take it from her.

As Faith and Precious walked towards the entrance of their dormitory, a woman approached them. The woman looked familiar, but Faith could not place her in a specific time or location. The woman was strikingly beautiful—tall, willowy, with a face that would be difficult to forget, yet Faith could not remember where she'd seen this woman.

She was dressed completely in black. Her jeans were covered by a baggy sweater, which seemed odd considering the warm late May day. The woman's hands clutched the straps of her purse. She looked directly at Faith.

"Are you Faith Maberley?" the woman asked Faith.

Precious stepped between Faith and the woman. "What do you want?" she asked.

Faith suppressed a smile. Precious was a good-hearted, Baptist woman, but she was also a Harlem girl. Whoever was going to approach Faith was going to have to go through Precious.

"I know you," the woman said to Precious, her voice quiet. "I met you with Rory after one of the games."

Precious looked at her but did not respond.

"Cherry," the woman prompted. "My name is Cherry Holland. I'm . . . well, I was one of the cheerleaders for the football team."

Precious' eyes widened with recognition. "I do remember you," she said, still wary.

Cherry turned to Faith and said, "We haven't met, but I know who you are . . . I've seen you at a few of the football games with Precious."

"What can we do for you?" Precious asked. Faith wasn't sure whether it was the association with the football team, or with Rory, that made Precious seem so anxious to get away from Cherry Holland.

Cherry looked as if she wanted to turn and walk away. Instead, she took a deep breath and said, "I was raped by Everton Rhodes."

Faith felt blood rush to her head. She felt sick. She felt her head pounding, as hard as her heart. Everton had done to this woman what he had tried to do to her.

"It was before he hurt you," Cherry continued. "He beat me pretty badly . . . I went to the hospital, but I didn't tell them who did it to me . . . I didn't tell anyone until last week . . . I told a friend and he told me to go to the police. He also told me to go to you . . . he thought that maybe I could help you with your case . . ."

Precious took a step towards the woman. She looked as if she wanted to hold Cherry Holland tightly in her arms, but instead she said, "I'm sorry for your pain, Cherry."

Faith struggled to keep her emotions under control. In that moment, standing in the pathway in front of her dormitory, all the terror, the helplessness, the anger, all those feelings she had pushed away again, and again, came flooding back. Everton had hurt someone else.

Cherry twisted the strap on her handbag with nervous hands.

"I should have gone to the police before . . ." Cherry said. "I was in his dorm room. I thought that maybe I asked for this . . . thing to happen to me . . . if I hadn't gone to his room . . ."

"Stop," Faith said, her voice sharper than she'd intended. "It's not your fault. Everton is the one who is responsible for his actions."

Cherry began to cry then. Long, keening wails, coming from somewhere deep within. She stood there, crying. Precious was the first to put her arms around Cherry. Precious held her, while Cherry cried. She did not try to soothe her. She did not try to talk her out of her pain. She simply held her while Cherry's wails rose up to a cloudless, blue sky.

Faith wanted to run away. She wanted to run away from the memories of Everton that were now crashing down around her. She wanted to run away from Cherry. She wanted to run away from Cherry's tears. She wanted to run away from all the mistakes that she had made in her life. She wanted to run away. Instead, she walked over to Cherry and held her hand.

Cherry wiped her face. "Thank you," she said.

Faith held on to Cherry's right hand. "Thank you, Cherry. Thank you for coming forward and telling me your story. Thank you for going to the police. The case against Everton just got a lot stronger and I thank you for that."

"It was Rory who gave me the courage to do what I should have done months ago," Cherry said. "He was the one who came with me to the police station."

Precious spoke up. "Rory was to the one who told you to go to the police?"

Cherry nodded her head.

Faith looked over at Precious and said without any hesitation, "Go and handle your business, girlfriend. I'll stay here with Cherry."

Precious looked at Cherry and said. "I don't want to leave . . ."

"I'll be all right," Cherry said. "Faith and I have a lot to talk about."

Faith stared at her friend. She knew that Precious did not want to leave her, but Faith knew that there was something else Precious needed to do.

"I'll be here with Cherry," Faith said to Precious. "You need to go to your man."

* * *

Rory opened the door to his apartment after the second knock. It was as if he had been waiting for her. She had rehearsed what she would say to him on her way over to his apartment. She would tell him that she was sorry. She would tell him that she had been wrong to put him out of her life. She would tell him that she'd felt guilty about what happened to Faith and she had turned that guilt into anger against him. Precious had no illusion that Rory would welcome her back with open arms. There were always consequences to certain behavior and she had hurt him. Still, she wanted him to know that she was sorry—that he had been good for her and good to her, that what Everton did wasn't his fault—that the few months they'd spent together were among the happiest in her life, that no matter where she went, no matter what she did in her life, she would always remember him as her first love.

She stood there in the hallway waiting for the right words to come, but nothing came. His expression was inscrutable. *What are you thinking,* she longed to ask. Instead, she stared at him and willed herself to say that she was sorry.

Finally, Rory spoke. "Just tell me one thing," he said. "Are you ever going to come back to me, Precious?"

Precious nodded her head and let Rory pull her close to him. He held her tightly for a moment and then he let go. Looking down at her, he smiled and said, "It's about damn time!"

Graduation

Chapter 36

Opal

"**P**recious Averyheart!" Dean Hambrick's words were lost in the rush of applause.

Opal watched as Precious walked across the dais with her head held high. She looked regal in her flowing black graduation gown. Beside her she could hear Precious' daddy, Roosevelt, crying. She understood that those tears were born of pride. The janitor who raised a crack baby, who today was Phi Beta Kappa on her way to France, had much to be proud of on this day. There was no sadness today. Opal had often dreamed of this day—the day when she and her girls would leave Middlehurst together—bound to blaze bright trails. Cancer had taken that dream from her, but it had given her other dreams, other goals. She was going to come back to Middlehurst next year and she was going to graduate. She was not going to follow her father's footsteps into law; she was going apply to a graduate program in social work.

Before she'd gotten cancer, she had been content to let others map out her life, her destiny, for her. She was smart and articulate. It was a given that she'd end up in law school. Now she realized that nothing was a given. She was not certain of how many tomorrows she would be granted—and she realized that no person had that certainty. She was only certain of today, just as she was certain that she did not want to be a lawyer. She wanted to be a social worker.

"Faith Maberley!"

Faith walked across the dais with a wide smile on her face. When she approached Dean Hambrick, she gave the dean a hug. Then, pulling away, she accepted the diploma from the college president. Opal rose to her feet, as did Faith's family, and applauded. Not many people could have gone through what Faith had and emerge undefeated. She had graduated; she was on her way to Fisk University; and she was going to face Everton Rhodes at the trial. Faith was going to be all right. As Faith now said, she was taking things, "one day at a time."

"Reva Nettingham!"

"That's my baby!" Sugar yelled out. She was sitting with Reva's father, his wife and Simon. Reva had finally gotten what she'd always wanted—a family. When it had just been Reva and her mother, Reva had always felt that something was missing. She'd wanted a relationship with her father, even though in time she'd learned to accept that her father was not a part of her life. Now, there was a chance for her and her father to start anew. Opal watched as Simon stood up and took pictures of his Reva. He would be a good husband to her. He would be a good friend. He would be the man that Reva deserved—strong, supportive, with a healthy dose of unconditional love.

When the graduation ceremony ended, Reva, Faith, and Precious surrounded Opal. Their families, boyfriends and soon-to-be husbands, joined in the circle. At that moment, Opal's definition of family expanded. She understood that these women, and those they loved, had crossed the line from friendship to family.

"Girl, we are going to come back here next year to watch you get your diploma!" Reva said as she hugged Opal.

"We'll have a party—a celebration!" said Faith.

"We'll always be here for you, Opal," said Precious.

In life there were few guarantees, but Opal knew that their friendship, their ties, although they might be tested, they had a bond that would never be broken.

"I know," said Opal. "I know."